KILLER COIN

KILLER COIN

A TOBY WONG NOVEL

A VANCOUVER ISLAND MYSTERY

ELKA RAY

SEVENTH
STREET
BOOKS®

Published 2020 by Seventh Street Books®

Cover images © Shutterstock
Cover design by Jennifer Do
Cover design © Start Science Fiction

Inquiries should be addressed to
Start Science Fiction
221 River Street, 9th Floor
Hoboken, New Jersey 07030
Phone: 212-431-5455
www.seventhstreetbooks.com

10 9 8 7 6 5 4 3 2 1

ISBN: 978-1-64506-015-4 (paperback)
ISBN: 978-1-64506-016-1 (ebook)

Printed in the United States of America

*For Sol, who makes me laugh
like a twelve-year-old boy*

CONTENTS

1   Chapter 1: The Femme Fatale

7   Chapter 2: A Bad Feeling

11   Chapter 3: A Bit of a Mess

22   Chapter 4: Coming Up Short

27   Chapter 5: Who's Stephen?

33   Chapter 6: Unfaithful

37   Chapter 7: Dining à Deux

54   Chapter 8: Portents

60   Chapter 9: Getting Somewhere

70   Chapter 10: In Shock

75   Chapter 11: Tough Questions

84   Chapter 12: A Bad End

91   Chapter 13: With Regret

99   Chapter 14: The Black Sheep

110   Chapter 15: Half Truths

114   Chapter 16: Bad News

121   Chapter 17: Replaced

133   Chapter 18: Connecting the Dots

138   Chapter 19: A Step Back

145   Chapter 20: The Other Women

149   Chapter 21: True Lies

162   Chapter 22: Crumbling

170   Chapter 23: A Slap in the Face

176   Chapter 24: A Sorry State

183   Chapter 25: Dark Shape

191   Chapter 26: A Bad Aftertaste

197   Chapter 27: Eavesdropping

204   Chapter 28: First Strike

217   Chapter 29: Seeing Double

221 Chapter 30: Alone

226 Chapter 31: Down and Out

240 Chapter 32: Good Medicine

252 Chapter 33: On a Knife's Edge

263 Chapter 34: Home Safe

CHAPTER 1:

THE FEMME FATALE

The jeweler beneath my office has been blasting Christmas carols since October in an attempt to inspire us all to spend money. Now, with December looming, he's tired of the classics and moved on to sellout pop stars' renditions: Maroon 5's heinous cover of "Happy Christmas (War Is Over)," Bruce Springsteen's groaner "Santa Claus is Coming to Town," and—just when you thought it couldn't get worse—John Denver's jaunty classic "Please, Daddy (Don't Get Drunk on Christmas)." Talk about depressing.

I'm trying not to moan along in my head when my phone beeps—a reminder of my 4:00 p.m. appointment.

I straighten the papers on my desk. According to my day-planner, a Mrs. Butts is scheduled to see me. A new client. Anticipation sends a buzz through my belly. After five years spent clawing my way up the career ladder at a big Toronto law firm, it was a hard decision to move home to Victoria last summer. While I love being closer to my mom—and am thrilled to finally have a social life—the slower pace at work is driving me a little crazy.

In Toronto, I had clients who really needed me—most of them women, unhappily married to Type A assholes determined not to share a red cent. Stopping these women from being beaten to financial and emotional pulp was hard but satisfying. I loved forcing bullies to share. Of course, some of my clients *were* the jerks, which was interesting too. Every day was a challenge.

In contrast, here on sleepy Vancouver Island, even estranged couples are chilled out. They're all about caring and sharing, determined to settle things *amicably*. Nobody contests anything. While that should make me happy, I'm bored stiff. Any more uncontested divorces and my brain cells might take early retirement.

As it is, my brain seems to be working on island-time. When someone knocks on my door, it takes me too long to answer. It can't be the firm's receptionist, Pamela. She just barges straight in. I smooth down my jacket. "Yes?" My throat sounds rusty.

Downstairs, mercifully, the John Denver tune warbles to an end. It might be time to buy the jeweler some new tunes as an early Christmas gift. The knock comes again, or rather three knocks: fast but quiet. I get to my feet and head for the door. Some clients are too timid to let themselves in. I cross my fingers—please, please, let Mrs. Butts bring a challenge, before I expire of boredom.

I am reaching for the doorknob when the door opens, forcing me to step back. A glossy red high-heeled shoe strides through the gap, followed by another. The buzz in my gut flares into a spine-straightening jolt. I take another step backward.

The woman smiles. I do too. One look at Mrs. Butts and I know my wish has been granted: She is the femme fatale in every noir movie ever made. There's no way she's here to end anything amicably. All she needs is a pearl-handled pistol.

From her cascade of dark curls to her luminous skin, Mrs. Butts is a vision in high gloss. I blink, dazzled.

She stops to survey me too. "Ms. Vong?"

I extend a hand. "Yes, hello. I'm Toby Wong."

"I am Vonda." Her voice is husky with an Eastern European edge, the kind of voice that would make men melt. Even my knees have softened. She's definitely not local.

We shake, her hand so cool and soft I'm surprised by the strength of her grip. Beneath lashes like palm fronds her cool grey eyes take me in.

I point her toward my desk. We both cross the small room and sit. Vonda sets her purse on her lap. She leans forward. "I vant a divorce. As quickly as possible."

I nod. No surprise there, divorce being my specialty, although most new clients start with small talk. "Okay. How long have you been married?" I ask, pen in hand.

"Three months." Her candy-apple lips contort. "He is a liar," she hisses.

Before she gets into it, I extract the basics. Name: Vonda Butts nee Sokolov. Age: thirty-three. My age, although that's where the similarity ends: me petite, attractive-enough, and Vonda like the cover girl of a men's magazine, only prettier. Citizenship: Russian. Occupation: this elicits a blank look and a pause, followed by a shrug that says it should be obvious: Model and Influencer. She's got 782,000 Instagram followers. Spouse's name and job: This gets her going again.

"Dennis Butts." She spits the name angrily. Her shiny red talons grip my desk. "Vine-dealer," she says. "If that's even true. He is a liar. A professional liar. He misleaded me."

As a grammar nerd, I almost blurt "misled," but manage to stop myself: English is her second language, for god's sake. Plus there's no time. Insults are flying like shrapnel from a homemade incendiary device: lazy-good-for-nothing-no-good-lying-scum . . .

I manage to break in. "Are you separated?"

"Not yet."

This surprises me. She's so angry. How could she still be living with the guy? "Why not?" I ask.

She crosses her shapely arms. "Financial reasons."

I fish out my usual forms detailing the divorce process in Canada and slide them across my desk. "What's called a No Fault Divorce is by far the easiest and cheapest way to get divorced in Canada. You can apply as soon as you and your spouse separate. Your divorce will go through after you live apart for one year."

One of Vonda's perfectly groomed eyebrows gives a horrified twitch. "One year? I cannot vait one year!"

"Um, why not?" I ask.

Again, her look says I've missed the obvious. "Vhat if I vant to remarry?"

"Ah," I say, trying to hide my dismay. "So there's someone else?" Adultery is grounds for Fault divorce. But since she's my client I'd prefer she's not the one doing the dirty.

"Not yet," says Vonda, coyly.

She glances at my brochures, her frown deepening, then waves a slender, ring-bedecked hand. "I do not vant a No Fault divorce," she says, through gritted teeth. "This is all his fault. I leaved my home, come all the vay here and . . ." Strong emotion has weakened her English. A single tear rolls down her smooth pink cheek. "He deceived me," she whispers.

I hand her my trusty tissue box. It's time to delve into her marriage. "How?" I ask.

"I meet him online," says Vonda. "Vhen I vas living in my homeland, Vladivostok. He vas so charming and . . ." Her eyelashes dip. "I trusted him."

Without meaning to, I click the pen in my hand. "So, did you meet in person before you got married?"

Vonda's slims nostrils flare. She sounds affronted. "But of course. Ve met in Paris. During Fashion Veek. I vas there on business."

Guilt makes me look down. I misjudged her, and succumbed to prejudice—the poor, Russian mail-order bride, with nothing going for her but good looks and a killer set of onion domes. Having spent my whole life battling racist assumptions, I should know better. Just because she looks like a caricature doesn't mean she's not a person of substance. Plenty of savvy women—models, actresses, the Kardashians—have leveraged their looks into business empires.

Lost in memories of Paris, Vonda's gaze turns misty. "Ve stayed at the George V. Strolled on Les Champs Elysees. It vas vonderful, very romantic."

I nod. It's always vonderful, at the outset. "So how did he betray you?" I ask. Surely, he couldn't be cheating on her yet. Look at the woman! And they've only been married for three months. Although who knows? Maybe he's a sex addict. I wonder what he's like, this Dennis Butts. He must be quite something to have landed Vonda.

Vonda's eyelashes dip, then flip open. Her eyes narrow. "He said he vas rich. Very rich." She tosses her head. "But he vasn't!"

Without meaning to, I start clicking my pen, trying to sort this out. Soooo. My new client is a gold digger who wants out because the mine's a dud. "Is he a gambler?" I say. "Has he mismanaged your money?"

Vonda waves a hand, her bejeweled fingers flashing. "Money? There is no money. It vas all for show. All this time and energy I put into him. All this!" She waves a hand toward her chest, showcasing her enviable assets. "All for nothing!" Her lip quivers and her voice drops. "I even posted about him! On Insta and Tumblr!"

"Uh, that's not really grounds for a Fault divorce," I say. "Is he cheating on you? Is he cruel to you?"

"Cruel!" cries Vonda. "Yes, so so cruel!" She sticks out her hand to show me her diamond engagement ring—the stone the size of an igloo. Her chest heaves with indignation. "I vent to the jeweler to get it assessed and it is fake!" she cries. "Cubic zirconia. Vorthless!" Fresh tears fill her eyes. "That is fraud! Such betrayal! Can you imagine?"

Seeing her so upset, I'm unsure how to respond. "Er, does he agree to a divorce?" I ask, once she's calmed down.

Vonda shrugs. "I don't know. Maybe. Probably." For a moment, she looks genuinely sad. "Perhaps he is also disappointed."

"Why?"

A tiny embarrassed pout. "Oh, vell, maybe he thought I had money too."

My pen clicks. What? This is a first. Mr. versus Mrs. Gold Digger. "So he married you for your money?"

"Perhaps," says Vonda. She clasps her hands primly. "But in truth I am broke. It is very difficult, being an Influencer. Instagram has changed its algorithm." She pronounces this last word with extra care. Her doleful gaze turns steely. "But not for long, don't vorry."

Seeing my questioning look she gives me a game smile. "I vill find a rich husband," she says. "I just need a divorce." She clicks her fingers. "A-SAP."

"One year," I say. "And No Fault. Unless there's adultery or physical or mental cruelty." Seeing her look of hope, I head her off. "I mean real cruelty. And it's hard to prove. I recommend you separate imme-diately and file for No Fault. It's the cheapest . . ."

She breaks in. "No vay. He must pay. I am humiliated. He has harmed my *brand image*." Another toss of her glossy dark head. "I vill vait. Sooner or later, he vill cheat on me."

"How do you know?"

Again, she looks at me like I'm thick.

"Because he has the same plan," she says. "To find a new vife and marry for money."

CHAPTER 2:

A BAD FEELING

From the way my mom says my name, I know she's upset. "Toby? Can I come up?" The intercom crackles.

I stab at the button. "It's open."

I live on the fourth floor of a 1950s building in Oak Bay. There's no elevator. Not that that's a problem for my mom. Although she's turning sixty next month—and underwent chemo last year, she's in better shape than most women half her age, myself included.

I step into the hall just in time to see her sprint up the final stairs. Back before the chemo my mom's hair was long and black. It now swirls around her face like a storm cloud. Dressed in black leggings and a purple sweatshirt, she's carrying a tote bag and a yoga mat. Her pretty face is flushed. She must have come straight from hot yoga.

I hold the door open. "Hey Mom. How's it going?"

"Put the kettle on. I'm parched," she says. She deposits her mat and giant tote in my nonexistent front hall. "I need your help." She kicks off her pink Birkenstocks and leans in for a kiss. Even sweaty, my mom smells good, like cinnamon and a warm kitchen. Her toenails flash sparkly turquoise as she heads for my postage-stamp living room.

I put the kettle on and surreptitiously check my watch. I have a date with Josh Barton and still need to shower, dry my hair, and do my makeup. What's brought my mother to my door on a Wednesday night? Isn't this her regular Mystical Book Club evening down at the Metaphysical Bookstore?

My mom is pacing the room. "What's up?" I ask, carefully setting two cups—chamomile for her, English breakfast for me—onto coasters on the coffee table. Not that my mom will use hers. She has no regard for fine furniture.

She throws herself into an armchair. "Something's happened," she says. "I can't find Daphne."

Daphne Dane is one of my mom's closest friends, as well as a long-term client. "What'd you mean?" I say. "Did she miss an appointment?"

My mom nods. "Yes, her three p.m. reading. I've been trying to call her ever since but there's no answer."

I fight back a sigh. So Daphne missed a reading. So what? People forget stuff.

But my mother looks agitated. She pushes a wisp of hair from her eyes and rewraps the brightly colored scarf around her neck. "It's not like her. The only time Daphne's ever missed a reading was the day Walt died," she says. "Remember Daphne's late husband, Walter?"

"Um, yeah," I say, although I barely knew Walter Dane. I know his face, though, off the cookie boxes. Walter and Daphne founded the biggest cookie brand in Western Canada. When I was a kid, Daphne seemed straight off *Dynasty*—a large, big-haired glamor queen who'd sweep into my mom's tiny kitchen once a week to get her cards done. It was Daphne who'd encouraged my mother to read fortunes for a living. I didn't know it at the time, but without her financial help, my mom might have lost our house after my dad stopped paying alimony and child support.

"Her phone is off," continues my mom. "It's never off."

I check my watch. I'm meant to meet Josh in forty-five minutes.

My mother wrings her hands. "And her home phone's always busy. It must be off the hook."

I blow on my tea. My mother and Daphne Dane are unlikely friends—Daphne a mega-rich, mega-blonde socialite, and my mom a tarot-reading, Chinese-Canadian hippie. I know why Daphne's important to my mom. What I don't get is why she's freaking out. People miss appointments. They turn off their phones. Maybe Daphne is having a long nap. It's only been a few hours. I say this to my mom and she waves her hands. She hasn't even touched her tea.

"You don't understand!" she says. "I read her cards anyway and . . ." She chews on her lip. "They were horrifying! So then I consulted the I Ching. Even worse." She jumps up and starts to pace around the boxy room. From the couch to the fish tank and back. "I also did the Kau Cim." Her voice quivers.

I bite my tongue. The Kau Cim are bamboo sticks that you shake from a tube. Each stick has a number associated with a line of obscure and badly translated Chinese verse that, supposedly, offers insight into life's important questions. About as scientific as a fortune cookie. Like the rest of my mom's divination methods.

"Is there anyone else you could call?" I ask. "Do her kids live here?" I have vague—and vaguely unhappy—memories of being forced to interact with Daphne's kids at various parties as a child. What were their names? It doesn't matter.

"They do," says my mom. "I tried to look them up in the phone book, but their numbers aren't listed. I'm going over to her place to check on her."

I nod. While I'm sure Daphne's fine, my mom will feel better after she's checked. "Good idea," I say.

My mother stops pacing. "Can you come with me?"

"I have a date," I say.

Her pretty face falls. She runs her hands through her messy hair. "Oh. With Colin?"

"No, Josh."

Normally, my mom would be full of questions. My love life, or lack thereof, is one of her favorite topics. She must be really worried because she doesn't even react.

I chew on my lip. I ought to help. Guilt kicks in, followed by resentment. Why does she need *me* to accompany her to Daphne's house? This thought brings more guilt. I take a deep breath. My mom doesn't ask for much. Even when she was going through cancer treatment last year, she never complained. When I moved home to Victoria she was absurdly grateful. Accompanying her to Daphne's is the least I can do.

Another quick look at my watch. "I'll call Josh," I say. "And tell him I'll be late. Does Daphne still live in Rockland?"

"Yes. The same place."

Good news. That's not far. I can go there first, then continue downtown to meet Josh. As usual, just the thought of him gives me a buzz. We're going to a fancy French restaurant, the chicest place in town. "Just let me freshen up," I say. While Victoria is the provincial capital, it's a casual sort of town: even in a fancy restaurant, my dark work skirt suit will do fine. And I can live without doing my hair. Josh has seen me looking much worse. Sparkly earrings, high heels, and some lipstick will more than suffice.

For the first time tonight, my mother smiles. "Thank you." Her look of gratitude intensifies my guilt. She flops onto my small 50s-style couch and reaches for her now-cold tea. "I know you think I'm crazy," she says. When I don't deny it, she wiggles a skinny finger at me. "I hope I'm wrong," she says. "But the cards . . ." The way she's staring into her cup, I'm scared she's reading her tea. She sighs. "I have a really bad feeling."

CHAPTER 3:

A BIT OF A MESS

pull up behind my mom's yellow Honda hatchback. It's a miracle it's still running. She bought it second-hand back when I was in law school.

Standing before Daphne's arched gate, my mother looks small and nervous. Her legs—which I've sadly inherited—are so thin that her spandex yoga pants are baggy. It's late November, and far from warm. I button my wool coat and tuck my scarf in at the neck. My dark tights are flimsy and the wind is biting.

Surrounded by high laurel hedges, Daphne Dane's house could pass for a historic hotel, with a black and white Tudor facade, various elaborate, steeply pitched roofs, and dormer windows. There's even a turret, which naturally reminds me of a madwoman in the attic.

My mom unlatches the gate. I follow her through it. The front garden is massive, the perfect grass bordered by flower beds and landscaped shrubbery. A well-lit stone walkway leads to broad front steps and an open-fronted porch. Since I'm wearing heels, I tread carefully. In the center of the lawn, an old monkey puzzle tree rises as high as the house.

We're climbing the front steps when something squeals.

I stop and clutch my mom's arm. "What the—?"

She keeps climbing. "Oh, that's Daphne's potbellied pig, Kevin. He's like a guard pig. Anyone arrives, he makes a racket."

"She has a pig?" I say, aghast. "In Rockland?" Her poor neighbors. Those high-pitched squeals carry.

"A miniature pig," says my mom. "Although he's a bit larger than expected."

I peer at the imposing front door, the carved wood inset with stained glass. The pig's aria continues. It sounds gigantic.

We've now reached the top of the stairs. When I press the doorbell, the pig's squeals turn to grunts. The front door shakes like something heavy has smacked it. As the bell's chimes fade, I listen for approaching footsteps.

While we're both focused on the door, a raspy voice comes from behind. "Hello?"

We both swing around. A young man is walking our way, slowly, like he's exhausted. Slung across his thin torso is a saffron cloth bag like those carried by monks. On his back is a massive backpack.

At the bottom of the steps, he stops and gapes up at us. Despite the cold, he's dressed in frayed board shorts, flip-flops, and a faded sweatshirt with an image of Ganesh on the front. He rubs his wispy hair from his eyes and squints in recognition. "Mrs. Wong?" he says, slowly. "Hey? How's it going?"

My mom smiles. "Hi, Lukas," she says. "I'm well, thanks. Did you just get back? Daphne said you were traveling."

Lukas nods. "Um, yeah. India," he says, vaguely. He yawns. "I'm beat. Such a long flight. And Mom's and Grace's phones were off, so I had to hitch a ride from the airport." He peers up at the house, disgruntled.

I have a sudden, vivid memory of him as a spoiled, chubby kid—ill from gorging on chocolate cake at some fancy hotel buffet. He's certainly lost the baby weight. Twenty years on, he looks malnourished, as well as scruffy. He's got a beach bum's ragged blond hair but the pallor of a teenage gamer.

He adjusts the straps of his pack. "Is my mom home?"

"She doesn't seem to be," says my mom. "She missed an appointment so I got worried and came over. I couldn't reach her either."

"Oh," says Lukas. "I thought it was just my phone, 'cause it's like, out of cash." He starts to climb the stairs. "My van's in the shop. I came over to borrow one of Mom's cars."

My mother nods. "Can we check indoors? It's not like Daphne to miss a reading."

"Sure," says Lukas, now joining us on the porch. He shrugs off his heavy pack. Like every other Canadian who's ever backpacked anywhere, he's sewn a small Maple Leaf flag onto his pack. We wait as he rummages slowly through various pockets. Unlike my mom, he doesn't look worried.

I grit my teeth. At this rate, I'll be here all night. My stomach rumbles. I skipped my usual late afternoon snack to leave more room for tonight's saucy French dinner.

Finally, Lukas extracts a set of keys. Behind the door, the pig is still grunting.

Lukas has just stuck his key in the lock when a woman calls out from behind us. All three of us turn to see a skinny blonde striding our way. She's trailed by a dumpy man holding a man-bag. They're both dressed for golf in matching aqua polo shirts and beige and aqua plaid slacks. Even their shoes match. These outfits seem especially absurd on account of their size difference—the woman is a Chihuahua and the guy a well-fed bulldog.

The woman's hands clasp her narrow hips: "When did you get back?" she barks at Lukas.

He doesn't answer.

I look from Lukas to the blonde, whom I now recognize as his sister. I struggle to recall her name. Ingrid? Annabel? The last time I saw her she was about fifteen, with a velvet headband and a haughty determination to ignore me at some lame holiday party.

She's got Lukas's sharp nose, slender frame, and narrow face. But despite their physical similarity, they couldn't look less alike—Lukas in his ratty, beach-tourist garb, and his sister in her preppie golf-wear.

"Why are you here?" she snaps.

"Geez. Nice to see you too, Isobel," says Lukas. His sister's frown deepens. "I'm here to see Mom. I just got back," continues Lukas. He shifts from foot to foot. "From, you know, that meditation retreat?"

Isobel's blue eyes register me and my mom, then dismiss us. She stomps up the steps toward us. "Just listen to that pig!" Her voice is sharp with indignation. "We need to stop it!"

"Isobel?" says my mother.

Isobel's plucked eyebrows rise in confusion before dipping with annoyance.

"I'm your mom's friend, Ivy," explains my mom. "It's been a long time since we last met."

I'm sure Isobel knows exactly who we are. How many Asian friends does her mom have? Even as a kid she was rude and snobby.

My mom's smile never falters. She repeats her story about Daphne's missed appointment.

Isobel looks my mom up and down. Her thin upper lip curls. "Oh. You're the fortune teller?" Based on her tone, these last two words could be substituted with any number of insults.

My mom nods. "That's me." She sounds resolutely cheerful.

Faced with Isobel Dane's cold stare, I feel my cheeks redden. I know exactly how this snooty woman views my mom—as a charlatan, out to scam her rich, elderly mother. While I share Isobel's suspicion of the occult, Daphne Dane is no gullible fool. And my mom's not dishonest—just delusional. She loves Daphne like a sister.

I'm tempted to defend my mom's honor. But how? Isobel is looking straight through me.

Isobel's partner has now joined us on the steps. When he removes his cap, I see he's almost entirely bald. If it weren't for the golf wear, he'd look exactly like Alfred Hitchcock.

"Oh, listen to that pig!" he says, in a peevish French accent. "No wonder the neighbors have complained!" He pulls a hankie from his man-bag and mops his brow. "They have telephoned us, saying it is making noises all day! We must shut it up! Where is that woman who works for Daphne? Open the door, Lukas!"

Lukas shrugs. Maybe he's jet-lagged, or just really laid back, but he's moving in slow motion. "Geez, chill, Gerard," he says.

Already red, the Frenchman's scalp purples. Isobel shoots Lukas a poisonous look and lays a soothing hand on Gerard's arm. "The neighbors called us," she tells Lukas, haughtily. "While you've been off . . . wherever . . ." She waves a hand. "I've been dealing with Mom's issues."

The pig emits a particularly piercing squeal. Isobel flinches. "We have to convince Mom to get rid of it. It's absurd! Just because George Clooney had one!"

While I doubt Isobel and I would agree on much, she has a point. That pig seems like a crazy rich person's pet, like Michael Jackson's chimpanzee or Mike Tyson's tiger.

No sooner has Lukas opened the door when the pig comes barreling out. Miniature, my ass—or rather ten times bigger. Black, white, and hairy, it's shaped like a barrel on elf legs. It pounds down the front steps, squealing.

On the lawn, its squeals cede to happy oinks. After running in circles, it shoves its snout under the pristine green. Clods of dirt and grass fly. Before Gerard can yell *"Merde! Arrete!"* it has gauged out a meteor-strike-sized crater.

Isobel shrieks. Gerard tuts. Lukas can't stop giggling.

While everyone else watches the pig, my mother sticks her head around the front door. "Daphne?" she calls. "Hello? Daphne?" She gasps. "Oh my gosh! Look at this mess!"

I follow my mom into Daphne's wood-paneled hall. High overhead, an old crystal chandelier glints in the gloom. Beside a coat cupboard, an ornate side-table has been knocked over. An antique brass telephone rests in a puddle on the wooden floor. Nearby, lie a broken vase and a scattering of squished purple chrysanthemums. Soggy magazines litter the hall.

My mom bends to pick up a pink satin shoe, its high heel scoured with tooth marks. She looks around, wide-eyed. "Good gracious. What happened?"

Lukas steps inside and stops. He frowns down the dark hall. "Hey Mom?" he calls. "Hellooooo Moooooooom?" He sounds put out. "Hey, it's me! I'm home, Mom!"

Nobody answers.

Gerard and Isobel step inside too. Isobel gasps. "Grace?" she screeches up the stairs. "Grace?" Again, there's no reply. "She should be working today," says Isobel, crossly. Her voice rises: "Grace? Mommy?"

Gerard pouts. "That *cochon!*" he says. He lowers himself to an uncomfortable-looking squat and runs a finger along a scratched floor-board. "This is mahogany." He sounds outraged. "You cannot even buy this kind of wood anymore! It is endangered!"

Isobel ventures further down the hall. "Mommy?" Unlike her brother or her husband, she sounds genuinely worried. She turns: "Gerard?" He's still examining the wooden floor. She returns and tugs at his elbow. "Do . . . do you think the pig made this mess?" she asks him.

"But of course!" says Gerard. He rises, shakily, to his feet. "It is destroying the garden! And now this!" He points at the scratched floor. "I told her. A pig—it is not a suitable pet. She should get a little poodle. Or a cat . . . A Siamese." When he shakes his head in disgust, multiple chins quiver. "Look at those scratches!" He throws up his hands in the French gesture of outraged surrender.

Peering into the dark house, I'm not sure Kevin is to blame. Yes, he chewed the shoe. But did he knock over that heavy table?

My mom's already hurrying down the hall, calling for Daphne. Lukas and I follow.

Daphne's house has a lot of rooms. We search everywhere: main floor, upstairs, and even the basement. Everything is in order.

When it's clear Daphne's not here, we follow Lukas into the kitchen. Isobel and Gerard are already there, making tea. They don't offer us any. A trail of muddy trotter-prints leads to the back door, which contains what looks like a giant cat-flap.

"For the pig," says my mom, when she sees me examining it. I push on the flap but it won't budge. "The pig has a microchip that signals it to open," explains my mother. "Otherwise, burglars could get in."

"Wow," I say, wondering how much this contraption must have cost. "Daphne must really love that pig."

"Oh, she does," says my mom. "He was just a wee little piglet when she got him." She raises her hands to show me Kevin's then size, like a small rabbit. "A teacup pig. It's just bad luck he got so big." She shrugs philosophically. "That's the mystery of genetics."

Right, I think. And unscrupulous breeders. Kevin is to a teacup as a blue whale is to a bathtub.

I unlock the back door and step onto the back deck. My mom walks out behind me. It might be trendy, but it still seems insane to keep a potbellied pig in the house. Although Kevin must spend a lot of time outdoors. Surrounded by a high fence, Daphne's large back yard is crisscrossed by long furrows and giant craters. It's like a World War I battlefield, post-typhoon. That pig's been engaging in trench warfare.

In a far corner stands a small wooden shed with a red-tiled roof, like a rich kid's cubby house. "Kevin's cottage," explains my mother.

Gerard steps out behind us. His round cheeks puff in disgust. "This house, it is heritage-listed," he says. "Built in 1901. It's disgraceful to keep a farm animal in such a fine building!"

I make a sympathetic noise and introduce myself. "I'm Toby, by the way. And this is my mom, Ivy, an old friend of Daphne's."

"The lady clairvoyant?" enquires Gerard. Maybe I'm just imagining it, but I think I see mockery in his watery green eyes. But then he surprises me and grasps my mom's hand. "*Enchantée*," he tells her. "Daphne says you're very good. I should consult you."

Is he serious? While I wouldn't have pegged Gerard as a believer, I'm constantly surprised that seemingly smart and sane people will pay a stranger to make random guesses about their lives.

"I am planning a new business venture," explains Gerard. "And want to get off on the right foot."

My mom smiles. "I'm often hired to help choose an auspicious day," she says. "Timing is everything."

I try to conceal my skepticism. "What do you do?" I ask Gerard.

He looks surprised. Like I should know. "I'm a chef," he says, proudly. "And Isobel is a *hôtelier*." He pronounces this last word the French way. "We met years ago, at the Cordon Bleu institute in Paris."

Paree. This reminds me of Vonda Butt's romantic honeymoon and brief marriage.

The door cracks open. "Gerard?" Isobel's voice is sharp. Maybe she thinks he's out here flirting, or maybe she's just upset about her mother. She runs a hand through her thin bob. "Mommy's phone is still off. What should we do?" she asks Gerard.

Despite my many attempts to make eye contact, Isobel still hasn't acknowledged my existence.

Lukas steps outside too. In one hand he's holding a bag of Dane jumbo chocolate chip cookies. He must have found them in his mom's kitchen. His other hand contains half a cookie. "I'm sure Mom's fine," he says, then shoves the rest in his mouth. He chews contentedly. "Wow, these are good," he says. "So chocolatey!"

My mom swallows hard. "I . . . I'm not so sure," she says. She fiddles with the scarf at her neck. "I'm scared something has happened." She tugs at her scarf's tassels. "I've got this bad feeling . . ."

While I doubt Isobel has any faith in psychics, my mom's misgivings must mirror her own. She wrings her skinny hands. "*Chéri*, should we call the police?" she asks her husband.

Lukas looks up sharply. He stops chewing. "For real? The police? It's only been a few hours. Mom's probably out getting a massage, or something."

"Of course you're not worried about a few hours," snaps Isobel. "You've been away for what—two, three weeks? Did you even call her?"

Looking at Isobel's creased face, I recall the mess in the front hall. Maybe the pig knocked that table over, or maybe it was the scene of a struggle. Daphne's not just a little bit rich. She's scary rich, like rich enough to get kidnapped.

I think of Colin Destin. He'd be happy to check things out. Getting his professional opinion would reassure my mom. More likely than not, Lukas is right: Daphne will walk in any minute now, fresh and shiny from some expensive facial.

"I have a friend who's a police detective," I say. "Colin," I tell my mom, who loves the guy. "I could call him?"

Lukas rolls his eyes. "You'd be wasting his time."

"I think you should call him," says my mother. "Please, call him, hon."

I reach into my purse and find my cellphone.

Lukas shrugs. "Whatever." He turns to his sister. "D'you know where Mom keeps the keys to her Audi?" He digs a hand in the bag and extracts another huge cookie.

Isobel's eyes narrow. "Why? You're not borrowing it."

"Says who?" He takes a big bite, his words muffled because his mouth is so full. "My van's leaking oil. Mmmmm . . ." He tilts the bag toward his sister. "You ever tried these? They're amazing."

She swats the bag away. "You can't just take Mom's car without permission!"

They're still bickering as I walk down to ground level. I sit on the bottom step. Is this a waste of Colin's time? I don't care. I want to call him.

To prevent the flutter in my stomach from reaching my voice, I take a deep breath, then press Call.

Colin picks up on the second ring. He sounds upbeat. "Hey, Toby! What's up? How are you?"

"Colin," I say. "I hope I'm not bothering you."

I can hear the smile in his voice. "Never."

There's something soothing yet buoyant about Colin's voice, alert yet optimistic. I can't help but smile too. "Colin," I say. "I'm with my mom. We need your advice." When I've finished explaining, he says he's nearby and can stop by in ten minutes.

"Great! Thanks," I say, gratefully. I'm glad he didn't pass me off to some beat cop, or even worse, tell me not to worry. I give him Daphne's address. It's been almost a week since our last date: Thai food and an action movie. The film was pretty lame, but we didn't watch much of it. I tamp down my smile at the memory of us cuddling in the back row. We're overdue for a repeat. I can't wait to see him.

It's only after I've stashed my phone that I remember my date with Josh. A look at my watch makes my stomach plummet. I'd better call him. I'm supposed to meet him in a few minutes.

I retrieve my phone. Back to recent calls. Josh and Colin's names come up a lot. I met them both this past summer, or rather re-met in Josh's case, since we'd had a brief, painful, and mostly one-sided teen-age romance—that is, I had a hopeless, childish crush on him that I couldn't shake, even as an adult.

Not long after I moved back to Victoria in June, Josh hired me to handle his multimillion-dollar divorce from a girl who'd made my life hell as a teen. She ended up being murdered, which is how I met Colin, the lead detective on her homicide case.

Both men are amazing: gorgeous, funny, interesting . . . More amazingly still, they're both interested in me. After years of Sahara-like dating drought, this double attention is overwhelming. I like them both. I like them a lot. Choosing feels impossible, like being asked to renounce booze *or* coffee.

Still elated from my chat with Colin, I wait for Josh to pick up. He answers on the fifth ring. "Hi, Toby. You on your way yet?"

"I'm so sorry but not yet," I say. "That problem I told you about with my mom. It's ongoing. I need another half hour. Maybe forty minutes?" I swallow hard. "I'm really sorry."

There's a pause. Is he mad at me? Will he tell me to forget it? I'm still not sure where I stand with Josh. He's so successful and good looking, the kind of blond god who stops women in their tracks, slack-jawed and drooling. It's hard to believe he's into me when he could choose anyone he wants.

"Okay," he says, slowly. I'm not sure if he's disappointed or angry or both. "Shall we make it another night?"

Now I feel disappointed. He's met my mom. They seemed to get along great. He could at least ask what's wrong, and if he could help. He could offer to meet me here. "If you prefer," I say. "I'm so sorry."

"Why don't you just call me when you're done and we'll see where we both are," he says. My stomach sinks lower. His tone sounds so clipped, like I just canceled some business meeting. I've never flaked out on him before. I'm reliable as an atomic clock, and obsessively punctual. He should understand that I'm well and truly stuck here.

"Okay." I apologize again and hang up feeling lousy. My shoulders slump. Have I messed things up with Josh? I sigh. Enough already. This insecurity must stop. It's ridiculous and pathetic. If he dumps me because of a family emergency, so be it. Not that this is a family emergency, but he doesn't know that.

I sigh again. Damn Daphne and her missed appointment, and damn my mom's crazy, pseudo-psychic *feelings*. If it weren't for them I'd be sitting in the best restaurant in town, eating haute cuisine, and drinking good wine with a guy who's at least partly to blame for global warming. Instead, I'm huddled on a hard step, freezing my bony ass off.

I hug my knees. When she shows up, Daphne had better have a damn good story.

CHAPTER 4:

COMING UP SHORT

advised Colin to come around back. If the front hall is a crime scene, which I highly doubt, the less people tramping through it, the better.

I'm still sitting on Daphne's back steps, feeling hungry and glum, when I hear the click of the side gate being unlatched.

Time to cheer up. I run a hand through my hair and rise to greet Colin.

He rounds the corner and stops. "Toby!" he says. His shy smile stokes mine. "Have you been waiting out here the whole time?"

I nod and stamp my high-heeled feet, which are frozen. In the glow cast by Daphne's path lights, Colin reminds me of a 1950s movie star, dark hair framing an expressive face, bright-eyed and serious. He studies me intently. "You okay?" he asks.

"Yes," I say, which is suddenly true. I push my shoulders back and walk toward him. "Thanks for coming, Colin."

He smiles and walks my way too. "How's the shoulder?"

"Good," I say. Two months back, Josh and I were both badly hurt fighting off his ex-wife's killer. Colin saved our lives. Having witnessed my recovery, he keeps reminding me to take things easy. Now, faced with his searching gaze, I find my hand going to my scarred shoulder. I force it down. When we're a few feet apart I stop walking.

I inhale, ready to bounce onto my toes and give him a quick kiss, only to freeze. He's not alone. A tall woman has rounded the house behind him. As she strides closer, her long ponytail sways. Despite the cold wind, she's not wearing a jacket, just black pants and a dark turtleneck that shows off her stunning figure. In the golden lights, she looks bronzed, impervious to the weather. I bet rain would bead off her.

The pig has noticed her too. Tail wagging, it trots toward her. Covered in glistening mud, it resembles a very fat slug, all its white bits now brown. When it gets close, I expect the woman to recoil in horror. Instead, she laughs and bends to pet it. "Ooh, a pig!" she says. "Did you dig up the garden? You naughty piggy!" Even her voice is lovely—deep with a sexy rasp, although with that perfect skin, there's no way she's ever smoked. The pig looks suitably charmed. She crouches to scratch its muddy chin.

When she stands, Kevin dives into a fresh mud puddle and starts to roll.

With a wide smile, the woman turns toward us.

"Toby," says Colin. He looks a bit awkward now, like he's not sure how to greet me. He touches my elbow, then gestures toward the tall woman. "This is Miriam Young," he says. "My new partner."

What? My stomach flips. He's partnered with this goddess? Miriam Young looks like she just stepped out of *Shape* magazine. She wipes the mud off her hand and extends a slim yet muscly arm. We shake. Even though I'm in heels and she's in flats, she towers over me. As do most people.

Her smile widens. Like the rest of her, her teeth are dazzling. "Toby. Nice to meet you." A quick glance from me to Colin, like she's trying to suss out our relationship. She turns to look up at the house. "So, who's missing?"

I explain about Daphne Dane. "Come inside," I say. "My mom and Daphne's kids are up there."

Colin and Miriam follow me up the back steps. The large deck lies empty. Lukas and Isobel have moved their argument indoors. Their angry voices float out of the kitchen: "You can't just borrow it without asking!"

"What's it to you?" says Lukas.

"I'll tell Mom."

"So? Go right ahead." Lukas sounds sulky. "She'd let me use it."

As an only child, I can't judge. I have friends with siblings who never outgrew their early family dynamics. That's clearly the case here: Lukas at least thirty and Isobel nearing forty, continuing a rivalry that's been raging for decades.

I step inside, Colin and Miriam behind me. "Hello?" says Colin.

Lukas and Isobel fall silent. Gerard and my mom are sitting at a long table. Recognizing Colin, my mom's face lights up.

He goes over and pecks her on both cheeks. "Hi, Ivy! Good to see you." He turns and introduces my mother to Miriam, then introduces himself to the others. He looks around the kitchen. "So what's the trouble?"

"We don't know where my mother's gone," says Isobel. She nibbles anxiously on a hangnail.

My mother jumps in to explain about Daphne's missed appointment. Thankfully, she doesn't mention tarot or the Kau Cim. Gerard is busy typing on his phone. Lukas is peering into the cupboards. He withdraws a box of Dane crackers.

I watch Colin and Miriam for some reaction, but their faces remain neutral. Do they think Isobel and my mom are overreacting? Will Colin be annoyed that I've wasted his time?

"Can we have a look around?" Colin asks the Dane siblings.

"Of course. Follow me," says Isobel, clearly relieved he's taking this seriously. "It's not like my mom to turn off her phone." She swallows hard. "And she's not getting any younger."

While Lukas stays seated in the kitchen, eating crackers, the rest of us troop around the house again. Even Gerard joins us, although he keeps looking at his phone.

Colin and Miriam start by surveying the front hall. Having seen the destruction wrought by Kevin outdoors, I can see they're unconvinced this was the scene of a struggle.

In each new room we enter, Colin asks if anything is missing or out of place. Library. Living room. Dining room. TV room. Office. Everything is neat and tidy.

Isobel keeps shaking her head. "No, it seems fine. No, it looks okay. No, nothing."

We all plod upstairs. Isobel's in the lead. We enter a bedroom with faded surfing posters on the walls. A shelf of model airplanes lines one wall. The narrow bed is covered by a bedspread in rasta colors. "Lukas's room," says Isobel, curtly. It's got a weird smell: like old, musty spices.

"Oh," I say, surprised. "Does Lukas live here?"

"He moved out last year," says Isobel—the *finally* there but unsaid. From the look on my mom's face, I sense there's a story.

Next up come two guest rooms, both decorated like five-star hotel rooms. Latte-toned quilts and cream pillows. Heather accents. Matching towels.

"And this is my mom's room," says Isobel.

It's not a room but a suite—a sitting room with pretty floral wallpaper, a cream and antique-gold bedroom, and a fancy, white, spa-style bathroom. An Instagrammer's dream. I'm reminded of my new client, Vonda. Can so-called Influencers earn a real living? What does Vonda actually model?

Colin peers into Daphne's walk-in closet. He repeats his standard question: "Is anything missing or out of place?"

Isobel starts to say no, then stops. She squints into her mother's vast closet. "One of her suitcases is gone," she says. "The medium-sized LV one. Not the big one or the carry-on. It's about . . ." She holds out her hands. "This big."

Gerard looks up from his cellphone. "Are you sure, *chéri?*"

Isobel nods. *"Mais oui,"* she says.

Miriam studies some shelves lined with expensive shoes. "How about her clothes and shoes?" she asks. "Is everything here?"

"Her green raincoat is gone," says Isobel. "And her black patent heels." She opens another drawer. "Plus her favorite robe, the cream velvet one."

Gerard shoves his phone into the pocket of his golf-slacks. "Well, that settles it," he says. "She's gone on a little vacation. Maybe Vancouver, or up island, for a few nights." He smiles at his wife. "All this worrying for nothing."

Miriam nods. "That does seem likely."

While Colin and Miriam seem convinced, I know my mom isn't. And Isobel? She still looks anxious, although that might be her normal expression.

Colin hands Isobel his card and smiles kindly at her. "Keep us posted," he says. "But from what we've seen, I'd say she's gone on a trip. Have you called her other friends? Is there anyone she might have gone on holiday with?"

Isobel's eyes slide to her husband. He doesn't meet them. "The housekeeper might know," she says. She frowns, crossly. "She should be here! Her phone's off. I'll try her later."

Colin nods. My mom offers to call her and Daphne's mutual friends.

We all troop downstairs.

We're on the front porch when Colin's phone rings. He answers it and looks grave, his high forehead creasing. "Just a second." He covers the mouthpiece with his hand. A meaningful look at Miriam, followed by a quick jerk of his chin. "We'd better go, Miri."

Miri? They've been partners for what, twenty minutes, and she's already got a pet name?

Miriam nods. I can see the excitement in her brown eyes. They have a real case. She says goodbye to everyone.

"Ivy, Toby—see you soon?" says Colin. He gives me a twinkly smile. I nod, suddenly breathless. He resumes his phone conversation.

Watching him and Miriam—Miri—walk away, I have a strange, tight feeling in my chest. Is that heartburn? But no, it's jealousy, stirred by the sight of two smart and beautiful people heading off to do what they do best. Together. Why couldn't his new partner be old, ugly, and male? Ew. I hate that I'm jealous. It's a nasty, petty feeling. I'm too old for this insecurity. Either I'm right for Colin as I am—short, scrawny legs and all—or he's not the one for me. End of story.

CHAPTER 5:

WHO'S STEPHEN?

We are on Daphne's front porch. My mother is bidding the Danes farewell. "Please let me know if you have news!" she begs Isobel. "And if I hear anything, I'll call you."

Lukas has joined us again. He takes a seat on the front steps, still clutching his box of crackers. "Sure thing," he says, then grins. "But seeing as you're psychic, can't you just tell us where she's gone?" He bites into a cracker.

While I'd snap out a reply, my mother responds with good grace. "I wish," she says. "Unfortunately, it's rarely that clear. I just have a bad feeling about Daphne. And the signs are worrying." She revives her tale about doing Daphne's tarot cards. And the I Ching. And the Kau Cim sticks.

While Lukas keeps nodding, his eyes look glazed. I don't blame him.

"Mom," I say, freshly embarrassed. Although my mom has been telling fortunes for almost twenty years, I'm still not cool with it. How could I be? It's humiliating to admit that your own mother has fallen for a load of crock—hook, line, and sinker. And she doesn't just buy it, she sells the stuff. It's worse than Amway. At least she's toned down her clothes. Back when I was a teen, she dressed like a fairground fortune-teller, her head, neck, and hips swathed in colorful scarves. An Arab bazaar's worth of beads hung off her small Asian body. These days, she looks almost normal. Or at least normal for Victoria, where most folk dress like affluent beatniks out hiking. I make a show of checking my watch. "Mom? Let's get going," I tell her.

We're walking toward the road, when a plump woman in her sixties opens the gate, carrying two bulging cloth shopping bags. At the sight of us, her steps quicken. Dressed in a long, quilted, rust-colored coat she reminds me of a gingerbread lady—all round and cheery. Despite her age, she exudes energy, her face ruddy beneath a pink woolen hat with a pom-pom. Gazing at my mom, her wide face cracks into a merry grin. "Why hello Ivy," she calls. "What a nice surprise! Is Daphne back then?"

"Hi, Grace," says my mom. "No. Where is she?"

Grace walks closer. We all stop. Her dark eyes twinkle. "I'm not sure," she says. "I'm terribly late. I was meant to feed the pig hours ago . . ." She sets down the bags. "But I had a wee emergency. My washing machine broke. It flooded my entire place! Water everywhere!" While most people would describe this as a catastrophe, this woman makes it sound like a great adventure. "I got so caught up I forgot about the pig." She smiles up at the house. "Has anyone fed him?" she asks my mother.

My mom waves a hand. "Oh don't worry. The pig's fine," she says. "He's out back." She peers at Grace. "But I'm worried about Daphne. When did you last see her?"

Grace rubs her mittened hands together. "Last night," she says. "But she texted me earlier today, said was going away for a few days . . . I was meant to fix Kevin's lunch."

Behind us, I hear fast footsteps. Isobel is walking to join us. "Grace!" she calls out. She eyes the housekeeper with cool disdain. "Grace!" Her tone is imperious. "Where have you been? Where's my mother?"

Grace repeats her story about the text message, and her washing machine, and forgetting.

Isobel checks her watch, pointedly. "The pig made so much noise the neighbors called us." She looks petulant. "Now we've missed our seven p.m. golf slot."

For a second, Grace's cheery face hardens. "Right. Sorry." She doesn't sound sorry. She stoops to retrieve her bags. "I'd best go fix Kevin's dinner. He must be starving."

"Wait," I say. That pig sure doesn't look starving. "I'm Toby, by the way, Ivy's daughter."

My smile is met with a hearty nod. "Oh right." She beams from me to my mom. "You're the spitting image of your mother."

"Thanks," I say. It's a compliment but not strictly true. I look fine. My mom has a face off a cameo brooch. "What time did Daphne text you?" I ask Grace.

She looks thoughtful. "Just after eleven," she admits. "I meant to come right away . . . but then . . ." She shrugs.

I nod. "Your washing machine."

"Right." She laughs. "It's been one of those days."

"She didn't say where she was going?"

Grace shakes her head. "No, but I figured it was somewhere with Stephen."

I glance at Isobel. Her hands are curled into tight fists. "Who's Stephen?" I ask.

Isobel's narrow lips pinch to oblivion.

For a moment, there's silence. Grace looks at my mom, like she fears she's said too much. Isobel glowers.

Finally, Grace answers: "Stephen Buxley, Daphne's new boyfriend. I figured they'd gone off for a romantic escape. To a B&B, maybe."

I look at Isobel, her eyes now as thin as her lips. Is it the mention of Stephen Buxley that's made her so tense? Or does she dislike her mom's jolly housekeeper?

Flip-flops flapping against the stone path, Lukas saunters over to join us. "Yo, Grace," he calls out. "I needed a ride. I've been trying to call you!"

Grace looks worried. She starts to apologize but Lukas cuts her off. He eyes her shopping bags with a hopeful look. "Ooh. I'm starving! You cooking?"

She beams at him, then clicks her tongue. She sets down her bags. "Oh, Lukas. You're not dressed warmly enough for this cold weather!"

Lukas shuffles closer and hugs her. Grace gives him a bear hug. She steps back to study his face, then shakes her pom-pommed head. "You okay? You look tired." Perhaps remembering the rest of us, she clears her throat. "Your trip went well?" she asks, brightly.

"Oh, great," says Lukas. He nods manically. "I learned so much about, er . . ." He shrugs. "Meditating and stuff. Thanks for asking."

He nods toward his sister. "But Izzie's freaking out here. She thinks Mom's missing."

"Who's this guy, Stephen?" I repeat, before Isobel can snap at Lukas.

Lukas rubs his eyes. Isobel glares at me, like she wishes I'd mind my own business.

"Her new . . . friend," says my mom, hesitantly. "She was very excited when they first met, but then seemed rather . . ." She pauses to find the right word. "Private. Because it's so new, I assume." She directs her next words to Grace. "I haven't met him yet. What's he like, this man, Stephen?"

Grace's smile slips a notch. "I, ah . . . I barely know him. He's from England, I believe. Ex-RAF. Or maybe SAS? Something military." She nudges a spray of snowy hair behind one ear. "They've only been dating for a few weeks." While Grace's tone is neutral, it's clear she's no fan. She described a flooded apartment with more enthusiasm than she's describing Stephen Buxley. Her voice trails off. "He's younger . . ."

When no one responds I have to ask. "How much younger?" I'm picturing Daphne with some hot toy boy stud. Like JLo and her back-up dancer.

"He's about fifty," snaps Isobel. "So it's no big deal, really."

I bite my tongue. It seems like a big deal to her. And Daphne must be at least seventy, so it's a twenty-year age gap.

Lukas wheezes out a peeved snort. "What? Mom's just run off with some strange man?" He looks petulant, clearly put out that his mom's not here to welcome him home with open arms, lend him her car, and do him all the other favors he obviously expected. He turns to his sister. "Mom's got a boyfriend?" He sounds incredulous. "Why didn't you say so, Izzie?"

I study Isobel, too. Her arms are tightly crossed. Lukas asked a good question. Why didn't Isobel mention Daphne's new man to the cops? Does she hate the guy and hope he'll just fade away? Is he embarrassingly awful?

Isobel's eyes slide down and left. "I . . ." She shuts her mouth and changes tack. "So Mom's dating again? So what?" she snaps at Lukas. "They only just met. I didn't think he was important!" The tight chords in her neck belie this statement. "Does everyone need to know our family's business?" she continues, shrilly.

She spins on her heels and calls out: "Gerard! Gerard! It's late! Let's go! *Chéri!*"

He comes bustling down the walkway.

Seeing Grace, his frown deepens. "Ah," he says. "Where have you been?" Then, before she can answer. "The floor in the front hall. It is scratched! It will need to be polished, maybe resanded!"

While Grace's smile doesn't change, her eyes narrow. "Resanded? I don't—"

Gerard cuts her off. "From now on, that pig stays outside. Understood? It is ruining the house! Outdoors only!"

Short as she is, Grace looks down her nose at him. Her smile has a dangerous edge. Gerard doesn't seem to notice.

"Ah, *bon*," he says, as if she'd agreed. He reaches for his wife's hand and turns to go. "We must be gone. Good night, all." They bustle off toward the street. The rest of us watch them go in silence.

My mom gives Grace a sympathetic smile. "You won't really leave Kevin outside all night long?" she asks quietly. "Will you?"

The housekeeper snorts. "I'd sometimes like to," she admits. "He makes such a mess. But no, of course not." She casts a pointed look toward the gate through which Gerard and Isobel have just vanished. Her smile rights itself. "Luckily, that man's not my boss." She winks at Lukas. "And neither is your bossy-pants big sister."

Lukas shakes his head. "Just ignore them," he tells Grace. "They have some nerve." He eyes the groceries on the ground. "What you got in there?" He bends to peer into the closest bag. "I'm starving."

"Well, we're off," says my mom. "Grace, if you hear from Daphne, please call."

"Sure thing," says Grace, cheerily. "But don't worry, Ivy. I'm sure she's off somewhere nice with Stephen."

Lukas mumbles goodnight. My mom and I walk toward the gate.

As it clicks shut behind us, I feel glad to be out of there, but also troubled. "Mom?" I say, as we turn toward our cars. "Don't you know some way to contact this guy Daphne's dating? Do you have his phone number? Or are you like, Facebook friends, or something?"

My mom sounds vague. "Daphne's not on Facebook. And neither is he, so far as I know."

Nor is she, really. I set up a profile and page to promote her business. I doubt she posts on it monthly. And when she does, it's always something weird and random, like a GIF of square-dancing penguins, or a story about volunteer-tourism in the Amazon Basin.

My mother sighs. "Stephen Buxley. Maybe he's in the phonebook? I really know next to nothing about him."

That is weird, I think. But is it? They haven't been dating for very long. Maybe they're taking things slowly.

"I'm sure Grace is right," says my mom. "And she's off with Stephen." I can hear her determination to be hopeful.

I agree. That's most likely. But who is this guy? No one knows him—or his motives for dating Daphne. I think of Vonda and her soon-to-be ex, both hoping to land loaded spouses, both ending up disappointed. We think lots of dosh will protect us from harm, and bring respect, security, and comfort. But wealth and luck are double-edged swords that can also attract greed and envy.

CHAPTER 6:

UNFAITHFUL

My office at Greene & Olliartee is smaller than Daphne Dane's walk-in closet, although at least it's got a window. There's a view of the office building across the street and—if you lean really far out—a sliver of ocean.

After days of rain and cold, the sun has broken through. Out of the wind, it's surprisingly warm. With sunlight streaming in, my teeny room is stifling. Luckily I wore a black tank top under my turtleneck sweater.

I've just shed my sweater when there's a knock on the door. I smooth back my hair. My next appointment isn't due until three. Pamela Powell, the firm's past-retirement-age secretary, never knocks. If it were her, she'd already be owl-eyeing me around the door in her giant Tootsie glasses. Maybe one of my bosses, Mel or Philippa, have stopped by for some postlunch chit chat.

I sit up straighter and use my toes to feel around for my shoes, abandoned somewhere beneath my large desk. "Come in," I say.

Pamela must be out powdering her already over-powdered nose because it's a client, unannounced. Her perfume hits me first.

She looks around the door: "Hello, Toby Vong."

As before, her voice gives me chills—that mix of fire and ice, wood smoke and cold vodka. I sit up straighter. "Hello, Vonda."

I have to remember to shut my mouth as she sashays across the room. While it hardly seems possible, today's black patent heels are even higher than the red ones she wore last time. Her stilettos click like black lacquered chopsticks.

Clad in a red dress so tight it's a wonder she can breathe, let alone sit, she twists into a chair and crosses her killer legs. With one eye overhung by a swathe of glossy curls she reminds me of a sexy pirate.

"You said I must prove cruelty or adultery for a Fault divorce," she begins. Her uncovered eye glints in triumph.

I nod, determined to do my duty. "Yes, but a No Fault would be cheaper and . . ."

She raises a hand and bats this point away. Her fingernails, now gunmetal grey, flash like knives. "No. I vill prove this is his fault." I wait as Vonda leans closer. Just for a moment, her big grey eyes well with sadness. Then she rallies. Her perfect teeth grit back into a grin. "He is seeing someone else," she says. "Another voman."

"Oh," I say. "How do you know?"

Vonda's fingernails tap my desk. "His credit card statements." Her eyes narrow dangerously. "Charges at Agent Provocateur, Victoria's Secret."

Seeing my blank look her top lip curls. "He is buying sexy lingerie," she hisses. "And not for me. There is nothing he can buy for himself at those stores. Nothing! Vhich means he is shopping for another voman!"

"Maybe it's your Christmas present," I suggest. Some people actually do shop early, instead of waiting until the last second.

Vonda snorts. Both her eyes and her engagement ring glitter. "No vay! He is cheating on me!" While her ring is fake, it's still eye-catching. She glares at me. "Can you believe it?"

Not easily, I must admit. If she's right, her husband's got balls, no doubt about it. I'd hate to make Vonda angry.

I open my mouth to ask who this other woman is but she's off again. "There is more." She swings her small red snakeskin purse off her shoulder and deposits it on my desk, then opens it with a click that makes me jump. "This!" Pinched between the blades of her fingernails is a matchbox. She tosses it to me.

I try but fail to catch it, which leads to an inelegant rummage beneath my desk. I'm about to give up when my sweaty fingers find it.

"It's from L'Escargot D'Or," says Vonda, as I resurface and regain my seat. I nudge my almost shoulder-length hair back out of my face, which is also sweaty.

I study the matchbox. Its swirly gold font and snail logo elicit a trickle of regret—this is the place where Josh was planning to take me last night. If only I hadn't gotten stuck looking for Daphne.

"It is the most romantic and expensive restaurant in town," continues Vonda, clearly convinced I've never been there. Her voice now has an angry swish, like the rustle of tall, dried grass as a cheetah glides through it. "He never took me there!"

"Okay," I say, satisfied she's probably right: Dennis Butts, her husband of just three months, may very well be unfaithful. "Do you know who she is?" I ask.

Vonda's glossy hair tosses. "Not yet," she says. "But I vill find out."

I shake my head. What's Vonda planning to do? Follow her husband? It's not like she doesn't stand out. Women like Vonda might blend in at the Playboy Mansion, but here, in Victoria, everyone else is in fleece and Hush Puppies. Maybe a private investigator would be the way to go, if she can afford one.

When I suggest this, a hand flies to her white throat. "No vay. It vill be easy to follow him, once he gets back."

By now, I'm having to make a conscious effort to pronounce my Ws correctly. "What do you mean?" I ask. "Where is he?"

Beneath her swept-over bangs, Vonda's scowl deepens. Her gaze turns to my window. Mine follows. In the red brick building across the street I can see into a dentist's office. A white-robed lady dentist is bent over a guy with buzzed hair, his mouth open and his eyes squeezed shut, as if he's screaming. My gut twists in sympathy. I look away, as does Vonda. There's another dentist in my building. I can sometimes hear the drill, when my window's open.

Vonda licks her glossy lips. "I don't know vhere Dennis has gone," she says. Her voice drops. "He didn't come home last night. He must be off, vooing this other voman."

"Er, okay," I say. That's suspicious. "Has he ever done this before?" I ask. "I mean, not come home?"

Her pout would make any trout proud. "He usually calls to make excuses," she says. "Dennis has endless excuses. He vould tell me some story: he is off meeting VIP investors, blah blah blah." She waves a hand. "But this time . . ." Just for an instant, her bottom lip quivers. "No call. No text. Nothing." She wags a single, glinting finger and leans closer. "But don't vorry. I vill find him."

CHAPTER 7:

DINING À DEUX

L'Escargot D'Or is smaller than I expected, with a cozy, almost homely feel. There are little tables draped in crisp white tablecloths and tea lights shining from cut-glass holders. The walls are covered in old Mucha prints and black and white photos of Paris. Since we got here so early, Quinn and I snagged a window seat. The facades of the old downtown buildings glow jewel-toned under the street lamps while the last office-workers scurry homeward.

Settling across from my best friend I feel a wave of happiness. Since Abby's birth two months ago we haven't seen much of each other. While I love my new goddaughter and am thrilled for Quinn, I fear we're drifting apart. Quinn seems distracted these days, too consumed by new motherhood to know what's happening in my life. I miss her, my best friend since kindergarten.

As I shrug off my coat, Quinn meets my smile with her own. She looks tired, dark dents beneath her blue eyes, her blonde hair, so full and glossy when she was pregnant, now dry and ragged. I know her husband, Bruce, had to talk her into coming out tonight. Both of us are concerned: Quinn hasn't seemed her upbeat, confident self since Abby was born. Not having had a baby myself, it's hard to know whether this is normal postpartum tiredness or something darker. Shouldn't this be the best time of her life? She seems so down lately.

Hopefully, tonight will be what she needs—a chance to dress up and relax, with no breastfeeding or poo-talk. In a loose black dress and low heels, she's even dredged up some lipstick, the first cosmetic I've seen her wear since we went to prom, a million years ago. While she rifles through her purse for her phone, I study my oldest friend. Despite her efforts, Quinn looks wan, her dress unironed and a splotch of what might be baby puke near her left shoulder. Her citrusy perfume has a faint undertone of sour milk, with notes of wet wipes.

After checking her messages, Quinn spreads her napkin over her still slightly rounded belly. She glances around the near-empty restaurant. Her eyes meet mine. There's a brief uncomfortable pause, like she doesn't know what to say, or would rather be elsewhere. Then she gathers herself and manages a smile. "I've always wanted to come here, but burgers and pizza are more Bruce's style. Wait, didn't you just come here with Josh a couple nights ago?"

"We were supposed to," I say, grateful she remembered. "But it didn't happen." I tell her about my mom showing up at my door, all aflutter, and our failed attempt to find her friend and client, Daphne Dane.

"The cookie lady?" says Quinn. She stifles a yawn.

"Yeah, she's one of my mom's best friends."

"Mmm, I remember meeting her," says Quinn. "Tall woman." This is coming from Quinn, who's five ten. But she's right, Daphne Dane is an Amazon, or rather Glamazon, like an eighties supermodel. Everything from her hair to her smile to her jewelry is larger than life. I wonder where she's gone. Despite Colin's reassurance, my mom won't stop fretting.

"So what's new?" asks Quinn. She toys with her phone. "You still out on hot dates every other night?"

I shrug. Dating-wise, things have slowed since September, when my relationships with Josh and Colin started to simmer. Colin is flat out at work. And Josh . . . I swallow hard. He hasn't called to reschedule our date. Has he lost interest in me? A guy that rich, charming, and good looking must spend his days wading through a sea of interested women. Maybe he's found someone better—or at least easier.

Rather than share this self-pitying thought with Quinn, who's definitely on Team Colin, I focus on work. "I have a new client," I say. I describe Vonda Butts—Russia's sexiest export since that hot blonde tennis star. This reminds me why I'm here. Vonda gave me a photo of her husband, Dennis, who looks surprisingly nondescript, given his bombshell wife. When I get the chance I'm going to quiz the staff.

Someone might remember seeing him here, getting romantic with some other woman.

As if on cue, our server appears—a skinny, shifty-looking young guy with a ghost of a mustache. His name tag identifies him as "Jean-Luc" and his accent as Anglo-Canadian. I bet he's called Dave and inherited the name tag from some long-departed Quebecois. He's bearing a wine list and a wicker bread basket.

"Evening, ladies," he says. Quinn practically rips the bread from his hands. She starts to toss chunks into her mouth. The waiter passes me the wine list.

Keeping a wary eye on Quinn as she tears into her second slice, Jean-Luc launches into tonight's specials: Moules Marinieres made with local honey mussels. Confit de canard, which I actually recognize, and something called Flamiche that Quinn has him explain. She orders that, plus three more dishes, before Jean-Luc can put shaky pen to notepad. His eyes goggle.

"Ah, maybe we can share?" I suggest to Quinn.

She looks aghast. "I'm starving," she says. "Breastfeeding does that." TMI for the waiter.

After ordering a carafe of red (no need to go wild and get a bottle, as Quinn won't drink much) and my own helpings of mussels and Flamiche—a kind of puff pastry quiche, stuffed with leek—I whip out my photo of Dennis Butts.

"One more thing, Jean-Luc." I hold the picture aloft. "Any chance you recognize this guy? He ate here about a week back."

Jean-Luc peers at the photo, as does Quinn.

"Who's he?" she asks me.

"The husband of one of my clients."

Jean-Luc wipes his fingers on his dark green apron before taking the photo. "Hmmm, I'm not sure."

"He was with a woman," I prompt.

"Ahhh. Ah!" He nods, his ghost-mustache twitching. "Yeah, I remember him." He frowns. "Lousy tipper."

"And the woman?"

"Older," he says. "Like fifty-something? Attractive. Blonde." His narrow forehead crinkles in concentration. "I recognized her from somewhere."

I nod, hopefully. "You knew her?"

"No, I didn't know her," he says. "But she looked familiar. Like maybe from TV? An actress or a newsreader?" He peers toward the door, which has opened to emit a couple walking arm-in-arm. The smiling hostess leads them to a low-lit table near the back. "Or a politician? She looked," he shrugs. "Important. Now, excuse me." He nods toward his new table and hands me back Dennis's photo.

Quinn pinches it out of my fingers and squints at it. "Why're you asking about him? No wait, let me guess." She shakes her head. "He's cheating on his wife. Right? And you're trying to find the other woman."

I spread my own napkin across my lap and try to decide how much to tell Quinn. While I shouldn't divulge details of my cases, she's known me for so long she always knows what's up anyway. Given how preoccupied she's seemed of late, her nosiness is a relief. This is the Quinn I know and love: always chock full of questions and opinions.

"Maybe," I say.

She rolls her eyes. "All your clients are getting divorced," she says. "It's always the same old story. People cheating and lying to each other. Fighting. I don't know how you handle it. It's depressing." She reaches for the bread basket and frowns, finding it empty. "Maybe that's why you're still single."

Seeing my face, she looks contrite. "Sorry. I didn't mean that." She sighs, her pretty face crumpling. "Oh god, Toby. I really am sorry. There's nothing wrong with being single. I mean, maybe it's for the best. Lots of people are happy being single. Happier. The statistics back that up . . ." She stops talking and rubs her eyes. "I'll shut up now. I'm just so tired and . . ." She hangs her head. "Snappy."

"It's okay," I say. I lay a hand on her arm. Quinn's always been there for me: when I was a scrawny kid, growing up without a dad and getting bullied for being small and Asian. And as an adult, the stresses of law school and the bar exam, career troughs and triumphs, dud romances, my mom's breast cancer . . .

While I lurched from drama to drama, her life seemed charmed: the child of happily married and successful parents, blessed with the lithe blonde beauty of Venus rising from the sea, her single-minded determination to be a marine biologist, and her love-at-first-bear-hug romance with her big cop husband, Bruce, who could not be prouder of her.

She's never, ever faltered. Until now. It breaks my heart to see her so vulnerable, especially now she's got everything she ever wanted. A secure tenure-track position at the university. A devoted husband. A perfect baby girl. I squeeze her hand. Why this sudden praise for the joys of singlehood? "Are you okay, Quinn?" Is she struggling with her marriage?

"I . . ." She swallows hard. "Yeah, I think so. I'm just exhausted." Her chin quivers. "This is harder than I thought it'd be. I'm not sure if Abby's happy. If she's comfortable. She cries and I just want to scream. I get so . . ." She hangs her head, voice low with guilt. "I get angry. I miss going to work. I resent Bruce because his life hasn't really changed. He's still working. His body isn't a stretched-out mess." She swipes at the tears on her cheeks. "I mean, how awful is that? Our baby is barely two months old and I . . . I resent her. I don't even deserve to be her mother."

"Of course you do," I say. "It's normal to miss work. To be tired and scared and frustrated. And you're right. Bruce's life hasn't changed as much as yours. That's not fair, but right now, that's how it is. Things will get better. You're a great mom, Quinn. Abby's so lucky."

Blinking back tears, my friend smiles. "Thanks, Tob." She squares her shoulders. "Sorry to be so silly."

"You're not silly," I say. "All of this is true. Everyone knows the first few months are brutal."

She nods. "I just thought I'd sail through it. I mean, how hard can it be? Women have been having babies forever, right? They used to have dozens of them. Like they gave birth in the morning and hoed the fields after lunch."

I snort. "You ever hoed a field?"

This warrants a tight laugh. "No, but I have spent weeks diving with Greenland sharks in dark, freezing water. I have a PhD. That takes stamina!" She rubs her eyes, which are full of tears. "I thought I'd be good at this."

"You are good at this," I say. "Have you talked to your mother?"

Quinn's mom, Jackie, is one of my favorite people. Elegant, gracious, and utterly sensible, Jackie is a successful criminal lawyer and the main reason I studied law. If Jackie knew Quinn was struggling, I'm sure she'd find some way to help.

Quinn takes a deep breath. "My mom means well," she says. "But her efforts to help just stress me out. She makes everything sound so simple, which makes me feel like a failure. She was in law school when she had me and still graduated at the top of her class. I'm home all day and look at me—a total basket case."

"You are not," I say. "But that could be the problem. Maybe you need to get out more. You should call me." I give her a lopsided grin. "I can babysit anytime you want. Then you and Bruce can get out together, have some fun."

Quinn blinks. "Thank you."

"She's my goddaughter, Quinn. I want to get to know her."

"I know," says Quinn. "Okay, I'll ask you to babysit sometimes." From the way her eyes slide back to her silent phone, I suspect she doesn't really mean it.

Looking at her anxious frown, I wonder if Quinn needs to see a doctor. Is she clinically depressed? How do I ask? I think back to the months before Abby's birth, Quinn so full of sparkle and excitement. Compared to that, she's a shadow of herself, a nervous wreck. If having a kid has done this to Quinn, imagine what it'd do to me. I'm already a hopeless worrywart, my mind perpetually palm-smacking my forehead. Maybe I'm better off staying single and childless. What if I pass this anxiety to the next generation?

Since I can't think of a good way to broach it, I just blurt it out. "Quinn, d'you think you might have postpartum depression?"

She blinks. Her big blue eyes fill with fresh tears. "Oh my god," she whispers. "Do I really look that bad?"

"No, of course not," I say, scared I've made her feel even worse. "I'm just worried, that's all. I mean, I know you. I've known you forever. And you just seem . . ." I bite my lip. "Sad," I say.

She nods. "I know," she says. Her voice sounds raw. "And I should be so happy, right?"

I hold my breath. Isn't that what I was thinking, earlier tonight? She has it all. She should be ecstatic. But is that true? Her hormones are bound to be a hot mess. She's getting next to no sleep. She's stuck at home, day after day, with a small creature who's insatiable and ungrateful. All babies do is take. They never say thanks. And all the while, Quinn's big, beautiful brain is spinning its wheels while she repeats the most mundane, crappy tasks.

The more I think about it, the worse it sounds. Why do people have children?

"I don't know. I think you're handling it way better than I would," I say. "I can't even keep my goldfish going. Remember when we were kids and I got given that hamster?"

This elicits a crack of laughter. "You meant well," says Quinn. "Building it that fancy house with all those toilet-roll tunnels."

"Too bad it chewed its way out and escaped," I say. "And lived in the vents for years, waging a campaign of guerrilla warfare."

"I remember when it chewed through your dad's cellphone cable." Her eyes crease with mirth. "Back when cellphones were total bricks. And crazy expensive."

I nod, recalling my dad's ire. "Maybe that was why he left," I say. I mean it as a joke, but it falls flat. What kind of person abandons their only child, there one day, then vanished? Or was my dad going through something like Quinn, crushed beneath some pressure he couldn't express? Surely not. My mom took care of all the grunt work.

I can feel Quinn eyeing me thoughtfully beneath her too-long fringe. At least now, twenty years on, I can make lame jokes about my dad's departure without feeling like the San Andreas fault is running straight through my heart, ready to crack at any moment.

Quinn shakes her head, serious again. "You're not your dad," she says. "You'll be a great mother." She fiddles with her spoon, looking wistful. "You might even love it. Some women are thrilled to stay home with a new baby. They feel . . . fulfilled."

I shake my head. "I'm pretty sure I'm not one of them."

A tight smile. "Me neither." She drops her head, like she's admitted something shameful. "That feels so ungrateful," she whispers. "So disloyal to Abby."

I roll my eyes. "It does not!" I say. "It sounds honest. Geez, Quinn, give yourself a break. It's not like you want to trade Abby in or hop on the next one-way flight out. You just want some of your old life back. Some time to yourself again."

My friend smiles. A real, Quinn smile, the kind that, just for a second, lights up the room. She sits up straighter. "I do," she says. Her next words are more hesitant. "I was thinking of going back to work in a month or two, just part time . . ."

"Brilliant," I say. "You'd be setting a great example for Abby."

Again, that flash of a smile. Her shoulders, which have been up by her ears all night, relax a little. "I . . ." Whatever she was going to say next is interrupted by the arrival of our starters.

Plate after plate. Everything looks and smells delicious.

"Bon appétit," I tell Quinn but she's already chewing.

"Thank god," she says, around a mouthful of French onion soup. "I am famished."

My mussels in white wine sauce are so tasty I'm tempted to pick up the bowl and slurp. If I were home alone, I'd do it.

The food seems to perk Quinn up. Maybe she was feeling extra low on account of being hungry. Or maybe our conversation helped. This thought and the wine warm my belly.

While Quinn eats her second starter, I look around the room. The restaurant is filling up, almost every table now occupied by couples on dates: men self-consciously pulling out chairs for women in little black dresses, who pick at their food like Jane Austen characters. Strained smiles. Stilted laughter. Peppered between the nervous newbies are couples with obvious chemistry. Forkfuls passed back and forth. Heads bent close. Legs entwined under tables. Lustful glances over tenderly held wine glasses.

Looking at these romantic couples, it's hard not to feel a little envious. I want to come back here, with Josh *and* Colin. God, I'm greedy. Surely, deep down I must know who's better for me, or—better than that—right for me. Or is it neither?

As the evening progresses, I have to keep biting my tongue. Quinn can't stop checking her phone, like she's scared it's stopped working. While Abby Rose isn't physically present, she may as well be. Quinn's obsessed. I can't distract her for more than two minutes straight. She keeps yawning too. I know she's exhausted but it's hard not to take it personally, like I've become stupefyingly boring. Should I admit defeat and call it a night? My energy is also flagging.

"Some more wine?" I ask. Quinn looks up from her phone. Seeing my disapproving frown, she stashes it under her napkin. I know she's both relieved and disappointed that Bruce hasn't called. She'd expected a slew of desperate calls: *Abby won't stop crying. She won't eat. She misses you too much.* In fact, the baby and Bruce are fine. Quinn's the only one suffering.

"I shouldn't," says Quinn. She looks torn. "I already had half a glass."

"So pump and dump," I say. In the past two months I've learned things I couldn't have imagined. If Quinn doesn't breastfeed regularly her breasts turn into hot, hard lumps—like giant, burning ten-day-old buns stuck to her chest. Even now, there's a breast pump stashed in her bulging purse. Oh, the glamor.

I tilt the carafe enticingly.

"Maybe a tiny bit more," she concedes.

Moments later, she's checking her phone again.

I'm about to signal the waiter for a second carafe when I see a plump balding man emerge from a swinging door at the back. He starts talking to the skinny waiter. Clad in a white jacket, the pudgy man is obviously the chef. His hands wave as he talks. The waiter bobs his head.

When the chef turns, I feel a jolt of recognition. It's Daphne Dane's French son-in-law, Gerard. He said he was a chef. Is he the owner of L'Escargot D'Or?

"Excuse me," I say to Quinn, whose head is bent over her phone, like it's a baby monitor and she just might hear her daughter shrieking for her mommy. She doesn't notice my departure.

Weaving between well-dressed couples on their best behavior, I feel like the only single person in the room. Or the universe, even. A little astronaut floating free, past planets of paired-up couples. I could be lonely, or lucky—bound for unforeseen adventures. Or maybe both, after talking to Quinn. A little lonely *and* lucky.

I'm about halfway across the room when Gerard turns and bustles off around a corner. Getting closer, I see it's a hallway that leads to the restrooms. Gerard is now standing at the far end, beneath a framed copy of "Kiss by the Hotel de Ville." He's talking to a skinny man with mussed blond hair sticking out from a green beanie. Beneath faded Thai fishermen's pants, this man's legs are twig-thin and the color of raw french fries.

Gerard looks cross, his cheeks puffing with displeasure. "What is so urgent?" he says. "It is the dinner service. I am busy."

When the blond guy answers, I step behind a potted plant. I know that voice—a low rasp. It's Daphne's son, Lukas.

"I need a favor," says Lukas. "Just a little loan. Until Mom gets back. I have to fix my VW van . . ."

Gerard sighs. "Again? You think I am what, made of money? I have bills!" He throws up his small, stubby hands. "The rent for this place, you would not believe it. And electricity. Plus all the staff." He shakes his large head dolefully. His jowls sway. "And Christmas is coming. Your sister, she is not one to economize . . ." He fingers the collar of his white jacket and looks sad but self-righteous. "*Non.* I'm very sorry Lukas but it is simply impossible." This last word is pronounced the French way—*im-poss-ee-bluh.*

"Aw c'mon, Gerard," says Lukas. He scratches under his ratty beanie. "It's only for a few days. As soon as Mom's back I can—"

Gerard's small eyes narrow. "You need to stop relying on your mother," he says. "She is fed up." He puffs out his chest to deliver this lecture. "She told Isobel that you treat her like an ATM. It is time you live on your own. Get a job. You must learn to stand on your own two feet."

Lukas's head rears back. "That's rich!" he says, "coming from Izzie. Who lent you guys the money to start this place, huh? What I borrow is peanuts! A few bucks here and there, just enough to tide me over, until my next exhibition . . ." His voice is an aggrieved whine. "She's given you guys so much, and you can't even lend me a couple hundred! I don't even have money to eat, Gerard . . ." His voice wobbles. "I'm gonna to have to ask Izzie."

Gerard's cheeks rise to new heights. He releases an exaggerated sigh. "*Alors*, fine, fine," he says. "Do not trouble your sister. She has enough to worry about with your mother." He takes a deep breath and smoothes down his white jacket. "I'll get some cash from the till." Gerard wags a finger. "Two hundred."

"Two?" says Lukas. "Aw c'mon, man . . ."

Gerard's floppy cheeks tighten.

Lukas must see his brother-in-law's face, because he backs down. "Fine, fine," he says, quickly. "Two hundred is great. You're the best, man." He rubs his hands. "You got any leftovers around here? Like, you know, some of that good bread? The stuff with the herbs and nuts?"

Gerard's next sigh is even louder. "I will get you some bread," he says stiffly.

Lukas nods. "Thanks, thanks. I owe you, man. Say, maybe I could paint something for this place to pay you back? Some original art instead of all these lame prints." He squints at the closest frame. "Something bright and modern."

Gerard gives a tiny shudder. "Ah, *merci* but no need. The prints fit the theme. You know, Paris . . ." His voice lifts with nostalgia.

Lukas shrugs a skinny shoulder. "Sure. Whatever. Suit yourself, man." He claps Gerard's back. "Don't worry. I'll pay you back. The minute Mom gets home." He pauses. "Any idea where she went?" he asks Gerard.

Gerard's frown deepens. "No," he says. "And Isobel is terribly worried. "Those police, they are useless. They fail to understand she could be in trouble, being off with that . . ." His round nose scrunches as if from an unpleasant smell. "That charlatan."

"Charles-what?" says Lukas. His already thin voice stretches further. "I thought his name was Stephen!"

Gerard looks confused, then shrugs. "Yes, Stephen. I forgot, you haven't met him." He rings his hands. "He is a charmer. A smooth-talker. Your *maman* is vulnerable to a man like that. He says all the right things . . . Why, just three nights back, at her house for dinner . . ." His jowls shake ominously. "Your sister fears they've eloped," he says, glumly.

Lukas snorts out a laugh. "Oh c'mon. Mom's not an idiot. She's only known him for what, a few weeks?" He smirks. "Iz thinks she'll marry him?" He tugs off his beanie.

Gerard throws up his hands. "Ah *mais l'amour*! It can turn us all into fools. Isobel fears he's a con artist. You weren't there to see them, behaving like teenagers . . ." His mouth forms a moue of distaste before his prominent eyes widen, like something's just occurred to him. "The Sooke cabin," he says. "Perhaps they went there. Someone should check it."

Lukas's head jerks up. "The old summer cabin?" His reedy voice cracks. "She wouldn't go there. It's falling apart. Nobody ever goes out there."

"But the coins," says Gerard. "Maybe for once Daphne actually listened to Isobel. Perhaps she went to fetch them and met some accident. Some fall or . . ." He fiddles with the hem of his white coat. "Perhaps a stroke. Dementia . . . She is aged, your mother . . ."

Lukas passes his beanie from hand to hand. "Wait. What coins?" he asks.

"Your father's gold coins. His collection. He left them in the safe in that old cabin. A ridiculous place, of course. Totally insecure. Isobel found some old papers of Walt's and questioned Daphne, who'd forgotten all about them. Imagine! Just forgetting! It caused quite a scene at Tuesday's dinner."

Lukas twists around. From where I stand, peering around the corner, I can now see his face, eyebrows high in amazement. "I remember those coins!" he says. "Dad used to show them to me when I was a kid. He loved those things. They were like pirates' treasure." He stops twisting his beanie. "I just figured they were in the bank. You mean all this time . . ." He laughs. "God, that's ridiculous! They were just sitting in that crappy summer cabin?"

"*Exactement*!" says Gerard. "Some of those coins are worth thousands, even tens of thousands of dollars! In that unprotected cottage! And now Daphne has gone off and nobody else knows the code to the safe. Unless she went out there? The *cabine* . . ." He rubs his hands on his pants and swallows nervously. "Isobel cannot remember how to get there. Do you know the way? It is quite isolated, no?"

Lukas is still shaking his head in amazement. "I'll go," he says. "It's in the middle of nowhere, but I'm pretty sure I can still find it." He tugs on his beanie. "But I highly doubt Mom went there."

"Why not?"

He shrugs. "She hasn't been in years. It's a dump. She's probably gone someplace nice with her new man. Someplace sunny . . ." He tilts his beanie. "Look, I gotta go, Gerard. Can I get the bread?" He laughs again. "And the dough? Haha!"

Gerard obviously misses the joke. He instructs a passing waiter to fetch some herb bread.

As Gerard and Lukas come closer, I retreat. I grab a menu off a counter and bury my face in it. There's no need. They walk past without glancing my way.

Peeking over my menu, I see Gerard pull two bills from the till. He looks sour, Lukas elated. I'm too far away to hear what they're saying. Lukas pats his brother-in-law's shoulder, pockets the money, and heads for the door. There's a spring in his step. Outside, he turns right, toward the harbor.

When I get back to our table, our mains have come—and are mostly gone. "Sorry," says Quinn, her cheeks full of my Flamiche. She leans closer and lowers her voice. "These portions are tiny! No wonder French women are so skinny."

"Um, no problem," I say. I cut into the surviving sliver. The leek tart, like the mussels, is amazing.

As I chew, I feel Quinn studying me. "What just happened?" she says. "You look excited."

Even more than usual, I'm amazed by how observant Quinn can be—and gratified she's taking an interest. I decide to fill her in on what I just overheard, adding some backstory about Daphne Dane's new romance.

"Hmmm, so Daphne's daughter thinks her new man's just after her cash?" says Quinn. "That's sad."

"Yes." I had the same thought. But who knows? Is Stephen a grifter or do Isobel and Gerard merely begrudge Daphne her happiness, scared some of their inheritance might end up with her younger lover?

Quinn pats at her lips with a napkin. She looks thoughtful. "I guess that's one good thing about not being loaded. You don't have to worry about guys chasing you for your fortune."

This makes me think of Josh, whose wealth is actually an obstacle, creating a power imbalance that makes me uneasy. Wealth is the ultimate pink elephant. Everyone notices but nobody says anything, acting like it doesn't matter. Am I just deluding myself in thinking Josh's lavish lifestyle isn't part of his charm? Would I still want him if he lost everything and lived in a tin-roofed shack? Money bestows power, which brings confidence. Confidence is attractive. Without his fortune, would Josh be someone else? Someone more ordinary? Would that much money change me? The vast difference in our net worth raises all kinds of unsettling questions. I'm not sure I'm cut out to be the lady of his manor.

These thoughts are interrupted by Quinn. "I haven't asked," she says. "But how's it going with Colin?"

My best friend adores Colin and doesn't much care for Josh. She wishes I'd just hurry up and choose the guy she likes, settle down, and produce a playmate for Abby.

"Good," I say, only to think of his beautiful new partner, Miriam. "He's just been really busy at work." Did this sudden new busyness coincide with Miri's arrival?

My response must be off because Quinn tilts her head. "Oh yeah?"

"Well, he has a new partner," I say. "Who looks like a Sports Illustrated swimsuit model." I'm embarrassed to even admit this is an issue. But it is. How could it not be? Miriam—Miri—is beyond gorgeous.

Quinn takes a sip of wine. "Oh yeah. Have you talked to her?"

I nod. "She seems very nice," I admit.

My best friend studies me. "Colin's crazy about you," she says. "But it's got to be tough for him."

"How d'you mean?"

"Well, you haven't committed. You're still seeing Josh, aren't you?"

I think of my last conversation with Josh, the night before last, after I finally left Daphne's. He'd sounded annoyed and told me we'd make it another night. I ended up eating cereal standing up in my kitchen, feeling guilty for missing our date and put out by his lack of concern. I don't usually bail at the last minute. He must have known it was important yet asked nothing.

Again, my best friend must detect something in my response—or lack thereof—because she looks thoughtful. "Trouble there?"

I hope that's not a hopeful glint in her eyes, but suspect it is. Quinn finds Josh self-absorbed—and maybe some part of me does too. Other parts, however, feel a buzz whenever he's close. Beyond his success and good looks, there's just something about him. You can't buy chemistry. Can you?

"We haven't talked since the night we were meant to come here," I admit.

Quinn swallows her last gulp of wine. "Colin had your back that night," she says. "Coming over to look for Daphne."

I know she's right but don't want to hear it. "Dessert?" I say, to change the subject.

It takes a minute to catch Jean-Luc's attention. He doesn't even ask if Quinn wants dessert but just hands her a menu and steps back, lest she jump him. I take a menu too. Being naturally skinny, I eat dessert whenever I want. Plus I'm hungry. Quinn stole most of my dinner.

After deciding—crème brûlée for me, mousse au citron (with extra whipped cream) for Quinn—we sit in silence for some minutes. I'm thinking about Josh and Colin. I know Quinn's thinking about Abby. When a phone beeps nearby, Quinn's onto hers like a seagull on a dropped donut. I bet she's dreading—and hoping—it's Bruce begging her to come home. Peering at the screen, she looks confused, then crestfallen. "Not mine," she mutters.

I dig my phone out of my purse to find a message from Josh. My heart lifts.

Hi. Want to go out on the boat tomorrow? There are two little emojis: a sailboat and a smiley face in sunglasses.

"It's Josh," I say. "Inviting me out on his yacht, tomorrow."

Quinn's full lips tighten. Just two months ago Josh and I were attacked on that very yacht. While boating doesn't hold great memories for me, Josh runs a yacht charter business. If we do have a future together, I'll need to get over my misgivings. Josh loves being out on the water.

"I'm going to go," I tell Quinn.

She nods. But it's a disapproving nod. For what seems like a long time, she chews. Finally, she swallows. "Where to?" she asks.

I shrug. "I don't know. Maybe a cruise around the Gulf Islands."

At just that moment the waiter reappears with our desserts. The dishes are tiny but beautifully presented. "This is the chef's special," he says, setting my crème brûlée before me. "The raspberry coulis is to die for."

As Quinn and I dig in, my thoughts return to Gerard and Lukas. What was it Gerard said, about a Sooke cabin?

"Have you been to Sooke recently?" I ask Quinn.

She licks some whipped cream off her spoon and shakes her head. "It's been a few years. Bruce and I went out to the potholes." Her eyes narrow. "Why?"

"Oh, well, Daphne Dane's got a cottage out there."

Quinn scoops out another spoonful of yellow mousse. "And?" she says. "What's going on? Why are you so preoccupied with this cookie lady?"

"I'm not preoccupied," I say. "Just kind of . . ." I struggle to find the right words. "A little worried. Mostly about my mom." I think of our most recent conversation: my mom still twittering on about Daphne's ominous cards. "She wants to file a Missing Person Report . . ."

My best friend licks her lips. "Well, if both you and Ivy feel anxious, maybe there's something to it." She chews on her cheek, studying me. "Your mom's definitely psychic, and you've got a bit of it. Maybe you could learn to . . ." She shrugs. "You know? Enhance it."

I swallow another mouthful of crème brûlée. How does Gerard make it so smooth and creamy? As always, I'm amazed by Quinn's enthusiasm for my mom's New Age mumbo jumbo. Crystal therapy. Color healing. Herbal lotions and potions. Quinn's a scientist. She ought to know better. Quinn knows me well enough to know how I feel about psychics, including and especially my mother.

Seeing my scowl, Quinn laughs. "Ivy's instincts have been right before." She scrapes out the last of her mousse. "And so have yours," she says, pointedly.

I nod. Instincts. I'm okay with that word, and all my instincts say there's something wrong with the Danes. Too much money and too many grubby hands hoping to reach into the giant pot of Daphne's fortune.

Sooke isn't far, less than an hour's drive westward. It's practically a bedroom community now, part of Victoria's ever-expanding suburbs.

I'll call my mom tonight and see if she knows how to find Daphne's cabin. Is it on the coast? If Josh and I are going on a boat cruise, we may as well have a destination.

CHAPTER 8:

PORTENTS

My mom's phone rings twice before she answers in her most chirpy, professional voice: "Ivy Wong's psychic services. How may I help you?"

I roll my eyes. Shouldn't she already know? "Hey, it's me, Mom."

"Toby!" She sounds pleasantly surprised to hear from me. "How are you?"

"Good. Sorry to call so late," I say, although it's actually only ten-past-nine. Quinn scurried out of the restaurant at nine on the dot, desperate to get home to Abby.

I'm in the back of a cab, heading up Fort Street, past rows of twee faux-Tudor shop fronts displaying antiques and old-lady knickknacks. I'm tipsy enough not to mind the cabbie's Classic Rock radio station. Every second song is the Eagles. Welcome to Victoria—you can check out any time, but damn, it's hard to leave.

"Oh you know me," says my mom, which I do indeed. "It's still early." My mother is both a night owl and an early bird but likes a good, long after-lunch nap. "I'm just listening to Joni Mitchell and cleansing my crystals."

I nod, picturing the scene perfectly: my mother's vast collection of minerals—rough, shiny, faceted, smooth—spread across her kitchen table, my mom soaking the stones in spring water, then drying and polishing them with a silk cloth while thinking positive thoughts, before setting them out in the moonlight. As a kid, I found her crystals mesmerizing. I really believed in their magic.

"What's up?" says my mom.

I tell her about my dinner with Quinn tonight.

"I miss our Friday nights," says my mom, referring to our pre-Abby ritual of dinner at her place on Friday evenings, when Bruce works the night shift. "How is she?"

"I don't know," I admit. "She's tired and seems kind of . . ." The cab's radio crackles. "A little down," I admit.

"The first few months with a new baby are exhausting," says my mother. "I'm going to call her tomorrow. Maybe stop by, see if I can help."

"That'd be good. I offered too."

"Well, she's probably scared to let the baby out of her sight."

"It sure seems that way," I agree. There's a plop of a crystal dropping into water. "Have you heard from Daphne yet?"

My mom sighs. "No." Her voice tightens. "I know Colin and his lovely young partner said not to worry but I still feel . . ." Another plop. "I think she's in trouble."

"The restaurant we went to," I say. "Is owned by Daphne's son-in-law, Gerard." I recount the conversation I overheard between Gerard and Lukas. "Lukas was there to borrow money." I sway a little as my taxi rounds a corner.

My mom's voice hardens. "Those kids! Daphne doesn't say much, but I know she's at her wits end. Isobel and her husband had another restaurant that went bust. And Lukas . . ." Water sloshes. "I don't think he's ever worked a day in his life."

I struggle to remember what Lukas does. "I thought he's an artist."

Another plop. "Even wonderful artists have trouble earning a living," says my mom. "And as for him . . ." More sloshing. "He's like a little kid. He only moved out last year, after Daphne insisted."

"You ever been to her cottage in Sooke?"

Joni Mitchell warbles in the background. The Eagles are competing in the foreground. "Mmmm, years ago," says my mother. "Why?"

"Gerard thought Daphne might be there."

"Oh, I doubt that," says my mom.

"Why not?" My taxi slows to turn into my street. I click open my purse to find my wallet.

"She and Walt used to go there when the kids were little, but it hasn't been kept up. I can't imagine she'd want to stay there. She was planning to have it torn down and rebuilt, maybe next year. Either that or sell it."

"Hold on a sec," I say. I count out the right change, then hand it to the driver, an older, smiley South Asian man who hasn't said a word the whole trip. We nod and grin at each other. I climb out and slam the door. "I'm just getting home," I tell my mom. "Did you know about Walt's coin collection?"

"He did collect coins for a time," she says, sounding surprised. "I remember him showing me some book, all about antique money. He had some extremely rare coins, I recall. But he lost interest, eventually. Walt was like that. Full throttle into some obsession, then a total change of direction. It was tropical fish for a while, then Vespa scooters. And those gold coins." More crystals plop. "Why? What about them?"

"Gerard said Walt's coins are in the Sooke cabin," I say. "In an old safe. Apparently Daphne forgot they were there. Isobel found out and got angry."

"Oh," says my mom. Another little plop. She sounds troubled. "When was this?"

"Just before Daphne dis . . . left," I say. Do I really believe Daphne has disappeared? That she's in trouble?

On my quiet street, my heels ring loud on the cement path leading to the front lobby. A four-story, flat-roofed block on the edge of Oak Bay, my building is full of retirees. Judging from the lack of lights, the majority are already in bed. Unless they're all out getting fleeced at the seniors' bingo.

I dig my keys out of my purse only to find there's no need—the door's been propped open with a brick to allow Mrs. Van Dortmund's incontinent cat to get in and out.

"Do you know how to get there?" I ask my mom, pausing to kick the brick out of the way. I lock the door. Oak Bay's safe but still. Judging from the smell of cat pee in the lobby, Mrs. Van D's cat isn't making it outside anyway. As usual, the lobby is tropical sweltering.

In honor of the looming holidays, someone has stuck an ancient artificial Christmas tree in one corner, held together by molting tinsel garlands. The tree is surrounded by a scattering of fake, mall-style presents. Surveying this sad scene is a squashed angel that looks like Chucky.

"Out where?" asks my mom. I hear the gentle plop of more crystals.

"To Daphne's summer cabin."

"Oh. It's out on the water, past East Sooke Park. Why?"

"I'm going out on the boat with Josh tomorrow."

There's a slosh of water and the sharp sound of something striking a hard surface. "Oh dear. I dropped my fluorite palm stone."

"Is it okay?" I know that stone—a smooth, round cabochon that fits perfectly into your palm, its domed surface like a crystal ball full of swirling green, blue, white, and violet, supposed to neutralize negative energy and boost concentration.

"It's fine," she says. I can picture her cupping the stone as lovingly as she would a baby bird. She takes a deep breath. "So, another boat trip." Her voice is tight with trepidation. "Not too many bad memories?"

"It'll be fine," I say. I stop to check my mailbox, then wonder why I bothered: bill, bill, junk mail. A red and green flyer full of "Holiday Savings." "No," I correct myself. I toss the flyer into the recycling bin. "It'll be fun."

"Well, that's . . . nice," says my mother.

I grit my teeth and head for the stairs. Is my mom's hesitation merely linked to what happened in September: me and Josh being attacked on the *Great Escape*? We both ended up in the hospital, which was obviously scary.

Or is my mom, like Quinn, hoping I'll pass up on smoking hot Josh and choose adorable, dependable Colin Destin? I think my mom likes Josh. The few times they've met they've acted like old friends. I wish I could ask. But what if I don't like her answer?

My apartment is on the fourth floor. The lack of an elevator usually doesn't bother me, but tonight, in heels, my ascent is slower. "I'm almost up the stairs," I tell my mom. I try not to breathe too heavily into the phone. "So I'll say goodnight now."

"Okay. Goodnight hon." A tiny intake of breath. "Wait. Tob?"

"Yes, Mom?"

"Just tomorrow. Be careful. Okay?"

Her warning puts me on edge. When Mrs. Van Dortmund's cat flashes past my shins, I jump and clutch the banister. This jolt of fear is quickly followed by annoyance. Careful of what? What happened two months back was a one-off. Me and Josh are taking a cruise on a totally safe, modern luxury yacht. That's pretty much a dream date. Can't Quinn and my mom just be happy for me? I'm going out with one of the most eligible bachelors in town, if not all of Canada. Josh—aka Adonis—Barton!

"What's that supposed to mean?" I blurt out, before I can stop myself. Immediately, guilt kicks in.

"I just . . ." My mother sighs, her voice tremulous and apologetic. "I'm sorry. I'm just feeling anxious. About Daphne, I guess, and now it's spilled over onto you." She takes a deep breath, then sounds more resolute. "I'm being ridiculous. You go and have fun. Tomorrow's forecast is decent, so hopefully you'll have good weather."

Her apology makes me want to apologize too. Instead, I just say goodnight as I climb the final steps.

"Sweet dreams, sweetheart." A pause, followed by a couple more plops as brightly colored stones slide through her fingers. "Just promise you'll wear your lifejacket, okay?"

I roll my eyes. What am I, six? "Of course, Mom."

Across the hall, I can hear tinkly feminine laughter waft out of Mr. Garlowski's place. One of the building's few widowers, he's a hot commodity amongst Oak Bay's countless single senior ladies—despite bearing a resemblance to a gargoyle.

I unlock my door. Stepping inside, I kick off my heels, then try to sound less like a teenaged brat. "I love you, Mom."

"I love you t—" A little gasp makes me stop.

"Mom?" When she doesn't answer right away, I can't help but imagine the worst: a heart attack, an aneurysm, a fall . . . "Mom?" I say again.

"It's the turquoise!" says my mother. "It's . . ." Her voice drops to a stricken whisper. "Oh my goodness! The color! It's faded . . ."

I swallow hard, torn between relief and teeth-clenching annoyance. While I have no idea what she means, she will surely inform me.

"Turquoise can sense danger," says my mom. "And infidelity and poison. When it changes from dark to light . . ." Her voice shudders. "That's a very bad sign."

Not wanting to encourage her, I stay quiet. I head into my tiny kitchen to fill the kettle. My mom's Sleeping Beauty turquoise has always been one of my favorite stones, a wonderful smooth, robin's egg blue. I used to press it to my eyelids as a kid, convinced some color might rub off, like Barbie's powder-blue eyeshadow.

"Toby?"

"Yeah, Mom?"

"Honey, this is terrible. You gotta be c—"

Since it's obvious what's coming next, I cut her off. "I know, Mom. Don't worry. I'll be careful."

After hanging up, I wonder if my mom's eyes—or head—need checking. Pouring my tea, I can't help but sigh. While rocks don't change, people do. Is old age making my mom even less logical and prone to wacked-out, magical thinking?

The tea is scalding. I open and slam some cupboard doors, unable to find the honey. While it seems my mom beat her breast cancer, that scare changed me, opening up a new, inescapable reality: sooner or later our roles will flip, caregiver turned dependent. My mom, who's always supported me, will need me to support her. I don't feel ready for this role, which seems impossibly adult. But like it or not, it's coming. As my mom gets older, weaker, and nuttier, I'll have to be the strong, sane one.

CHAPTER 9:

GETTING SOMEWHERE

The morning dawns cool and overcast. The days are rapidly getting shorter and the temperatures lower. While there's no wind, it'll be cold on the water. I don thermals under my jeans and a thick wool sweater.

Stuffed with a thermos of hot chocolate, a package of ginger snaps, a warm hat, and four bottles of Corona, my backpack clinks as I descend the stairs to the lobby. From his tree-top perch, Angel Chucky leers down at me. Someone has trod on one of the fake presents. Half squashed, it looks sadder than ever.

Rather than inhale the lobby's standard odors of cat pee and Vicks VapoRub, I wait outside. I sit on the low, mossy wall that runs along the sidewalk.

As usual, Josh is late—something else I don't like about him. But no one's perfect, least of all me. When he pulls up my stomach does its customary gymnastics routine. Ten out of ten at the Crush Olympics.

"Hi," I say, breathless as a schoolgirl jumping into her first boyfriend's first car. In both good and bad ways, Josh's presence transforms me into an adolescent—excited and insecure in equal measure.

"Morning," he says. He leans in for a quick kiss. As always, he smells wonderful, like spice and the ocean. With his bright blue eyes, tanned face, and mussed blond curls, the man is summer personified. It's like he travels in his own sunbeam. Sure enough, despite the cool day, the Porsche's sunroof is open.

Doing up my seatbelt, I feel shy. When we talked on the phone last night, I told him about my hopes of finding Daphne Dane's summer cabin. "You still want to head out past Sooke?" he asks. "There's a high chance of rain. Should we risk it?"

"Yes," I say. I don't care if it rains. "That'd be fantastic." I hand over the road directions I got from my mother.

Josh squints at my handwriting. "Wait, let me check." He turns on the car's sat nav. "Hmmm," he says. On the screen, grids of neighborhoods give way to sparse lines and white space. "It must be around here someplace," says Josh, pointing at a blank spot. "There's no road access, right?"

"You have to walk in," I say. "But there's a bay with a jetty."

"Great." Josh takes out his iPhone and opens Google maps. "So it's somewhere around here," he says. I examine the smaller screen. "We should be home before dark. Want to stop at Subway to grab lunch?"

"Good thinking."

The last time we went out on his boat he'd prepared a fancy picnic with strawberries and champagne. I'm glad he hasn't tried to recreate that romantic scene. It feels better to keep this casual—subs, hot chocolate, and cold beer. I get a six-inch tuna. He opts for a foot-long pepperoni.

By the time we reach Oak Bay Marina, some blue sky is peeking through the clouds. We park near the restaurant and walk through the coffee shop's large outdoor deck. Looking out at the docks and boats, it's hard not to think of Josh's estranged wife, Tonya, who was murdered here last summer.

Maybe Josh is thinking about her too because his steps slow. I wonder if I should bring her up, and give him the chance to talk about her death, or if it's better to leave it.

I'm saved from having to decide by the arrival of a large black standard poodle. It bounds up to Josh with its tail wagging. "Hi, Claude," he says. He bends to pet its wooly rump. The dog spins in happy circles.

I look around. "Is Mike here?" The dog, formerly Tonya's, now belongs to Josh's brother.

"He must be." He scratches Claude's ears. "We're looking into buying another boat." He grins. "To take out more charters."

"That's great," I say, pleased to hear their charter business is expanding. Josh made his money in the States, on a tech startup, but moved back to Victoria for a more outdoorsy lifestyle. He and his brother Mike haven't always had an easy relationship. I'm glad their partnership's thriving.

We descend the ramp, which is steep at low tide. I look for the seals that hang out under the ramp, waiting for tourists to throw them frozen fish, but both the water and dock lie empty. Even in the harbor, the water's clean enough to see the rocky bottom.

Claude follows us some way along the dock, only to veer off and start chasing a seagull. We turn toward the Customs station. As we get further from shore, the boats grow larger. Josh reaches for my hand and squeezes it. At his touch, my insides squirm. I can't stop smiling.

Near the *Great Escape*, my steps falter. It's impossible not to recall my last, terrifying trip. I thought we'd both die. Josh gives my hand another squeeze. I turn his way. Does he know how I'm feeling?

But no, a look at his face reveals he's studying his boat. "The new boat will be even bigger," he says. "It'll be ready for the spring tourist season." He looks delighted. He climbs onboard, then gives me a quizzical look. "You coming?"

I nod. I can't back out now. And I don't want to. I must get over this fear. With a deep breath, I follow him onboard. A brief, dizzying flash of déjà vu strikes as I climb the spiral stairs. I touch the wall to steady myself and keep going.

As before, I'm hit by how bright it is up on the bridge— everything gleaming white—the floor so clean it's like it's never been walked on, the table and chairs also shining. I fight back a memory of the bloodstains. There's nothing to be afraid of.

Josh unlocks a cupboard and pulls out two floatation jackets. We both put them on. Mine comes down to my knees. He laughs. "Want to try a kid's size?"

I'm not sure if he's joking. "This one's fine," I say. If I ever want a pumpkin costume for Halloween, all I'll need is this jacket and a black marker.

Josh starts the engine. "Are you okay to go down and untie us?" he asks.

"Aye, aye Captain."

I follow his shouted instructions.

"You learn fast," he says, when I regain the bridge. "You'll make a fine first mate, after all."

I fight back a smile. "And you thought I was just some feeble land-lubber." I sink into a large white swivel chair. "Know any good pirate jokes?" I ask him.

Josh shrugs and turns the wheel. "You got me stumped." The boat edges smoothly away from the dock.

I curl up in my chair. "Neither do ayyyye," I say.

He groans. "Any more jokes like that and you'll be walking the plank."

"You know there's an official Talk Like a Pirate Day?" I say. "I think it's in September."

Josh rolls his eyes. "You and I are never going boating on that day."

As we motor out of the harbor, I start to relax. I like the implica-tion that we'll still be together next fall, that pirate talk will be an in-joke we share, part of our couple language. This is fun. I'm glad I'm here, seeing another, important side of Josh's life.

We cruise around the breakwater and turn toward the golf course. The wind is cold and damp on my face. Out to sea, I spot some seals on the rocks, fat as bratwurst. There's the little beach where Quinn and I used to play as kids, skipping rocks and collecting sea glass. With no wind, the ocean is smooth and shiny as a high-grade sapphire, set beside the polished emerald of the Victoria Golf Club. From this angle, the familiar landmarks look different: McNeill Bay, the Chinese Cemetery, Beacon Hill Park, Ogden Point. I feel excited each time I recognize a place. Past Esquimalt, nothing looks familiar, although I know we're passing Colwood and Metchosin. Victoria's suburbs keep spreading westward.

"You having fun?" calls Josh, from behind the wheel. His blond curls bounce around his smiling face, eyes covered by black Ray-Bans. He looks even hotter than usual.

"Yes!" I yell. It's invigorating to be out on the water, moving at speed. Up ahead, in the distance, I can see a fishing boat. More of the clouds have blown away. Currents of multicolored blue crisscross the sea. Where the sun hits it, the ocean sparkles.

"That's East Sooke Park," says Josh. He slows to consult some charts and his iPhone. I see grey rocks, backed by dark green forest. Once we've passed the park, the occasional cabin comes into view, little matchboxes set by the water. We pass three sailboats headed the opposite way. All their passengers, also dressed in orange, wave at us. We wave back. Out toward the States I spot a hulking cargo ship.

"Want to steer, matey?" calls Josh.

I walk to his side. "I'm a little green, m'hearties."

"Here." He moves over so I can take the wheel. "There's nothing to it." With him standing so close, it's hard to follow directions. Before I know it, my hands are off the wheel and on him. He slows the boat and pulls me close. It's suddenly much hotter in my giant survival jacket. Our kiss sets my heart racing.

When we finally lean back, Josh grins. "Shiver me timbers."

I laugh. "See, you'll love Talk Like a Pirate Day."

Back on track, we see less traffic. The coast looks more desolate now. I see dark trees and grey rocks with some ribbons of beaches.

Josh slows the boat and checks the GPS. "We must be close," he says. A few minutes later, he points toward a narrow cove gripped by steep cliffs. "That should be it, just ahead."

I squint to follow the line of his finger. Thick trees come right down to a rocky beach. There's a rickety jetty but no sign of a cabin.

We slow further and turn into the cove. Above the trees, I spot a circling bald eagle.

As we draw closer to shore, I peer overboard. The water is crystal clear. Down below, I see rocks and seaweed. "Is it deep enough?" I ask.

Josh nods. He studies the depth sounder's small screen. "Yes. Plenty deep."

Josh's obviously had lots of experience; he makes steering this big boat look easy. "Now heave ho," he says. "I need you to run down and tie us up."

I give him a mock salute, then grab my backpack and descend the spiral staircase.

When we're safely tied up, I peel off my floatation jacket. Now that we're stationary, I'm sweating.

Josh trots down the stairs.

As I step onto the thin dock, it shudders beneath me.

I shade my eyes as I walk. Negotiating this rickety dock I feel a sense of misgiving. This is private property. We're uninvited. What if Daphne's here and doesn't want visitors? Am I being invasive?

But then I recall my mom's worry. She thought it was a wonderful idea to check Daphne's cabin, just in case. As Daphne's best friend, surely my mom has a right—no, a duty—to look for her. Or has my mom lost the plot? After all, even the turquoise looked ominous. If you're convinced of something, you'll see signs everywhere. Ordinary things become omens. Every bird, bug, or rock is a messenger. That's the danger of magical thinking.

I step off the dock. Josh's right behind me. "So, where to?" he says. Our feet sink into the pebbled beach. I squint into the trees, looking for a trail. There's a faint gap in the woods, up ahead.

"That way," I say, pointing. We start to walk, our feet crunching through the pebbles.

Josh glances my way. "I'm glad we came today," he says.

I nod, suddenly tongue-tied. "Same." Our hands find each other's as we walk. As usual, I get a charge from his touch. Everything around us looks suddenly brighter.

"Whose place is this, again?" asks Josh, scanning the bay. Our feet stir up loose pebbles. Some long, shiny strands of kelp litter the beach, like snakes from some alien planet.

"Daphne Dane's," I say. I'd explained the whole saga last night, on the phone. I guess he wasn't really listening.

One of his golden eyebrows rises. "As in Dane cookies?"

I'm surprised. "Yes. Do you know her?"

"We've met at the marina," he says. "She keeps her yacht there."

"Oh," I say. I didn't know Daphne had a boat.

"How do you know her?" he asks me.

"She's an old friend of my mom's," I say. "From way back." What I don't say is that Daphne helped my mom stay afloat, back when my dad deserted us. Without Daphne's aid, we might have ended up in a shelter. Or on the street. Daphne also introduced Ivy to all her rich, gullible friends, who—with more cash than sense—became devoted clients. I bet half my mom's customers have some link to Daphne Dane.

"Daphne seems like a smart woman," says Josh. "Not the flighty type. I think your mom's right to be worried."

"Really?" I say, surprised. I'm mostly here to appease my mom, not because I think Daphne's in real peril. Except what if she is? "Col—," I stop myself from mentioning Colin. "The cops think she's gone off on holiday, maybe with her new boyfriend."

Josh bends to pick up a reddish pebble. He examines it before tossing it away. "Well, I think it's strange," he says. "Leaving without telling her kids or friends. No note, nothing."

I think of Daphne's kids: disapproving Isobel and lazy Lukas, both eager to milk their mom for cash. Maybe she's not that close to them. And my mom? That's a little weird, although maybe Daphne's feeling secretive about her new romance. It's very recent, after all. Maybe she's scared it'll all go wrong and she'll end up feeling foolish. It's hard enough dating at my age. Imagine doing it as a senior! Even the language—boyfriend, girlfriend—seems absurd. We need new words to match today's reality: it's not just kids who are dating.

We walk along the beach in silence, then scramble over some large driftwood logs. Josh steps onto a big rock. He shields his eyes to look around. "What a great spot," he says. "A deep protected harbor with good views." He examines the tall cliffs bookending the bay. "Does Daphne own those points too?" Twisted pines and cedars overhang the cliffs' edges.

"I don't know. My mom said it's a big property." Whatever that means. Given the Danes' wealth, it could be gigantic. It's isolated, that's for sure. And Josh's right: the aspect is lovely.

We follow a narrow path into the dark trees. The ground is springy beneath our feet. Apart from our footsteps, it's utterly quiet. Under the trees, the light is greenish-grey. Thanks to my teenage stint at summer camp, I recognize pine, spruce, and mountain hemlock. I recall being in the woods with Josh, our first kiss, at the age of fourteen. Time for a repeat, only better. I stop and pull him toward me.

"Nice," he says, when we pause for breath. He smiles down at me, his eyes shining. "What was that for?"

"I just felt like it."

"Mmmm, well, I feel like this."

Our next kiss leaves me dizzy.

We start to walk again, both of us grinning.

A bend in the trail reveals an old log cabin with a low front porch and a sagging roof. While Mom described it as rundown, I'm still surprised by the state it's in. Because of the Danes' great wealth I'd expected something much grander. This place looks derelict, the front porch littered with dead leaves and pine needles. There's a dusty table and a few hard-backed wooden chairs. The welcome mat looks rotten.

"Yikes," says Josh. "You ever see that movie, *The Cabin in the Woods?*"

I shake my head. "A love story?"

Josh laughs. "Yeah, if you find zombies romantic."

We both slow down. I shiver. The cabin's small dark windows remind me of staring eyes, its gaze sullen. I'm glad to be holding Josh's big, warm hand. This place is creepy.

My feet feel heavy. I force myself to keep pace but can't shake my misgivings. I tell myself to get a grip. It's just an old, unused cabin. I'm being ridiculous. But with each step, my chest tightens.

Before stepping onto the sagging porch I call out. "Hello?"

"Hey? Anyone home?" calls Josh.

For a beat there's dead silence. A sparrow shoots out of a chink between the logs. I jump. The bird darts into the trees. I stare after it, feeling shaky.

Josh releases my hand and walks to a front window. He presses his forehead to the glass and raises his hands as blinkers. I join him.

When my eyes adjust, I see a dark room. Everything is brown. Unpainted wooden floors. Fake-pine-paneled walls and ceiling. A sagging brown couch. Even the mug resting on the wooden coffee table is brown, as is the man's shoe discarded in the middle of a brown rag rug. A shiny brown dress shoe.

While there's nothing scary about a shoe, the sight of it fills me with horror. I see a man spin around and cry out. I close my eyes, feeling dizzy.

"Toby?" Josh grips my elbow. "Hey? You okay?" His tanned forehead creases.

I realize I'm bent double. I grip the window frame. "I . . . Yes." I say. "I'm just a little lightheaded."

He frowns down at me. "Maybe you're hungry."

I nod, but the thought of food flips my stomach. I'm not hungry.

Still holding my elbow, Josh leads me to a chair on the rickety porch. I sink down gratefully and rub my forehead. What just happened?

He crouches beside me and holds my hand, blue eyes dark with worry. "You've gone all pale," he says.

I look at the front door, then look away. It'd be better to leave, as fast as possible. But we came all this way. I should look inside. What if my mom's right and something's happened to Daphne? What if she came here and met some accident? That brown mug niggles at me. It's like someone just left it there. And that shoe . . . My mom's fretful voice floats into my head. "The turquoise . . . be careful."

I rub my forehead as if to scour this thought away. If I don't watch out, I'll end up as loony as my mom. Don't they say girls end up like their mothers? It might be genetic.

"I better look inside," I tell Josh. "Just in case."

He looks skeptical, but shrugs. "Okay. But it looks empty."

When I stand, he does too. We both walk to the peeling front door. It's locked. I rattle the handle.

Part of me wants to give up. I can say I tried. But I know I could try harder. I check under the front mat, just in case. No key. Now Josh looks uneasy. "Want to get going?" he asks.

I shake my head. I'm going to try the windows. Something about this place has me repulsed but curious. I need to see what's in there.

CHAPTER 10:

IN SHOCK

We walk around to a side window, obscured by olive-green curtains. A tug on the glass reveals it's unlocked.

Josh raises an eyebrow when I slide one pane behind the other. "Toby?" He sounds incredulous. "What are you doing?"

"Climbing in," I say. I explain about Walt's gold coins, which might be out here, forgotten in some hidden safe. I want to check if anything's been disturbed. And I want to be sure Daphne's not inside, ill or injured. "Can you boost me?"

Josh glances around, like he's worried we're being watched, then steps closer. He looks both amused and disbelieving. "Really?"

"Really," I say. "It'll only take two minutes. Just so I can tell my mother."

With a shrug, he knits his fingers and extends his joined hands to form a step. His blue eyes twinkle. "Did Nancy Drew have a boyfriend?"

I smile. "Yeah, Ned Nickerson."

Josh snorts. "Ned Nickerson? What kind of name is that?"

"Ned and Nancy," I say. "I bet those were super trendy names in the 1930s." I step up onto his hands and hold his shoulder to steady myself. After finding my balance, I clamber from his hands to the window frame. Perched birdlike on the windowsill, I pull back the dusty curtains.

The room looks dim and dusty. There's a saggy bed with an orange crocheted cover, two 1970s-style bedside tables, a lamp with a tasseled mustard shade, and a brown and orange shag rug.

I jump down, as lightly as possible. As a kid I did gymnastics. But I'm rusty. I land on my feet but fall forward.

Josh sweeps the curtain aside and peers in. "You okay, Nancy?"

I get up and brush off my knees. "Yeah, super. Thanks Ned," I say.

Except it's a lie. I feel like one of those oblivious kids in a horror movie, the ones determined to explore places that are obviously haunted. The audience in my head is covering their eyes, just waiting for some ghoul to grab me.

I try to shake off this feeling. As a teen, I watched way too many crappy mad-slasher films. And I ought to lay off the late-night, true crime podcasts. This is just an old, empty shack. On a peaceful island. In a peaceful land. There's nothing to be scared of.

"Let me in through the front door, okay?" says Josh.

I nod, relieved to have a partner in crime. "Sure thing." It's an effort to keep my voice steady.

Exiting the bedroom, I turn left. A dark narrow hall leads to the front room, with its brown couch and rag rug. I give the dress shoe a wide berth, like it's a grenade, or could come alive and fly at me—a possessed shoe, à la Stephen King.

I unlatch the front door. In true haunted-house style it creaks open.

Josh is waiting on the porch. Seeing me, he smiles, then, wrinkles his nose. "Ew. What's that smell?" he asks. He puts a hand to his face and steps backward.

As soon as he says it, I don't know how I didn't notice. I must have been too intent on the sick feeling in my stomach. Now, like Josh, I cover my nose and mouth. The smell is sour yet sickly sweet, like damp fabric and rotting food. Whoever was here last must have forgotten to empty the garbage.

"I'll be quick," I say. Behind my hand, my voice is muffled. With the smell, I don't expect Josh to follow but he does. I love him for it. *Who's got my back now, Quinn?* I think. He follows me down the dark hallway.

Past the first bedroom lies a door. I force myself to open it and flick on the light. A dim bulb reveals an avocado-colored toilet and a tub with a moldy gold shower curtain. Ugh. No wonder Daphne doesn't come here anymore! This place is disgusting. It must have been overdue for a renovation even when the Dane kids were little.

Josh peers over my shoulder. "Yuck. They need to tear this place down and start again," he says. "It's a great piece of land." His voice is pinched, like he's holding his nose. "It must be worth a fortune."

I flick off the light. We continue down the dark hall. Another door lies to my left. It's partly closed. I pause before pushing it, my chest tight as a drum. If Josh weren't behind me I might turn and bolt. When I grab the doorknob, my hand trembles.

Another bed, another orange cover. Another tasseled lamp. Another shag rug. In the middle of this rug lies the other shoe—shiny and beetle brown. It looks expensive.

I blink. Not far from the shoe lies a dark blue sock. It's half inside out. I turn my head. Some steps away lies a large, bare foot. It's sticking out of a mirrored closet. My breath scrapes the back of my throat. Oh my god. Is it Daphne?

Josh steps into the room behind me. I see his face reflected in the closet's speckled mirror. His mouth sags open with shock. He clamps his hand to his mouth, gagging.

My legs turn to badly set Jell-O. I take a tiny step forward. I reach for the closet's door and pull it back. Another bare foot comes into view, the toes white and uncallused. I blink and edge forward. Two long, strong legs are clad in navy blue dress pants.

Another shaky step and I can see him: a big man, lying facedown on the floor. He's got one arm curled under him, the other outstretched, like he was reaching for something. His hair is neat and sandy blond. He looks very fit. I feel a moment of hope. He might be asleep. Except there's a black, tarry patch on the back of his head. In the center of this mess sits a large, shiny green fly. More flies circle lazily. Their buzzing fills my head, deafening.

I jump back and crash into Josh. He yelps and grabs my arm. His fingers dig in. "Is he . . . dead?"

I blink, unwilling to believe my eyes. My head swims with horror and questions. Should we check for a pulse? Or leave the scene undisturbed? Is there a chance he's alive? Who is he?

Josh inches closer. He crouches. Beneath his tan, his face has a weird pistachio tint. With one shaking finger, he touches the man's bare foot. "Cold," he whispers.

I shuffle sideways to get a view of the dead man's face. Only the left side is visible. On his white cheek lies a red welt, with a cut running through it. His eye is blue and half open.

My stomach tilts. I start gagging.

I back away. My foot lands on something that rolls. I stagger backward. Bending low, I see a gold tube of lipstick. I tilt my head: on the base, a tiny sticker bears the name—*Scarlet Woman*—and a color sample. Blood red.

I lift my head, feeling dizzy. Sticking out from under the bed is an iron poker. Its tip is gummy. A few strands of fair hair bristle out. A fresh wave of nausea strikes me.

My gaze lurches around the room. The bed is made. There's no sign of a struggle. Above the bed lies a painting—a seascape, roiling waves in dark colors. The frame hangs at an angle. I feel a crazy urge to straighten it but resist.

"Jesus, let's go," says Josh. We both back away.

I follow him down the dark hall and through the living room. We both avoid the shoe. It's a relief to step through the front door. When it creaks shut behind us it sounds like a reproach: *Fool kids, I told you not to go in there.* I can practically hear the Scooby-Doo theme song.

On the porch, Josh skids to a stop. I do too. He raises his hands to his head, grabs two fistfuls of hair and pulls. "Shit. We need to report it." His voice is shaky.

I look around, breathing hard. Is the killer still here? This thought strikes me hard, in the gut. But no, the corpse—my mind skitters away from this ugly word—wasn't fresh. The smell . . . I start gagging.

Josh pats his pockets, finds his phone. He squints at it, frowning. "No reception."

My stomach sinks lower.

He steps off the porch and paces around the small clearing, trying to find a signal. Finally, it connects. I can hear him talking to the 911 operator. The line must be bad because he's yelling.

My legs are liquid. I collapse onto a wooden chair only to jump back up. I can't sit still. I can't stay here. But there's no choice. We'll have to wait for the police. We found a dead man. A dead body. A murdered dead body.

As Josh tries to explain our whereabouts, I reach for my phone. Without even thinking, my fingers have found Colin's number. Except what would I say? One, I'm on a date with another guy. Two, while not exactly breaking and entering, it might look that way. Instead of dragging Josh out here, I should have called Colin in the first place and told him about the conversation I overheard between Gerard and Lukas. I shouldn't be here.

I stash my phone and sink back onto the rickety chair. I hang my head between my knees. Colin will be livid. What was I thinking?

I rub my temples. While Colin's bound to hear about this case, I can only hope my name doesn't crop up. If I'm lucky, he'll never know. My heart lifts a little. I don't want to lose Colin's respect. I like him too much for that. His opinion of me matters.

CHAPTER 11:

TOUGH QUESTIONS

The 911 operator instructed us to stay put. Rather than wait on the porch, we huddle under a tree. From here, we can see the trail that, presumably, leads to the road. It looks overgrown. We don't talk. I want to hold Josh's hand or, better yet, press him close. But he keeps pacing in erratic circles.

Earlier, the woods seemed quiet. Now, they're full of rustlings and slitherings. Branches sway. Twigs snap. I keep thinking I hear footsteps but know it's only my stressed imagination.

After what feels like hours, two figures appear on the trail. In front marches a woman. She's short and freckled, in her mid-fifties. Behind her strides a stocky, freckled man in his mid-twenties. Dressed in matching black uniforms, they have matching expressions of flushed, nervous excitement.

Seeing us, the woman waves. She looks friendly.

Josh and I wait awkwardly as the pair approaches. Ever since we saw the dead guy I've felt cold all over.

The police officers stop. The woman introduces herself as Sergeant Jane Brock. "And this," she points at the young guy, "Is Pete." Seeing his frown, she corrects herself. "I mean Constable Peter Gardener."

Judging from their similar features, identical coloring and familiar manner, they're clearly related. Mother and son? Aunt and nephew?

After asking some basic questions, they tell us to stay put, then vanish into the cabin. They reemerge in record time, looking pale beneath their freckles.

"It's a homicide," confirms Sergeant Brock. She compulsively zips and unzips her jacket. "We gotta call in help." She gestures vaguely toward the cottage. "Don't go anywhere." We both nod. "You got the tape?" she asks the young constable. "We need Doc Cassidy out here pronto."

I raise an ironic eyebrow at Josh but he doesn't seem to notice. Doc Cassidy? While we're only a short drive from Victoria's five-star hotels, wine bars, and international airport, this feels like another, much more rustic planet.

As Sergeant Brock retreats out of earshot, Constable Gardener starts to wind police tape around the old cottage. With his pink cheeks he looks like a kid with a new toy. "Last murder out here was before my time," he cheerfully informs us. "The Jennings cousins. Drank too much Jim Beam and got into a fight about a downrigger." I grit my teeth. What are the chances of this being solved? I bet these cops spend their days busting speeders and underage drinkers.

By the time Constable Pete finishes with the police tape, Daphne's decrepit cabin resembles an old shoebox held together by yellow ribbons. Sergeant Jane reappears. "The coroner and murder guys are on their way." The good news is they've called in professionals. The bad news is this will take longer.

I stomp my feet to keep warm. I want to ask where these new cops are coming from but don't dare. Up island? Or from Victoria? My stomach bottoms out. I certainly hope not. Colin is a "murder guy."

Sergeant Jane checks her watch. "They shouldn't be too long," she says, cheerfully. "They're coming by speedboat." She withdraws a notepad from her jacket. After some patting, she locates a pen in her breast pocket. "I'll start with the basics," she says. "Names. Ages. Reasons for being here."

I go first. My reason for being here is complicated. Jane has trouble keeping up. When it's Josh's turn, his answer is simple. "Because of her." He jabs a thumb my way.

"Right," says Sergeant Jane. "And what's your relationship?"

Again, Josh directs his thumb my way. "Ask her."

Jane peers at me expectantly. There's an uncomfortable pause.

"We're friends," I say. I give Josh a tentative smile, which he doesn't return. I feel hurt. Is he upset that I brought him to a crime scene? But how was I supposed to know we'd find a dead guy? Or is it the word "friends" that's pissed him off? I think of Nancy Drew's boyfriend. Even when stuff went wrong, I don't recall Ned getting narky.

Jane is taking an awfully long time to write everything down in her tiny black notebook. Finally, she lowers her pen. "Okay. You two can wait on your boat until the detectives show up. Constable Gardener will walk you down there."

Thank god. It's a relief to get away from the cabin. I follow Josh back to the beach. There's no hand-holding this time. The young constable walks behind us. He talks the whole way, all about his latest triumph—catching a guy who was stealing crab traps. It's like he found Malaysia Air Flight 370, nabbed JonBenét Ramsey's killer, and ID'd Jack the Ripper. Normally, I'd admire his enthusiasm, but right now, I have a headache.

While Constable Pete keeps watch below, Josh and I climb onto the bridge. We turn our chairs to look out to sea, as far from the dead man as we can get. Out of sight, out of mind. Except he isn't. I keep reseeing that grim head wound . . .

Neither of us talks. Josh keeps checking his watch. My stomach rumbles. Wherever the detectives are coming from, they're taking their time. My definition of "not long" does not match Sergeant Jane's. Luckily, we brought lunch, although I have no appetite. Still, we should eat, to keep our strength up.

"Want your sandwich?" I ask Josh.

"Not really."

I unpack them anyway and hand him his. We both pick at them. I know we're both thinking about the dead guy. Who is he? Or rather who was he? And why would someone kill him? How did he get here?

We can hear the boat before we see it. It rounds the rocky point, moving fast. White water V's out from its grey prow. As it gets closer, it slows. I can make out the letters RCMP—Royal Canadian Mounted Police—stenciled onto its side. The word POLICE is written across the windshield in bright blue letters.

We both stand and walk to the rail, watching in silence as it pulls up to the skinny jetty. It's lower and smaller than the *Great Escape*. A fit-looking man jumps out and ties it up, followed by two chubby guys in matching square glasses. Bearing boxes and bags of equipment, they must be the crime techs. A thin man in a long dark coat steps carefully onto the dock. He's clutching a briefcase. Is he the coroner? Next out is a tall, slim woman in tight black pants and a black baseball cap. Her shiny red-brown ponytail swishes behind her.

Josh shades his eyes. Like me, he's noticed the woman—and how could he not? She's got legs like a pantyhose model, legs like . . . I can't swallow.

Oh God, no. It can't be. But it is. Miriam Young. My stomach—still unsettled from finding the dead guy—flips and sinks even lower.

And lower. It hits my pubis and ricochets. My jaw jolts up.

Behind Miriam strides Detective Colin Destin. I'd know his walk anywhere. Chin up, shoulders back. Relaxed yet purposeful and watchful.

I want to run, hide, shrink. But it's too late. Colin's eyes slide from the shoreline to the *Great Escape*, then narrow. After reading the boat's name he looks up. He frowns when he spies Josh. Spotting me, his jaw tightens.

After walking closer, he sets down the bag he's holding and shades his eyes. He cranes his neck to peer up at the bridge. "Toby?" he calls sharply. "What are you doing here?"

While I never hid the fact that I'm still seeing Josh, faced with both of them, I feel guilty. Colin's hands find his hips. I start to answer but he cuts me off. "No, wait." He shakes his head in disgust. Even from way I up here, I can see the reproach in his eyes. "Let me guess," he says. "You found the body."

I nod, blushing.

"Right," says Colin. His clipped tone makes me want to cry. "Well, stay put. We'll come speak to you soon." He retrieves his bag.

"Come on," says Miriam. "We'd better see what we've got." The crime techs and coroner have long since vanished.

We watch Colin and Miriam walk along the dock and down the rocky beach. After they've vanished into the trees, Josh sits back down.

He folds his arms. His lip is curled in annoyance. His foot keeps tapping. Is he just on edge after finding a corpse? Or is he upset about seeing Colin?

He starts to fiddle with his phone. From the way he's sitting, with his back slightly turned, it's obvious he doesn't want to talk. Shaky and miserable, I dig out my thermos. "Hot chocolate?" I offer.

He just shakes his head, an irritated shake, like a fly landed on him.

I guzzle lukewarm hot chocolate in a lame attempt to feel better. Talk about a crappy date! It's hard to imagine how it could get worse. I've set a new personal record.

Waiting for Colin and Miriam to reappear, I feel like a small kid sitting outside the principal's office. How long will I have to wait? What will Colin say to me? Why oh why did he have to get this case? Will Josh and Colin forgive me? Of all the bad luck. I can hardly believe it. And yet it's so typical.

We wait for what feels like eons but is actually closer to twenty minutes. Finally, when I've worked myself into a nervous lather, Colin and Miriam reappear. Watching their approach, I feel sick. My anxiety is tinged with jealousy. They look so good together, both so tall and athletic. Why did I have to inherit Ivy's lack of height? Half my casual wardrobe hails from the Girls' Department. Compared to Miri, I'm a midget.

"Hello?" calls Miriam. "Can we come up?"

Josh looks up from his phone and frowns. "Of course," he says. He stands. Colin and Miriam climb the boat's spiral staircase.

Colin and Josh met last summer, back when Josh was a suspect in his ex-wife's murder. Now, the two men shake hands. They seem cordial, even friendly, but I can feel their tension. Colin's polite smile doesn't reach his eyes, while Josh's appears frozen.

"Josh," says Colin. He casts a real smile toward Miriam. "This is my new partner, Detective Miriam Young."

Josh shakes Miriam's hand with considerably more enthusiasm than he'd shaken Colin's. "Hi, Detective." He flashes her his megawatt smile: white teeth, blue eyes, bronze skin, golden hair. The effect is dazzling. Again, jealousy stabs through me.

While Miriam doesn't return Josh's smile, she doesn't look unfriendly either—just observant and neutral. Her hair is in a French braid. A dark pink scarf circles her elegant neck. Whoever said redheads should avoid pink has never seen Miriam Young. But then, natural beauty goes with everything.

When she turns my way, her big brown eyes search my face. "Toby." A quick smile. "Fancy meeting you here." It could sound snide but doesn't.

I shrug. Believe me, I wish I were just about anyplace else. "Hi, Miriam."

Her gaze seems to soften. "Are you okay? It must have been quite a shock, finding that guy."

She seems so likable. Or is she just trying to get me to lower my guard? But why? Surely Josh and I aren't suspects. We don't even know the dead guy. I hate feeling so suspicious of Miriam, and so envious. If only she weren't partnered with Colin—and so attractive. If only she were a crusty old man. Or some young kid, just out of the police academy, covered in pimples.

I nod, warily. "Yes, it was a shock."

Josh drags a couple more chairs across the deck.

"Do you mind if we record this?" asks Colin. He pulls a tiny recorder out of his coat's pocket.

I'm surprised but just nod. He sets it onto a nearby table and takes a seat. He looks from me to Josh, like he's weighing something up.

I drop my gaze. Sitting here, with both men, I feel guilty and uncomfortable. But why should I? I'm just getting to know them both better. Taking things slowly isn't a crime. I'm not lying to anyone. I really do like both of them. A lot. I want to blurt this out but bite my lip. A man died. This isn't about me and my stupid romantic indecision.

"We'll do this one at a time," says Colin. He turns to me, uncharacteristically serious. Normally, his green eyes dance with light. Right now, they're hard and flat. "Let's begin with Toby." He glances at Josh. "Do you mind waiting downstairs?" It's an order not a question.

Josh gets up without a word and descends the stairs. I watch Colin's finger depress the ON button on his tiny tape recorder. He states the time and my name, then turns my way. "So why are you here?" Am I only just imagining the accusation in his voice?

I remind him about my mom's concern about Daphne Dane, and how, since she hasn't shown up, I decided to search her holiday cabin.

"Did the Danes know you were coming?"

I shake my head, blushing. My mom knew. But she's not a Dane. Even though it's true, saying she and Daphne are *like* family won't hold water from a legal standpoint. It's a scary realization. You can be someone's best friend for thirty years but, in a crisis, their relatives get to make the key decisions, even if they're motivated by self-interest. Looking for Daphne was the right thing to do, yet technically, I'm a trespasser. My blush deepens.

The next questions are easier. What time did we leave Oak Bay Marina? What time did we arrive here? Did I see anyone or have the sense someone might be around the Danes' cabin?

"No. It looked abandoned," I say. I glance toward the woods and shiver.

"So why did you go inside?"

I shrug, recalling the dread I felt upon seeing that discarded man's shoe. "I felt I had to," I say. "Just in case Daphne was in there. In trouble . . ." I know it sounds crazy. "My mom's so worried."

"The deceased," says Colin. "Did you recognize him?"

"No." I fight back the image of that awful head wound. And the flies. His empty blue eye. My stomach twists. "Do you know who he is?" I ask Colin.

He shakes his head. But would he tell me even if he did?

"Did you find the safe?" I ask him.

"What safe?" asks Miriam. There are dark hollows beneath her eyes today. Still, it would take a lot more than looking tired to mar her astonishing beauty. With her luminous light brown skin and coppery hair she's got extraordinary coloring. It's hard not to stare at her.

I explain about the coins. Colin and Miriam exchange a meaning-ful look. "We'll check on that," says Colin, tightly.

When he speaks to Miriam, there's more warmth in his voice: "We'd better get one of Daphne's kids out here to open the safe."

I shift in my seat. "They don't know the combo."

Colin turns to me with a frown.

"Only Daphne does," I explain. "And she's still missing. Do you think the dead guy, whoever he is . . ." My voice drops. "Maybe he was out here trying to steal Walt's coin collection?"

Again, Colin and Miriam lock eyes.

"Who knew those coins were out here?" asks Colin.

"Only the family, from what Gerard said." I explain how Isobel had learned of the coins' whereabouts and caused a big stink at a family dinner, the night before Daphne went missing.

"Oh yeah?" says Miriam. She licks her full lips. Colin's eyes brighten.

Seeing their avid expressions I know what they're thinking: Gerard, Isobel, and Lukas Dane are about to get visits from the cops. From what I heard, they're all short of cash. Did one of them hire this blond guy to come out here and crack the safe? And then what, they argued about how to split the loot and bashed him?

My far-fetched musings are interrupted by Colin, whose own brain—I can see from his glinting eyes—has been spinning. "That family dinner," he says. "Where was it?"

I think back to the conversation I overheard in L'Escargot D'Or. "At Daphne's house."

He nods, as do I, because, just a for a moment, we're connected again. We've both had the same thought: the list of people who knew about the coin collection has expanded, a little. Daphne's housekeeper, Grace, would likely have been there. And her new boyfriend, Stephen . . . Gerard had whined about him and Daphne acting like teenagers that night. With a start, I remember that Colin and Miriam don't even know about Daphne's new man. Isobel failed to tell them.

"There's something else," I say. "Daphne has a new boyfriend. A British guy named Stephen Buxley. He was at that dinner too . . ."

Miriam rubs her hands. "Oh yeah? Any idea where we could find him?"

"With Daphne, I guess," I say. "That's what Daphne's housekeeper, Grace, figured. That they're off on a romantic vacation."

Colin tilts his head. "This man, Stephen Buxley. Any idea what he looks like?"

I shake my head. "No. All I know is he's younger. Like around fifty." I struggle to recall what else Grace had said about the man. "Grace said he was ex-military." Unbidden, an image of the dead man's head pops into my mind. That short, perfectly trimmed hair . . . His fit torso . . . A dead middle-aged white guy.

From the stillness that's descended, I know we're all wondering the same thing. Could the dead guy be Daphne's younger lover? And if so, where's Daphne?

CHAPTER 12:

A BAD END

The first time I went out on Josh's boat, we almost died. The second time, we found a dead body. Talk about bad luck. While I don't want to believe in signs and omens, it's hard not to feel like I'd be better off avoiding the *Great Escape*. Unless it's third time lucky.

It's close to five by the time we're allowed to leave. We're both quiet on the homeward trip. As if to match our mood, it pours the whole way back. Plus it's gotten rough. We both retreat to the glassed-in cabin. It's too dark to see the scenery. My lame attempts at conversation are met by one-word answers. I want to scream. Yes, today sucked but there's no need to make it worse. Why is Josh being so distant?

Finally, I snap and ask what's wrong.

"I'm tired, that's all."

So am I. But that's not all. The tension between us is as heavy as the rain. I hate it when people are angry but won't admit it.

After that, I stop trying to melt the ice. Rain twists down the windows.

I feel limp with exhaustion when we finally motor into Oak Bay Marina. The docks lie dark and deserted. No pirate jokes as I tie us up. *Back we arrrrrrrr,* I think sadly, aware that my inner pirate has morphed into Yoda.

Josh's car looks lonesome in the huge, empty lot. Even Beach Drive is deserted. We run hunched against the rain, skirting puddles.

We're back in Josh's Porsche when my phone rings. It's my mom, asking about our trip. I don't want to tell her about finding a dead man. She'll freak out. But I can't lie. She always knows when I do. It's uncanny.

"We, er, found something," I say. "Out at Daphne's cottage." I inhale. There's really no good way to say it. "A strange man died out there," I say. "We found his body."

As expected, she's shocked. "Holy moley!" she says. "Someone died out there? Who was he?"

"The cops don't know yet."

There's music playing at my mom's—the sort of soft, chiming tune they favor in fancy spas. It sets my teeth on edge, the musical equivalent of cheesy social media affirmations: *If you love something, set it free etcetera.* Does anyone find these tunes relaxing?

"Oh how dreadful. What'd he look like?" asks my mother.

I describe the John Doe as best I can—a tall, well-built white guy with short, neat, fair hair, dressed in a white button-down shirt and navy slacks. I clear my throat. "What does Daphne's boyfriend look like?"

"Stephen Buxley?" says my mom. She sounds alarmed. "I don't know. I haven't met him yet."

I fight back a sigh. That's the thing about people my mom's age: they don't share photos documenting every moment of their lives. Daphne's not even on Facebook, which is popular with older folk.

"Why?" asks my mom. Her voice is breathy. "Do the police think it's—"

I cut her off. "They don't know. Or aren't saying."

Josh speeds up to catch a yellow light. I wish he wouldn't, especially in this weather.

"I knew it," says my mother. Her voice thickens. "I just knew something awful had happened. The cards . . ."

I cut in, fast, suddenly, absurdly hopeful. "Any word from Daphne yet?"

There's a pause, filled only by tinkly music. A fake bird twitters. "No." Her voice is fearful.

"Well, at least now the police are looking for her," I tell my mother.

There's a pause as she takes this in. "Do they think she's been . . ." She gulps for air. "Injured? Did they search the cabin?"

"They did," I say. "They're trying to find her, Mom. Try not to worry. There might be no connection. For all we know, the dead guy could have been a squatter, killed by some other squatter."

It sounds plausible, except even as I say this, I recall those shiny brown shoes. Since when do squatters wear dress shoes? Or navy trousers with perfect creases?

We turn onto my street. "Mom," I say. "Can I call you back? Give me ten, fifteen minutes?"

She says sure. I stash my phone in my coat pocket.

Josh pulls up in front of my building. In the gloom, various tenants have turned on their lights. The old place looks warm and inviting. As usual, head-busybody, Mrs. Daggett, is staring down from her second-floor window, half obscured by a lace curtain. She's got a lisp, hair like something pulled out of a shower drain, and one facial expression: pinched disapproval.

One floor up sits Mrs. Van Dortmund's cat, kept indoors by the rain. It's got one foot in the air and is licking its butt, like it's doing cat yoga.

I undo my seatbelt and turn to Josh. In the dashboard light, his face is taut and slicked sickly green. I take a deep breath. Everything about today has felt off, but then it would. We found a dead man.

Or did the uncomfortable feeling precede our grim discovery? I don't think so. We were having such fun . . . I'm not sure what to say. Another deep breath. "Are you okay?" I ask him.

Josh zips up his red jacket. "Sure. Why wouldn't I be?"

"I . . . I don't know." I shudder, trying to repress the memory of that shiny shoe. The empty navy sock. The unnaturally pale foot. "It was just . . . shocking."

While his head is twisted my way, his body isn't. Both his hands are still on the wheel. He's not looking at me, but out the window behind my head.

Is he mad that I got him involved in another murder investigation? Did the police interview rattle him? Or is it something else? I bite my lip. There's a cold, empty feeling in my belly.

The windshield wipers sweep back and forth. "Okay. Well, see you soon?" I hate that I sound so plaintive. Why's he being so cold? We just found a dead body—a grim experience but a shared one. Shouldn't this visceral reminder of death make us feel even more alive, more determined to live to the fullest? Shouldn't it bring us closer?

My head throbs. I don't understand his reaction. We should be taking comfort in each other. I want to hold him and be held, to feel his warm, living body.

Finally, he meets my gaze. I see a flash of resentment in his deep blue eyes. I freeze. "Toby, I want to be with you," he says. "All the time. I need you."

I blink. He's saying stuff I've always longed to hear, stuff I spent years imagining. So why do I feel like I'm being chastised instead of cherished? And why are his eyes so angry?

His chin juts out. "This has been going on too long," he says. "When are you going to decide if you're my girlfriend or not?"

I lean back, stunned. This is about Colin. I blink. Josh Barton's jealous.

"I . . ." I open my mouth, then close it. All of a sudden, I feel beyond tired. I'm depleted.

"I like you, Josh," I say, dismayed that it sounds so lame. "You know I do. I mean, ever since we got together as kids . . ." Just for a moment I'm fourteen years old, back at that crappy summer camp. There was Josh, emerging from the lake, spraying drops of water like spilled diamonds. The eyes of every girl in camp were glued to his tanned, toned chest, everyone hoping he'd look their way, that he'd choose them. Pick me. Yes, me. And then he'd seen me and smiled his lottery-winning smile. Straight at me! I hadn't—and still can't—quite believe it.

I press my lips shut and push my palms against the Porsche's smooth leather seat. I've never admitted it out loud: it wasn't just some teeny teenage crush. When he finally, inevitably rejected me, it was crushing. He broke my heart. Yes, it's pathetic but I spent years obsessing about him. Nobody else measured up. Ever. When we met again, this past summer, it was like a dream come true. And now he's here, in my life, close enough to touch. A living god.

He said he needs me. I got what I wanted. So why do I feel so empty?

Josh's knuckles are white against the wheel. His jaw is rigid.

I realize I stopped talking mid-sentence. He's waiting for me to finish. I swallow. "For years and years, I still thought about you," I admit. "I couldn't get you out of my head. When we met again, I couldn't believe it."

He's still staring straight ahead. "Then why are you still seeing Colin?"

I study his square chin, glints of gold stubble against his tan. He's so beautiful. How come I'm not sure? I like Colin too. I love things about both of them.

But Josh is right. I should know by now. What's wrong with me? I should be sure. Quinn claims she loved Bruce from their very first date. Why am I so indecisive?

I take a deep breath, unsure how to say it. "I'm taking this seriously," I say. "I just want to be sure."

He frowns. "It feels like you're playing games." His voice is harsh.

I lean back, shocked. "I'm not!" Does he think I'm that shallow and manipulative? If I were deceitful, I'd just tell him what he wants to hear. That I'm in love, that he's the One. I know there's a long line of women who'd kill to take my place. If he gets sick of waiting, I might be kicking myself for the next two—or six—decades. But I can't lie and promise—without a doubt—that we're meant for each other. If we get there, and I hope we do, I want it to be wholeheartedly.

"I haven't been in many relationships," I say. "Not serious ones. I don't enter into things lightly. And I don't play games." I lay a hand on his arm. I will him to turn to me, to reach out. But he sits frozen. "Please Josh." I take my hand away. Maybe it's the lack of food, or the stress of today, or this tense conversation, but the ache behind my eyes has expanded. "Just bear with me. Okay?" I shake my head and attempt a smile. "It's been a rough day, hasn't it?"

His frown deepens.

"Please," I say, again, trying to lighten the mood. "Can we talk about this some other time? Soon, I promise. Okay, Captain?"

A muscle in his jaw tightens.

I remember Quinn's misgivings about Josh—that he's so charming, so rich, and so good looking that he feels entitled to adoration, that people *that* blessed can't help but be arrogant and selfish.

A large oak tree stands some feet from his car. Somewhere overhead, an owl hoots softly. I hope it's sheltered from the rain. The car's windshield wipers have started to squeak.

Josh's voice is low. "I think we're done," he says.

Done? For tonight? Or forever? I swallow hard, unable—or unwilling—to take this in. I feel chilled to the bone. The smooth leather is cool beneath my hands. "You . . . you don't want to see me anymore?"

"Not deciding is a decision," says Josh. "Your decision. So don't pin this on me." He sounds so bitter I don't know what to say. This is not my decision.

I pull my backpack up off the floor. My hand feels leaden as I reach for the door's lock. I'm desperate to get out, and equally desperate to fall into his arms.

He sits like a statue, staring straight ahead at the rain-flecked windshield.

I paw the lock open and crawl from his fancy car, dragging my backpack behind me.

When I shut the door, he's still frozen.

Standing out there, in the rain, I want to take it all back, to tell him I was wrong. I want to scramble back into his car, to say I love him. I want to beg for forgiveness.

Except I'm too sad to speak and too angry. How could he do this, today of all days? He's still staring straight ahead, his face like a waxwork in the dashboard light. He looks like a zombie.

Rain and tears fill my eyes. I hunch my shoulders and take a step back, dragging my backpack. Rain leaches under my collar. It's raining harder than ever.

When Josh's car pulls away, it's like a gate slamming down on my heart. He speeds off down the street. I'm too shocked to believe it.

He'll stop. He'll turn around. He'll reach the corner and regret it. Couples fight. It's part of being in a relationship. They fight and realize they were wrong—or at least half-wrong. They wake up. They make up.

I wait for his brake lights to glow red. I'll give him another ten seconds. One Mississippi. Two Mississippi.

When his car rounds the corner my head drops. But I force it back up and look the other way. No problem. He's just going around the block. Three Mississippi. Four. I stop counting at sixty.

He's not circling back.

It's over.

I swipe the wetness from my eyes and turn away. Rain is dripping, icy cold, down my spine. I look up, blinking.

Skinny arms crossed against her sunken chest, Mrs. Daggett glares down at me from her window. As usual, she looks poised to give me the finger.

Usually, I wonder what I've done to piss Mrs. Daggett off. I tell myself she hates everyone under age sixty-five or all Asians. But tonight, for once, her disapproval feels justified. It's like Mrs. Daggett knows I screwed up. She sees me for who I am: an indecisive, socially awkward loser—the kind of cowardly, neurotic girl who had a clear shot at love but blew it.

CHAPTER 13:

WITH REGRET

I'm woken at what feels like dawn by my ringing phone. It's my mother. "I'm downstairs," she says. She's talking fast. "Is your buzzer not working?"

I sit up, blearily, and rub my sore head. I had a horrible night's sleep, plagued by recurring dreams about Daphne's cabin, interspersed with replays of getting dumped by Josh—an endless loop of dread and disappointment.

My bedside clock reads 7:42 a.m. I knead my forehead. It's not even early.

"I'm coming," I say. I stumble out of bed. Despite my thick terrycloth robe I feel cold and clumsy.

When the buzzer sounds afresh it takes me two tries to admit my mother.

I slouch by my front door and try to psyche myself up. She mustn't know I'm depressed. She'll want to talk about it. I can't even bear to think about it.

My throat tightens. I messed everything up. When Josh said he *needed* me I should have leapt into his muscular arms and declared my never-ending passion . . . Instead, I froze.

Tears cloud my eyes. The man of my dreams just dumped me.

"You won't believe—" says my mom, as I open the door. Seeing me, she falls silent. Her eyes widen. I must look like death warmed up. "Honey? Are you okay?" She sounds worried. "Is it the shock of finding the body? Oh, it's so terrible! Did you have nightmares? I should have brought the Bach flowers rescue remedy!"

I attempt a smile. "I'm fine," I croak. "But I just woke up."

My mom looks skeptical. She steps inside. In one hand is a cute wicker basket, covered by a gingham tea towel. She could have stolen it off Little Red Riding Hood, except I can guess what's in there: her dreaded "healthy" breakfast muffins.

I shut the door, resisting the urge to lean my forehead against it.

My mom steps out of her purple Crocs. She tilts her head, a cute, bright-eyed budgie surveying a sad little sparrow. "Hmmm . . . Have you had breakfast yet?"

I manage to nod.

"No you haven't," says my mom. Her basket swings ominously. "Look!" She smiles, thrilled to be of use. "I brought you muffins!"

I mumble my thanks, but there's no disguising my lack of enthusiasm. As well as being fat free, gluten free, dairy free, and egg free, my mom's muffins are—unsurprisingly—free of flavor.

"I'll heat them up," she says. She motions toward my oven. My mom mistrusts microwaves. At night, she turns off the Wi-Fi. "I put quinoa in these ones. And teff. It gives them a lovely nuttiness. Do you want one or two, sweetie?"

I rub my eyes. What the hell is teff? It sounds like some pricey new high-tech fabric. Head wrapped in a turban printed with tropical fruit, my mom blinks at me expectantly. She is a vision of lovely nuttiness.

"Um, one, please," I say, trying not to sound reluctant. The only thing worse than being woken suddenly from a deep sleep is being woken suddenly by my mom, who's hideously chirpy in the mornings. I didn't inherit this trait. No one should speak to me precoffee.

You'd think that by now my mom would have figured this out, but she hasn't. As she heats a couple of nutty muffins, I stumble toward my espresso machine. I can't hear a word she's saying over the whir of the machine, but that doesn't stop her from chattering.

I don't bother to offer her a cup. My mom thinks coffee's poison.

I watch the black liquid gush into my cup and inhale its rich smell. It smells better than chocolate, or honeysuckle, or Josh. Well, maybe not Josh, but I mustn't think about him now. The back of my throat burns. I want to cry. I bite my lip. Just focus on the damn coffee.

Meanwhile, my mom hops around my tiny kitchen, twittering.

She's keyed up about something. I lack the strength to ask what. I take a desperate gulp and scald my tongue. I swallow anyway. Another sip and some of her chirps begin to make sense. I upend the tiny cup. So good. So bitter.

"I just consulted the I Ching and the answer was crystal clear. Daphne's been misled. She feels alone and brokenhearted."

Oh God no. No I Ching before noon. There should be a law. The last grainy drops of coffee land on my seared tongue. I lick the sides. It's all gone—as is Josh. My eyes well up. I squeeze them shut.

Too much self-pity and not enough caffeine. I need more coffee.

After two doubles, I feel capable of speech. My mother is still chattering nervously, all about cards and bad feelings. Her real news, whatever it is, has yet to come. She's working up to it, slowly.

"Right?" says my mom. She tilts her head, clearly expecting an answer.

I make a noncommittal sound and rub my forehead. I have a headache.

She peers at me. "Does your head hurt?" she asks, then, before I can deny it, "Well no wonder! Drinking that poison on an empty stomach!"

She opens my fridge. From the look on her face, you'd think she was peering through the gates of Hell. She sounds aghast: "Ketchup, yogurt, Nutella, and beer?" I know what she's thinking: I raised you better than this! "You know, Nutella is full of palm oil," she says. "It's killing the rain forests."

I hang my head, guilty that I don't feel sufficiently guilty. Those poor homeless orangutans. I am a heartless, unenvironmentally-friendly bitch. No wonder Josh dumped me.

My mom pulls out the produce bin and extracts a flaccid carrot and a bunch of sad-looking spinach. She proceeds to wash and chop these vegetables before tossing them in the blender with some yogurt. I enjoy the quiet that's descended. Whatever she's concocting has her full attention. She opens and shuts various cupboards in search of my spice rack, then tosses in colorful pinches. "Turmeric.

Cinnamon. Ginger," she says. "All anti-inflammatories." She spoons in some honey.

I wonder if another espresso is a bad idea. Probably. My heart seems to have sprouted its own tiny, offbeat heart.

The blender whirs. Gazing at the whirring sludge, my mom looks pleased with herself. She can't seriously expect me to drink that.

"A smoothie," says my mother. She holds out the glass. It looks exactly like baby poo—a substance I've grown familiar with since the arrival of Abby. She smiles encouragingly.

I shake my head. "Thanks but no—"

"C'mon, Toby." It's her Mom voice. I haven't heard it in ages.

I take the glass.

Her smile doubles in size. "You'll feel much better after this."

I highly doubt that.

Strangely, I do. While the smoothie tastes like it looks, the pounding behind my eyes subsides. I feel awake enough to question what my mom's doing here. It's Sunday morning. Isn't this when she usually does Tai Chi in Windsor Park, near the rose garden?

I force down another sip and follow her into my box-like living room. There's no space for a table in my kitchen.

She opens my curtains to reveal a view of some poplars and the building behind mine, separated by a parking lot. I blink against the sudden glare. My mom pads across the room and sits cross-legged in an armchair. I sink onto the couch across from her.

"Lukas called," she says.

It takes me a moment to recall who Lukas is. When I do, I lower my glass in surprise. "Lukas Dane? Has his mom turned up?"

"No," she says. "The police came to see him and his sister." From the tight pitch of her voice, I know she's finally getting close to the reason she's here. Her bright eyes float around the room before settling back on me. "They ID'd the dead guy." She clutches at the dark blue beads around her throat—kyanite, I see, a stone meant to ward off lies and ill will. "It was Daphne's new boyfriend, Stephen Buxley."

I push my smoothie away. I feel freshly sick. Even though I sort of suspected it was him, it's still a shock. The discovery of Stephen's body makes Daphne's disappearance a lot more worrying. What was her lover doing in that decrepit cabin? They were meant to be together . . . Were they there together?

"He wants my help," says my mom. "My professional help."

For one dreadful moment, I think she means Stephen, who is dead. But then I understand: she's referring to Lukas.

"Lukas wants to hire you?" I say. "You mean, as a psychic?"

My mom crosses her skinny arms and pouts. "Don't sound so surprised, Toby. That's what I do. People hire me all the time."

I rub my forehead. "Sorry." I shouldn't belittle my mom's métier. She is passionate about it. "I'm just . . ." I choose my words carefully. I know psychics get used in murder and missing persons investigations. If someone I loved vanished, I'd try everything too. But Daphne's been gone for what, four days? And she took a suitcase. "It just seems early in the day to hire a psychic," I tell my mother.

My mother sniffs. "Lukas is a very spiritual young man."

Okay. I guess that's possible. He was off meditating, after all. My head is pounding again. "So how does it work?" I ask. I hope I sound interested, rather than dubious.

"I'll go to her house and hold a piece of her clothing or jewelry," explains my mom. She twists the large chrysocolla (healing, calming) ring on her right hand. "Of course I've been thinking about her nonstop, trying to get a sense of where she might be." She shakes her head in frustration. "But beyond this deep . . ." She touches a hand to her chest. "Deep sadness and sense of betrayal . . ." My mom sighs. "I can't see where she's gone."

I study my fish tank, unsure how to respond. "Well, maybe going to her place will help."

My mother jumps up, like she's been reminded of her purpose. She rubs her hands on her jeans. "Right. We'd better go," she says. Then she remembers the muffins. I stay seated as she retreats to the kitchen and deposits them—clink, clink—onto two plates. "Voila!" she says. She bounces across the hardwood floor. "Hot from the oven!"

I hold my breath. Her muffins look like rocks—something I imagine an archeologist pulling out of the ruins of a two-thousand-year-old bakery in Pompeii.

"Eat fast," she says. She passes me my muffin-slash-fossil. I doubt eating fast is possible. It would take hours to gnaw through it. As for digesting—years would be my guess.

My mom grabs hers. "I said we'd be right over."

I sink deeper into the sofa. "Um, pardon?"

My mom bites into her muffin. She's always had great teeth. "To Daphne's house," she says. She chews with gusto. "To meet Lukas."

"I . . ." I shake my head. "You want me to come?"

"Well, you said you'd give me a ride," she says, with a tiny frown. I blink. I did? When? My mom looks nonplussed. "My car's in the shop," she says. "Weren't you listening?"

Oh no. I must have nodded or said uh-huh back before the espressos. "Um, of course," I say. "Sorry. I, ah, I meant inside. Of course I'll give you a ride." I'll drop my mom off and get the hell out of there.

My mom's frown reappears. "But you promised to stay. You said you'd have a quick look around, while I was doing the reading."

I frown too. I did? I think of Colin and how unimpressed he was by my visit to Daphne's summer cottage. He more or less told me to butt out and let him and Miriam do their jobs. "Look for what?" I ask. "The police already looked . . ."

My mom's pointy chin goes up. "We told the police she was missing days ago! They didn't take us seriously! There might be clues they've missed!" She shakes her head. "I know it's their job. But they don't know Daphne. They're not family!"

I start to say I'm not Daphne's family either but don't. The truth is, Ivy is my only real family, and she considers Daphne part of hers. Like Quinn and her parents are part of mine. Blood ties aren't always the ones that count. My dad's not family, after all.

My mom checks her bright pink Swatch. "We should get going."

I fight back a sigh. I planned to spend my day on this couch, moping. But I can't not drive my mother. Maybe it's better to get out and about anyway. Otherwise, I'll just wallow in self-pity. If I stay home alone I'll spend all day rehashing last night's scene with Josh, swaying back and forth over whether or not to call him.

He dumped me. I cannot, will not, call him. It'd be wiser to help my mom and focus on someone else's problems.

I haul myself off the couch and run a hand through my tangled hair. "Okay. Do I have time for a quick shower?"

My mom nods. "Yes. But skip the conditioner."

In the shower, with hot water gushing down on me, I feel a little better. I try to breathe deeply. Even if me and Josh are through, I still have a good life. Plenty to eat. A safe, peaceful place to live. Friends and family who love me. A job I'm happy to go to. I should count my blessings. Being single might be a blessing. It's so much better to be alone than to feel lonely with the wrong person. Maybe I'm better off staying single.

I raise my face to the rushing water and try to roll my shoulders down and back. Ouch. It's like they're carved from hardwood. I dig my fingers in to massage them.

My mom's voice penetrates the bathroom door: "Toby? Honey? You almost done yet?"

"Yes Mom!" I yell. I give up on massaging and turn off the water, only to spin the lever the wrong way. A blast of ice water hits me.

Still swearing, I reach for a towel. Damn. There aren't any. That figures. I shake dry like a dog, then dab my damp body with my pajama-top. I drop the lid of the deodorant and can't find it anywhere. How is this possible? My bathroom is airplane sized. It's like the lid's been sucked into another dimension.

"Toby?" It's my mom again.

I grit my teeth and get up off the floor. Peering under the sink has cricked my neck. "Ready in a second," I yell.

Pulling jeans up over damp skin is hard work. By the time they're on, I'm out of breath. My comb must be hiding with the deodorant lid. I rake my fingers through my unconditioned hair and glance in the mirror. I look like some kid's long-forgotten rag doll.

As much as I mock my mom's signs and portents there's no deny-ing that this feels like a bad day—a day I should hide away in bed. A day that can only get worse.

"Toby?"

I open the bathroom door. My mom's fist is raised, ready to knock. Seeing me, she lowers her hand. "Ready?" she says, briskly.

I nod. It's a lie. Whatever's coming, I'm not ready.

CHAPTER 14:

THE BLACK SHEEP

Yesterday's rain has continued, although it's slowed to a drizzle by the time we pull up out front of Daphne's. I try to stay in the car but my mom won't have it. My feet drag as I follow her down Daphne's long stone path. The garden smells of wet earth and cedar. The cool, damp air clears my head, a little.

When we climb the broad front steps, the pig goes wild, grunting and squealing in the front hall. There's no need to ring the bell.

Lukas opens the door. The pig barrels out. My mom jumps out of the way fast, but it almost hits me.

"Woops," says Lukas. He squints against the light. Like me, he looks like he just woke up. His eyes are red and his hair resembles a scant haystack. I wonder if he spent the night here.

He steps onto the porch and calls after the pig. "Kevin! Come Kevin!" The pig disregards him. Seeing me, Lukas blinks. He fights back a yawn. "Oh. Hey, Toby." I'm surprised he remembered my name. He turns back indoors and calls down the hall. "Hey, Grace. The pig's out! Sorry."

Grace bustles into view. Dressed in a long red skirt, a white blouse, and a red apron, she could pass for Mrs. Claus. Her downy white hair is even styled in a bun. As if to complete this Christmassy look, in one plump hand, she clutches a green feather duster.

"Hello dears," she says, brightly, then coos at the retreating pig. "Here boy! Kevin! Kevin Bacon." When the pig pays no heed she bounds down the steps. Lukas descends more sedately.

"We'd better help," says my mom.

I'd rather not but give in. The lawn is mushy.

At our approach, the pig eyes us warily. A game of tag ensues. The pig waits until someone gets close before darting off, grunting. When it's not running, it's digging. Daphne's lawn is soon dotted with molehills. Even Grace starts to look fed up, her round cheeks pink with exertion. She waves her duster.

We try to herd Kevin toward the side gate but it's hopeless. Despite its girth and short legs, the pig is nimble, as well as cunning. Its black eyes twinkle as it trots just out of reach. I swear it's mocking us.

Finally, Grace has an idea. Reaching into the pocket of her skirt, she withdraws a pack of Mentos. She places a mint on her palm. Kevin is over like a shot. It snuffles the mint off her hand and chews daintily, its tail wagging. Grace pats its hairy head. It leans up against her. When the pig's not wrecking stuff, it's endearing. Although it's a ridiculous house pet.

It takes three mints to lead Kevin back up the front steps and into the hall. Lukas, my mom, and I follow. When we're all in, Grace shuts the door firmly. Seeing the pig's muddy footprints, her smile slips. "Oh dear." She sighs. "All over the carpet."

My mom and I nod in sympathy. Keeping this place clean would be a full time job even without a pet pig. And Grace is no spring chicken. My mom mentioned she's worked here for over three decades. I hope she's well paid for her efforts.

For a moment, gazing at the muddy trotter prints, Grace looks tired. But then her shoulders go back. "Excuse me," she says. "I need to clean this up." She trots toward the kitchen.

I take off my blue raincoat and hang it beside my mom's purple one. Kevin curls up on the hall rug for a nap and starts snoring.

My mom looks at Lukas. "Shall we start?"

He jumps, like he's just remembered why we're here. He rubs his hands on his shorts. "Oh yeah," he says. "Ivy, thanks for coming. I figure with your talent, plus being Mom's friend, you might figure out where she went." His prominent Adam's apple bobs. "I really need to find her."

I can't help but notice how he's phrased this—so it's all about him, as usual. Is he worried about Daphne or just out of cash and in need of a top up?

"The police came by," he says. "Asking all sorts of questions about the dead guy . . ." He glances at me sideways. "I heard you like, found his body."

I nod. My name—and Josh's—were reported in the local paper.

Lukas's throaty voice drops. "That's, uh, intense. So what'd you like, see out there?" he asks me.

I suppress a shudder. "He was in one of the bedrooms," I say. "On the floor . . ." I shrug and stop talking. The police asked me not to discuss details with anyone. I wonder who gave my name to the press. "I just saw him and ran out of there," I tell Lukas.

Lukas picks at the beaded necklace circling his skinny neck. "Oh," he says. Like me, he shivers. "I'm gonna make tea," he tells my mother.

We follow him down the long wood-paneled hall toward the back kitchen.

In the doorway my mom stops in surprise. I stop too. The top cupboards have been taken down and the tiles over the counters and sinks stripped away. The cupboards' contents are piled in boxes and stacked near the back door. Everything's dusty.

"What's happening? Is your mom renovating?" asks my mother. It seems weird that any planned renovations would proceed in Daphne's absence but who knows? Good builders are hard to find. Maybe this job was booked way in advance. My mother frowns. "She never told me."

Lukas squints up at the walls, like he's just noticed the ravaged tiles. "Oh, naw, that's Isobel." He sounds vague. He runs water into an electric kettle. "Step one of her master plan." He sets the kettle on its stand and clicks it on.

I give my mom a questioning look. "What plan is that?" I ask.

Lukas throws two teabags into a cobalt teapot, then sets three cups on the kitchen table. Thanks to the ongoing renos, the table is grey with dust. Lukas ignores the mess. Despite the cool weather, he's still wearing board shorts, although he's got a fleece jacket over his ratty old t-shirt.

When the tea is made, we all sit at the large table.

"This is a historic building," says Lukas. He pours the tea. "It was one of the first houses built in Rockland. Some old coal baron. Or was it timber? He might have been the mayor, or something like that." He tugs at his bleached fringe, blue eyes more unfocused than usual. "Anyway. It's heritage-listed. Izzie wants to turn it into a fancy B&B. With a fine-dining restaurant. Gerard is a chef, ya know?" He slides us our teacups.

Over her cup, my mother blinks. She looks slowly around the kitchen. "This place?" She sounds incredulous. "But Daphne loves this house."

Lukas peers at the pocked walls. "Yeah, last I heard Mom wasn't too keen. But I've been away . . . I guess she agreed. Iz and Gerard think it's too much for her and Grace—I mean looking after this place. It's a lot of work. They want to build Mom a separate granny flat." He scratches his stubbly jaw and frowns. "I offered to move into the basement," he says. "To help out. That seems like a way better idea than turning this place into a hotel."

My mom sets down her cup with a thoughtful look on her face. I remember her saying how relieved Daphne was when Lukas finally flew the nest. She's probably none too eager to have him move back in. How much "help" would he actually be, after all?

I take a sip of tea. Has Daphne really agreed to her daughter's B&B plans? It seems outrageous that Isobel would take advantage of Daphne's absence to defy her mom's wishes.

Armed with a giant basket of cleaning supplies, Grace reappears in the kitchen. She's been down in the basement. Seeing the dusty table, she retrieves a wet cloth to wipe it. We raise our cups and the teapot.

"These workmen are so messy!" says Grace. She scrubs at the grime. "I don't have time to supervise them! I didn't even know they were starting!"

My mother tilts her head. "Daphne didn't mention this?"

I look around. I don't know what style's coming, but the kitchen looks fine, with oak cupboards, a brass range hood, and a stone-topped island.

"No," says Grace. "I guess it slipped her mind." Her placid face clouds. "Oh, where could she be? It's just not like her not to call! And now, the police have been here, asking all sorts of questions . . ."

She turns and rinses the dusty cloth, then points at the missing cupboards. "This is Isobel's doing. Her silly talk of a hotel . . ." She tuts. "She's constantly hassling Daphne about it. Heritage-listed this. Historic that. Who cares? Why doesn't she rent some other old pile?" She wags a finger at my mom. "I'll tell you why, Ivy. It's because she wants this place for free! She wants to drive her own mother out of her home! Into a granny flat. Soon, she'll be talking about a rest home! Assisted living! Maybe that's why Daphne left—to escape the endless nagging!" Cloth hung to dry, she retrieves her duster and starts dabbing at the plaster-flecked counters.

Lukas gives her a goofy smile. "Poor Grace," he says. "What would we do without you?"

Faced with his smile, the housekeeper laughs. "Oh, don't mind me," she says. "I'm just wound up after those police officers poking around, making awful insinuations." She snorts, then smiles at Lukas. "You're a good boy," she says. She shakes her fluffy head. "But sometimes, your sister drives me crazy."

Lukas's smile widens. There's obvious love between them. But I guess there would be. Having spent thirty years here, Grace has known Lukas since he was a baby. They're family.

When the counters are spotless, Grace heads toward the front hall. She's halfway across the room when Lukas calls out to her. "Grace?" She stops and turns. He clears his throat. "What did the cops ask about that dead guy?"

Grace's cheeks flush. "Stephen." Her round nose wrinkles in distaste. "They asked what I thought of him and I told them, flat out. Good riddance to bad rubbish."

Her vehemence leaves me shocked. Her reaction seems harsh, given that he was brutally murdered.

Perhaps she notices my stunned expression because she looks contrite. "I know that sounds mean," she says. "But that man!" She pats at her puffy bun. "I'm sorry he's dead, of course." She doesn't sound sorry. "Just thank goodness he's out of Daphne's life! He was no good. No good at all." Her duster shakes with indignation.

"How so?" I ask.

They say the best way to solve a murder is to know the victim. But what do we know about Stephen? Next to nothing. If only my mom had had the chance to meet him. For all her flakiness, she's a good judge of character. Would she have liked him, as Daphne did? Or loathed him like Grace here?

Grace looks torn. She studies her red slippers. "One shouldn't speak ill of the dead and all that."

My mother snorts. "Really, Grace. The man's been murdered. And Daphne's missing. Now's not the time to hold back."

Grace nods. "No, you're right, Ivy. It's obvious I couldn't stand him." She sets down her basket. "I didn't trust him one bit! He had this BBC accent and these fancy Saville Row suits. Like he was really posh!" She waves her duster. "But he wasn't." Her eyes narrow. "I saw him licking his knife!" She shudders.

I wait. There must be more—beyond bad table manners—to have made Grace hate him.

She shrugs. "He was a cad," she says. "A chancer. I think he was after Daphne's money."

As Lukas and my mom finish their tea, I excuse myself. That scary smoothie, and/or the "healthy" muffin, seem to have gone right through me.

"Sorry, dear. The downstairs bathroom is also under renovation," Grace informs me.

I follow her instructions and ascend the polished staircase.

Second door on the right. I push it open.

Painted a pretty shade of plum, the bathroom smells of lemons. There's a watercolor of a forest that I'm pretty sure is an Emily Carr, one of Canada's most revered (and expensive) artists.

As I wash my hands, I study myself in the mirror. A wrinkle seems to have formed in my forehead overnight, etched by insufficient sleep and chagrin. Rubbing it has no effect. I recall Josh's closed-down face, staring straight ahead, in his fancy car. Why did I wreck things with him? For twenty years he was my vision of male perfection. My dream guy.

Should I call him?

My fingers are crab-walking toward my purse when I stop, attention caught by the toiletries pouch beside it. Brown and rectangular, it looks manly, totally plain but for two embroidered cream letters: SB. Son of a Bitch. Or Stephen Buxley.

Josh momentarily forgotten, I lift the pouch off the shelf and set it on the sink, then unzip it. Part away along, the zip catches. I curse under my breath, and tug. It's stuck on a piece of paper. After a lot of wiggling, I free the zip and pinch out the offending scrap. It's been ripped from a yellow notepad.

I turn the square over. It's written in heavy black block-printed letters:

GRACE

STOP GOING THROUGH MY BELONGINGS! I KNOW IT'S YOU AND WILL TELL DAPHNE THEN YOU'LL BE SORRY.

SB

The word STOP has been underlined twice, while SORRY is extra thick and a bit jagged.

Hmmm. I slide this note into my handbag.

The pouch holds nothing of further interest, just the sort of toiletries I'd expect from a posh, middle-aged, British man: a toothbrush and whitening toothpaste, hair wax, Burberry cologne, Molton Brown black pepper deodorant—a sniff of which starts me sneezing.

But that note. I recall Grace's obvious glee that the man met a sticky end. Not surprising if he threatened to get her fired. Thirty years of service down the drain. Did she take matters into her own competent hands? No wonder she disliked him.

I head back down the hall. Mind brimming with my recent discovery, I don't watch where I'm going. My foot hits something soft. I stumble, but steady myself on the wall. I've tripped over an old, army-green backpack, the lid of which has flapped open. Some contents have spilled out: a Swiss army knife, a cheap cigarette lighter, a pack of rolling papers, a plastic bag, about as big as a loaf of bread, full of what could be tea leaves, but isn't.

I bend and sniff. This must belong to Lukas. No wonder he seems so out of it, so much of the time. I poke the bag with a finger. That's a lot of pot for just personal use! Does he deal it? Or just smoke non-stop? Addiction would explain his need for cash. Might his problem extend to harder drugs too? Could that be a motive for killing his mom's lover?

I straighten up. I'm being judgmental. Just because the guy's a pothead doesn't make him a killer. And it's hard to imagine a weedy little guy like Lukas attacking the big, strong man I saw dead in his mom's cabin.

I'm about to stuff everything back in the pack when there's a sound behind me. I turn to see Grace at the top of the staircase.

Seeing the spilled items at my feet, her eyes widen. "What are you doing?" she cries. She sounds accusing.

I flush. It looks like I'm in the midst of snooping. "I tripped," I say. "And the bag spilled open."

Grace marches closer. She's still wielding her duster.

Her usually smiley face looks grim. I recall the note I just found—and Grace's resentment of Stephen. Were his threats the final straw that made her snap? For a moment, I imagine the duster transformed into an iron poker, smashing down on Stephen's fair head. I gulp. Beneath her grandmotherly padding, Grace looks strong as a wrestler.

Her footsteps slow. She examines the items at my feet. The anger in her eyes has turned to shocked disappointment. "Oh dear," she says, softly. She stops walking, one hand pressed to her ample bosom. "Is that . . ." She swallows hard. Her voice trembles. "Is that the weed?" she asks me.

"Er, yes," I say.

Grace blinks. She looks stricken. "But he went to rehab," she says. Tears have sprung into her eyes. "For alcohol and marijuana."

I keep quiet, unwilling to point out the obvious: it didn't work. The guy's a stoner.

Grace is still blinking back tears. "He said he was better," she laments. "He said he was cured! That he'd stopped!"

I bend to put everything back into Lukas's pack. "Well, it could be worse," I say, trying to cheer her up. "I mean, at least now pot's legal." Or is he into harder stuff too? There's an opioid epidemic. Plus crystal meth. Lukas sure is skinny.

Grace nods. "Yes," she says. "I'm sure he's cut way back!"

I stuff the loaf of pot back into the pack and stay silent.

"It's just recreational," continues Grace, her voice brighter now. "And you're right. It is legal! Like tobacco!" She's clearly trying to convince herself, as well as me. "Lots of young people do it!"

I nod. So do lots of old ones. I don't think pot's worse than booze—it's just a question of moderation. Lukas, unfortunately, does not seem like the now-and-then type. I close the pack's lid and set it back against the wall, then straighten.

Grace's eyes are now dry. She licks her lips. While some color has returned to her face, she still looks shaky. "Your mom," she says. "Are her powers real?" Her voice is hushed, almost fearful.

"I don't know," I admit. "But a lot of people think so."

Grace shivers, as do her duster's green feathers. "All that stuff gives me the willies."

I smile. We have that in common. "Same," I admit.

Grace runs her duster over a picture frame. There's a thoughtful look on her plump face. Her dark eyes meet mine. "But sometimes, it'd be good to know the future. Wouldn't it? To get some answers."

I think of Josh. And Colin. I nod. Yes, if only we could see the path ahead, and make the right choices. We could get answers to darker questions too: Who killed Stephen? Where's Daphne?

She wipes her hands on her apron. "I just want to know he'll be alright," she whispers. "That he'll get through this."

It's like she's forgotten I'm here and is muttering a prayer. She sounds so sincere and solemn—the archetypal mother praying for a lost child to come home. The Grandmothers of the Plaza de Mayo.

She sighs. "Lukas has always been fragile," she whispers. "Even as a baby. He was a preemie. He was always so sensitive. Not like Izzie."

The hall is totally quiet. I want to reassure Grace, to tell her Lukas will be fine. But do I really believe that? I recall Lukas and Isobel as kids: spoiled yet peevish.

Being born too rich can cause almost as much damage as being born too poor, robbing a kid of motivation. Endless cash. Endless thrills. Until nothing has value or seems thrilling. There's nothing to strive for and no way to surpass your elders' shining achievements.

Lukas was spoiled rotten. I recall him as a fat kid stuffing his face with cake. He must have moved on to booze and pot as a teen. Now, aged thirty-something, he's still at it. Not working, sponging off his rich mom. Does he actually paint, or just talk about his art? I've never seen paint flecks on the guy, or smelled turps. Who knows how much pot he's smoking?

Seeing Grace's fretful frown, I feel bad for her. Again, I want to reassure her. "Well, at least he acknowledges he has a problem," I say. "And he's been getting treatment." Plus it could be worse, I think again. Hopefully he's not on oxys. Or heroin.

Grace nods. "You're right," she says. "I'm just feeling anxious. With Daphne gone. And the police poking around. That nasty man ending up dead . . . " She sighs. "It's been a strange few days. If only Daphne would come home!" Her voice lifts. "Oh, I hope your mom can help find her."

I can hear my mom and Lukas coming up the stairs, chatting. I lower my voice: "Me too," I say. "And you know, Grace, Lukas is lucky to have you."

Grace beams. Again, her eyes shine with tears. She looks both thrilled and embarrassed. "I did my best," she says. "But he was spoiled. They both were."

I nod. Poor Grace. She seems a sensible woman, but raising the Dane kids can't have been easy. She must have had so much of the responsibility and none of the power. The best she could do was mitigate her excessive employer's excesses.

Now, smiling like that, I see her as a young woman. A young mother. Clapping her hands at a small boy's first, faltering steps. Proudly sticking crayon drawings onto the fridge. Cheering when's he up to bat. Reading good night stories. She blinks. "Thanks for saying that, dear."

I nod. There's more than blood that ties people together. Love is stronger. And Lukas is lucky. Whatever the shortcomings of his childhood, this good lady loves him.

CHAPTER 15

HALF TRUTHS

My mom decides to do the reading in Daphne's bedroom. She claims this room has the strongest "essence" of Daphne. I don't bother to ask what this means. As my mom and Lukas take a seat, I watch from the doorway.

Perched on a cream loveseat, my mom holds a silk houndstooth scarf that's a favorite of Daphne's. Lukas is hunched in a beige armchair. His eyes are still red. Now that I've seen his stash, I wonder how I missed the signs earlier.

"I'll be out in the car," I tell my mother. Finally, I can get out of here. I'm going to recline the seat and have a nap while I'm waiting.

My mom frowns. "Oh honey, no," she says. "Could you just stay here for the reading?"

I grit my teeth. Why? My mom knows I hate this stuff. Plus she asked me to snoop around. This would be my chance—not that I'll use it.

She tilts her head, like she can hear faint, distant music. Her forehead wrinkles. "It's strange but I just feel more energy when you're nearby."

My teeth clamp a little tighter. Great. That's all I need, my mom convinced my presence heightens her imaginary powers. Like I'm a psychic mascot. I'm still hanging in the doorway. "Really?"

My mom nods. She smoothes down her long violet skirt. Violet, the color of intuition. My head is full of this nonsense. No wonder I can't recall dates or phone numbers: my brain is jam-packed with New Age bullshit.

I fight back a sigh and take a tiny step closer. Lukas tugs at his bead necklace. He looks antsy. I wonder when and where he went to rehab. Was that in India? Maybe some alternative kind of place, involving meditation and yoga? I sink onto a chair next to Lukas.

I'd like to ask but don't know how to broach it without sounding too nosy.

My mom shuts her eyes. She holds Daphne's scarf to her forehead. The third eye. She bends her head and hums. I cringe. Lukas's eyes are shut too. He's rocking gently. I squeeze my eyes shut. Whatever my mom's up to, it's better not to watch. The humming grows louder, as does my discomfiture. Jaysus. Enough already. I'm glad no one's here to witness this, besides Lukas, who's probably too stoned to care. Or am I being judgmental? Maybe he's stone-cold sober. He looks more sober than my mother.

"Daphne?" whispers my mom. "Where are you, Daphne?"

Hearing her sound so weak, I feel worried. She sounds like she did last year, in the midst of chemo. Thank god we found out early, and her breast cancer is in complete remission, although the fear lingers.

I open my eyes and study my mom's heart-shaped face. She looks serene, if somewhat pale. The amethysts (healing) in her ears glisten. If only they really ensured healing.

I grip the wooden arms of my chair. So far, so good. My mom's doctors seemed really pleased with her latest test results. But her cancer was a big scare. I'm still worried about her getting physically or emotionally depleted. All this anxiety about Daphne can't be good for her health. Where is Daphne?

A tear drips down my mom's round cheek. Her dark eyes pop open. She shakes herself. I look around for tissues but she motions me to stay seated. She wipes her cheek with the back of her hand and composes herself. "I'm fine," she says. But she doesn't look fine. Seeing her trembling lips, I reach out for her. Again, my mom shakes her head. "Don't touch me," she says. "Not yet." The way she says it, scares me. It's like she's contagious.

Lukas's eyes are still closed. Has he nodded off? My mom says his name gently. His chin jerks up. His eyes blink open, blue as topaz in his pale face. "I . . . Hey Ivy." He looks worried. "Is it finished?"

My mother nods. "I don't want to alarm you but your mom's in a bad state," she says. "I sensed such sadness. And anger." She shivers again, as if to shake off these feelings. "She's feeling heartbroken." My mom drops her chin. "I . . . I saw black mist filling the air." Her voice quivers like she's trying not to cry. "It was . . ." She swallows hard. "It was hard to breathe." Her dark eyes meet mine, and her voice drops to a whisper. "She's in danger."

Lukas pulls at his shaggy bangs. "What?" His eyes bulge. "But . . . but where is she?"

My mom straightens. "That's the good news. I feel she's close. And getting closer." She clasps her hands. "I believe she'll soon be ho—."

She's interrupted by a knock on the bedroom door. Lukas jumps. "What is it?" he calls. His voice is even thinner than usual.

Grace peeps around the door. Lit by a grin, her dark eyes are bright. "Daphne's back! She's just getting out of a taxi!"

We all spring to our feet and follow Grace. Four sets of feet clatter down the long staircase. High overhead, the chandelier twinkles.

In the hall, Kevin is going nuts, squealing and running in circles. The pig keeps pressing its flat nose up against the door like it wants to dig through it.

I'm about four steps from the bottom when the front door swings open. Daphne steps inside, a set of keys in one hand. Her face is impossibly smooth and tanned nutmeg brown, framed by fresh-from-the-salon platinum highlights. She is dressed in an elegant dark green raincoat. An orange Hermes bag hangs from one arm. Behind her rests a bulging brown LV suitcase.

At the sight of us, her plumped mouth falls open. She sweeps a hand over her silky blonde mane. "Oh," she says. "Hello there."

All four of us stand fanned out on the stairs, open-mouthed. After all this worry, here she is, alive and well in her own front hall, redolent of Poison perfume and hairspray. If she's changed since I was a kid it's impossible to say how. All the usual signs of aging—the dips, puffs, and wrinkles are absent on her high-cheekboned face. Yet weirdly, she doesn't look young—just artificial.

I turn to my mom, who's got deep crinkles around her eyes, her eyebrows and mouth in constant motion. While there's none of

Daphne's smooth perfection, my mom's face is dynamic. Daphne's is frozen. All the work she's had done makes it hard to read her emotions.

Daphne steps into the light cast by the chandelier. She slowly sets down her handbag. I see what the tan, makeup, and surgical touch-ups can't hide. Her eyes—as blue as Lukas's—are full of sadness.

My mom was right about one thing: she looks heartbroken. Thank god she was wrong about her being in danger.

CHAPTER 16:

BAD NEWS

Daphne shrugs off her coat and hangs it next to my mother's. She bends to pet Kevin. The pig snuffles happily around her feet. "Hello Kevi," she coos. "Hello my little piggy. Hello my baby. I missed you."

"Where have you been?" demands my mom. She descends the final steps. "We've been so worried! When you didn't show up at my place on Wednesday . . ."

Daphne straightens, a hint of confusion on her smooth face.

"The police are looking for you," says Lukas.

Daphne's pink-painted mouth falls open. One perfectly arched eyebrow attempts—but fails—to lift. She loosens the cream scarf around her neck. "The police?" She looks past Lukas and my mother to a small table, where an antique telephone rests. She turns to Grace. "Didn't you read my note?" she asks her.

Quiet until now, when Grace starts talking, the words gush out: "What note? All I got was that text message, which said nothing! Where have you been? All these days! We've had the police here . . . and . . ." She rings her hands. "Isobel and Gerard have been in and out. And those builders, making a racket! Poor Lukas here has been worried sick! Haven't you, honey?"

"Well," says Daphne, huffily. "I left a note right there." She jabs a shiny red fingernail toward the telephone table. "I said I was going away for a few days, to the Sanctuary Spa in Colorado. I left a contact number and everything."

She strides over to the table and lifts the phone to look under it. "And I asked you to call Ivy and cancel my appointment!"

Grace puts her hands on her wide hips. "There was no note," she insists.

"Wait," I say. "Remember how the hall table was knocked over?" I look at the pig. "The note must have fallen on the floor."

"So where is it?" asks Daphne. "The whole notepad's missing!"

Looking at Kevin's soft pink snout, I remember Daphne's chewed satin shoes—and the mangled flowers. A notepad would be a tasty snack. "Do you think Kevin ate it?" I ask.

A thorough search of the hall reveals some scraps of yellow paper, wedged down between a giant vase and the skirting boards. I hold these crinkly shreds aloft. "Was your notepad yellow?" I ask Daphne.

"Hmmph," says Grace. She wags a finger at the pig. "Naughty beast!" She laughs. "He missed you! Did you see the front garden?" She shakes her head. "But thank goodness you're alright! We've been going crazy!"

Daphne hangs up her scarf. "Well . . ." she says. She peels off her gloves and looks at each of us in turn. "This sounds like a story! You'll have to tell me all about it."

"You look tired," says Grace. "Go and sit down. I'll put the tea on."

The mystery of the missing note solved, we migrate into Daphne's living room—a large formal room with gleaming rosewood floors, cream and blue silk rugs, bay windows overlooking the front yard, and oversized floral sofas.

Lukas sprawls into an armchair printed with irises and butterflies. My mom and Daphne take the matching couch. The pig follows us in. It requires three comical attempts to scrabble up beside Daphne. I perch on a jade-cushioned Rococo chair. The room smells of orange-blossom-scented candles.

Soon, we should call Colin Destin to tell him that Daphne has shown up, safe and sound, fresh from the medi-spa.

Daphne crosses her legs. "Well, what a big fuss for no reason!"

It's hard to tell if she's in a huff, or finds it funny. She shakes her head. Her glossy lips twitch into a smile. "You really called the police?" she asks, laughing.

My mom explains how the front hall was in disarray, which left everyone worried. "And I did a reading," she says. "A few, actually."

She tugs off her bright turban and runs a hand through her steel-grey hair. "It was awful," she says. Her eyes are big and bright as an owl's. "Someone's been lying to you. I saw deceit and a lot of pain." My mom leans closer to her friend, her voice urgent. "Even danger, Daphne!"

Daphne's wide shoulders slump. All of a sudden, she looks old and tired. Her lower lip quivers. A tear trickles out of one heavily mascara'd eye. Soon, a wiggly trail runs through her peachy foundation.

"You were right," she whispers. "I've been such a fool. He lied to me . . . My new boyfriend, Stephen." Just saying the name seems to hurt, and yet she says it again, like poking a bruise to confirm it's still painful. "Stephen Buxley." She winces.

She looks from my mom to Lukas, whose eyes are heavy-lidded. Beneath the blush, Daphne's cheeks flush. She turns back to my mother. "I didn't tell you more about him, Ivy, because I didn't want to jinx things. It was going so well." She twists her hands as if to scrub off something sticky. "I was so happy, so excited." Her pouffed blonde head droops. More tears overflow her blue eyes.

My mom pats her friend's shoulder. "I'm so sorry Daphne. What happened?"

Daphne looks up. Her eyes harden.

I recall her in the eighties or early nineties, a larger-than-life billboard of a woman. All shoulder pads and teased hair. Colorful power suits. Earrings like hard candies.

Now, she looks equally arresting. Her back straightens and her chin lifts. "He asked me to marry him." She stares angrily into her front yard. "And like a fool, I said yes."

Lukas gapes at her, suddenly roused from his haze. "M . . . married?"

Daphne tosses back her Barbara Walters hair. Her eyes mist over. "That's right." She smiles sadly at her son. "I was going to ask you to give me away and . . ." She turns to my mom. "You'd have been my maid of honor. I had it all planned. The reception at the yacht club. Honeymoon in the Seychelles." Her rueful smile turns upside down, and her eyes glitter dangerously. "There was just one little problem." She snorts. "The lying bastard was with another woman!"

My mom's mouth pops open. "Oh! Who?" she asks.

"I don't know her name," says Daphne. Her shiny lips purse with distaste. "But he called her 'Hotsauce.'" She glares at the carpet. "He sent a text message meant for her to me by mistake. It was . . . graphic."

My mom's mouth opens even wider.

Lukas leans forward. "Whoa. What a jerk. So what did you do?"

"I confronted him," says Daphne. "Of course he tried to deny it, said it was some telecommunications glitch and he'd never sent that message. But please." She rolls her eyes. "I wasn't born yesterday. Or in the 1800s."

"When was this?" asks my mom.

"Last Wednesday. Just before I left for my reading." At the memory, fresh tears fill Daphne's eyes. "After I threw him out, I just fell apart. I was so shocked and humiliated. I decided to get out of town, go somewhere quiet to think." She reaches for my mom's hand. "I'm sorry I didn't call but you'd have known something was wrong. I couldn't face talking about it yet. I was in such a state! I just packed a few things and headed straight for the airport, got the first plane off the island." She bites her lip. "How could I have let myself get sucked in by that cheating scumbag?"

Lukas toys with the frayed hem of his fleece vest. "I guess Izzie and Grace were right," he says, slowly.

His mom rounds on him. "What does that mean?"

"Well, they didn't like him," says Lukas. "They thought he was after your money."

At just that moment Grace reappears. She's bearing a lacquered tea tray.

Daphne glares at her. "You didn't like Stephen?" she asks. "Why didn't you say so?"

Grace sets the tray onto the gleaming coffee table. "You were happy," she says, flatly. "And would you have listened?"

Daphne looks taken aback. "Of course I would have . . ." She swallows hard.

Grace tilts her head. "No you wouldn't have!" she says. "Love is

blind! Everyone knows that. There was nothing I could say. And besides, what if I was wrong?" She pours the tea and hands a cup to
Daphne. "Maybe I was just . . ." She gulps a little, like what she's about
to say next has shocked her. "A little jealous."

"Oh Grace!" says Daphne. She looks shocked too. "You were jealous?"

"Not of him," says Grace. "I didn't much like him. But seeing you
so happy made me wonder. I mean about my life's choices. Maybe I was
letting life pass me by. I've always thought I was happy being single,
but maybe . . . even at my age . . ." Her round cheeks flush. She emits
an embarrassed little titter. "Ignore me," she says. "I'm being silly. I'm
far too old for this. It's been a strange few days, that's all." She sets out
a plate of homemade cookies.

"That's not silly," says Daphne. "I can teach you to internet date.
There's nothing to it."

I blink. What?

"There's this website called seniormatch-dot-com," continues
Daphne. My eyes flick to my mom. Holy crap. And here I thought
they weren't online. Does she do it too? "You can meet all sorts of
interesting people," continues Daphne. Then her eyes harden. "Or total
assholes."

My mom reaches for her tea. Clearly reminded of Stephen, Daphne is chewing on her over-full lips. "I wish you'd mentioned your
misgivings about him," she tells Grace. "Were there clues I missed?
He seemed so charming." She rings her be-ringed hands. "I've been
such a fool," she moans. "It's like they say, there's no fool like an old
fool."

Grace sighs. "Well, what's the use of dwelling on it now?" she says,
kindly. She stirs a spoonful of sugar into a cup of tea. "The man's dead
and gone." She crosses herself and mutters something under her breath,
then passes the teacup to Lukas.

Daphne's already frozen face permafrosts. Only her blue eyes wid-
en. Her gaze darts from Grace to my mother, then back. "D . . . dead?"
she stutters.

The ensuing silence is broken by Lukas. "Dead as a doornail," he says. "Poor Toby here . . ." He nods my way. "She found his body."

All the color that's not painted on leaches from Daphne's face. She presses a finger to her temple. Her voice rises to a desperate question. "What? All . . ." She swallows hard and falls silent.

I search her stricken gaze. I may be wrong but I think the word on her lips was "already." But that can't be right. Did she know about Stephen's death and think it'd take longer to find his corpse? I recall the poker. Daphne is a tall, strong woman. And not one to mess with.

Perhaps sensing his mistress's disquiet, Kevin crawls closer. He lays his snout in Daphne's lap. She rubs his ear absent-mindedly. Her hands are shaking.

Looking into Daphne's glassy eyes, I see heartbreak. And shock. But also rage. And satisfaction. Like Grace, she's not sorry Stephen's dead. Not really. She's sad. But she thinks he had it coming.

Leaning back against the sofa, Daphne shuts her eyes, shutting me out. With her hair spread around her, her flawless face appears regal.

"Daphne?" says my mother.

Daphne's eyes flick open. "I feel old," she says. "Old and tired."

My mother nods. "You've had a big shock." She sighs. "Or several, in fact. But the police need to know you're back. So they can stop looking for you."

Daphne tilts her head. "Sure," she says. "Grace, could you please inform the police that I'm alive and well? Or at least . . . alive," she says, sadly.

"They'll want to talk to you," says my mom. She twists the amethyst in her left ear. "About this man." She speaks his name with distaste. "Stephen Buxley."

Daphne sits up and pats at her stiff hair. "Why?" she asks. Her forehead tries to wrinkle. Then she turns my way. "How did he . . ." She coughs. "Pass away?" she asks.

I set down my teacup, reluctant to be the bearer of such bad news. But there's no way to sugarcoat the truth. "He was murdered," I say. "In your cabin, out at Sooke."

"W—what?" Her eyes goggle. She bows her head and starts laughing.

I blink. Whatever reaction I expected, it wasn't raucous laughter, now bursting out in throaty gusts, a sexy bar room laugh—full of cigarettes, dirty jokes, and good whisky. She laughs until fresh tears fill her eyes and cascade down her cheeks. Is this shock? Hysteria? I glance at my mother.

Just as quickly as it began, Daphne's laughter stops. "Jesus. That bastard," she says. "Getting himself killed in my cabin and making me a suspect!" She swipes the tears from her eyes and pats at her still-perfect hair. "No doubt the cops want to grill me!" She rolls her eyes. "I wish I had killed him!"

Grace tries to pooh-pooh this, but Daphne waves her protests away. She smoothes down her knee-length turquoise skirt, and sits even straighter. "Call them now," she instructs her housekeeper. "Yes, I've been foolish, but that's not a crime." She takes a sip of tea. "I'm going to tell the cops all about that cheating scoundrel! Let's get this over with! Grace! Call them!"

Over the rim of her teacup, Daphne's eyes blaze with determination. This is the Daphne Dane of my childhood memories, the Cookie Queen, going into battle.

I think of Stephen Buxley, lying dead in that decrepit cabin.

At any age, Daphne's not someone to mess with. Did he pick on the wrong rich old lady?

CHAPTER 17:

REPLACED

As much as I'd like to see Colin, this isn't the time or place. He made it glacial-lake clear I'm to avoid the Danes until Stephen's killer has been found. And yet here I am . . . I'd better slink away before he arrives to quiz Daphne.

I bid them farewell. My mom stays to lend moral support. Not that Daphne needs it. War paint retouched and freshly armored in a teal suit, she looks ready for anything. I hope Colin survives the interrogation.

As I climb into my car, I feel cut adrift. All morning I was tethered by the Danes' drama. Now, I'm free to float. Or sink.

I check my watch: 11:42 a.m. It feels much later in the day. I do the math in my head and check my phone, just to be sure. The time is right. I've had no missed calls or messages. I fight back a sigh. It's going on eighteen hours since my fight with Josh, and still no word from him. Is it really over?

My stomach twists. I'm not sure if it's sadness, hunger, or both that has caused the hollowness in my gut. So far, all I've consumed today is my mom's smoothie, a few bites of rock-hard muffin, two double espressos, and countless cups of tea. It's not surprising my stomach is in knots. I feel both jittery and lackluster.

Part of me wants to drive to Josh's house. But then I recall his officious tone, and how he'd refused to listen. What would I say? That I was wrong and am now ready to commit? So what about Colin? I put the key into the ignition. I can't think about men right now. I need food—real food—first.

I retrieve my phone. Quinn picks up on the sixth ring, just when I was ready to give up.

"Hey? Quinn?" I say. My best friend mumbles a hello. "Can I come over?" There's more unintelligible mumbling. It sounds like her phone is squished right up against her mouth. Or else she's being smothered. "Hey Quinn?" I say. "I can't hear you."

After a few squishy sounds her voice grows clearer. "Sorry, I don't have any free hands," she says. "Oh shit. I just tipped Abby's diaper and spilled poop everywhere."

Well, there goes my appetite. "Ew," I say. "I was going to ask if I could come over."

Maybe it's my imagination, because the line's not good, but I think there's some hesitation in her voice. "Um. Sure. Bruce is at work. I'm just here at home with Abby."

"You sure?"

Again, she misses a beat, then tells me to come over.

I do up my seatbelt. "Have you eaten yet?"

"There's leftover mac n' cheese in the fridge," says Quinn. "My mom made it."

I perk up. Quinn's mom, Jackie, is a great cook. I've loved that mac n' cheese since I was a ravenous kid. She makes it with five kinds of cheese—and a whack of butter to boot. Just thinking about it gets my saliva glands going. "Great," I say. "Do you need anything?"

"A pack of Huggies. Size extra-small."

"Okay, no problem."

"And some ice cream."

I don't need to ask what brand and flavor. "Sure thing. See you soon, Quinn."

As I pull away I see Colin's unmarked police car turn into Daphne's tree-lined street, framed in my rearview mirror. I feel a twinge of regret at this missed chance to see him, yet oddly gleeful to escape in the nick of time.

Just before turning the corner, I recheck my rearview mirror. A tall woman climbs out of Colin's car. Miriam. My spirits plummet afresh. I'd managed to forget about Miriam. Dressed in fitted, dark clothes, she looks like an unusually statuesque ninja.

Who'd have guessed that extra-small Huggies could be such a hot commodity? I stop in two 7-Elevens and a Save-On-Foods before managing to find a bag. By then, the caramel ice cream I bought in the first 7-Eleven is half-melted. Tough. Quinn will have to eat it that way. In fact, she'll probably be thrilled. It's too melted to refreeze, giving her the perfect excuse to polish off the whole tub.

By the time I get into Gordon Head, my stomach is more than empty. It's aching. I'm tempted to eat the ice cream myself but lack a spoon. I wish I'd bought a snack in 7-Eleven.

While my mom's neighborhood is dominated by houses built in the early 1900s, around Quinn's place, the houses are slightly newer, mostly from the 1950s through 1970s. Most places look simpler, with less fancy wooden trim painted in contrasting colors. The lawns are less pristine. There are less elaborate flowerbeds. Gordon Head is full of younger families instead of the cashed-up seniors who dominate Oak Bay. But they're both respectable, middle class neighborhoods, with minimal traffic.

Set on a quiet dead-end street, Quinn's house is pure 1970s: single-story stucco, the shape as simple as a kid's drawing.

No one's in sight as I park and climb out of my car. Abby's stroller is sitting near the bottom of Quinn's front steps. I stoop to collect the junk mail off her open porch. The living room curtains are partially drawn.

When I knock, Quinn yells for me to come in. The door is open.

She's sitting in a patch of sunlight in her kitchen, holding Abby. At the sight of the ice cream, her eyes light up.

I tell her about the run on Huggies.

"Thanks for doing that," she says. "Can you grab me a spoon, Tob?"

Abby's leaned up against Quinn's chest. Her tiny face is peeking over Quinn's shoulder. I walk around to get a look at her. She's grown in the week since I last saw her. Her hair is thicker. It's the same honey blonde as her mom's. I play peekaboo but she doesn't react. She yawns and her tiny eyelids sag. Quinn strokes her small back. I start to say something and Quinn lifts a fingertip to her lips. She crosses her fingers.

Moments later, the baby's asleep. Still carrying the Huggies, ice cream, and spoon, I follow Quinn as she walks down the hall. She lays Abby into her crib and pulls a blanket up to her chest. I set the diapers on a shelf below Abby's changing table. A painting of two smiling orange cats hangs nearby.

After Quinn turns on the baby monitor, we both tiptoe out of the room. "Thanks," she whispers. She takes the ice cream and spoon off me. We retreat to her orange kitchen.

While Quinn starts on her ice cream, I heat up Jackie's famous mac n' cheese. The smell makes my mouth water. I pull a fork and another spoon from the cutlery drawer, then fill two glasses of water.

There's a weird, almost uncomfortable silence when I join Quinn at the table, like she's got something unpleasant to tell me. I wait but she just keeps eating. "How are you?" I ask. She shrugs. I take a hot, cheesy bite of macaroni. It's the best thing I've ever tasted.

"Tired," says Quinn. "Abby was up half the night."

I study my friend's face, and note her pallor. She runs her fingers through her unbrushed hair. "I'm not sure what's wrong," says Quinn. "She seems extra restless."

I look around the kitchen. Dirty dishes are piled in the sink, while crumbs dot the old orange Formica countertop. A packet of prunes is sitting open on the table. Quinn yawns into her ice cream.

Again, I study her, her eyes fixed upon the ice cream tub. Is this just the normal fatigue of new motherhood or something more sinister? I'd get depressed being stuck inside with a baby, day after day. And Quinn's so smart and inquisitive. She must be bored half-to-death. She loves being outdoors. She craves nature.

Quinn fights back another yawn. "How about you?" she asks.

Blowing on a spoonful of macaroni I realize we haven't talked since our fancy French dinner. I haven't told her about my fight with Josh, or about finding a dead body, or that Daphne Dane has reappeared. Where to start? It's been a crazy weekend.

I take a deep breath. "Josh doesn't want to see me anymore."

A whole symphony of emotions plays across Quinn's tired face:

concern, anger, and yes—relief. She bites a cuticle. "Oh," she says. "What happened?"

I swallow. Saying it out loud has made it depressingly real. I spent close to two decades obsessed with this guy, who seemed as unobtainable as a movie star. And then he wanted me. Me! The dream came true but I couldn't quite believe it was real. So I wrecked it.

The mac n' cheese feels like a shot put in the bottom of my gut. I rub my eyes. "We had a fight," I say. "About Colin. Josh wanted me to commit."

I tell Quinn about our boat trip to Sooke and how we found a corpse in that desolate cabin. "We were both upset," I say. "About finding the body. It was horrible, Quinn." I shudder at the memory of Stephen's crusty head wound. "I felt Josh was unreasonable, making those demands then." I set down my fork. "I kept trying to explain how I felt, and he wouldn't listen . . ." I blink the tears from my eyes.

Quinn sighs. "I'm sorry." She, too, stops eating. "Bruce told me how you and Josh found that guy's body."

"Oh yeah?" I say. As well as being colleagues, Bruce and Colin are good friends. I hold my breath, waiting. "So, ah, what'd Bruce say?" I ask, when the silence is too pressing.

"Colin was pissed you went out there by yourself."

I start to say I wasn't by myself—I was with Josh—but don't bother. I know what Colin means: I should have told him about Daphne's cabin and let the cops handle it.

Quinn's been studying her scarred pine tabletop but now meets my eyes. I wait. Is she mad at me too? Maybe this is why she seems so cagey today. Am I in for a lecture?

"A man's been murdered," she says. "This is serious, Tob. I know you were just trying to help, but Colin's really worried. You need to stay out of this. Okay?"

I nod. Quinn doesn't need to be worrying about me. "Daphne's back," I say. "So it's all good. My mom's happy." This last bit isn't true. My mom remains inexplicably fearful, convinced Daphne's in deep trouble—which she is, I guess, if the cops think she killed her cheating lover.

"Good," says Quinn, although her tone is more reluctant than relieved. She stirs her melted ice cream and bites her lip. "There's something else," she says. She rakes back her mussed hair and frowns. "Something I have to tell you. And it's . . ." She stares into her bowl, looking gloomy.

I push my bowl away. "Quinn? What's going on?" Is something wrong with Abby? Are she and Bruce having trouble? Or is it something I've done or failed to do? It feels like bad news is looming.

My friend moves her chair away from the table. She folds up her long legs and hugs her knees. "Bruce and I took Abby for a walk," she says. "On Willows Beach. Early this morning."

I nod, mystified. Quinn and I often go for walks on that same beach. As kids we used to swim there, never cluing in to why the water was so much warmer near the end of the long sewage pipe that empties into the ocean. As they say, what doesn't kill you makes you stronger.

Quinn takes a deep breath. "We saw Josh in a parked car, on the Esplanade."

I wait, the shot put in my belly now a wrecking ball. Swinging.

"He was with a woman," says Quinn.

When I fail to react she tries again. "I mean *with* a woman."

If I were standing I'd stagger backward. Instead, I just lean back. I want to say she's wrong. She misunderstood. That's impossible. Only yesterday he told me how much I meant to him. He said he needed me! He gave me an ultimatum: me and him, exclusively.

Maybe him and this woman are just friends. Or he went on a date, just to distract himself from me. He's allowed to date other women, after all, given that I'm still seeing Colin. It's only fair. This isn't such a big deal. Or maybe it was staged and he was trying to make me jealous.

Quinn's blue eyes flash. "I wanted to run over and smack him," she says. "But Bruce held me back." She shakes her head. "Now, after hearing you guys ended it yesterday, I'm glad I didn't."

I nibble on my knuckle. "What did you see?" I say. "Describe it."

Quinn waves a hand. "You don't want to know," she says, firmly.

"I do." My voice is equally firm.

My best friend looks around her kitchen, like it's all new to her. Finally, her eyes swing back to me. Her top lip curls. "They were making out."

"Like a little kiss?"

She shakes her head and bites on a cuticle. While she's trying to spare my feelings, I'd rather know. When I tell her this, she shrugs. "Okay. Fine. We're talking major tongue. And I didn't even look at their hands." She makes a face. "Yuck," she says.

I grimace. "Maybe it's a rebound thing," I say, hopefully. "Like he's brokenhearted and trying to drown his sorrow."

"Right. In another woman's spit," says Quinn. Seeing my crestfallen face, she looks contrite. She tugs at her ear. "Sorry."

Quinn has never liked Josh. She never forgave him for breaking my heart as a teenager. Talk about holding a grudge. Despite his best efforts to win her over, she's remained suspicious of his motives. So of course she'd see this incident in the worst possible light. Although it's hard to cast a good light on it. Slightly more than twelve hours after declaring his *need* for me, he's getting down and dirty with another woman in a car, parked by a public beach.

"Where were they parked?" I ask. I feel a masochistic need to picture the scene.

"Down by Cattle Point," says Quinn. "They were in a red convertible." She makes a face. "I mean talk about tacky. It was like a teenage-boy, midlife-crisis type of convertible."

I wince. I can imagine the scene all too well. Except Josh's Porsche is grey. It must have been her car. I try to picture her: the kind of woman who drives a flashy red convertible. "What'd she look like?" I ask.

Quinn shakes her head. "Seriously, Tob. Who cares? Just forget about Josh. And her, whoever she is."

I nod. This is sound advice. If our roles were reversed I'd say the same thing. As did Daphne's housekeeper, Grace, only this morning. Forget about the guy. He was bad news. Move on.

But like Daphne, I need to keep poking this bruise. "Was she blonde?" I ask. Josh's ex-wife and ex-mistress were both beautiful, buxom blondes. My physical opposites. He has a thing for curvy blondes.

Quinn gives me a look of disgust. "No. A brunette."

"Pretty?"

She rolls her eyes. "Jesus, Toby. You seriously want to know?"

I nod.

"Okay." She lowers her knees and sits cross-legged on her wooden chair. She's wearing jeans and an old blue sweater of Bruce's that's slightly paler than her eyes. "She was sitting down so I couldn't tell if she's tall, short or average," says Quinn. "Slim but curvy. Hard to tell her age. Maybe late twenties? Early thirties? Very attractive, with long dark brown hair. Stylishly dressed in a black leather jacket. She was wearing a hat—a dark raspberry beret. And it looked good on her."

I frown. Now Quinn's being mean. I look dreadful in hats, like a kid playing dress up.

Her eyes narrow. "Enough?" she asks. "Can I stop, please?"

I nod but feel ill, like I've just gorged on fast food. I know I asked for the quarter pounder with super-sized fries, but it was a bad, bad idea. Quinn should have kept saying no. I rub my eyes.

"Do you want a drink?" asks Quinn. She unfolds her legs and stands up. I nod. She pulls a red tin from a high cupboard. "Tea?"

"Um, no thanks." After this morning's tea-a-thon, I want something else. Like a liter or two of scotch. Too bad it's only midday. Quinn pours herself a glass of milk. "Just more water, please," I say.

She refills my glass and reclaims her seat. I take a sip. The cool water feels good going down. Thinking about Josh and this brunette beauty has heaved a boulder onto my chest. I take another calming sip. Quinn is watching me carefully.

"Toby," she says. "You might not agree, just yet, but trust me—this is for the best."

I scratch my head. How? I'm sure she'll enlighten me, soon enough.

"You couldn't decide," she says. "Well, the decision's been made."

I nod. That's true. But what if it's the wrong decision?

She leans forward. "You like Colin, right?"

I nod again. I really do. But I spent so many years wanting Josh.

"Well, he likes you too. A lot. He's in love."

I wonder how she can be so sure, especially now, with Miriam on the scene. Why would he choose me, with a woman like that by his side? Shared cases. Shared interests. Both of them equally fit and fabulous. Like two perfect peas in a pod.

Maybe Quinn sees the doubt in my eyes because she intensifies her efforts. "He's crazy about you, Tob. You guys are so good together. A really good fit."

I stay silent. Colin is one of Bruce's best friends. Of course Quinn wants me and him to be together. It'd be like a happy sitcom, the four of us best buddies. Cue the cheery theme song. She has Bruce and Abby and wants the same things for me. And she wants a best friend for Abby, as soon as possible.

"So maybe this is a sign," says Quinn. "And you can focus on being happy with Colin." She tilts her head and stops talking. Her eyes narrow. "What are you thinking?"

"I think you're right," I say. It couldn't be clearer. Before the dust from my fight with Josh even settled he was all over another woman. He's not sitting around missing me. He's not broken-hearted.

I think of Daphne's housekeeper and how she'd described Stephen Buxley as a "cad." Is Josh a cad? It's such an old-fashioned term. What's the modern equivalent? A jerk? An asshole? A love-rat? Yes, anyone who can move on that fast is a love-rat.

I should forget Josh. If Quinn is right about Colin, I'm a very lucky woman. Colin is awesome. Except I don't feel lucky.

I feel kicked to the curb and deflated. Like a cheap discarded toy. A trinket—briefly admired, then forgotten. Worse still, this feeling is so familiar. I felt this way aged fourteen when Josh dumped me for a sexy mean-girl. I'm thirty-three but have learned nothing. And poor Daphne's seventy-something. Brains, beauty, and wealth couldn't protect her. It might be safer to stay single.

I don't say this to Quinn. "I guess I just need some time," I say. "To feel better. It just came out of the blue."

Quinn nods. "Maybe you should do something fun with Colin."

The way I'm feeling right now, I don't think I'm capable of having—or being—fun. "He's really busy these days," I say. "With Stephen Buxley's murder still unsolved."

"He still needs to eat," says Quinn. "You could stop by his place with Chinese takeaway sometime soon."

I nod. Thoughts of Colin and the case lead to thoughts of Miriam. I feel even lousier. Colin's never been this busy before. Despite Quinn's claims otherwise, has he lost interest in me too? Will I be single forever? With each passing year there are fewer available—let alone desirable—men in my age bracket. Already, a high percentage of the guys giving me second glances are old enough to get seniors' discounts. At the same time, my standards keep rising. I'm too old—and too settled—to settle. Let's face it: no one is perfect. We all have bad habits and worse moments. Perhaps *I'm* too old to compromise and that's why I couldn't decide between Josh and Colin.

At this sobering thought, Abby starts to bawl, her cries magnified through the baby monitor. Quinn climbs tiredly to her feet. I carry our dirty glasses and dishes to the sink. All this thinking is wearing me out. What a never-ending day. And according to the clock on Quinn's stove it's only 1:42 p.m. I should just go home, have a long bath, binge-watch trashy TV, and hide away until this weekend's officially over. How sad is that? I'm actually wishing it were Monday.

I've just explained my plan to Quinn, who's busy breastfeeding, when my cell phone rings. I'm tempted not to answer, but it's my client, Vonda Butts.

I try to keep the sigh from my voice as I greet her.

"Toby Vong?" Her voice is breathless. "I need your help, right away."

I'm surprised to hear her sounding so upset. "What's going on?" I ask.

"The police vant to see me."

"The police?" I exit Abby's room so as not to disturb Quinn and the baby. "Why? What's happened?" I'm confused and concerned. What has Vonda failed to tell me?

"Vhere are you?"

I walk out of Quinn's front door and take a seat on her front steps. The front yard is pretty basic: a square of lawn that could use some more watering and three spindly maple trees. I guess gardening hasn't been Bruce and Quinn's top priority since they bought the place three years ago.

"Toby Vong?" barks Vonda.

I force my attention back to my client. "I'm at a friend's place in Gordon Head." She never answered my question. "Why do the police want to see you?"

"Gordon Head," she says, again ignoring my question. "That's vhere I am! Vhat address? I vill come get you."

I rub my forehead, which hurts. Vonda is not one to take no for an answer.

I squint out at the street, lined with seventies bungalows a lot like Quinn's. Flat roofs. Faux Tudor. Faux Spanish. Seventies style was like a Boston Terrier—so ugly it's endearing. "It's Sunday," I tell Vonda. "Can this wait till tomorrow?"

"Vait?" She sounds outraged. "The police are on their vay! You are my lawyer! I need you there vhen I talk to them." A click of her tongue. "I thought that's vhat lawyers do!" she adds.

I start to formulate an excuse but stop. My hot bath and Netflix binge vill have to vait. Argh—my Ws have gone again. It happens whenever I talk to Vonda. She's right. She is my client. It's my job to help her. Plus I'm curious. What has she done to interest the police? Possibilities flash through my tired brain. Immigration violation? Unpaid parking tickets? Shoplifting? Does she actually earn a living from modeling and "influencing"? What the hell does that even mean? I've checked out her Instagram. She seems to spend a lot of time drinking detox teas and flouncing around in yoga clothes.

I tell her Quinn's address.

"So close!" She sounds pleased. "Vait two minutes."

I go indoors to say goodbye to Quinn only to find both her and Abby asleep. I write a short note and stick it on the fridge, then toss the empty ice cream container in the garbage.

After tiptoeing back down the hall, I shut the front door quietly behind me. Sitting on Quinn's front steps, I'm tempted to call Vonda back. My car's right out front. I could just drive over to meet her. I'm so tired I wasn't thinking straight.

Sitting with my head in my hands, I shut my eyes. I hope whatever Vonda's done, it can be cleared up fast. Does she need a criminal lawyer? If so, I'll have to call Quinn's mom, Jackie. Geez, Jackie should give me a finder's fee. Who else in my life needs a good criminal lawyer?

I wrap my arms around myself to stay warm. All I want is to go home and wallow in peace. What a day. Not only did I get dumped, I found out Josh's already moved on. All this time and angst for nothing: I meant nothing to him. The thought of him pashing some other woman is like a squirt of lemon juice in my eyes. My nose starts to stuff up, leaving me furious. I need to stop dwelling on this. Any second now, Vonda will show up. Do I want her to find me sniveling on the curb, like a kicked puppy?

Hearing an approaching engine, I look up to see a shiny red car. It turns into Quinn's cul-de-sac and slows.

I rub my eyes. It's a convertible. Despite the cool day, the top is down to reveal a woman with long, glossy brown hair. She's wearing a raspberry beret. Seeing me, she smiles. She looks fabulous.

The wrecking ball that was in my gut goes into free-fall. What are the chances? It can't be. And yet, it must be . . . Josh Barton and my sexy client . . . This can't be happening.

I want to turn and bolt, but it's too late. Vonda has seen me. She pulls up and waves. When I don't move, she calls out. "Hello?" A toss of her head. "Vhat are you vaiting for, Toby?"

My knees shake as I rise. There's no choice. I must face her. Could today get any vorse? She might be Josh's new voman, but she's still my client.

CHAPTER 18:

CONNECTING THE DOTS

Eyeing my red-rimmed eyes, Vonda frowns. "Vhat is wrong vith you?" she asks. I climb into her flashy little car.

"Allergies," I mumble, unable to meet her eyes. I fumble through my purse to find my sunglasses.

Once we start moving, I understand why Vonda's wearing a hat. With the top down, my hair keeps blowing up my nose. In the depths of my purse I manage to find a hair-elastic and fashion a messy pony-tail.

Vonda turns onto Arbutus Road. While she sounded distraught over the phone, in person, she looks cool and collected, her eyeliner perfectly drawn into sexy cat eyes. It takes a steady hand to get that look right. Was her distress just an act, so I'd agree to meet her?

I wonder if Vonda knew that I was seeing Josh. Is that why she hired me? There are women who don't want a man unless they can lure him away from someone else, women whose whole reason for being is to compete with other women. It's hard not to feel like I've been drawn into some twisted Machiavellian plot. Or is it just a co-incidence? I'm probably being paranoid. Both Josh and Vonda are su-pernaturally good looking. Like attracts like, by and large. Victoria is not that big of a town. They probably just saw each other someplace, and it was lust at first sight. She is Josh's type, after all, with boobs like cantaloupes and a butt like a newly discovered, sexy planet. His ex-wife and ex-girlfriend were similar. I was the anomaly. The one not like the others.

Beside me, Vonda shifts gears. Her voice is ominous. "They are coming to my house."

Because my mind was sunk deep in self-pity, it takes a moment to resurface. She means the cops. I need to wake up. "What's going on?" I ask her.

Vonda slows to take a corner. "I don't know," she admits. "A detective called. A voman."

"A detective?" So it's not just some traffic violation.

"What'd she say? Exactly?"

Vonda chews on her pillowy bottom lip, painted the same raspberry red as her artfully tilted beret. I sit on my hands, lest I'm too tempted to rip it off her head.

"She asked if I vas home and said she vanted to see me."

"That's it?" I say. I note the little crease of worry in Vonda's flawless forehead. "Why are you so worried?"

Vonda's eyes flick my way in surprise. "It is the police!" she cries, like this explains everything. "That is never good!" When she brushes back a stray curl, I see her fingers are shaking.

Looking at Vonda Butts, I realize how little I know about her. Maybe this is a cultural thing. The police do more harm than good in many parts of the world. Suspects get bundled into vans and never seen again. She did grow up in the KGB era. Or maybe she's been up to no good.

I speak gently in an attempt not to sound accusing. "So there's nothing you've done?" I shrug. "Nothing illegal?"

Vonda shoots me a dark look. "Vhat? You think I am some criminal? Is this vhat you think of Russians? Ve are all mafia or selling drugs! Or I am vhat—a prostitute?"

Her reaction is so extreme I can't help but laugh in shock. "No!" I say. "I didn't say that! I'm your lawyer, Vonda. I'm just trying to figure out why the police want to see you. So we can be prepared when we meet them."

Her furious pout recedes a little. "I see," she says, then, with a tiny shrug. "Then no, I am in the dark." She looks at me when she says this, one glossy eyebrows rising as if to check she's used this idiom correctly.

"Okay." I check my watch. "Did the police say what time to expect them?"

With a flick of her wrist, Vonda also checks her watch. We've been turning onto smaller and smaller streets, and now pull into a road that dead-ends at a small park. The car slows, then stops in front of a non-descript single-story house. It looks a lot like Quinn's. Painted green, it appears mildly unkempt, like a rental.

"My house," says Vonda. She kills the engine. Given her ultra-groomed appearance, I'm surprised. I pictured her living in some sleek, uber-modern condo, full of touch screens and metallics.

We've just stepped out of her car when another car turns into her street. A dark sedan, unmarked, but obviously a police car. Colin drives one just like it.

Beside me, Vonda's breathing quickens. My head pounds as I watch the car pull closer.

When Colin steps out, he looks as shocked to see me as I am to see him. Miriam looks surprised too, but handles it better.

"Hi, Toby," she says. She strides our way. "What are you doing here?"

I shut my gaping mouth. What is this, the Day of Coincidences? Of all the cops who could come to see Vonda, why is it Colin and Miri? Aren't they busy enough trying to track Stephen Buxley's killer?

I go to run a hand through my hair, only to remember that it's still piled in a snaggly ponytail. Great. So as well as looking exhausted, old, and like I've been bawling, I'm homeless-lady disheveled. Especially next to Vonda, who looks airbrushed.

"Er, hi, Miriam. Colin." My voice sounds sticky. "This is Vonda Butts." I motion her way. "My client."

Against his pale skin, Colin's dark eyebrows dip. His expression says that-figures. He turns to Vonda. "Mrs. Butts?"

Vonda inhales, like she's scared of what's coming next. "Yes. Vhat do you vant?"

"You called your lawyer?" says Colin. He sounds more disappoint-ed than anything, his tone and manner somber. "We're not accusing you of anything, Mrs. Butts." He motions toward Miriam. "This is my partner, Detective Miriam Young. I'm Detective Colin Destin." He glances up at her house. "Could we just come in and talk to you, briefly?"

Vonda looks at me, unsure. I nod. "Of course."

We all troop up Vonda's front path and climb her peeling steps, then wait as she unlocks the front door. I know the detectives have noticed: her hands are shaking harder than ever.

We sit in her living room. Like the house's exterior, it looks plain and uncared for. Vonda and I sit side-by-side on a sagging beige sofa, the two detectives on matching armchairs. We all perch on the edges, like we'd rather not be here.

Miriam clears her throat and crosses her long legs. As usual, she's wearing dark, fitted pants. Today, her turtleneck is charcoal. "I'm afraid we have bad news," she tells Vonda.

Again, Vonda looks at me, as if she needs me to interpret. I wait and Miriam goes on. "It's about your husband."

Vonda's grey eyes narrow. "Dennis?" she says, with a frown. "What has he done, this time?"

Both Colin and Miriam exchange a glance before Miriam continues. Hands clasped, she looks sympathetic and serious, her hair scraped into a tight bun. As usual, her brown skin is luminous and free of makeup. "I'm very sorry, Vonda. But he's dead. He was murdered."

While Vonda doesn't react, I recoil in shock. Victoria is not a hotbed of violent crime. Two men murdered, in less than a week? It seems unreal. Are the deaths connected?

Vonda blinks in slow motion. "Dennis, dead? But how?" Then, before they have a chance to answer. "It cannot be him!"

Colin sighs, his green eyes sympathetic and watchful. I know they're tracking Vonda's every move, judging her. Her husband was murdered. The spouse is always a suspect, right? And she wanted a divorce. She said he deceived her.

Colin withdraws something from his coat pocket and shows it to Vonda: a B.C. driver's license, sealed inside a little plastic bag.

Even though the photo's tiny, I recognize it as the same image Vonda gave me the night I went to L'Escargot D'Or. A neat, trim, rather nondescript middle-aged man with fair hair, wearing a light blue dress shirt. He is not smiling in the photo but looks pleasant, his blue eyes friendly.

"We found this in his pants' pocket," says Colin. "And contacted his dentist."

Vonda's shoulders start to shake. She presses a hand to her mouth, as if to hold back a sob. Today, her nails are painted dark blue, like the background in Van Gogh's "Starry Night." The color doesn't suit her pale skin, the effect macabre. Or maybe it's just the feeling cast by this dreadful news.

"I'm sorry," says Colin. "But the dental records match. The dead man is definitely your husband."

I hold my breath. Two deaths, close to home. It hardly seems possible.

Vonda bows her head. She covers her face with her hands. On her right hand, two long nails have snapped off. How did that happen? When she lowers her hands, I see her lipstick has smudged across her teeth. Blood on snow. My head is full of creepy thoughts. Like how was her husband murdered?

"Mrs. Butts?" says Colin. "Are you alright?"

She stares at him, pewter eyes wide and desperate: "Oh, my Denny!" Her other hand finds her heart, the picture of a heartbroken young widow. "Who vould do this?" she cries. "And vhere vas he?"

Miriam leans closer. "Do you know anyone who lives in Sooke?"

My mouth unlatches. It can't be. It just can't be. But I know it is. First Stephen Buxley. Now, Dennis Butts. Two cheating men. And two women being cheated on. Except that math might be wrong. I never did like geometry. This isn't a square but a triangle.

What if Daphne's unfaithful fiancé is Vonda's cheating husband?

CHAPTER 19

A STEP BACK

C olin is poised to walk down Vonda's front steps when he catches my eye. "Toby?" he says, quietly. He lays a hand on my arm. "Can I have a word, please?"

I nod, elated by his touch, yet dreading what's to come. "Of course." I swallow hard.

Miriam is already striding toward their car. Vonda is indoors, on the sofa, sobbing. I'll need to go back to her soon and try to console her.

Colin studies my face, his scrutiny making my cheeks color. "Are you okay?" he asks.

"Um. Yeah, just allergies," I mutter.

"Oh," says Colin. He sounds relieved. "That's good. I was worried it was more serious."

Great, I think. That's how dreadful I look—like I've got the flu. Or I'm dying. But, despite my embarrassment, the concern in his eyes sparks a warm glow, deep in my belly.

"I slept badly, too," I admit. I flush even brighter. "Look, Colin, I'm really sorry about going out to the Danes' cabin. I—"

He cuts me off, his forehead furrowed. "Listen, Tob."

I freeze, unable to breathe. Given my day, it's obvious where this is heading. Any moment now, he'll tell me it's over. He can't go out with someone who disregards property law. Who's so terminally nosy. And indecisive. And short. Plus allergy-ridden.

Colin looks stern. "I should be lecturing you about the legal side of things, arguably breaking and entering." I hang my head, waiting. "Except I won't," he says. "Because that's not what upset me." I hold my breath. "Toby?" He lays his big hands gently on my shoulders.

"Yeah?" I still can't look at him. I'm too embarrassed and remorseful and sad. If only I hadn't gone to Daphne's stupid cottage. I wouldn't have found Stephen's body, or rubbed Colin and Josh in each other's noses. Josh wouldn't suspect me of playing games. Colin wouldn't think I'm a natural-born meddler.

"Toby? Look at me." I do as he asks. Colin looks like I feel: tired and stricken. "I'm sorry I got angry," he says. "But I worry about you. I see awful things at work, things I can't fix. There are real dangers out there . . . Even here, on the island . . ." His Adam's apple bobs. "I don't want you anywhere near that."

I blink. So he's not ending it? I can hardly believe it. Relief has left me dizzy. "I . . . I'm sorry," I say, again. "I feel like an idiot for having gone out there uninvited. I should have called you. And as for Josh—"

He raises a fingertip to my lips. "It's okay," he says. "We don't have to discuss that right now." Deep in his green eyes, there's a flash of something—maybe anger, or anxiety—but then his gaze softens. "We will discuss it soon though. Right?"

I nod. "Yes."

"Good," he says. "When you're feeling better."

Without thinking I lean forward and press my forehead to his broad chest. I squeeze my arms around him. He smells of chocolate and mint, a warm, Christmassy smell, fresh but cozy.

His arms close around me and his lips find the top of my head. He inhales. "I've missed you so much, Toby."

"Same," I mumble, although it comes out as "shame," because my nose is squished up against his chest. Pressed against him, I can't remember when I last felt this good, like the clouds filling my heart have suddenly parted. This very grey day has a silver lining.

Vonda is still on her couch. She looks somber but dry-eyed. Were the sobs just an act to impress the cops? She is hard to read, fragile as a Fabergé egg one minute, hard as nails the next.

I sit beside her. "I'm so sorry," I say. "Do you want me to stay with you?"

She shakes her head. "I am fine." She rises smoothly to her feet. "I vill drive you back to your friend's now."

I'm worried she's in no state to drive, but she assures me otherwise. "I am not a divorcee but a vidow," she says. "It is easier, no?" She retrieves her purse and gives me a tight little smile. "Not so much paperwork . . ."

I'm unsure whether to be appalled by her callousness or impressed she's already seen the bright side. She tosses her hair and strides toward the front door: "You coming?"

As we walk to her car, I watch her carefully. It's like her earlier breakdown never happened. She betrays no sign of shock or grief— chest out, shoulders back, like she's strutting down a catwalk. Her makeup has been retouched to its former perfection. Even that damn beret is back in place, tilted jauntily. I'm torn between dislike and admiration. What must it be like to be Vonda? She reminds me of a lion or a tiger, utterly intent on her own desires, utterly immoral. Utterly capable of murder.

She turns the radio until she finds an upbeat pop song. Her head bops to the beat. I grit my teeth. Her husband is dead! Is she in shock and denial? Or is she really this cold-blooded?

"You sure you'll be okay?" I ask, as we pull up out front of Quinn's. Abby's stroller is no longer in the yard. Quinn must be out for a walk. I'm relieved. I wouldn't want to introduce them to Vonda, whose ability to suppress—or manufacture—emotions scares me.

"I am fine," says Vonda. Her clipped tone makes it clear the topic's closed, although, just for an instant, her lower lip quivers. Then she regains control of herself. Or is she acting? Her grey eyes are steely. "He vas not a good husband," she says tightly. "Remember? He deceived me."

"Still," I say. I unclick my seatbelt. "He was your husband. It's a big shock . . ."

"Yes, shock," agrees Vonda. She pronounces it with a "ch." She's still nodding to the beat. "Vhat a shock!" she says.

Instead of climbing out, I stay put. Knowing that Stephen was a liar and a conman makes it easier to not feel his death, to think he had it coming. But even if he wasn't a saint, he didn't deserve that end, bludgeoned to death, and left to rot in that horrible cabin.

What was he like, this man, to have attracted two strong women like Daphne and Vonda?

"Tell me about Stephen, I mean Dennis," I say to Vonda.

She sighs. "He vas . . ." She bites her lip. "He vas funny. He loved cats. Not dogs, no he did not like dogs at all. But cats, they always came to him, always vanted a cuddle." Her smile widens a little. "As a little boy in Texas he had a big brown cat named Leia, you know, like the princess in Star Vars?"

"Texas?" I say. "I thought he was British."

Vonda looks surprised. "He vas American, grew up in Houston. His parents died vhen he vas six. So tragic . . ." Her voice tightens with emotion. "A train hit them." She wipes a tear from one eye. "Poor little Denny."

"Huh," I say. "So how'd he get a British accent?"

Vonda frowns. "He spoke like George Bush," she says. "The younger von. He vas definitely not British."

"But I heard . . ." I begin, then stop.

"You heard vhat?" She balls her hands into tight fists.

I shake my head. "It doesn't matter."

Vonda pounds the steering wheel with one fist. Her perfect teeth clench together. "My god. He lied about everything, didn't he?" she says, quietly. "Even the orphan bit." More tears have appeared in her grey eyes. I'm not sure if they're from sorrow or frustration. She bends her head, her shoulders heaving.

I pat her back. "I'm sorry," I say. "I'm really sorry."

Vonda nods. "Is okay." She dabs at her eyes. It's obviously not. When she speaks again, her voice is softer than it's ever been, her accent less clipped. "The vorst thing," she says, "is that I don't even know who he vas. And now . . ." She hiccups. "Now I never vill. I vill never, ever get to know him." A tear slips down her cheek. "Who vas he?"

What can I say? I stroke her back. I guess it's healthy that she's crying. But is this for real? I fight back a sigh. God, I hate this: seeing everyone as a suspect. Poor Vonda—people respond to loss in different ways. Grief has no map. The bereaved go up and down and around in circles. Her emotions must be tugging her in every direction.

I rub my forehead. Poor Colin—this is how he must live, all the time, seeing the worst of human nature, questioning everyone's motives. It's a miracle he's not jaded.

I dig a pack of Kleenex out of my bag and hand it to Vonda. She thanks me, blows her nose daintily, and stops crying.

"The police," she says, watching me out of the corner of her eye. "Do you think they believed me?" She daubs at her mascara.

"About what?"

She looks surprised. "About everything."

I shrug. "I guess so." Let's hope she has a great alibi for whatever day the coroner decides Stephen died.

When I ask if she's ever been to Sooke, Vonda looks vague. "Vhat for? It is countryside, no? I am city girl." She blinks, like some fresh mascara has flaked into her eyes. "Vhen you found him," she says. She blinks even harder. "Vhat did he look like?"

While there aren't many sentimental bones in Vonda's body, despite her tough act, and her fury at Dennis Butts, I suspect she loved him. That being so, I don't want to tell her about the flies, or the missing shoe, or the crusty head wound.

"He looked, er, peaceful," I say. A blatant lie. "Like he was sleeping."

Vonda tilts her head. Her smile is sad. I don't know what bad things have happened to Vonda to make her so hard, but I do know she doesn't believe in fairy tales. "This other voman," she says, softly. "The von who owned this cottage. Do you know her?"

"Yes," I admit. "She's a friend of my mom's."

Vonda's jaw clenches. "Oh? Is she old?"

"Ah, older." They say fifty is the new thirty, which makes seventy the new fifty. By this scale, "old" starts at ninety.

"Rich?" says Vonda, still smiling sadly.

"Kind of." Another lie. Daphne's beyond loaded.

She shakes herself. Her blue fingernails tap on the steering wheel. "Vell." She pats at her hair. "I vant to meet her."

"Meet Daphne?" Surprise makes me blurt out her name, then regret it.

What if Vonda's the vindictive type, who'll blame Daphne for her husband's transgressions? Daphne's a tough old bird but Vonda's no pushover. In a fight, I don't know who I'd put my money on. It wouldn't be pretty.

"Vhat is she like, this Daphne?" asks Vonda. To my surprise, she doesn't sound bitter, merely curious and a little wistful.

"She's smart," I say. "And successful." I bite my lip. "She didn't know he was married."

"Of course not," says Vonda. "That vas Dennis's vay." She sighs. "This voman is a victim too . . . And she's not the first. Denny vas a . . ." She pauses, as if unsure of the right word. "A svindler. A professional svindler."

She lays a hand on my arm, eyes wide and beseeching. "Please Toby. Please tell this voman, Daphne, that I vant to meet her. Okay?"

"Okay," I say. I'll tell Daphne and see what she says. Maybe it'd be good for them to compare notes and sort the truth from the lies—if that's even possible. As it is, they're stuck with aching hearts and unanswered questions.

"Take care of yourself, Vonda," I say. I unlock the car's door. "Call me, if you need me."

Vonda raises a hand in farewell. "Oh don't vorry about me," she says breezily. "At least I am saved the hassle of getting divorced. And I have met a new man . . ." She winks. "He is rich and handsome."

I fight back the ensuing image: Josh in the very seat where I'm now sitting, all over Vonda. How did I forget? Vonda doesn't need my sympathy: she's got Josh to console her.

Feeling freshly punched in the gut, I stagger out of her car. What a day. It's felt endless, and full of awful surprises.

I pause on the curb. My headache has gotten worse, like there's not enough space in my skull for all these jumbled thoughts and feelings. There are so many overlaps, so many layers blocking my vision. It's like a kaleidoscope—confusing patterns everywhere I look, depending on how I twist things. Is Stephen's death even related to the Danes? It seems so because he was found in their cabin. But maybe someone else followed him out there, someone else he scammed or lied to. Another victim. Or his wronged wife.

She pulls away from the curb and turns up her car's radio.

Half-drunk with fatigue, I stumble toward my car. Vonda's little red convertible rounds the corner. The cul-de-sac lies empty. A dog barks in the distance.

I unlock my car and sink into the driver's seat.

My car smells ever so faintly of my mom's perfume—a mix of vanilla and sandalwood she brews herself. I shut my eyes and inhale. It feels like years since this morning at the Danes' place.

Finally, I can go home and hide—and leave Josh, this endless day, and Stephen's murder far behind me.

Daphne is home, safe and sound. And Vonda's right: she no longer needs a divorce. Which means she's no longer my client, or my problem.

CHAPTER 20:

THE OTHER WOMEN

Before I forget about Vonda forever, there's one last thing I must do. As promised, going via my mom, I approach Daphne Dane about a possible meeting. Daphne is surprisingly keen to meet her romantic rival. I guess they're both curious about the other woman.

While I'd rather just leave them to it, both Vonda and my mom beg me to introduce them in person. Why they want me there is unclear. Am I supposed to referee? I have no desire to watch the fur flying.

Perhaps fearing I'll bail, Vonda shows up at my office just before closing, then follows my car out to Rockland. My mom promised to join us too, although when we pull up out front of Daphne's front gate, there's no sign of Ivy's beater. I hope it hasn't broken down again. I try to call her, but her phone rings out. She's probably on her way over.

It's now dark well before I leave work. It's also freezing. As I step out of my car, a blast of frigid wind makes me shiver.

Not surprisingly, Vonda's got the top up on her red convertible. Looking back, I see she's still in her seat, applying one last layer of war paint. At my approach, she gives her hair another fluff, opens the door, and steps out. She's wearing a short red skirt. In my mind, the paparazzi go wild. She looks even sexier than usual.

"Ready?" I ask.

Vonda grits her teeth. She nods. "Ready."

How she can walk in those red snakeskin boots is a mystery. Everything about her—boobs, butt, bouncy hair—seems to defy the laws of gravity.

Walking beside her in my sedate navy suit I feel short, bony, and dowdy. No wonder Josh moved on. I bat this thought away. This is not the time for self-pity. Plus let's face it: Josh likes 'em trashy. I was never his type and never could be.

Beside me, Vonda's pantyhose swish. She peers up at the huge house. Her scarlet lips tighten. "Vhat did this voman do to get so rich?"

We climb the steps side by side. "She owns Dane cookies," I say. "You ever heard of them?"

Vonda shrugs. With that tiny waist, she's probably never had a cookie in her life.

I explain how Daphne and her late husband founded a highly successful confectionary company. Vonda looks unimpressed. "She is a baker?"

Indoors, the pig starts to squeal. "Kevin! Stop!" says a sharp voice. To my surprise, the pig does. This is a revelation: it actually listens to Daphne.

I've raised my hand to knock when Daphne speaks again. She sounds irate. "I said no," she says. "End of story."

A whiny voice answers: "But you agreed, Mommy! I showed you all the B&B plans. You said yes!"

Daphne's reply is clipped. "I did not! I never wanted those renos, and there's no way I'm giving up my house!"

Even through the door, I can hear Isobel's sigh. "But you said yes, Mommy. You approved it all. And now you've forgotten."

"Forgotten?" Daphne's voice rises. "How could I forget?"

Another long-suffering sigh. When she speaks again, Isobel sounds plaintive. "You've been forgetting stuff, Mommy. It's getting worse and . . ."

Daphne cuts her daughter off. "Bullshit!"

"Oh Mommy, it's not! You just can't remember . . . You need help. Maybe we should go to the doctor, try to find a specialist . . ." She coughs. "I've been worried for a while but now this thing, with this man, Stephen." Her voice has a hysterical edge. "The police think he was a conman, Mommy . . . A conman trying to take advantage of you. Don't you see it's time to . . ." Her voice quivers. "Time to get some help with the company. I could take on more responsibility, take charge of more assets. You know, just to double-check everything."

Daphne's voice is icy. "There's nothing wrong with my intellect. Nor my eyesight."

Isobel sounds taken aback. "Uh, eyesight?" she says. "What d'you mean? How is that . . ."

Daphne's voice drops menacingly. "What I mean," she says. "Is that I saw you there, at the cabin, the day Stephen died."

I hold my breath. Holy crap. As far as I know the police haven't released an estimated time of death. How does Daphne know what day Stephen was murdered?

There's a little thud, like Isobel dropped something. Her voice is now a strangled croak. "I was not!" she cries. "I haven't been to that cottage in years. I can't even remember how to get there!"

"I know what I saw," says Daphne. "You ran into the woods, headed toward the road." Her voice drops so low I have to strain to catch her next words. "I know what I saw! I remember that perfectly!"

Isobel gives a strangled sob. "Seriously, Mommy? You're going crazy!"

Footsteps pound down the hall. The front door opens so fast Vonda and I are forced to jump back.

Isobel rushes past us, her face pale as old snow. While she stares right through me, as usual, Vonda is harder to ignore. Isobel gasps but doesn't stop. Her blue eyes goggle. She staggers past us.

Vonda and I watch in silent amazement as she stumbles down the steps. Thin shoulders hunched, she hurries down the lit path. Her coat flaps around her.

As Isobel nears the gate, it opens to emit my mother. Ivy stops in surprise. She's clutching a brown paper bag. "Isobel?" she says.

Isobel rushes right past her.

My mom shrugs. Looking up at the house she spots me and Vonda on the front porch. She raises a hand and waves. "Sorry I'm late," she calls. She gestures behind her, toward Isobel's retreating back. "Is everything okay with Isobel?"

Behind us, Daphne steps out onto the porch. Beneath her carefully applied makeup, her face is as bleached as her daughter's. She looks so dazed and shaky I wonder if she's been drinking. For some moments, Daphne stares toward the road. Then she shakes herself. Her look of angry dismay smoothes into a gracious smile. She nods to me and Vonda.

"Why hello," she says. She extends a perfectly manicured hand. "You must be Vonda." Her face is a mask of polite and polished calm.

I'm amazed by how she hides her emotions. In that way, she's like Vonda. Their ability to compartmentalize is astounding.

As they shake, the two women assess each other. They're like boxers, prefight. Or a pair of dogs, both poised and alert. I hold my breath. I half expect to see hackles rise, to hear growls. Instead, in perfect sync, their smiles widen with approval. It's as if they've recognized kindred spirits: two women as tough, practical, and ruthless as they are beautiful to look at. They could be the sort of mother and daughter who'd pass for sisters.

"It is very nice to meet you," says Vonda.

"Thank you for coming," says Daphne.

I follow them inside. Killer legs. Killer heels. Killer curves.

Holy crap. Talk about biting off more than you can chew. What was Stephen/Dennis thinking?

CHAPTER 21

TRUE LIES

Following an exchange of pleasantries in the hall, we move into Daphne's formal living room. With a fire burning in the grate, golden light glints off the chandelier and various crystal ornaments. On the coffee table rests a huge vase of irises that complement the sofa set's iris motif.

Vonda looks suitably impressed, until she spots the pig, curled up asleep on the sofa. She stops. A hand flutters to her chest. "Is that a . . .?" Words fail her.

"He's a potbellied pig," says Daphne. She sits beside her pet. The pig grunts sleepily. "He's friendly. And very clean. Most people don't realize that pigs are cleaner than dogs. And much easier to toilet-train than small children."

Vonda sits daintily in an armchair. "Ve eat pigs," she says. "Where I come from. But not dogs." She looks at me. "Don't they eat those vhere—"

Since I'm not in the mood for racist assumptions, I cut her off before she can say "where you come from." Which is the Jubilee Hospital, not far from my place. "Daphne," I say. "These flowers are stunning."

Daphne nods, distractedly. "Yes, that wonderful blue. Irises were always Walt's favorite."

While I take a seat too, my mom remains standing. Dressed in leggings and an oversized sweatshirt with an image of a bright, smiling unicorn, she looks twelve, at most. She pulls something out of her brown paper bag: a bundle of dried leaves. Ignoring my look of dismay, she smiles. "Sage smudge sticks," she says. "For dispelling bad energy."

I think back to the argument I just overheard between Daphne and her daughter. That was bad energy for sure. But I know my mom is referring to Stephen, aka Dennis Butts. Aka the dead guy.

Ivy smiles sadly at Daphne and Vonda. "I'm sorry for both of your losses," she says. "It's such a . . ." She struggles to find the right word. "A real tragedy." (I'd have replaced *tragedy* with something far less polite.) She glances around the room. "The energy's off in here," she tells Daphne. "Sage is wonderful for removing bad memories."

I try not to roll my eyes. If it were that simple, I'd smoke the stuff. How much sage would it take to make me feel fine about Josh and Vonda making out, mere hours after he dumped me?

Daphne nods. "How thoughtful," she says. "Thank you, Ivy."

Vonda cocks her head, like she's watching two unknown creatures at the zoo. Her expression says: *Vhat-da-fuck?* I cross my arms. Me and Vonda don't have much in common, but I recognize a fellow skeptic.

My mom lights a bundle. It emits not-unpleasant-smelling smoke. She retreats into a corner and waves the smoking wad. My eyes start to burn. A little of that smoke goes a long way. It's very fragrant.

Grace strides into the room bearing a tray laden with cookies and tea things. "Hello," she says, cheerfully, then does a double take at the sight of my mom waving her smudge sticks.

I fight back a laugh. Poor Grace. Her surprise looks so comical. No doubt she's envisioning ash stains on the Persian carpets.

Grace's eyes pop. "Is that . . . the weed?" she whispers to Daphne.

Again, I fight the urge to laugh. Oh no. As if she doesn't have enough to worry about with Lukas smoking up, now she's scared Daphne's at it.

"No," I reassure Grace. "It's just sage. You know, the spice? Good with chicken?"

Grace flushes. She puts a plump hand to her mouth and starts to giggle. "Oh," she says. "Now that it's legal, I just thought . . ." Her voice peters out. I'm pretty sure where her thoughts were headed: my mom looks like the kind of old hippie who'd be growing it in her herb garden.

Grace sets out a plate of homemade cookies and pours the tea.

"Thank you, Grace," says Daphne. She beams at her. "Those biscuits look amazing."

Grace's eyes twinkle. "They're your recipe."

Daphne eyes the tea with less enthusiasm. "Perhaps some wine?" she suggests. "Or a cocktail?" She looks around at the rest of us. "Grace makes wonderful martinis."

My mom and I decline, but Vonda says vhy not? I don't blame them for wanting some lubrication. This is a pretty weird situation.

"Two martinis, coming right up," says Grace, then retreats.

Daphne turns to my mom. "Hmmmm." She inhales. "Thank you, Ivy. That sage is wonderful. The room does feel lighter."

Amidst clouds of spicy smoke, my mom takes a seat. "Ooh, one more thing," she says. She reaches into her boho bag and withdraws a fist-sized blue rock. "Sodalite aids communication." She deposits it on the coffee table.

"Lovely," says Daphne.

Vonda eyes the rock warily, like it might contain some hidden surveillance device. Grace reappears with two giant martini glasses. "Here you go," she chirps. "With extra olives."

Both Daphne and Vonda's eyes light up. Daphne grabs hers lightning-quick. Again, I wonder if she's already sauced up. Or maybe she's just agitated thanks to her recent fight with her daughter, or the stress of meeting her younger love rival.

Vonda takes a sip. "Delicious," she says, approvingly. "Just like Moscow."

Grace retreats, beaming. Vonda pulls her cell phone from her purse and jumps in close to Daphne. She points the screen their way. "Selfie!" she says, brightly, holding her martini aloft. Daphne grins in surprise. I fight back a laugh. I wonder how Insta-Vonda will caption that photo. Perhaps something about Girl Power and Sisters Sticking Together.

When the selfies meet Vonda's satisfaction, she stows her phone back in her purse. There's a brief pause, like we're all waiting for the curtain to rise, before Daphne addresses Vonda. "So," she says. "How did you meet Stephen, I mean Dennis?" She waves a ringed hand and frowns. "Your husband."

Vonda studies my mom's ridiculous blue rock, like she's trying to work out its value. "It vas a vhirlvind romance," she says. Perhaps it's just the sage smoke, but her gaze looks suddenly wistful. After a brief description of their meeting in Paris, her voice hardens. "I should have known he vas too good to be true." She sits up straighter and tugs down her tight red top. "I vas fooled for too long." Her ruby lips pout. "Vhat made you suspicious?" she asks Daphne.

"I got a text message," says Daphne. "About looking good nude in some red boots. And how he couldn't wait for a replay." She eyes Vonda's knee-high, red snakeskin footwear. Fighting the Botox, her forehead struggles to wrinkle. "Since I don't own any red boots, I knew it wasn't meant for me." She swallows hard, as if the memory pains her. "But for some other woman."

Vonda's nostrils quiver angrily. "Hmphphft," she says. "One time I vear red boots vhen ve—" She waves a hand and looks coy. She leans closer to Daphne. "Then vhat?"

"I called him right away," says Daphne. Her voice is taut, regret tugging against righteous fury. "And he denied everything. Said it was some telecommunications glitch." She makes a throat-clearing sound much like Vonda's. "But come on! I'm not some tech-challenged old grannie who can't work the remote!"

Vonda nods angrily. "Men!" she says. "Always underestimating us!" She toys with her silky red skirt. "Then vhat?"

"He rushed over," says Daphne. "To try and convince me." Her pink nails flash as she opens and shuts her hand to mimic a talking mouth. "You know. Blah blah blah."

Vonda snorts. "Yes," she says. "He vas a smooth-talker."

"So smooth," agrees Daphne. "But I knew he was lying. I didn't want to believe it but . . ." Her hands shrink into tight fists. "Deep down I knew. So I followed him." She licks her lips. "I thought he'd go see this other woman. You." She smiles tightly at Vonda. "I wanted to catch him in the act. So I could be a hundred percent sure." She studies the sodalite. "It's always better to know. Isn't it?"

Vonda nods over her teacup. "Yes," she says. "The truth vill set you free." It's a Biblical quote, but I bet she got it off Instagram. My mom smiles. Vonda lowers her cup. "So vhere did he go?" she asks Daphne.

Daphne's cheeks are bright pink. She is talking fast. "He drove out of town, on the Juan de Fuca Highway. Out to Sooke."

My mom frowns. The unicorn on her top is made of sequins that change color—pink to white—depending on which way you brush them. My mom keeps stroking them back and forth. The unicorn looks like it has a rash. My mom's face is tight with worry. "What? Sooke?" she asks Daphne.

I hold my breath, fearful that the self-revelatory spell cast between Vonda and Daphne has been broken. But I needn't have worried. Daphne is drunk and dying to continue her story. "At first, I figured this other woman, the one with red boots, lived out that way . . ."

Again, her eyes slide to Vonda's feet. I stare at her boots too. Are they real snakeskin? How many snakes had to die for those?

"But eventually it became clear," continues Daphne. "He was heading to my old summer cottage!" She gazes into her dark yard, her eyes far away. "I thought maybe he was meeting her—you—there."

"Had he been there before?" asks my mother.

Daphne shakes her head. "No, but the night before we'd talked about it, at a family dinner. Isobel was complaining . . ." She waves a be-ringed hand, like she's getting sidetracked. "Anyway, there's a framed map of the area up in Walt's office. I figured maybe Stephen saw it and decided to check the place out, maybe go find Walt's coins . . ." She swallows hard, as if still unwilling to believe Stephen Buxley was a thief, as well as a cheat. "Or just use the cabin for some private liaison."

My mom curls up her legs and rubs her sequined top. If she doesn't stop, all the sequins will wear off. "What happened next?" she asks Daphne.

"I couldn't follow too closely," says Daphne. "Or he'd spot my car. His was already parked when I got to the trailhead." She crosses her legs and smoothes down her magenta skirt. "I wasn't wearing the right shoes so it took a while to walk." Whatever she remembers next makes her grimace. She clasps her hands in her lap. Beside her, the pig snores. Daphne's false eyelashes flutter. "When I got there he was already dead," she says, softly.

My mom gasps. Vonda's eyes glitter. I'm not sure if she believes Daphne or not. Does she think Daphne killed him? Would she blame her if she had, or just wish she'd beat her to it?

Daphne blinks, like she's seeing something terrible. "He was still warm," she whispers. "And his head . . ." She touches the back of her own head and shivers. "I . . . I felt for a pulse but . . . nothing."

I take a deep breath. "When was this?" My mind is racing: Why didn't she call for help? Has she told the cops this story? Why didn't she admit to this sooner?

"Last Wednesday," says Daphne. Five days back. "Early afternoon." She pats at her frosty blonde hair. "I . . . I panicked and ran out. I knew it looked bad." She looks at Ivy, beseeching. "I'd just found out he was cheating on me and here he was, dead at my feet. I should have called 911, but I instead . . ." She blinks. "I just ran back to my car in a panic."

My mom's dark eyes are wide. She keeps rubbing at her top. The poor unicorn looks mangy, pink and white sequins stuck in every direction. "Oh dear," she says. "Then what?"

"I drove home, packed a small case, and went to the airport. Took the first flight to Vancouver I could get. From there, I flew to Denver and checked into The Sanctuary."

I nod. The flights and spa-stay will be easy for the cops to check. It's what happened before she left that matters. "Did you see anyone?" I ask.

Daphne casts her cool blue gaze my way. "At the spa?"

"No," I say. "At the Sooke cabin." This is the moment of truth. Will she admit to having seen her daughter? I wonder how much booze Grace put in that cocktail.

"I . . ." Daphne frowns down at my mom's rock. She inhales. "No." When she meets my eyes, her gaze is unflinching. "It was deserted. I saw no one."

Vonda leans back, against a fluffed pillow. My eyes find hers. On her lips is the hint of an ironic smile. We both know Daphne's lying.

I keep checking my watch, waiting for Vonda to depart. I need to talk to Daphne in private.

It's quarter to seven when Vonda finally rises, citing another engagement. A date, no doubt, with some rich, potential husband. Is it Josh? I imagine them kissing in that little red car. The thought twists my stomach.

Daphne, my mom, and I see Vonda to the front door. She shakes my hand, and Ivy's, then embraces Daphne warmly. "He vas a liar," says Vonda. "But at least he had good taste." She shrugs on her fitted leather jacket.

Daphne nods. "Yes. He was a cheating piece of shit." Her voice quivers. "But he was charming." She sighs. "I will miss him." Is this for real, or merely to convince us she wasn't mad enough to bash his head in?

Vonda nods. "Yes. Me too." She gives Daphne a sad smile. Either she's a great actress, or her regret is genuine. But no, it's not either/ or. She might be regretful *and* a great actress. Vonda clasps the older woman's elbows. "It vas good to meet you, Daphne."

The three of us watch her sashay down the lit walk. When she's reached the gate, Daphne turns to go indoors. My mom and I follow.

"Vow," says Daphne, approvingly, then realizes her mistake. "I mean wow." She shuts the door. "That Vonda is quite something."

Despite having eaten almost all Grace's homemade cookies, my stomach is growling. Maybe Daphne actually hears it because she asks us to join her for dinner. I hesitate. Since yesterday's pity-party didn't materialize, I'd been planning to go home, watch some tragic movies, and gorge on chips, red wine, and caramel ice cream. I might look at old photos of Josh. Or obsess over Vonda's Instagram, which is full of photos of Vonda looking glowing yet perfectly groomed while posed on beaches or climbing mountains. Given how urban she seems, I suspect the backgrounds are photoshopped. Her captions are equally suspect, being all about "positivity," "self-love," and "eternal gratitude." Does she come up with it herself, or has she hired an Insta-ghost writer?

Lost in thoughts of eternally grateful, self-loving Vonda, I forget Daphne asked me a question.

My mom answers for both of us. "Oh Daphne, dinner sounds love-ly," she says. "I'm famished." She gives me a nudge. "You're staying too, right, Toby?"

"Um, yes please," I say to Daphne. A postbreakup dinner of chips, wine, and melted ice cream is too big a cliché. But then, breaking up *is* a cliché. The shock, bitterness, and regret . . . The self-loathing . . . It's like being back in some crappy motel after swearing you'd never, ever stay there again. In my head, an old neon Vacancy sign blinks on.

I fight back a sigh. Enough self-pity already! Dinner with my mom and Daphne will do me good. Plus I really need to ask Daphne some hard-hitting questions.

"Great," says my mom. "Can we help, Daphne?"

Daphne leads us into the kitchen. Her heels tap on the stone floor. "No need," she says. "Grace prepared it all in advance. I hoped you'd be staying."

I expect to see Grace in the kitchen, but perhaps she's gone home. Daphne lifts the lid off a pot on the stove. The smells of tomato sauce and oregano seep out. Wow. That Grace can cook! Kevin comes run-ning. Like me, he's drooling.

"Pasta," says Daphne. "Ivy, can you grab the bowls." She gestures toward the wall only to remember that the cupboards are no longer there. "Dammit," she mutters. "I think the bowls are in there, some-where." She points to a box near the back door. My mom bends to rummage through the box. It takes her some minutes to locate the bowls. I find the cutlery and set the table. Grace has also made a big tomato and fresh mozzarella salad.

"Wine?" asks Daphne. My mom and I both nod. That will help my mood more than sage.

Daphne selects a bottle from her wine fridge. She digs in another box and locates three glasses.

We all take seats. "To closure," says my mom. She lifts her glass aloft. "And no regrets." We all clink.

I'll drink to that. Although it hardly seems possible. Who can honestly say they regret nothing, besides Edith Piaf? The wine is delicious—not the cheap plonk I usually buy. This reminds me of Josh. I take another gulp, and another.

During dinner, we keep the conversation light: my mom's latest attempts to brew the perfect kombucha (god help me); all the "noninvasive" skin rejuvenation treatments on offer at Daphne's fancy medi-spa; my uniquely smart and beautiful goddaughter, Abby.

I wait until we've all finished eating before raising the question that's been bothering me. "Daphne," I say. "Have you told the cops about finding Stephen's body?"

Her face tightens. "Not yet," she admits.

In the living room, her grandfather clock strikes eight times. It's later than I thought. I wait for Daphne to explain but she doesn't. Her face is taut.

"Well, you'd better tell them," I tell her.

Daphne bites the inside of her cheek. She looks at her empty plate and pats at her mouth with a napkin. "I know," she says. "I just . . ." She shakes her head. "I should have called 911 right away. I shouldn't have raced off. It looks so bad." She twists the napkin in her hands. "How could I have been so stupid?"

My mom sets a comforting hand on her friend's arm. "You were in shock," she says.

"I still am," says Daphne. She hangs her head. "I can barely believe he was married. And now he's dead. Murdered." A tear drips down her trembling cheek. Again, I wonder if this is all for show. But her heartbreak looks convincing. Poor Daphne.

"The longer you wait, the worse it looks," I say. It already looks awful. I clear my throat. "It might be a good idea to call Jackie." This comment is directed at my mother.

Ivy frowns. "Quinn's mom?"

Daphne reaches for her wine glass. "You mean Jackie Andriesen?"

I nod. Quinn's mom, Jackie, is one of the best criminal lawyers in town, if not the province. At this point, Daphne might need her.

Daphne swallows hard. "You . . . you think I need a lawyer?"

I shrug. "I don't know. But she might have some good advice." I drink the last of my wine. "For you and Isobel."

Daphne lowers her glass so hard that some wine splashes out. She starts to protest but stops. Her face is bitter. "So you overheard."

My mom stares from me to Daphne. "I don't understand." She blots at the spill with a napkin.

Daphne sighs. "I saw Izzie out at the cabin." Her voice shakes. "Just before I found Stephen's body."

"Oh." My mom's eyes go wide. "Oh," she says again. "Oh, Daphne."

"I'm sure it's not what you think," says Daphne. "I mean why would Izzie . . ." She trails off. "What possible motive could she have?" She coughs and reaches for her wine glass.

I can think of a few. Isobel is jockeying for control of her mom's finances. Did she know Daphne was planning to remarry? Or if both Isobel and Stephen were out to find Walt's coins, they might have fought. "Where are Walt's gold coins?" I ask Daphne.

She looks surprised. "Uh, in a safety deposit box in the TD Bank. Why?"

I'm surprised too. "So they weren't in the Sooke cabin, after all?"

Daphne reddens. "Oh, well, they were. I took them out last week, after finding . . ." She drains the last dregs of wine from her glass. "After finding Stephen's body."

I picture this new scenario. The way she told it before, she found Stephen's body, went into shock, and ran. Now she's admitted to sticking around long enough to unlock the safe. How practical. She didn't race off in a blind panic.

I try to keep my tone neutral. "The coins were in the safe?" I ask.

Daphne nods. I think back to that decrepit cabin. "Where was it?" I ask her.

"In the bedroom where Stephen was l . . . lying."

Daphne reaches for the bottle and tops up her wine glass. She turns to refill Ivy's glass but my mom puts her hand over it. "No thanks. I have to drive," she says.

"Me too," I say, when Daphne swings the bottle my way.

After setting the bottle down, Daphne regains her glass. She takes a big swig. She shuts her eyes, like she's trying to remember the scene in the cottage. "The safe's on a shelf, hidden behind a painting," she says. "A seascape."

A jolt of recognition makes me nod. I remember that painting—the way it was tilted at an angle. "Did anything look disturbed?" I ask Daphne. "When you got there?"

"Uh, no," she says. "Well . . . The safe . . ." She extends both hands to show its approximate size—about as big as a large microwave. "It was a bit twisted, like someone might have been tugging at it."

"But it was still locked?" I ask.

"Yes," says Daphne.

"And the painting," I say. "Was it hung straight when you got there?"

Daphne knuckles her brow, like it's hard to recall. "I . . . I think so. Everything looked normal, except for Stephen's b . . ." She swallows hard. "Body."

"Okay," I say. "So you took the coins and then what? Did you re-hang the painting?"

"Y . . . yes," says Daphne, although she doesn't sound too sure. "I relocked the safe. There were some old papers in there. And yes. I rehung the picture." She takes another swig of wine. "Then I got the hell out of there." Her lip quivers.

"Why do you think Stephen and Isobel were there?" I ask.

Tears fill Daphne's eyes but her voice sounds stubborn. "I don't know," she says.

I think she does but is in denial. Who wants to think that both your fiancé and your kid were trying to rip you off? Were they colluding?

"Please," says Daphne. Her tone is beseeching. She looks from me to my mom. "You can tell the police about me being there. Let's call them now. But please don't say anything about Izzie. I mean, maybe I was wrong." She swallows hard. "I . . . Please," she begs.

I shake my head. "We're not going to tell them," I say. "You are."

Daphne shakes her head even harder. "I . . . I can't. What if they get the wrong idea? What if—"

I interrupt. "Daphne," I say. "Do you think Isobel killed Stephen?"

"No!" she looks aghast. "Never! Well, maybe in self-defense . . . If she surprised him out there and he jumped her." She bows her head. "Oh God. It's so awful."

"Toby's right," says my mom. "The police are bound to find out. If it was self-defense, Iz has no reason to worry. She's never been in trouble in her life. The man was a fraudster. And a bigamist. He was breaking and entering, by the sound of it, trying to rob you."

Daphne nods. She blinks back tears. "Okay," she takes a deep breath. "I'll call the police—and Jackie—in the morning."

"Why not now?" I ask.

Daphne shakes her head even more vehemently. "I'm tired. And I've had too much to drink," she says. "I need my wits about me when I talk to the police. In the morning. I promise."

I study her strained face. Do I believe her? But what's she going to do—head back to the airport and flee the country? Even if she killed Stephen, I think she'd stick around to defend Izzie.

I rise to clear the table. "I've got some more sage smudge sticks in my bag," my mom tells Daphne. "We should smudge the upstairs. Drive out all this negativity! Then you'll be in a good place to talk to the police and get this all sorted out in the morning!"

Daphne rises shakily to her feet. "Okay," she says.

I keep quiet. It's going to take a lot more than sage and positivity to stop this train wreck. The cops are going to zero in on the Dane women. Daphne had better call Jackie.

While they're busy smudging, I load the dishwasher. Pretty soon, the whole house smells like the inside of a stuffed turkey.

It's close to nine when my mom and I exit the house. The temperature has dropped, the lawn sparkly with frost. We walk up Daphne's long path. The wind whips right through my thin pantsuit. My mom pulls up her jacket's hood and ties it under her chin, the effect elfin. "What a mess," she says. I latch Daphne's gate behind us.

Turning, I can see my mom's Honda, Easter egg yellow under a street lamp. I've hugged her and am turning to go when she stops me. "Honey?" She grasps my cold hand. "Wait."

"Yes Mom?"

Beneath her peaked hood, her face looks tiny and anxious. "You don't think she did it, do you?"

"Who?" I say. "Daphne or her daughter?"

My mom swallows hard. She jiggles her car keys. "I . . . Either, I guess."

I shrug. "I have no idea. Do you?" Why couldn't my mom be psychic, just this once? It'd make everything so much simpler.

"I think Daphne would confess if she had," says my mom. "If they'd fought. If it was a crime of passion." She chews on her lip. "She'd have gone straight to the cops and owned up."

I don't respond. We all want to think the best of those we love. "Yeah, maybe," I say. "Good night, Mom."

With a final squeeze, she releases my hand. "Get some sleep, hon." She peers into my face. "You look tired. Your aura, it's really squashed and dark tonight."

I just nod. While I don't believe in auras, squashed and dark pretty much describes how I feel. I square my shoulders and trudge to my car. All I want is a long hot shower and a good night's sleep, with no dreams about Josh and Vonda, or her and Daphne's mysterious, murdered lover.

CHAPTER 22:

CRUMBLING

It's the kind of gloomy day that give West Coast winters a bad name. The glass in my office's window seems to have been replaced by a sheet of rain. At ten to eleven, it feels like dusk, like the sun took one look at the clouds and refused to get up today.

I wish I could have stayed in bed too. All night long I dreamt of Josh and Vonda and Colin and Miri. It was like watching a kissing scene on TV as a kid, through splayed fingers: gross yet riveting. I didn't want to watch but had to.

I yawn. A double espresso barely dented my fatigue, its effects worn off, long ago. I wish I could hibernate until April.

Rather than sit and mope, with a lull between clients, I call Colin. Five rings. Six. I'm about to hang up when he picks up. "Toby!" This word is spoken with surprised joy. But his next words sound cautious. "Hey. How's it going? Are you feeling better?"

"Yes, thanks," I say. "Any chance you're free tonight? Maybe dinner and a movie?"

"Ah, I'd love to," he says. His tone is heavy with regret. "But I, uh, sorry. Just a sec." There's a squishy sound, no doubt from his hand covering his phone. "Hey, Toby?" He sounds frazzled. "You still there? Yeah, sorry about that. Um . . ." There's another pause. He sounds totally distracted. "Hey, about tonight. I'm really sorry but I'm snowed under and have to . . ." A thud, like he just dropped the phone. In the background, some new noise starts up. Hectic music. Is that cartoons? Where is he?

"Er, Toby?" He's talking really fast. "I'm really sorry but I have to go. I, um, I'll call you soon."

I can barely say "bye" before he's hung up.

I set down my phone. That kind of sucked. Him being free tonight was a long shot—it's late notice. But why didn't he make future plans? It's been ages since our last date. I hope he'll call back soon. It's hard not to feel like Colin's lost interest in me too. Has my lucky romantic star sputtered out? It barely had time to shine.

I imagine a gloomy little cartoon cloud hovering over my head, dispersing grey raindrops.

Feeling glum, I watch the rain glaze my window. It'll soon be Christmas. Another year over. I'd better make plans soon. Quinn is going to Bruce's family this year, in Calgary. And my mom always hosts half her yoga class for a big vegan Christmas dinner. They're all nice enough, just a little weird—plus about forty years my senior. And after dinner, when I just want to chill, they all sing interfaith folk songs. Kumbayfuckingya. Lord help me. I can't face it.

I sigh. The holidays. They're meant to be fun. Time for glamorous parties in metallic sweaters, cuddles beside a twinkling tree, and champagne-soaked kisses. It's not the greatest season to be single.

When my phone rings I'm on it in a flash. I'm so sure it's Colin I almost say his name. But it's my mom. "Hey hon," she says. "Want to come over for dinner tonight? Quinn's coming."

Before Abby was born, once a week, Quinn and I had dinner at my mom's. I'm pleasantly surprised that Quinn's coming tonight, leaving Bruce with the baby. "I'm making eggplant parmigiana," says my mom. My mouth is already watering. "Are you free?"

With Colin unavailable, I have no plans. "Sure, what time?" I ask. I was planning to call her soon anyway, for an update on Daphne's police interview. I wonder how it went. This is perfect: I can quiz my mom in person.

"Oh, Jackie should be here by six-thirty," says my mom. "Alistair's at a conference in Toronto."

"Oh, Jackie's coming too?" I say, surprised. I hope Daphne took my advice and called her.

"Yes," says my mom. "She's bringing her famous cheesecake. And Quinn's making a salad."

I fight back a groan. Bad luck. It's potluck. I did not inherit my mom's skills in the kitchen. My culinary talents max out at assembling a sandwich or making a salad—with store-bought dressing. And Quinn's stolen the salad option. Damn her.

I switch my phone to my other ear. Downstairs, "Last Christmas" is blasting from the jewelry shop. "This year, to save me from tears . . ." It's hard not to warble along in my head. "Er, what can I bring?" I ask my mother.

"Wine," says my mom, who's fully aware I can't cook. "Red, I think."

I nod, gratefully. "Okay. Sure thing. Thanks, Mom." I'll stop by the liquor store on the way over. Out in the lobby, the secretary is singing along to Wham! with gusto.

I'm about to ask whether Daphne has already spoken with the police when there's a knock on my door. I check my watch. My eleven o'clock: a new client. Slowly, I'm starting to get busier. "Mom," I say. "I have to go. I've got a client."

"Okay," she says. "Bye hon. Tonight will be so much fun." She sounds excited.

I force my lips into a smile so she won't hear a frown in my voice. My mom's right. I should cheer up. I love Jackie and Quinn and my mom. Tonight *will* be fun. And yet I still feel sad and rejected. First Josh, now Colin . . . I shake my head. I've got to stop being self-defeating. I should take a lesson from Insta-Vonda and embrace positivity and self-love. As they say, fake it until you make it. But ew, that sounds exhausting.

"See you soon, Mom." I set down my phone.

There's another knock, louder this time. I run a hand through my hair and sit up straighter. "Come in," I say. Time to get back to work and focus on my clients' woes, instead of my sadly flagging love life.

When I pull up out front, I see my mom has strung up her Christmas lights. Her front bushes are striped red and white. Icicle lights drip from the rafters. In the window stands her tree—potted and dragged in annually from the back porch. It makes Charlie Brown's tree look lush. I'm surprised it hasn't collapsed, given all her homemade decorations. Many of them date from my childhood.

Cradling my wine bottle I climb the red-painted front steps. I try to psyche myself up. If my mom senses I'm feeling down, she'll worry. Or ply me with revolting herbal pick-me-ups. The last thing I need is another "healthy" smoothie.

"Hello?" I turn the knob. The door's open. I peek my head around. "Hey Mom?"

The smell of molten cheese makes my tummy growl. I can hear women's laughter in the kitchen.

Quinn and Jackie are already there, both seated on my mom's mismatched chairs. I only saw Jackie's car parked out front. They must have come together. "Hi, sorry I'm late," I say.

At the sight of me, they both smile: a matched set of tall, pretty blondes. My mom is peering into her oven. "Hi, hon," she says. She extracts a casserole dish. "Perfect timing."

I wash my hands and open the wine, then select glasses from the cupboard.

"Only a taste for me," says Quinn, holding her thumb and forefinger an inch apart. I know. I know. She's still breastfeeding.

I pour a regular-sized glass for her and three supersized ones for the rest of us. After handing Jackie her glass, I lean down to kiss her. "You look great," I say. She smells of citrus and chamomile. Her eyes match her cornflower sweater.

Last summer, Jackie tripped over a dog while jogging and broke her foot, thumb, and collarbone. Luckily, she's now fully recovered and back to her usual energetic self. She and Alistair just got back from a trip to Hawaii. Unlike the rest of us, who are Arctic pale, she's glowing.

When I tell her she looks wonderful, Jackie smiles. "Thank you, dear. There's no cosmetic like a good vacation." I think of Daphne and her frozen face post–medi-spa.

I hand Quinn her wine. Compared to her mom, she looks wan and too thin. Pulled into a messy ponytail, her hair is lackluster. "How are you?" I ask.

"Great," she says, a little too brightly. Right. "How about you?"

"Oh good!" I say. Right. I doubt I'm fooling her. She lets it go, as do I, on account of our moms' presence.

I sit across from my mother. She lights some candles. "Bon appétit," she says. In the candlelight, her dark eyes and ruby earrings sparkle. She looks at each of us. "It's so lovely to have us here, all together."

Quinn is the first to dive in. As usual these days, she looks ravenous. I wait for Jackie and my mom to dig out squares before taking the spatula. My mom's eggplant parmigiana is the ultimate comfort food. After just one bite, I feel better. Tonight feels special. Great food. Decent wine (better still, it was on sale!). And the company of three wonderful women. This beats a night of moping in front of the TV, or checking my phone every two minutes.

After hearing about Jackie's trip to Kauai, I maneuver the conversation to Daphne Dane. "Did she call you?" I ask Jackie.

For a second, Jackie's face tightens. She takes a sip of wine and nods. "She did indeed. We went to the police station this morning."

"She sounded relieved to have gotten it off her chest," says my mother. "She called me shortly after."

Since Quinn's in the dark, I fill her in. She looks aghast. "So Daphne found the body before you did?" she asks me.

I nod, then look at Jackie. "How did the cops take it?"

Jackie toys with her wine glass. "Hard to tell," she says. "The detective we met with. A woman. Tall. Long reddish hair." I grit my teeth. Miri. "She was very polite but she's got a real poker face," says Jackie. "I guess that's her job." She sighs. "Daphne did well," she goes on. "She was calm and not too emotional."

I'm tempted to have more eggplant parmigiana. But what if another serving leaves me too full for Jackie's cheesecake? A dilemma. I don't want to miss out. Finally, I decide on a small helping. I maneuver the eggplant onto my plate. My stomach is already straining against my pants' waistband.

"How about Isobel?" asks my mother.

I sever the long strings of gooey cheese linking my serving to the pan. Quinn tilts her head. "Who's Isobel?" she enquires.

"Daphne's daughter," I say. "Remember? The skinny blonde from the Easter egg hunt."

"Ah," says Quinn, like all is clear. At some long-ago Easter egg hunt, Isobel went whining to her mom because Quinn and I found more candy than her—not surprising since we ran around searching, while she couldn't be bothered. Despite our superior talents and efforts, we ended up having to share our stash evenly. The resentment still lingers, which is why Communism failed miserably.

I explain how Daphne admitted to seeing her daughter at the Sooke cabin, just before finding her lover's body.

"Oh. Wow." Quinn looks at her mom. "What was the daughter's story?"

Jackie sets down her knife and fork. "She flat out denied it," she says. "She said her mom was wrong. She'd gone nowhere near the place. And her husband, Gerard, gave her an alibi."

I lower my fork. "Oh yeah?" I guess it doesn't mean much. Spouses must lie for each other all the time. "Did the police confirm Stephen's time of death?" I ask Jackie. Daphne says she went out there on Wednesday. Josh and I found the body on Saturday. That means he'd been dead for three days when we found him.

"They were asking about Tuesday and Wednesday," says Jackie. She looks somber. Her eyes slide to my mom. "Isobel claimed Daphne's been forgetting stuff, that her memory's going . . ." She sounds apologetic. "She more or less implied she's losing it."

My mom blinks angrily. "That's absurd! Daphne's sharp as a tack." She turns to me. "You saw her, yesterday." Her cheeks have colored.

I shrug. Daphne seemed fine. Finer than fine. A force of nature. But then I recall the conversation Vonda and I overheard on Daphne's front porch: Isobel's claim that Daphne approved her B&B plans, then forgot all about it.

When I recount the argument, my mom looks furious. "What a load of crock," she says. "Isobel's always been sneaky! She's after the family fortune."

I blink. That's a serious accusation. Is Isobel lying to her mom, trying to make her doubt her own sanity, just to gain control of her money? It seems so cruel, gaslighting your own mother. I recall her encouraging Daphne to see a doctor. What's she trying to do, get Daphne declared mentally unfit? Or does Isobel have a sound reason to worry?

"Are you sure?" I ask my mom. "Has Daphne said anything about this?"

My mom sets down her fork. "Isobel and Gerard have been pressuring Daphne to move into a grannie flat. Or a condo." Her lips purse. "Assisted living."

I shudder. Like most euphenisms, the phrase has a scary undertone, evoking iron lungs or robotic nurses. Surely, Daphne's a long way from needing *that*. She's more energetic than I am.

From the way Jackie's studying her empty plate, I fear she's mulling over something unpleasant. She clears her throat. "Isobel gave the police an example," she says. We all wait.

"What do you mean?" asks my mother.

"Well, apparently last month Daphne bought a giant new barbecue at The Bay." She takes a small sip of wine, like her throat's too dry to continue.

"And?" says Ivy.

"It was top of the line," says Jackie. She tucks her blonde bob behind her ears. "All the bells and whistles. We're talking a barbecue the size of a cow. Six thousand dollars." I blink, as does Quinn. Who spends that much on an outdoor grill? My mom's car isn't worth that much. "So," says Jackie. Another throat clear. "When The Bay delivered it, Daphne said they were mistaken. She claimed she'd never bought the thing. But it was paid for with her credit card. And the slip bore her signature." Jackie scratches her ear. "Daphne insisted she never bought it. Isobel says she did but forgot."

My mom looks stunned. "I . . . I don't believe it."

Looking at my mom's stricken face, I feel a quiver of fear. Daphne's only ten years her senior. How hard must it be for my mom to accept: her longtime friend and protector is getting older and weaker?

I faced a similar shock last year when my mom had breast cancer—that sudden, blinding awareness that the person who'd always been there for me, my tower of strength, could be toppled. Daphne Dane seems indestructible. But what if she's not? She looked awfully shaky yesterday, watching her daughter's angry retreat. What if the Cookie Queen is crumbling?

Jackie addresses me: "You must have seen this in Family Law," she says. "Older people making increasingly irrational decisions, getting estranged from family and old friends who are just trying to help . . . And their loved ones are left powerless . . ." She looks at my mom. "I'm not saying this is what's happening with Daphne." She sighs. "But it could be."

I nod. Jackie's right. A lot of older people won't admit they're in physical or mental decline, going to great lengths to hide the decay, even from their best friends and doctors. Someone has to be pretty far gone before a Power of Attorney will be granted against their wishes. By then they've probably racked up a slew of disastrous personal, medical, and financial decisions.

"You're wrong," says my mom. "I *know* Daphne. She might forget the odd little thing but . . ." She taps her temple. "She is not making irrational decisions."

I rise and start clearing the plates. No one wants to contradict her. But I know Jackie, Quinn, and I are all thinking the same thing: Daphne was planning to marry a guy she'd only just met, a guy determined to milk her hard-earned fortune. Conmen are predators. Like lions or wolves, they zero in on the weak, cut them away from the herd, and attack. It seems cruel to blame the victim, but one has to wonder: What was it that drew Stephen Buxley to Daphne?

CHAPTER 23:

A SLAP IN THE FACE

t's now been raining for three days straight. Today, the wind is up. Rain batters my office's window. Despite the thermals under my suit I'm still cold. Gazing down at the wind-lashed street, I can just make out the posters in the travel agent's across the road. While it's raining too hard to see the details, there's no mistaking that tropical-ocean blue. What I wouldn't give for an escape to some Caribbean island . . . Warm water. Pina coladas. Romantic couples. This vision grinds to a screaming halt. I sigh. I will not think of romance.

A knock on my door heralds the intrusion of Pamela Powell, the firm's sixty-something secretary. The grimmer the weather, the brighter Pam's outfits. Today, she's in head-to-toe fuchsia. A hot pink bow circles her bleached blonde bouffant. She whistles under her breath. "Guess who's back?" This is followed by a wink. Or it could be an eye tic. That fuchsia eyeshadow makes her look like a burn victim.

Just moments ago, I studied my day-planner: no clients scheduled until 10:15 a.m. I'm in no mood for guessing games. "Pardon?" I say.

Pamela's fuchsia lips twist into a sly grin. "Ooooh," she says. A mock sigh. "If only I were younger."

With that, she retreats. I remain standing by my window. Another knock, softer this time. "Hello?" I say. The door opens.

My breath catches in my throat. It's Josh. He peers into the room, like he's scared something might jump out at him. "Hey. Can I come in?" he asks.

I swallow hard. How good does he look? Rain is beaded on his red jacket and in his blond hair. Despite the lack of sun, he looks lit from within. I can barely speak. He'd look so great on a tropical beach, shirtless, bare chest shining in the sun . . . His eyes are the same color as that holiday ad ocean. "Sure," I say.

Josh steps in and shuts the door. He unzips his jacket. "Hi, Toby." His grin widens. "Sorry to show up unannounced but I've missed you."

I want to stagger across the room and collapse into his arms. Cue the romantic music—violins and piccolos lilting toward the crescendo: a kiss . . . Happily ever after.

Instead, some wariness holds me in place. I recall that scene in his car, the night we found Stephen's body. Josh's angry refusal to listen. And then him and Vonda, hot and heavy in her flashy red car. My stomach and fists tighten. No calls. No messages. No apology. Nothing. Why is he here now, acting like nothing happened?

Faced with my stillness, his smile slips a touch. "I . . . I'm sorry," he says. "Can you give me another chance? I overreacted. We can take it slow. Take our time getting to know each other more . . ." His gaze is laser-hot.

I feel myself starting to melt. I am moving toward him.

He meets me half way. His strong arms encircle my back. I am lifted off the floor, his chest warm and solid against mine. Oh my god. His lips are hot. That kiss. Like the first kiss I ever had, as a teen, me and Josh, in the woods, the air redolent with passion and pine sap. We are fourteen again, everything happening for the first time, all brand new. A fresh start. My knees buckle.

The kiss goes on and on, both of us drinking each other in. Like we were parched. Dying of thirst. We cross the room, pressed together. My back is now up against my desk. He lifts me onto it. My arms and legs circle him. His fingers twist in my hair. I squeeze him like my life depends on it. We belong on the cover of a Harlequin romance.

Until my door opens.

"Toby?"

A swish of silk and a tap-tap of stilettos. A furious gasp. "Vhat? I don't believe it!"

I turn in dismay. Beneath her raspberry beret, Vonda's face is livid. Her eyes flash gamma rays. Her raspberry lips snarl with fury.

Oh shit.

Josh lets me go. He straightens. I sit up. My feet hit the floor with a dull thud, like an echo of my sinking heart.

Vonda strides closer. "Men!" she spits. She points a red talon at Josh. "How could you?" Her dark mane sways ominously. "You vere vith me!" She lunges closer.

Josh shrinks back but is too slow.

The sound of her palm striking his cheek makes me flinch. "Bastard!" she hisses.

Josh raises a hand to his face. He takes a step back. "Vonda, please!"

Again, he's too slow. Another loud smack. This time, her ring gouges his cheek. It draws blood. "Ow!" gasps Josh. He cups his face.

"Vonda!" I say. "Stop it!"

She rounds on me. "You?" She looks me up and down. "He is vith . . . you?" A dismissive wave, like I'm a bug, unpleasant but harmless, not worth the bother of squishing. She turns back to Josh, eyes flashing like a ninja's knives. "You vill regret this!"

She spins on her heels and strides out of my office.

I blink. The door slams behind her. In her wake, the room is dead quiet. The smell of her perfume—too heavy, too floral—lingers.

Josh is still holding both cheeks. I pluck a tissue from the box on my desk and hold it out to him. He takes it with a frown. After some hesitation, he presses it to his bleeding cheek. "I . . . I'm sorry about that," he says. His voice is deep with regret. He steps closer.

I cross my arms. The spell of desire has broken. I feel angry and embarrassed. But why am I embarrassed? He's the one who deceived Vonda.

Josh rakes a hand through his blond curls. "I . . ." He looks shocked. "Do you know her?"

"She was my client," I say. "When did you meet her?"

He shrugs. "A few weeks back."

Immediately I'm on red alert. Did his liaison with Vonda precede the night he dumped me?

"We recently had a . . ." He pats at his cheek. "A thing," he says.
"A thing," I repeat.

"Yeah, I mean, after you and I agreed to stop seeing each other."
He frowns. As do I. I never agreed to anything. It was all his decision.
"Look," he says. "That was awkward. I'm sorry. But she doesn't mean
anything." He looks toward the door, like he's scared she'll come back.
The office's front door slams. Josh looks relieved. When he speaks
again, he sounds more confident. "Me and her," he says. "It was nothing."

Once again, I feel cold all over. While I don't like Vonda, there's
much to admire about her. She is a tough and resourceful woman. If
Josh can dismiss her and her feelings just like that, he could do the
same to me. It shows a lack of respect—for her, for me, for others.

I recall Quinn's dislike of him. Her assertion that he's selfish. I
know she's right. And yet. How can I not want more of those kisses—
like that moment in a dream when you discover you can fly, before
Vonda barged into my office?

I shiver. Josh steps closer. His arms reach out to me. "Please Toby,"
he says. His hands grasp my elbows. "I really missed you."

At his touch my misgivings crumple, reason no match for chemistry. Every cell in my body pulls his way in a tide of pure longing.

I'm just about to embrace him when my phone dings. A reminder
of my 10:15 appointment. Out in the lobby I hear Pamela greet someone. I wonder where she was when Vonda stormed in and out. Probably
cowering under her desk. Or adding a fresh layer of fuchsia cosmetics
in the restroom.

I lean back, torn between relief and regret. I'm at work. This is not
the time or place to make up or break up. Romantic dramas have no
place in my office. My clients deserve my full attention.

Seeing Josh's eager gaze, I'm tempted to apologize but don't.
There's polite and there's being a pushover. "Look, I can't deal with
this right now," I tell Josh. "I'm at work. I have a client. She's outside,
waiting."

His jaw tightens. He lets go of my elbows. Then his smile returns, dazzling me. "Okay. You're right. I'll call you soon." His confidence shines bright, catching me in its spotlight.

I nod. Do I want that?

My mind says *no, it's over.* Everything below my neck shrieks *hell yes.*

At my door he turns. "I really care about you, Toby."

I stare at the closing door. My stomach is in knots. Is this love? Such intense highs and lows . . . I realize I'm shaking.

Out in the lobby I hear Pamela coo a goodbye. I walk to the window and look into the street, as if this might clear my head. I don't feel ready to see a client. It's like I just crawled off a rollercoaster.

The street is empty. No cars. No people. But then a man comes into view. Tall and fit. He has short, dark hair. When he gets closer, I realize it's Colin Destin. There's a splash of warmth deep in my gut. Is he coming to see me?

Colin is walking fast. I see him look up at my window. He looks serious and determined.

Then Josh emerges from my building. Colin stops in his tracks. A look of uncertainty crosses his face. Josh turns the opposite way. He strides toward View Street. I don't think he saw Colin.

I wait for Colin to start walking again. Instead, he just stares at Josh's retreating back, then studies my window. Can he see me? I feel a bit silly, like I've been caught spying on him. I raise a hand and smile. But no, there's some special clear-coating to stop people from looking in. I am invisible, or a blurry shape at best. I lower my hand. And cross my fingers.

I know he can't see me, but Colin keeps looking up, like he can sense me. There's a strange, sad look on his face. Or am I just imagining that? He gazes back down the street toward Josh's retreating back. Colin's broad shoulders hunch. He shoves his hands deep into his coat. His chin rises, some decision made. I watch, bewildered, as he spins and walks back the way he came. He is walking away.

Was he planning to come see me and then, seeing Josh, changed his mind? Regret courses through me like cold rain. I uncross my fingers. It didn't work. I want to call him, ask him to come back but there's no time. There's a knock on my door.

I turn away from the window.

I'm unsure what to feel about Josh but have no doubts about Colin. Tonight, I will call him, when I'm done work. The thought warms me. Finally, I'm sure. I need to let him know that I miss him.

CHAPTER 24:

A SORRY STATE

'm eating a bowl of tomato soup in front of the TV when my phone rings. My first thought is Colin. I've tried to call him repeatedly, without success. Or it might be Josh. At the memory of today's kiss, my stomach spins. I do want to talk to him, yet know I shouldn't. Maybe, just like Lukas, *I* need rehab.

There are no mixed feelings about Colin. Colin is good for me. Please let it be him.

"Hello?" I sound hopeful.

"Honey?"

My heart deflates a bit. It's my mother. Instantly, I feel guilty. My mom is not second best. "Hi, Mom!" I speak with extra good cheer. I pat the couch in an effort to find the remote. It's under a cushion. I turn down the TV's volume.

I'm about to ask how she is but don't get the chance. "It's Daphne," she says. She's talking fast. "There's something's wrong. She's . . ." The line fades and crackles.

"Mom?" I say. I deposit my bowl on the coffee table and jump up, like that might help our connection. My mom's tone was all wrong. "Mom?" I stare into the receiver.

"Honey?"

I'm relieved she's back. "Mom? Are you okay?" I'm scared we'll be cut off again. "Mom? Where are you?"

"I'm at Daphne's," says my mom. "She's in trouble."

"What? How?" I ask, already imagining the worst. Daphne fallen down the stairs. Or worse. My voice is sharp. "What's going on? What happened?"

"I . . ." The sound deadens again. I hear my mom say something. Her voice is muffled. Then she's back. "Hon?" she says. "I need your help. Please come over."

"Now?" I say. It's a wild night. You wouldn't send a dog out in this weather. But given her tone, there's no choice. She sounds more than worried. She sounds fearful.

"Mom?" My alarm spikes. "What's going on?" My heart starts to thud. Maybe she should be calling 911 instead of me. What if Stephen's killer has come after Daphne? I envision some dark, shadowy figure creeping through that huge old house. "Mom!" Why isn't she answering? "What's going on there?"

I can hear another voice now, like Daphne's but slurred. Is she drunk?

"Don't worry," says my mom, in a tone that increases my worry. "I'm fine. Really. I swear. Just come over."

The rain feels apocalyptic, Victoria's streets even emptier than usual. My windshield wipers can't keep up. Every street seems extra dark. Through the deluge, the street lights glow as feebly as gas lamps.

I perch on the edge of my seat, trying to peer through the torrent. The heat's on high but I'm freezing. The radio whines. Every station except Golden Oldies 101 has bad reception. They're counting down the Eagles.

My mom's car looks forlorn out front of Daphne's place. I park behind it.

Seen from the street, Daphne's house belongs in a Victorian ghost story, all dark, pointy roofs, wrought iron trim, and flailing shrubbery. I eye the creepy turret. Most of the many windows are dark. On cue, lightning flashes. I grab my purse and my umbrella. Thunder crashes.

When I step out of my car, rain splashes up from the pavement. My feet slosh through deep puddles.

It's a mad scurry to Daphne's front porch. I knock. The pig squeals. I collapse my umbrella and shake it out. I toss it down, kick off my squelching shoes. My socks are wet.

The door opens to a fresh roll of thunder.

"Toby!" My mom looks relieved. "Come in." I slip inside. The door clicks behind me. After sniffing me, the pig retreats toward the kitchen. "What a night!" exclaims my mother. She's dressed in a long, sedate charcoal knit dress with pink tights underneath. From her neck hangs a long leather cord and a smooth, heavy, rose quartz pendant—a stone to relieve stress and resentful feelings.

I study her face, note the strain in her jaw. "What happened?"

She doesn't answer but motions upstairs. I shrug off my raincoat— wet, despite the umbrella—and hang it from the coat rack. "She's up there," says my mother.

I follow her upstairs, down the long hall, into Daphne's room. While the sitting room looks pristine, Daphne's bedroom is in disarray. A nightstand has been knocked over. A lamp—still lit—lies on its side, its shade tilted. Light spills across the floor to illuminate a small Persian carpet, its intricate cream and gold pattern stained with some dark liquid.

Is that blood? I bite back a gasp. But then I see a mug. A larger stain spreads around it.

My mom ignores the mess and walks to Daphne's bed. I follow.

Surrounded by ornate pillows Daphne's face looks as small and pale as a sick child's. Only her face and hands peek over the sheet. Eyes shut, she is almost as white as the Egyptian cotton. I clutch my purse. Is she—? I don't even dare think it.

"Daphne?" says my mom. "Toby's here."

Daphne's eyes flutter open. She blinks in confusion. "Ivy?" she says. "I feel sho shtrange . . ." Her head shakes, feebly before it flops down. It's like her neck lacks the strength to hold her head up.

"I . . . What happened?" I ask. Has she had a stroke? Is she drunk? Or drugged? This looks serious. "I think we should call an ambulance!"

Daphne's eyes and mouth gape in horror. "No!" she exclaims. "Ishobel will find out! Pleashe! No!" She struggles to sit up but can't manage.

The violence of her reaction makes me pause. "Find out what?" I ask.

"My medsh," says Daphne. "I . . . I shink I took too many pillsh. A double doshe. Ishie shays I'm forgetting shtuff." Her face crumples. She starts to cry, quietly.

"There, there," says my mom, gently. "Please, Daphne, don't worry."

"What pills are those?" I ask.

My mom retrieves a jar off the floor. It must have fallen off the toppled nightstand. She hands me the jar. I squint at the tiny print. A long name that means nothing to me. "What's it for?" I ask Daphne.

"My blood presshure . . ." says Daphne.

I look around. On Daphne's other nightstand rests a wine glass. Maybe she mixed the pills with booze. "Daphne?" I say. "Did you drink anything alcoholic?"

Daphne's forehead tugs against the Botox. "A glash of wine," she says. "And shome cocoa."

Cocoa. That might explain the stain on the rug.

"Pleashe," croaks Daphne. "I'm sho thirshy."

While I fail to understand her, my mom does. "She's thirsty," she tells me. I look around for a glass. That mug will do just fine.

I bend to retrieve it and carry it into the en suite bathroom.

I'm about to rinse it out when I notice some residue in the bottom. Along with a brown sludge of undissolved cocoa there's a gritty white powder. It's not sugar.

Was Daphne drugged?

I can still hear her crying.

There's a bottle of Evian and two upturned glasses in the bathroom, just like you'd find in a fancy hotel. I grab a glass and the Evian.

The bedroom is just as I left it. I hand the water to my mom, who guides it to Daphne's shaking lips. I watch her drink. I think we should call 911. But when I say this, Daphne grows hysterical. She keeps repeating the same thing: "No! Pleashe, no! Don't tell Ishie! She'sh convished I've got Alsheimersh!"

It's heartbreaking to see Daphne like this—so unwell but even worse, so afraid of Isobel's condemnation.

I'm still trying to decide what to do when I hear a door shut downstairs. I freeze, freshly reminded of the gruesome scene in Daphne's cottage. Did my mom lock the front door after letting me in? Stephen's killer is still out there, somewhere. My ears strain. It's hard to swallow.

I tiptoe back through Daphne's suite and out into the hall. Is that just the pig or are those footsteps down below?

Outside, there's a fresh bang of thunder. Maybe I'm paranoid. Ever since finding Stephen's corpse, I've been on edge. I take a deep breath and call out: "Hello? Who's there?" My voice has a wobbly echo.

Something scuffles. My unease balloons into dread. My knees go shaky.

I'm pressed against the wall, considering my options, when a voice replies: "It's me. Grace." She sounds suspicious. "Who's up there?"

An exhale of relief propels me to the top of the stairs. I find the light switch and peer over the landing.

The antique chandelier blazes to life. I blink. It's like something off the Titanic.

In the sudden glare, Grace squints up at me. Clad in a green rain poncho, she's got a shopping bag in each hand. Beneath her shiny green hood, her round cheeks look like apples. "Oh Toby!" She sounds equally relieved. "Gracious! You scared me!" She deposits the bags with two clunks. "What are you doing here, in this weather?"

"Daphne's sick." I gulp. "My mom found her."

Grace's mouth gapes in alarm. Without bothering to remove her wet poncho she races up the stairs, two at a time. "What's wrong?" she cries. Calling Daphne's name, she rushes past me before I can answer.

"Grashe?" croaks Daphne, as Grace enters the room.

My mom's sitting on the bed, clasping Daphne's hand. There's more color in Daphne's cheeks, although her gaze remains vacant.

Seeing them, Grace stops, aghast. "Goodness gracious!" She yanks down her hood. "Oh Daphne! What is it?"

My mom fills her in. Grace strides closer. She pushes some wet hair from her eyes and turns to my mom. "We should call Dr. Wagner!"

"No! No!" whimpers Daphne. "Ishie wansh to put me in a home!" Again, she starts sobbing.

I feel helpless. It's so hard to reconcile this pitiful, trembling old lady with the strong woman I've always known. Her fear of Isobel is sad. No, it's more than sad. It's scary. If Daphne were incapacitated, her fate would be in her kids' hands. They'd have the power to order her resuscitated or not. Or to turn off her life support. This thought is chilling.

"Daphne, hush," orders Grace. "No one's calling Izzie. But I am calling Doctor Wagner."

We all watch her dial. She puts the call on speakerphone. "Dr. Wagner? It's Grace Hornichuck here. Daphne Dane's housekeeper. Sorry to wake you but it's urgent . . ." I listen as Grace explains. "No. I don't think she requires an ambulance. Good," she says. "Thank you."

After hanging up, Grace looks relieved. "He's on his way." She peels off her rain poncho and carries it into the adjoining bathroom.

I recall the mug sitting on the bathroom counter. That white residue troubles me. I don't want Grace to wash it.

I follow her in. As she turns to hang her wet raincoat in the shower stall, I grab the mug. Grace looks surprised. "Excuse me," I say, already retreating.

I carry the mug downstairs to the kitchen. It takes a while to find what I need: a box of cling film. I wrap the mug carefully and hide it in the depths of my purse.

In the living room, Daphne's grandfather clock strikes once. I check my watch: 9:30 p.m.

I set my bag on the stairs. I should pass that mug on to Colin Destin.

The pig starts to squeal. Footsteps shudder up the front steps. The bell rings.

"Hello?" I call out. I walk to the door.

"Hello," says a deep male voice. "I'm Doctor Wagner."

Through the peephole, I see a round, pink nose and a round, bald pink head. Beneath this, lies a round belly, shiny in a wet yellow raincoat. One tiny hand holds an old-style black briefcase.

"Thank goodness," I say and unlock the door. I'm relieved the doctor's here. I just hope I'm wrong about Daphne.

CHAPTER 25:

DARK SHAPE

My mom, Grace, and the doctor are in with Daphne. I shut the door to her suite and walk down the hall, then sit at the top of the staircase. Down below me, the chandelier twinkles. It has five tiers of sparkly, faceted crystals.

I dial Colin's number. It rings and rings. I can't help but count: Six, Seven. I hang up with a sigh and check my call log: I've called him four times tonight with no answer. A few weeks back, he never missed my calls. Ever. Is he trying to avoid me, hoping I'll take the hint and stop calling? Surely not—this isn't high school.

Moments later, he calls back. "Hi, Toby?" His voice is strained, like he's anxious or exhausted.

Despite his tone, I'm relieved he called—for both romantic and practical reasons. He's finally returned my missed calls. And as a policeman, he'll know what to do. "Colin," I say. "Sorry to call so late." It must be close to ten. "I'm at Daphne Dane's place."

I describe the night's events, and Daphne's condition. "Before she fell ill she drank a little wine," I say. "And some cocoa."

Just when I'm getting to the white grit in the bottom of the mug, Colin cuts me off. "Er, 'scuse me," he says. The line goes quiet. I peer at my screen. Have we been cut off?

The storm might be to blame. From here, I can see down the stairs to Daphne's front door. A flash of lightning illuminates the stained glass window. The line crackles.

Colin's back. He sounds impatient. "Hey Toby? Sorry, what were you saying?"

I backtrack a little.

"White powder?" says Colin. "Um. Okay, ah . . ." There's a loud crash on his end. Colin swears under his breath. I wonder what he's doing while he's talking to me.

Whenever he calls I give him my full attention. What's so important that he can't focus on me for three minutes?

He sounds so distracted I decide to spell it out. "This white residue," I say. "I'm worried she's been drugged. Or poisoned." I explain about Isobel's claim that Daphne's mind is deteriorating. "Can you test the mug?" I ask Colin.

"Um . . ." Again, the pause is so long I fear we've been cut off. "Test?" He sounds vague. I grit my teeth. Has he even been listening?

I start to explain again but he interrupts. "Toby, I, ah . . . Can I call you back?"

I'm ready to snap and tell him not to bother but the line is already disconnected.

Maybe five minutes later my phone rings. Should I answer? I take a deep breath. I need to calm down. Who knows what crisis he's facing? Maybe he's been chasing down some crook. Or tracking a ransom demand on the other line.

I pick up. "Hello, Colin?"

Down the line, I hear a woman laugh. Every muscle in my body goes rigid. It was such a teasing, delighted laugh. The laugh of a woman in love. Now she's talking, a low murmur, equally loving.

What she's saying is unclear but her identity isn't: Miri, her voice low and sexy. My vision swims. He's with Miri. They sure don't sound like they're working.

I clamp my eyes shut. My heart follows.

"Toby?" says Colin. "Can you hear me, Toby? Sorry, we got cut off."

"It's fine." My voice is as tight as my heart, a grey, curled-up armadillo. "Can you test that mug or not?" I say, stiffly.

"Okay, I think so," he says. Maybe he sounds a touch hurt, as well as confused and distracted. "I'm sorry but I'm, ah, occupied right now."

I fight back the ensuing image of Miri, stifling a giggle as she nuzzles his ear. "I'll send an officer over to bag it. You're at Daphne Dane's, right? Near my place?"

I don't answer. I've never been to Colin's place.

"In Rockland?" he continues.

"Right."

"Okay, right . . ." His voice goes quiet then loud. "Oh no, baby," he exclaims, like he's talking to someone else.

When the line goes dead I'm not sure whether I hung up or he beat me to it.

My mom and the doctor have both left. I'm still stuck here, waiting for the policeman to come and collect Daphne's mug. When a half hour has passed, I call Colin. It goes straight to voicemail. I call again. And again. He doesn't answer.

The longer I wait, the more aggravated I feel. He said he lived nearby. Should I drop the damn thing off? All I want is to go home and get a good night's sleep. It seems Colin forgot all about this.

I text Quinn. There's a high chance she'll be sound asleep, which is why I don't call.

hey quinn - what's colin's address?

To my surprise, she answers right away. She sends an address. A quick check of Google maps confirms his place is around the corner.

I'm about to stash my phone when Quinn texts again.

why? you going over?

This is followed by a winking emoji. I think of Pamela Powell.

maybe tomorrow - I reply. A white lie. This story is way too long to explain. And "maybe never" would raise too many questions I lack the energy to answer.

Quinn's response appears in a flash.

go now & surprise him. wear some sexy lingerie under your raincoat. More winks and sexy kisses.

I roll my eyes. Who is this woman? Next thing she'll recommend I wrap my naked body in cling film. This reminds me of the mug in my handbag.

I text back: **go to sleep u perv.** It takes a minute to find the snoring emojis.

Phone back in my purse, I go to find Grace. She's staying the night, which is reassuring. Grace is the sort of calm, competent pioneer woman you'd want by your side in a crisis, the kind who could chop firewood, bind a wound, and pickle enough cabbage to get you through the long, dark Canadian winter.

And yet . . . Am I naive to trust her? If I'm right about the white residue, who had a better chance to drug Daphne's cocoa than her beloved housekeeper? Although the why is hard to fathom. Plus, Grace seemed genuinely shocked to find Daphne ill. I recall her sprinting up the stairs.

Grace is in the kitchen, pouring detergent into the dishwasher. Despite her quick movements, she looks tired. Surely, that could wait until morning.

"Grace," I say. "You should call it a night. It's been a long day. You must be exhausted."

"Oh, it's no trouble," says Grace. She straightens and unties her apron. "I like things tidy. It's nice to wake up to a clean kitchen."

I agree. But still. I'd make an exception tonight. "Okay, well, good night," I say. "I'm going home now."

Grace pulls off her apron and yawns. "Good night. Lock the door, dear. And drive carefully."

I promise I will and retreat down the hallway.

After double-checking the door, I force my feet into my sodden shoes. I don't even bother to open my umbrella as I sprint to my car. The storm is still raging. The puddles are even deeper.

I slide my damp self into my seat and lock the car's doors. That short run has set my chest heaving.

Rain clatters against the car's metal roof and cascades down the windows. I should get going but need to gather my thoughts. Anxiety has stiffened my neck. I squeeze my sore shoulders.

I think of the doctor—who treated Daphne's husband Walt and has known her for decades. He seemed unconvinced that too many blood pressure pills were to blame. He guessed she took something else and drank more than she claimed. Daphne denied this, then admitted she couldn't remember.

I tried to question the doctor about Daphne's recent health but he clammed up, probably worried about patient confidentiality. He promised to stop by again in the morning.

I'm startled by a crash of thunder. The car's interior is bright with lightning. After that brief flash, the darkness seems even deeper. I peer into the rain. Daphne's street stretches desolate. Rain and trees are the only things moving.

I dig through my purse and pull out Daphne's mug, then set it on the passenger seat. I retrieve my phone to find Colin's address. Can I really face him tonight? What if he's there with Miri?

Eyes shut, I replay our last conversation: Colin's distraction, Miri's tinkly, delighted laughter. I rub my temples. What if I got it all wrong? Maybe they *were* working, sitting in their office, or side-by-side in their unmarked car.

Miriam might have been on the phone too, talking to her husband or boyfriend. I know nothing about her private life. Was that image of her whispering sweet nothings in Colin's ear just a product of my jealous, paranoid imagination? Maybe I got the wrong end of the stick. Or there is no stick, apart from the one I'm using to beat my own happiness into a soggy pulp. God, what's wrong with me, assuming the worst about a great guy? So Colin's busy at work. He's trying to find a vicious killer! I need to stop being so insecure about Miriam Young. She's his police partner. For all I know, she's happily married with a gaggle of kids. While this is hard to believe, given her perfect physique, it's not impossible. She might be the ultimate yummy-mummy. Or else she's just happily married. I try to picture Mr. Young. In my head he's a male version of Miriam. A fellow superhero. Long and lean. Wholesome but dashing. Oh no, I'm picturing Colin . . .

By now, I've forgotten Colin's street number, again. My brain is mush. I scroll back through Quinn's texts—all those winks and sexy kisses.

Am I brave enough to surprise Colin? I unzip my raincoat and peer down my top, see my black satin bra. I'm pretty sure I chose matching undies. That's more than sexy enough. But what am I planning—to strip in my freezing car? Even with the heat blasting, it's Siberia. The idea is so ludicrous I smile for the first time in ages.

I peer into my rearview mirror. While it's too dark to see much, I don't look so bad, considering my night—and recent dearth of sleep. I pinch my cheeks to add color. Maybe Colin will invite me in. I fluff the back of my hair and smile winningly into the tiny mirror. "Hi, Colin," I say and wink at myself. Over-tiredness is tipping into hysteria. I fight down a snigger.

I turn on the headlights and pull away from the curb. This could be a great night, after all. I imagine me and Colin snuggled up together, safe and warm while the storm rages. Finally, the car's heater seems to be working.

Between Daphne's and Colin's places I don't see a single moving car. No people. No dogs or cats. Even the raccoons are hiding. It's hard to see the house numbers in the deluge. But then I find it.

Colin lives in a big old mansion that's been converted into flats. I pull up out front. The building is set on a low hill, overlooking the street. I gaze up at it. Only two windows are lit: one on the second story and the other on the top floor. As I watch, a man walks in front of the second-floor window. He's holding a glass, his back turned to the street. My heart squirms. Even in silhouette, I recognize him right away: broad shoulders and narrow back. He moves his free hand, like he's gesturing to someone.

And then another figure appears, also silhouetted against the light. A woman. Tall and slender. Like a black ink drawing of the perfect woman. My stomach twists and drops. I recognize her too. Miriam Young. Perhaps she's tired, or upset, because her shoulders droop. She raises her hands to her head, in fatigue or frustration.

Colin strides closer. I grip the wheel as he enfolds her in a hug. She bends toward him. Her forehead rests on his shoulder.

I shut my eyes and bury my face in my hands. Of course he's with Miriam Young. I knew it. I knew it. And yet I let myself hope.

I shouldn't be here.

I feel a moment of sick panic. Colin knows my car. What if he looks out and sees me here, watching? I'll feel even more pathetic. Like some crazy, desperate stalker.

That mug be damned. I'll drop it off tomorrow, at the police station.

I pull away from the curb. My vision is blurry.

The whole way home I blink tears from my eyes. Why didn't Colin just tell me? The betrayal hurts worse than losing him. I thought he was a good person. An honest and upstanding guy. If he prefers Miri, why didn't he say so?

But then I remember him earlier today, gazing up at my office window. He must have been coming to tell me, then seen Josh and decided not to bother.

By the time I pull up outside my building my nose is clogged from crying. Before Stephen's murder, things with Colin seemed great. We had so much fun. I thought we were getting closer. Maybe I was wrong about everything. Maybe I misread every signal.

There are no tissues in my car. Typical. I scour my face on my sleeve. I pray the lobby is empty. Half my fellow tenants survive on digestive biscuits, prunes, and gossip. Meeting me in this state would make their week. I can't face their nosy, solicitous questions.

I bow my head against the rain and run down the walkway.

Luckily, the lobby is deserted, but for me and the leering Chucky angel. It looks more malevolent than usual.

I'm so tired I can barely climb the stairs, yet once in bed, sleep is a pipe dream.

That silhouette won't leave my head: Colin and Miriam like a cutout on a romantic greeting card. How long have they been together? And why didn't Colin tell me?

I thought he cared for me, at least enough to be honest. He's an old friend of Bruce and Quinn's. Quinn said he was crazy about me.

I can't help but feel resentful. I trusted Colin and I trusted Quinn. What if I'd actually followed her dumb advice and shown up on his doorstep wearing nothing but gonch under my raincoat? For a moment, I actually considered it! My cheeks burn at the thought. I curl into a ball. How could my judgement be so awful?

CHAPTER 26:

A BAD AFTERTASTE

I'm in the bath when my doorbell rings. I ignore it but it rings again. And again. Then my mobile starts buzzing. I shake the water off my hands.

My phone rests on the shut toilet lid. I grasp it carefully. It'd be just my luck to drop it in the bathtub.

It could be Josh. Or Colin. In the past few days they've both called repeatedly. Whatever they want to say, I don't want to hear it. At least not yet. I keep thinking of Vonda's shocked fury after catching Josh kissing me in my office. And Colin embracing Miriam. Maybe they're more similar than I thought—and not in good ways.

A glance at my phone's screen reveals I needn't have worried: it's my mother. "Toby?" The way she says it revives my worry. "I need to talk to you," she says. "Where are you?"

"In the bath," I say. "Where are you?"

"Outside your door."

I fight back a sigh. So much for my revitalizing soak. I even used the lavender bath bomb my mom gave me last Christmas. Lavender's meant to induce relaxation. "Hold on," I say. I feel anything but relaxed. "Give me two minutes."

I'm still half-wet when I slip on my robe and pad, dripping, to my front door. I crack it open. The towel that was around my hair slides to the floor. I bend to retrieve it.

My mom charges inside. Beneath her purple raincoat she's dressed for yoga.

"Hi, Mom."

She tosses down her umbrella, drops her yoga mat, and kicks off her wellies. "This weather!" she says. She peels off her raincoat. In her pea-green yoga tights, her skinny legs resemble a frog's. Overtop, she's wearing a baggy grey top with a yellow Smiley Face. Her own face is anything but.

"Half my garden is underwater!" continues my mom. She stomps into my small kitchen and starts opening and closing cupboards. "Where's the herb tea?"

I rewrap my hair. There goes my chance of sliding back into my hot lavender-infused bath. "Top left." I say.

Another cupboard door slams. What's gotten my mom so riled up? I slide past her and fill the kettle. "How are you?" I venture.

My mom frowns at a yellow box. "Chamomile?"

"Uh, sure," I say, although I hate chamomile. I only bought it for her. But I don't want tea right now, anyhow.

She locates two mugs and sets them onto the counter with two loud clunks. I bite my tongue. Those are fine china! Unlike her, I don't shop at Value Village.

"Is everything okay?" I say. I can't recall when my mom's next mammogram is due. What if she's had bad news? My throat tightens. I need to keep better track. I'm a bad daughter.

"I'm fine," she says, but doesn't sound it. "It's not me." She pours the boiling water. Some of it misses the mugs and puddles on my counter. She doesn't bother to wipe it.

I follow her, meekly, to the living room.

Of course, she sets the mugs right on the coffee table, ignoring my impressive array of coasters. She flops onto the sofa and tosses one, two, three pillows to the side. She turns one way and the other way but can't get comfortable. She's like a little flea-ridden dog—itchy and jumpy.

I take an armchair. I resist the urge to ask what's wrong. No matter what, she'll say she's fine. I need to wait her out. When she's ready, she'll tell me.

She grabs her tea and takes a long sip. Chamomile, like lavender, is meant to be soothing. Maybe it actually works. Although it's probably just the power of suggestion. Some of the tension drains from her face. She takes another sip. "It's Daphne," she says.

I wait. Now what? My mom said she'd recovered well, after that incident three nights back. Has she had another health scare?

"The police came to see her early this morning," says my mom. "That white powder you found in her cocoa. You were right. It was a sleeping pill called Ativan." Her knuckles are as white as the cup she's clutching. "She's never been prescribed it."

"Oh," I say. My throat's suddenly so dry I reach for my chamomile tea. It tastes awful, as expected, but at least it's warm and wet. I cough. "That's crazy."

I swallow. It's one thing to suspect something dreadful, and another to learn it's true. Someone drugged Daphne Dane. "Can it cause memory loss?" I ask my mother.

While she looks angry, I know it's fear she's feeling. "Yes," she says. Her lip quivers. "And death, at high doses."

I swallow harder. I recall the large stain on Daphne's cream rug. Most of that cocoa was undrunk. What would have happened if she'd downed the whole mug? I shiver. Was someone trying to kill her? Or just trying to make it seem like she's losing her marbles? Either way, it's unspeakably cruel. Someone hates Daphne enough to want to end her life, or destroy her peace of mind. Erode her self-worth and sanity. That's worse than just murdering her.

I recall her a few nights back, sobbing piteously. How scared and lost she seemed.

My mother starts to cry. "It's just . . . Who could do that to her?" she sniffs. "This man, Stephen . . . I tell myself he wasn't a good person, like that makes his death justified, somehow. I know that's not right but, well . . ." Her voice quivers. "You know, karma."

I nod, having done the same thing. I fetch her some tissues.

She blows her nose. "But Daphne." She hiccups. "Daphne's helped so many people, not just us. Her work for charity." She rubs her eyes. "I know life's not fair but this seems . . ." She shudders. "It seems evil."

For some minutes we sit in silence, trying to take this news in. Who would do such a thing? And who could do such a thing?

I clear my throat. "Who made Daphne's cocoa?"

My mom sighs. "She has no idea," she says. "The whole night is a big blank. She has no memory of us being there, or the doctor. She doesn't even remember that the whole family was over, earlier that night, for dinner."

I mull this over. "The whole family?"

"Lukas. Izzie and Gerard." My mom dabs at her eyes. "And Grace," she says.

I frown. "But Grace arrived after us," I say. Now that I think about it, that's odd. By then it was close to 9:30 p.m. Why was Grace stopping by so late—and on such a miserable night?

"She was working earlier," says my mom. "But ran out to the shops. They'd run out of dishwashing detergent. She didn't want the plates to get all crusty."

I recall Grace bent over the dishwasher as I was leaving. Couldn't she have just left the dishes to soak in the sink overnight? But Grace seems to take her job very seriously. She's an obsessive neat freak, I'd say. She was still cleaning when I finally left, close to eleven.

I tuck my feet up under me and shiver. "Do you know if the police have any theories? Do they think it's related to Stephen's murder?"

My mom chews on her bottom lip. "The police . . ." She balls her hands into fists. "They don't believe Daphne's story." She tugs at her blue lace agate (calming) choker. If she's not careful, she'll break it. "They insinuated that Daphne had a guilty conscience!" Her voice rises. "That she . . ." She waves a hand and scowls. Her dark eyes are bright with tears and fury.

I rub my forehead. I'm not following. While Daphne is a suspect in Stephen's murder, surely, her drugged cocoa suggests there's more to the story. It must be linked: one murder and one attempted murder. Both crimes must have been committed by the same person.

My mom keeps tugging at her choker. "The detectives suggested she took the Ativan knowingly," she says. "That she meant to, you know . . ." Her voice cracks. "It's absurd!" she cries.

I recoil in horror. "Oh," I say. "But that's crazy." The cops think Daphne attempted suicide. Do they suspect she did it in a fit of remorse or because she's scared they can prove she killed her cheating lover? Do they know something we don't? Daphne was at the murder scene. I bet she has a vicious temper. I can picture her swinging that poker.

"Daphne would never try to kill herself," says my mom. "It's not in her nature."

I nod. I agree with my mom. Even if Daphne bashed Stephen, and fears the cops are on to her, she'd fight to the bitter end. She's no quitter.

But then I recall her three nights back, sobbing hysterically, scared of Isobel's reaction. Maybe Daphne fears her mind is deteriorating, and decided to end her life before she's entirely at her kids' mercy. Someone as strong as Daphne couldn't bear being so dependent.

These grim thoughts—and the chamomile—have left a sickly taste in my mouth. Did Daphne snap? Or was I right before and someone else drugged her cocoa? Someone who was there that night, which means it was someone she loves and trusts. Family. I feel queasy. It's a horrific thought: Daphne betrayed by her lover and then by her nearest and dearest. If I'm right—and I hope I'm not—it's the ultimate betrayal, a Greek myth come to life.

"What does Daphne think?" I ask my mom, gently.

She sighs. "She refuses to believe it was Grace or her kids." She squirms on my sofa. "She suspects Vonda."

"Vonda?" I say, in disbelief. "Was she even there?"

"Not for dinner," says my mom. "Afterward. Grace says she stopped by. To give Daphne a book."

"A book?" I say, surprised. I wouldn't peg Vonda as a reader.

"Daphne doesn't remember Vonda's visit, but the book is there," says my mom. "On her bedside table."

"Oh yeah? What was it?"

"Self-help. *Women Who Love Too Much.*"

I fight down a snort, then tell myself off. There's nothing wrong with self-help. It might help me. I shouldn't be so judgmental.

My mom can't sit still. She's like a toddler on a long plane ride, crossing and uncrossing her legs, edging to and fro on the sofa. I try to picture Vonda crushing pills into Daphne's cocoa. "Why would Vonda want to drug Daphne?" I ask my mother.

My mom twists the damp tissue in her hands. "Daphne figures she's furious that she stole Stephen."

I keep quiet but don't buy it. Stephen's dead. I think Vonda's got new fish to fry, including a rich, blond, handsome one.

"Or maybe it was revenge, if Vonda thinks Daphne killed him," ventures my mother.

I shake my head. Vonda's about as sentimental as a Komodo dragon. If she did drug Daphne, it was for financial reasons. "I don't believe that."

My mom sighs. "Nor do I." Her anxious frown deepens. "But I can't say that to Daphne. She's so distraught . . ." Her voice falters. "Daphne's strong but I'm worried about her health. She'll be seventy-five next April." She keeps shredding the tissue. "Of course she'd kill me if she knew I was telling you her real age. She pretends she's still forty-something."

We both fall silent. Poor Daphne. Imagine the strain she's under, knowing someone either tried to kill her or wanted to destroy her sanity and reputation. No wonder she wants to blame Vonda. It'd be so much better to suspect a near stranger than the people you ought to trust the most in the world.

CHAPTER 27:

EAVESDROPPING

After lunch, the rain stops. I call Quinn to meet at our favorite cafe, which doubles as a nursery. When I pull up, I see her out front. She waves at me. She's wearing a yellow raincoat and a blue knit cap. Abby is sleeping in a sling on her mom's chest. She's wearing a pink knitted cap with cat ears. Her cheeks are like ripe peaches.

"Hi," I say. I grin at Quinn and Abby. "She's getting big."

Quinn nods. "Yes, she's changing so fast." She squints up at the sky. I do too: grey clouds with cracks of sun, like those Japanese ceramics that are broken and fixed with gold solder. "Want to risk sitting outside?" Quinn asks me.

While it's far from warm, we're all bundled up. And after days holed up indoors, I have cabin fever. "Let's," I say. "You save a table."

I order our coffees at the counter and carry them back outdoors.

Quinn chose a table set under the eaves, surrounded by greenery. The bushes glisten in the weak sun. Potted plants sit in shelves like bleachers. Even in December, some flowers are in bloom. Victoria is dubbed "The Garden City." All winter long, its smug residents post photos of flowers to rub it in the frostbitten noses of everyone else in Canada, who are snowed under.

At my approach, Quinn smiles. She's removed her hat. Abby is still asleep. I'm relieved to see Quinn looks good. Her eyes are bright. Her nose and cheeks are pink.

"I got you extra whipped cream," I tell her.

I set down our mugs and pull out a chair. They're heavy, with ornate iron legs. I move slowly, to avoid waking Abby.

Quinn shifts to reach for her cup. "So what's new?" she asks.

I take a sip of my latte. It's hard to know where to start. It's been one shock after another this week: Vonda confronting Josh. Colin and Miri. The scary lab results of Daphne Dane's cocoa.

I start with this last one. Having only found out this morning, I'm still processing it. Quinn frowns as she listens. She cups the back of Abby's head, as if to protect her from this grim tale.

When I've finished, she shudders. "That's beyond awful." She stirs her hot chocolate. "That guy, Stephen, of course it's terrible, him being murdered. But we didn't know him. And by all accounts he was up to no good . . ." She shrugs. "Not that he deserved it. But, you know."

"I do," I say. We *know* Daphne. She helped me and my mom. Each year, she donates a small fortune to Secret Santa and helps to buy, wrap, and distribute the gifts to poor families. Her and Walt's generosity built the local woman's shelter. She MCs the annual auction at the Empress Charity Ball. She has a great laugh and tells jokes that are off-color but funny. How could someone hate her that much?

"Bruce hasn't said a word," continues Quinn.

I nod. I wouldn't expect him to, seeing as Quinn's mom is representing Daphne. I tilt my head. "How about Jackie?" I ask her.

Quinn studies her daughter's head. "She's advised both Daphne and Isobel to stop talking to the police."

"Oh," I say. I wonder if one or both of them will actually be charged. Do the police have evidence that Daphne or her daughter killed Stephen Buxley?

My friend rolls her head, as if to relieve a stiff neck. Maybe the baby sling is digging in. She stifles a yawn. "Have you seen Colin lately?" she asks. There's no tension in her voice, nothing to suggest she knows or suspects.

My stomach clenches. "No."

That single word is like an exploding flare in the dark. Quinn's chin jerks up. She peers at my face like she expects more illuminating flashes. "Oh yeah," she says. "Why? What's happened?"

I sigh. Even talking about it is depressing. I explain what I saw through Colin's window.

Quinn looks shocked. "No. Come on! Are you sure?"

I nod miserably. "He was holding her."

"Like a friendly hug?" asks my friend. She sounds hopeful.

Eyes fixed on a potted fern I recall the silhouette in Colin's window. Could it have been innocent? "I don't think so."

Quinn sighs. "I don't know what to say. And he hasn't called?"

I admit he has but I haven't answered.

Quinn sighs again, this time with an exasperated edge. "Well, that's mature."

Immediately, my back goes up. "What's the point when he's just going to dump me?"

"You could talk about it," she says. "That's how relationships work. People discuss things."

I cross my arms. Why's she being so mean? I sobbed the whole way home from Colin's house. Next morning, my eyes were like currants in puff pastry. Can't she see I feel sick with disappointment?

"At least give him a chance to explain," says Quinn. She spoons out a glob of whipped cream. "And even if he did kiss Miriam, you've been seeing Josh all along! Doesn't that seem like a double standard?"

We've been talking quietly on account of Abby, but our increasing tension must have roused her. She stirs and frowns, as does Quinn. Moments later the baby starts squawking.

How can something so small be so loud? I shrink back.

Quinn unclips the baby sling and lifts Abby out. She digs through layers of blankets and fluffy clothes to check her diaper. From the look on Quinn's face, it must be fine. But Abby's still shrieking.

I watch as Quinn unzips her jacket. She fumbles under her sweater and unclips her maternity bra. There's a pale flash of boob as she maneuvers the baby closer. Abby lunges like a shark. Thank god she's still toothless.

All is quiet but for the puck-puck of sucking and swallowing.

"Where were we?" asks Quinn.

I shrug. It's impossible to berate a woman while she's nursing a baby. And maybe she's right. Kind of. "Okay, I'll call him," I tell her.

My friend nods. She eyes me speculatively, as if trying to gauge whether I mean it. "I will!" I say.

She spoons out more whipped cream. "How are things with Josh?" Her tone is casual.

I drain the last of my cappuccino. "Shit," I say. I recount the scene in my office: Josh begging for another chance, Vonda's dagger-eyed fury.

When I've finished, my best friend sighs. I would expect her to get a few digs in at Josh. Instead, she just shakes her head. "So, you going to keep seeing him?" she asks. She readjusts Abby to the opposite breast.

I rub my forehead. Behind my eyes, there's a dull ache. I think of before I met Josh and Colin. Sure, I was hoping to meet someone. But life was also peaceful, minus this drama and angst. Maybe I'm too old for it. "I'm kind of over dating," I tell her.

Abby rolls away from Quinn's chest, sated. She looks drunk.

Quinn shrugs her up onto her shoulder and rehooks her maternity bra. She pats the baby's back gently to burp her. "Well, plenty of fish in the sea," she says. "Whenever you do feel like fishing."

I nod but don't feel cheered at all. I don't want any old fish, I want *my* fish. I was sure either Josh or Colin was my perfect match—not just the catch of the day. Maybe my match doesn't exist. I stare into my empty cup. Is that so terrible? Has society brainwashed me into believing that single means lonely? My life is actually pretty full.

"You want another drink?" asks Quinn. "Or a cookie?"

I smile. A cookie would definitely cheer me up. This place makes killer white chocolate macadamia nut cookies.

"I'll get the cookies," she says. Her nose wrinkles. She lowers the baby and peers down at her. Sure enough, Abby's little face is bright red. "Can you pass me a diaper out of that bag?" says Quinn. She nods at the massive tote occupying our table's only empty seat. I hand it over. She stands. "I'll be right back." She heads indoors. At the door she turns back. "White choc macadamia nut?"

I nod. Maybe I don't need a boyfriend after all. I have Quinn. She knows me so well. I should count my blessings: a good job, that pays well enough. Friends and family to love. I'm young, healthy, fit. Okay, not fit-fit, but fit enough. I live in a beautiful place in a beautiful, peaceful country. Today, the sun is trying to shine. It's not raining.

I bury my nose in the potted lavender that rests on our table.

My eyes are shut, inhaling its scent, when I hear a familiar raspy voice: "Do you want to sit here?"

"Yes, this is lovely," says an older woman.

I look up. It's Lukas Dane and Daphne's housekeeper, Grace. I recognize her gingerbread coat and pink pom-pommed toque. They're headed toward the closest table.

Once they're seated I can't see them. A thick bush separates us. They didn't notice me.

"What will you drink?" asks Lukas. His voice is hoarse. "I'll get it."

"Just regular coffee, please dear," says Grace. "Nothing fancy."

Lukas goes off to order.

Quinn returns bearing a plate with two gigantic cookies. Abby is back in her baby sling. Now wide awake, she grins at me. Her gummy smile is adorable. It's impossible not to grin back and make goo-goo eyes. She looks so much like Quinn. I feel a welling of love for her.

Quinn doesn't give Grace or Lukas a second glance. She's never met Grace. And hasn't seen Lukas since childhood. "The cookies are supersized today," she says, happily. She sits back down and brushes back her hair.

"Thanks," I say, quietly. I keep making faces at Abby. The baby giggles.

For some minutes we're too busy chewing to talk.

I hear Lukas return to the table next door. "Thanks, dear," says Grace. "Oh, that's lovely."

There's a scrape of a chair. "So what did the cops say?" asks Lukas.

When Quinn goes to speak I raise a finger to my lips. I point in Grace and Lukas's direction. "Lukas Dane," I whisper, so quietly I practically mouth it.

Her forehead creases in confusion before she gets it. She shrugs and keeps eating her cookie.

Grace starts to recount everything the cops said to Daphne when they stopped by her house this morning. "Your mother was poisoned!" concludes Grace. "She could have died! But the police barely mentioned that! Instead they went on and on about that horrible man, Stephen. Except that's not even his real name. He wasn't even British but Australian! Can you imagine? He was wanted for fraud down there too, something to do with timeshare condos on the Gold Coast." She sighs. "The police kept asking your mom about the Sooke cabin. The same questions, over and over . . ."

"Jeez," says Lukas. "It's like they really think she did it." He sounds worried. "Did they talk to you too?"

"They did," says Grace. She sounds ominous.

Lukas's voice thins in alarm. "You didn't tell them she hit him, did you?"

"Hit him?" says Grace. "You mean Stephen?" Lukas must nod because she contradicts him. "No. They were just yelling at each other. And then he drove off and your mom did too. She never hit him."

I stop chewing.

"Oh," says Lukas. "It's just . . . that cut on his cheek. I figured she'd smacked him and . . . you know, she always wears those giant rings . . ."

All my Spidey-senses tingle. I recall that red mark on Stephen Buxley's pale cheek. And the cut. But how could Lukas have seen it? Stephen died the day Lukas got home from India. I saw Lukas that evening, still lugging his backpack. The cops must have checked his flight time by now.

Quinn's watching me closely. *What?* say her eyebrows.

I shake my head, still unsure. Then I get it. What if Daphne didn't see Isobel heading into the woods but her son? Similar build. Similar blond hair. Maybe Lukas wasn't fresh off a plane but at the cabin, the day Stephen died.

He could have been. And yet . . . Already, my mind is debating. Why would Lukas be there? He was the only one who didn't know about the stash of gold coins. He wasn't at that family dinner the night Isobel found her dad's papers.

Grace is talking again. Her voice is low and worried. "I don't trust the police," she says. "They're desperate to pin that murder on someone. Anyone. Whatever we tell them, they'll just twist things . . . You have to be careful, Lukas."

I'm listening but my mind is buzzing. Something else Lukas said is bothering me. I picture the red welt on Stephen's waxen cheek. The gash below it. My stomach clenches. I study the crumbs on my plate. Oh. Wow. Of course it could be a coincidence, but I saw a similar injury just days ago, when Vonda smacked Josh in my office.

I rub my eyes. Did Vonda slap Stephen, aka Dennis, just before he died? If so, was she also at the murder cabin? So much for the place being deserted. It was like that intersection in downtown Tokyo. I recall the gold tube of lipstick I saw near Stephen's dead body. *Scarlet Woman*. Vonda loves bright red lipstick. *Scarlet Woman*.

The last bite of cookie gets stuck in my throat. Quinn hands me her water bottle. "What's wrong?" she asks, frowning.

I'm spluttering too hard to answer. Of all the potential killers, who had a better motive to bash Stephen than his feisty, wronged wife? Hell hath no fury, etcetera. Plus Vonda stopped by Daphne's house, the night of the drugged cocoa. Maybe Daphne saw something that day in Sooke that Vonda fears she'll remember!

Quinn tilts her head. "You just realized something?" I shrug. Her blue eyes narrow. "Something you'll tell the police," she says, sternly.

I nod again. The police might want to shift their focus from Izzie to Lukas, and from Daphne to the other scorned woman.

"I'll tell them," I promise Quinn. But will they listen?

CHAPTER 28:

FIRST STRIKE

Saturday night, home alone. Even my mother is out on a date, with some guy she met at the Oak Bay Library. He was in the Self-Help section. I'd have run a mile. But my mom is a kinder, more optimistic woman than me. She found his eagerness to self-improve charming. I guess I should be glad she didn't find him on pensioners-dot-com.

They're going to see some artsy foreign film up at the Cinecenta—no doubt one of those movies where the question "what happened?" is impossible to answer if you're not a 23-year-old Philosophy post-grad.

I sit on the sofa. Get up. Sit back down. I pick up the phone. Put it down. Pick it up. Drop it. I recall Quinn's impatience when she told me to call Colin. Her implication that I was being immature. Or did she actually say it?

As far as Colin knows, Josh and I might have gone from just see-ing each other to being head over heels, joined at the hip, planning our yacht club wedding . . . Maybe I overreacted about Colin and Miriam. Maybe I need to discuss things.

I find his number. Just the thought of him makes me hug my knees. I miss him. Quinn's right. I should have returned his calls—both for personal and Dane-related reasons. I have to tell him that Lukas and Vonda might have met Stephen the day he was murdered.

My belly is fizzy with nervous excitement as I dial Colin's number. "Hi, Colin. It's Toby," I say. The words come out in a big rush.

"Toby." He sounds worn out, and like he's fighting a cold. "I've been trying to call you."

"Yeah," I say. "Sorry."

I take a deep breath, suddenly, truly contrite. I should have called him days ago. He sounds awful. Is he ill? Whatever is happening be-tween him and Miri, I've been a bad friend.

I'm about to ask if something's wrong but he beats me to it.

This is my cue. I inhale. How do I start? Do I just blurt it out, say how hurt I was seeing his and Miriam's embrace? How I felt like a kid waking up to a bare Christmas tree, every gift stolen? The decorations in smithereens . . .

Or do I explain that I'm no longer seeing Josh, that I'm hoping he and I could be together, like, seriously? A real couple. Boyfriend and girlfriend. Partners—but no, not like Miriam. I bite my lip. To say that would make me so vulnerable. What if he's already set on Miri?

I take the easy way out and procrastinate a little longer. It's easier to focus on the Danes, to tell him about the conversation I overheard between Grace and Lukas. "It's about the murder," I say. "I heard . . ."

He cuts me off, his voice tight with disapproval. "Wait. Look Toby, this is an open case. I think you should, you know, stay out of it."

I blink. For all he knows, I could hold the key to the whole mystery. "I'm just trying to help," I say, tightly.

"I know," he says. "But just . . . Don't. It's not your p . . ." He coughs. I swear he was about to say "place." If I were a cat I'd be hissing.

Instead, he says "problem." His voice softens a little. "Please Toby. Please let me deal with this. There's already been one murder." He sounds weary. " And what happened to Daphne . . ."

For what feels like ages the line is silent—the sort of heavy silence that follows the rattle of an earthquake. My desire to ask where we stand, to learn the truth about Miriam, is now buried beneath a layer of resentment.

"I'd like to see you," says Colin. He sounds wistful.

I hold my breath, waiting. Do I even want to see him? Yet again, my feelings are stirred up and murky.

"But right now, it's . . ." He sighs.

I shut my eyes, steeling myself for the coming blow. But. In any statement, it's what's after the "but" that counts.

"It's complicated," says Colin.

My nose wrinkles. Wasn't that the title of some predictable romantic comedy?

He coughs again. "I'm so . . ."

There's a crash so loud I almost drop the phone. "Colin?" I say in alarm. "Hello? Colin?"

"Hello? Hey, ah, Toby?" He sounds thoroughly fed up. "Look, can I talk to you later?"

"Fine," I say—the second most passive-aggressive word in the English language, after "whatever."

What I mean is "don't bother."

After hanging up, I lie down on the floor. Tears flood my shut eyes. If the lump in my throat were any bigger, I'd choke, right here on my pristine no-kids-no-pets cream carpet.

Whatever I had with Colin, it seems I've lost it.

My tears overflow. It's like hearing his voice ripped a scab off my heart. Why didn't I stop dithering months ago?

Behind closed lids I see his twinkling green eyes, the cowlick above his left eyebrow that he's always trying—and failing—to subdue, his little-boy smile, full of kindness and mischief . . . It all seems so poignant, so precious.

Do I only appreciate things when they're gone? I'm like a bad Country Western song. No love. No money. No dog. No pickup truck. I feel like howling.

It's so quiet I can hear the kitchen clock. Tick. Tock. Tick. Tock. It's doing my head in, every beat a reminder that I'm a second older, another second past my prime.

Or is this my prime? It should be. At thirty-three I'm hardly some old crone. Yet I'm lying on the floor, alone and mopey on a Saturday night. I blink back tears. It's hard not to picture a string of lonesome Saturday nights stretching before me like a sad, wilting daisy chain . . . I see myself older, wrinklier, and increasingly bitter, jaded by decades of divorce-lawyering, scanning the Engagements column with the smug satisfaction of knowing that I'll never run out of new clients.

I rake my fingers through my hair and tug. Jeez. Self-pity is worse than smack. And pessimism is poison. I need to quit both, cold turkey. This is my early New Year's resolution. No more dwelling on Colin. No more lusting after Josh. No more wasting time worrying about stuff that might never happen. It's time to grow up and be happy with what I've got, which is a lot. The energy I'm putting into men should go into financial planning. I ought to be saving up for my own place. I can't rent this place forever.

To prevent a woe-is-me relapse, I force my thoughts to Stephen Buxley. Who slapped him? Who killed him? Daphne, Vonda? Or neither?

Since Colin wouldn't listen, I'll have to ask Daphne myself. I'll stop by her place in the morning.

When my phone rings, I figure it's Colin. My heart lifts so fast I get the bends when I sit up. I leap onto the sofa, where I tossed my phone in despair. It's under a pillow. I snatch the phone. The pillow goes flying.

"Toby?" It's my mom.

If my heart bottomed out any harder, I'd be under a pile of rubble in the lobby. "M . . . mom?" I try not to sound too devastated. "Are you okay?" Maybe she's having a bad date. My throat is thick with unshed tears. "Aren't you at the movies?"

"It's about to start," she says. "I'm in the ladies." Sure enough, somewhere nearby, a toilet flushes. "I need a favor."

"Er, okay," I say, aware that tonight might get even worse. What if she wants me to come and meet Mr. Self-help? What if he's creepy? "What's going on, Mom?"

"It's Daphne," she says. I fight back a groan. I should have known. "Those lab results," says my mom. "I can't stop thinking about it."

I wait. It's been preying on my mind too—the possibility that Daphne's in danger.

"I have a really bad feeling," says my mother. "And all the signs." I grit my teeth, lest she elaborate. "I asked Daphne to stay at my place but she refused," continues my mom. "She's so stubborn. I was going to stay there tonight but . . ." She coughs. "Well, I might be out late." Another cough.

I squint at the phone. Is my mom planning to stay overnight with some guy she just met? What kind of self-help was he reading?

"And now Daphne's not answering her phone," says my mom. She swallows anxiously. "Could you please pop by and check on her? Just in case . . . Please, honey?"

I'm tempted to say no. But really, why not? I was planning to go there tomorrow, anyway. And it's not like I've got anything better to do. I make a face, as if to spit out this fresh shot of self-pity. "Okay, Mom," I say. "I'll drive over."

"Oh hon. You're the best," says my mom.

The gratitude in her voice makes me smile and roll my eyes. "How's your date?" I ask.

"Good!" Her voice drops to a whisper, as though he might somehow overhear. "He's a Cancer! And a Pig!" While this doesn't sound good at all, it must be, judging from her tone. "I'd better go. Bye, honey! Remember, drive carefully!"

After she hangs up, I try Daphne's number. Her machine answers. I sigh. Looks like I'll have to keep my promise and go check on her. Daphne's probably out, anyway. Doing something fun—unlike me. Ugh. Enough desolation already.

I wash my face, brush my teeth and hair, and add a dash of court lipstick, for confidence. Satisfied that my sunken spirits don't show, I open the balcony door to check the weather.

The night is cold but dry. I hesitate between my stylish charcoal wool coat and a tatty old navy raincoat before selecting the latter. The break in the rain might not last. But no. I swore off pessimism! I shrug on my nice wool coat. I retrieve my purse and keys off the coffee table.

As usual, when I get off the main streets there's little traffic. I consciously avoid Colin's street. There's optimistic and then there's plain dumb. The last thing I need is to see a loved-up silhouette of him and Miri in his picture window.

Daphne's house is well lit. She must be home, after all. I wonder if she's truly recovered from Wednesday night. It's scary knowing that whoever drugged her could try again. Do the police really think Daphne took the drugs knowingly? If so, they're not even trying to protect her.

Again, I feel mad at Colin. How can I not get involved when my mom's best friend—who gave us so much—is in danger?

I'm only halfway up Daphne's garden path when Kevin starts to squeal. By the time I knock he's like a siren. The longer I wait, the more anxious I feel. What if Daphne is unconscious, or worse? I'm even tempted to try another call to Colin.

The door cracks open, restrained by a safety-chain. A heavily made-up eye peeps through the gap. "Toby?" Daphne swings the door open. "Hey. What are you doing here?"

"Sorry to show up unannounced," I say. "But you weren't answering your phone. My mom got worried."

With a frown she ushers me indoors. Kevin sniffs at my boots. I bend to pat his back, which is covered in sparse, wiry hair. He feels side-of-ham solid.

"Oh, my phone's on the blink," says Daphne. "I dropped it and . . ." She waves a hand, dismissively. "I need a new one."

Clad in a quilted maroon dressing gown over matching satin pajamas, she resembles an aging soap-opera star lounging in her trailer. Despite being home alone, her makeup is camera-ready. Under all that foundation, it's hard to tell if she's less pale than she was the other night. I eye her bright red lipstick. *Scarlet Woman?*

"Would you like a cup of tea?" she asks. "Or wine, perhaps?"

"Tea, please," I say. I'll be driving home soon. "I wanted to ask you something, about Stephen."

Daphne's jaw tightens. "Right, well," she says. "Come on."

The pig and I follow her into the kitchen. Half the cupboards remain missing, their contents still stacked in cardboard boxes.

"Jackie advised me to stop talking to the police," says Daphne.

"They think I might have . . ." Her painted index finger rakes her throat. "You know."

"I heard," I say. "Are you feeling better?"

While Daphne nods, I see her hands shake as she fills the kettle. Her cheeks look sunken, like she's lost weight.

"Do you have any idea who could have drugged you?" I ask.

Daphne closes her eyes and rubs her smooth forehead. With her eyes squeezed shut, she looks gaunt and tired. "Izzy thinks I took it myself. An accidental overdose . . ." Her lower lip trembles. "Like I took a bit to sleep and then forgot and took more." She leans against the counter, as if standing straight is too much effort.

"Is that possible?" I ask.

For a second, Daphne's face sags but then she rallies. Her shoulders and chin lift. "Of course not," she snaps. "I don't even know where you'd get that stuff!" When she pours the hot water, her hands have steadied. "I don't know who did it, but don't worry. I'm watching my back." Her spine straightens a little more. "And I have my suspicions."

I suppress a shiver. How awful must it be to know someone wants to hurt you—or even kill you. "Such as?" I say.

Daphne's red lips clamp shut. "I'm not accusing anyone without proof," she says, tightly.

"Mom said Vonda came by that night," I say. "Did you tell the police that?"

This earns me a dirty look. "The police!" says Daphne. "I'm their number one suspect! Anything I tell them, they'll use against me." She sets the cups onto a silver tea tray.

Armed with the tea, she marches into the living room. I follow meekly.

A gas fire burns in the grate. She sets down the tray and bends to light some tall white candles. Again, I'm struck by the room's beauty, the ceilings high, with ornate, old-fashioned moldings. There's another chandelier in this room, almost as big as the one in the front hall. Its lights twinkle.

"Please, sit," she says, again the perfect hostess. I take a seat. She pours the tea and hands me a cup. It has a delicious smoky flavor.

"Now what was it you wanted to ask me?" asks Daphne. She smoothes down her dressing gown, waiting.

"The last time you saw Stephen," I say. "Did you hit him?"

Daphne's over-plumped lips tighten. She hesitates, frowning at her dark front yard. Then her eyes snap my way. "No," she says, stiffly. "Certainly not."

I'm not sure I believe her.

Again, Daphne stares out the darkened window. On her left ring finger is a ring she keeps twisting. It's got a dark red stone, so big I'd assume it was glass if I saw it on anyone else. On Daphne, I figure it's a Burmese ruby—darker than fresh blood, a stone that protects the heart. I grit my teeth as if to chew this last thought to bits. Is there no way to empty my mind of my mom's crazy crystal nonsense?

When Daphne notices my eyes on her ring she stops twisting it. Using her left hand, she reaches for her teacup. Stephen was struck on the right cheek. Is Daphne left-handed? But if she did slap him, wouldn't she admit it? I, for one, wouldn't blame her. He'd pretended to be single—and was after her fortune!

Although her reluctance to admit having lost her temper is understandable, given that he was murdered.

I consider sharing my theory that it was Lukas she saw in the woods instead of Isobel. But something stops me. "You told the police you saw Isobel there, right?" I ask.

Daphne nods tightly. "I said I thought I did," she says. "But maybe not . . ." She stares into her teacup. "That drug in my cocoa . . ." She clears her throat. "I don't think that's the first time someone drugged me. I've been having memory problems for a while. And . . ." She swallows hard. "Even hallucinations."

"Hallucinations?" I say, alarmed. "What about the past couple days?" Whoever spiked Daphne's drink could still be doing it.

Daphne shakes her head. "I'm being careful," she says again. "I feel totally clear-headed."

I nod. She does seem her shrewd old self. "The day you found Stephen's body, when you saw Isobel running away," I say. "How far away was she?"

Daphne's lips twist in annoyance. "Like I said, I'm not sure I saw anyone," she says. "I thought I saw her—or someone fair—slipping into the trees." She shrugs. "But I might have been mistaken."

There's no point asking again. It's obvious she wants to protect her daughter. I take a deep breath, unsure whether to show my hand or not. So far, I've learned nothing. What's stopping me? "Do you think it could have been Lukas?"

This comment hits home. Her pupils widen like bull's-eyes as she reassesses her memories. Daphne raises her teacup, as if to shield her thoughts. She takes a slow sip of tea and collects herself. "Of course not!" Her tone is haughty. "As you know, he was . . ." Her left hand finds the gold chain at her throat. "Away. At a . . . meditation retreat."

"Where was it?" I ask her.

Her eyes slide left. "In India. Goa . . ." She sighs, like she's too tired to keep telling this story. "Oh what the hell. We only lied because Izzie wanted it hushed up. She's embarrassed that her brother had a problem and doesn't want anyone to know." Daphne tugs at the heavy chain around her throat. "But to hell with Iz. Lukas was in Duncan. Getting treatment. For alcohol and marijuana."

I perk up. Given Lukas's pallor, I should have questioned his India story. I just assumed it was true, based on what he was wearing.

Daphne's eyes narrow. "I know what you're thinking. But by the time Lukas was released from the clinic, Stephen was already dead." She shudders. "I saw his body, remember?"

I nod, but wonder. Is that true? Duncan's not that far from Sooke. Could Lukas have skipped out of rehab early and hitched a ride to the cabin?

"The police will be able to check," I say.

A noise makes us both turn. "Check what?" asks Grace. She is standing in the double-wide door from the front hall. Lukas is beside her.

Dressed in her brick-red quilted coat, Grace looks warm and

cuddly. As usual, her hands are full of shopping bags. Beside her bulk, Lukas seems extra thin and weedy. In a wrinkled oilskin coat and brown wool toque, he could pass for a hobo. His green backpack hangs from one thin shoulder.

"Oh, nothing important," says Daphne, with a tight smile. She sets down her cup. The saucer rattles. She looks at me pointedly. "Toby was just leaving."

I stay seated. I suspect Daphne's defensiveness means one thing: I'm right. She saw her son at the scene of Stephen Buxley's murder.

"Lukas," I say. "Where did you go when you left rehab early?"

The way his eyes bulge tells me my guess is spot on. "Wh . . . what?" he stammers. He glares at his mom. "You told me not to tell anyone about rehab," he says, his voice like a spoiled child's. "And now you told Toby. Why—"

Daphne cuts him off. "Lukas, quiet!" she snaps.

Lukas looks sullen.

Still holding the groceries, Grace walks closer. Her round face is flushed and imploring. "Please Toby," she says, softly. "Please keep this quiet. If the police know about Lukas's problems they'll suspect him . . . They'll say he was high, that he's an addict."

I shake my head. It's obvious Grace and Daphne want to protect Lukas. What I want is the truth. "If Lukas didn't do it, he has nothing to fear," I say. "But he has some explaining to do. I know he was there the day Stephen died."

While Grace's face is pink, behind her, Lukas is ashen. He blinks, slowly. Grace starts to splutter.

I ignore her and get up, then walk closer to Lukas. "Who told you about the coins?" I ask him. "Is that why you went out there?"

"No!" protests Lukas. "No! It wasn't like that!" When he shrugs, his pack slips off his shoulder. Upon hitting the ground, the top opens, disgorging its contents: a family-sized Snickers bar, a bamboo bong, an orange lighter, and a brick-sized bag of marijuana.

At the sight of it, his mom jumps to her feet. "Lukas!" she hisses. "What is that? You promised you'd stopped smoking!"

The fury in her voice startles all of us, but especially Lukas. He shrinks back and starts to stutter out a response. But Daphne isn't finished. "You swore you quit!" she yells. "You swore on my life! When will you stop lying?"

Faced with his mom's ire, Lukas looks at Grace, as if for backup, but she has frozen. He spins toward me. His guilty expression changes to one of accusation. He jabs a skinny finger my way. "This is your fault!" he whines, like a six-year-old, claiming I tattled. "Why are you even here?" His voice rises. "Why couldn't you mind your own business?"

As he steps closer, one foot lands on his bong, which rolls. Lukas loses his balance. His arms pinwheel and his fist catches my jaw. It might be an accident, I'm not sure. The blow knocks me down and sideways. I put a hand out to catch myself.

Something cracks. Pain explodes up my arm. I curl up, my wrist clutched to my chest.

I expect Lukas to apologize, to try to help. Instead, he glares at me, wild-eyed. "You have no idea," he snarls. "How much rehab sucked! All those people kept talking at me!" His voice rises in pitch. "They wouldn't shut up! There were so many rules! I went and hid in the cabin!"

Bags abandoned, Grace tries to grab Lukas's arm. "Lukas, no," she begs. He shrugs her off and takes another step toward me.

"Lukas! Stop!" commands his mother.

Their pleas have no effect. It's like he's on angry auto-pilot, intent on telling his story. "That asshole thought I was a squatter!" he growls. "He threatened to call the cops on me! He called me a druggie loser! Who the hell did he think he was? He came at me—"

Daphne leaps toward her son, screaming: "Lukas! Be quiet!" There's a sharp thwack as her palm connects with his cheek. His head hinges back. He clutches his cheek and staggers.

"Owwww." He blinks at his mom. His next words are more whiney than angry: "Moooom, you hit me!"

When Lukas moves his hand, I see a smear of blood on his cheek. It's starting to swell around an angry, gouged cut.

I look from Lukas to Daphne. Two red dots have appeared under her blush, high on her perfect cheekbones. Her mouth opens and shuts, quietly, like a goldfish's. She falls into a chair. Her teeth clack.

For a moment, Daphne sits slumped, but then she straightens. "I did it," she says, her back ramrod straight. "I admit it. I killed Stephen."

I don't bother to answer. We all know she's lying.

Grace shakes her head. She unbuttons her coat. "No, no, no," she cries, like a disappointed babysitter who's caught the kids pulling each other's hair. "Both of you, stop it!" Her dismayed gaze swings from Daphne to Lukas. "You're both being silly!"

I have climbed to my feet, my broken wrist cupped to my chest.

At the sight of my hand, which is purpling fast, Grace's eyes pop. "Oh dear," she says. "Oh dear. You've hurt your hand. It looks dreadful."

Lukas's eyes swing my way too. He frowns.

I take a step backward.

Lukas pouts. "It wasn't my fault!" His voice rises. I keep quiet. "Listen," he hisses. "This is your doing! If you hadn't . . . Hey!" He reaches out to grab me. "Listen!"

I don't stick around to hear what's coming next. For all I know, he'll attack me again, just to prove it was my fault the first time. People like Lukas are never to blame. They're always the victims. I made him hit me. Stephen made him kill him.

I back away, using my good hand to protect my throbbing wrist.

Lukas steps closer.

I turn and dash past him.

Both Grace and Daphne have started to yell. They're calling for Lukas to stop and for me to come back. My head swims. I ignore them.

I slide into the hall and fling open the front door. I sprint through the front yard and out the gate, which bangs shut behind me. The street lies silent and empty.

My car. Thank god. I scurry toward it.

My good hand is on the door when it hits me: my purse is on Daphne's couch. My keys and phone are in it.

I look back, petrified I'll see Lukas, lurching through the gate. He looked crazy. Will he chase me? I recall the fury in his red-rimmed eyes. He wanted to hurt me.

I need to get out of here.

I turn left in the empty street. My footsteps ring loud against the pavement.

Legs pumping, I don't dare look back. Are those footsteps behind me or just echoes? Is that a car engine, starting up? I have tunnel vision. Everything is a dark blur. Panic drives me faster.

I spin into Colin's street. There's a stitch in my side. With each step, pain jolts up my arm, into my shoulder.

I pound up the long sloped drive, then up the staircase. I peer at the grid of buzzers. Names swim in tiny font. Finally, his name floats free: *C.M. Destin.*

Using my left hand, I stab at the button.

I know who killed Stephen. I need the police to take over.

Please let Colin answer. Or Miri. Right now, I don't care. I don't need a boyfriend. I need a police officer—someone to arrest crazy Lukas.

The buzzer sounds. I can barely talk: "Please help," I croak. "It's me, Toby."

CHAPTER 29:

SEEING DOUBLE

tug at the door. The lobby is bright. It has white-painted walls and white cement tiles. I run past some rows of metal letter boxes. A white door marked STAIRS lies to my right. To my left, two tall plants flank an elevator.

I hesitate. Loud footsteps pummel down the stairs.

"Toby?" Colin's anxious voice echoes downward.

I turn toward it.

I'm halfway to the second floor when I see him, careening down the stairs toward me. Seeing me, he stops dead. I stop too. My chest heaves.

He is holding a baby—maybe seven or eight months old. It's asleep, and wrapped in a blue blanket. In the fluorescent lights Colin looks duck-egg green. His eyes are ringed like a panda's. I wonder if he's ill.

He gapes. I guess I don't look my best either. "My god," he says. "Toby! What happened?"

I'm wheezing too hard to answer. Another step is impossible. My knees buckle, like a badly made jumping-jack. The sight of him has pulled the pins from my legs. I collapse onto a step and hang my head between my knees. My lungs feel empty, despite my heaving gasps. I feel dizzy.

Colin descends toward me.

"Your wrist!" he says. He moves the baby into one arm and crouches down. His hand finds my back. "Is it broken?"

"I don't know." My breath scrapes my throat. "Lukas killed Stephen!" Between gasps, I explain about Lukas's confession, and how he attacked me at his mom's place. "He's dangerous," I croak. "You have to stop him."

Colin helps me up the stairs. "This way." He guides me through

a partly opened door. His apartment smells weird: like camphor and
baby oil. "Come sit down," he says. His hand is on my back. "I need to
call for assistance."

He leads me into the front living room, which is dominated by
that broad picture window. For a second, I see it from outside, as I did
a few nights ago: Colin's strong arms around Miriam. My heart, still
straining, plummets.

We aim for a big dark green sofa. I sink down, then jump up.
Something poked me in the butt! Between two sofa cushions rests a
spiky plastic dinosaur. A half dozen small dinosaurs roar silently from
the coffee table. Do they belong to the baby?

I dig Buttpokersaurus out of the sofa and set it beside its buddies. My legs shake. I'm still panting. It's a relief to sink down onto
the sofa.

Colin finds his phone. He paces as he talks, still holding the baby.
Again, I'm struck by how tired Colin looks. He's paler and thinner
than when we last met. Is something wrong? I recall how his mom had
breast cancer, like mine. I hope she's not sick again. And whose kid is
that? The baby remains sound asleep in his arms.

As Colin explains, I survey the room. His place is messy, clothes,
towels, and bags strewn around. I see a woman's pink sports sock near
the radiator. My throat closes a little. Does Miriam live here? Is it her
baby?

"Toby?" says Colin. "What's Daphne's address?"

I struggle to remember. It's hard to think through the pain in my
arm.

The baby in his arms stirs. I think it's a boy. He has tawny skin
and a shock of pale brown hair. Again, I wonder who he belongs to.

Colin hangs up the phone and walks closer. He looks contrite.
"Tob, I need to go," he says. He gazes down at the infant in his arms.
"D'you mind taking care of—"

He is interrupted by a loud squall, which erupts from down the
hall. Colin's face plummets. I stare at the baby he's holding, like it's a
ventriloquist.

"Oh no," groans Colin. His tired face sags. "As soon as one goes to sleep the other wakes up. Can you . . ."

Before I can respond, he thrusts the baby into my lap. The baby frowns in its sleep, then settles. While my baby-know-how is slightly higher than it was a few months ago, thanks to Quinn and Abby, I hold it the way I'd hold a pipe bomb. What if it starts shrieking?

"Colin! Wait!" I say, but he's already speed-walking toward the wails. Jeez. I thought Abby was loud.

Moments later he's back with another baby—so similar to the first one I do a double-take. Same rosebud mouths. Same pudgy cheeks. Except they're like Baby Jekyll and Hyde—mine sweetly asleep, his apoplectic.

"I'm so sorry," he says. "But can you watch this one too?"

I blink at him, incredulous. I'm in shock and in pain, with one working hand! I've been assaulted. I need an X-ray! How am I supposed to mind two babies?

"Only for a minute," says Colin, quickly. His baby bucks and writhes, its face like a maraschino cherry. Any second now, its head will start to spin, Poltergeist style. "Help is on its way." His voice shakes. "I swear! Someone will stay here with them." He nods at the infants. "And someone will take you to Emergency. I have to run to the Danes."

He shoves the second baby into my lap. It head-butts my chest. "Please, Tob," says Colin. "It's urgent."

I'm saved from having to reply by the sound of footsteps in the hall. "Detective?" comes a man's voice. A uniformed officer peeks around Colin's door, then another. Not a moment too soon. The promised help. Two strong-looking men stride closer.

"Thank god," says Colin. He turns back to me. "I'll be back as soon as I can. I promise."

I watch as he races away. Is he going to arrest Lukas?

Roused by its twin's screams and kicks, the first baby wriggles. It opens its eyes, sees me, and frowns. Its face scrunches up like a troll's and turns red. It takes a giant breath and starts screaming.

The approaching policemen look alarmed. "Are you okay, Miss?"

asks the closest one. At least I think that's what he said. It's impossible to hear over the babies' shrieking.

"I'm fine," I yell, through gritted teeth. "Just please . . ." I nod at my lap. "Take them!"

I'd rather face Round Two with Lukas Dane than try my luck with these demon babies.

CHAPTER 30:

ALONE

The nurse taps my cast. "Almost dry," she says. "Can I just check your name?" I hold out my good hand so she can compare the name on my wristband to the name on the forms she's holding. She nods. "Okay. Can you sign here, please?"

I hold the pen awkwardly in my left hand. My signature looks like it was written by a three-year-old. Six weeks in a cast won't make life easier at work.

The nurse glances at the clock. "Another fifteen minutes and you should be good to go," she says, smiling.

I consider calling my mom for a ride but decide to take a cab. The policewoman who dropped off my purse refused to say anything about the Danes. Should I go back to Daphne's and retrieve my car? But no, I'm too tired. Plus they gave me painkillers. I shouldn't drive. It'd be better to go home and get my mom or Quinn to drive me over there in the morning.

I'm gathering my things when my phone rings. Colin's name makes my heart jolt, then flatline. This call is surely professional, not romantic. While the cop who brought me here questioned me, Colin will need to follow up. "Hello?" I say, tiredly.

"Toby? Are you okay?" He sounds tired, too. And anxious.

"I'm fine," I say. "You?"

"I heard your wrist is broken."

"Fractured," I say. "Did you get Lukas?"

He sighs. "He got away. We're looking for him now."

I reach for a wall to steady myself. The thought that Lukas is still out there gives me a weird, shaky feeling. I recall his crazed, menacing stare, the way he'd kept coming closer . . .

"Toby?" says Colin.

I take a deep breath. "Yeah?"

"Don't worry, we'll find him." He sighs again. He sounds utterly spent. "There's one more thing . . ." I wait, my shoulders tense. "Daphne confessed to the murder. Thanks to Jackie, she's already made bail."

I shake my head. "Daphne's lying," I say. "To protect her son."

"I . . . Hold on." There's some noise on the line, like someone else is talking to him. "Sorry, I have to go," he says. He sounds both frustrated and apologetic. "I need to question Mrs. Dane. I'll call you tomorrow. Is someone there with you?"

I hesitate. Admitting I'm alone sounds too pathetic. It feels shameful.

"Uh, yeah," I say. "I'm about to go home."

"You have a ride?"

I bite my lip. "Yes."

"Oh, okay."

I can't tell if he sounds relieved or disappointed. Does he think Josh is here, my knight in shining, solid gold armor? Or is he just happy I'm someone else's problem, so he doesn't have to feel guilty?

"Well then . . ." He clears his throat. "Please, take care of yourself, Toby." He sounds suddenly formal.

"You too," I say.

It's only after I've hung up that I realize I never even asked about the mysterious twins. Whose are they? But I'm too tired to dwell on it. All I want is my own bed. I stash my phone in my bag and stand up.

With aching muscles, I shuffle out of Emergency.

There are no taxis in sight. I sigh. Should I call one? I ran out of Daphne's without my coat. The wind cuts right through my wool sweater. Waiting around, I'll surely freeze to death. And by the time a cab shows up, it'd be quicker to walk.

I adjust my grip on my bag and set off through the dark parking lot.

With each step, my legs protest. Even though it's a busy street, and well lit, I feel anxious. My arm throbs. My entire body feels leaden. But my mind is buzzing. Lukas Dane is a killer. And he's still out there. Are the cops really looking for him? Or do they believe his mom did it? I'm sure Daphne and Grace denied everything I said. I can't help but feel bitter. They'd both do anything to protect their darling boy, Lukas.

When the streets get quieter and emptier, my unease grows. I keep seeing the loathing in Lukas's bright eyes, like laser beams, pointed straight at me. I won't feel safe until he's behind bars. I really need Colin to believe me.

It starts to drizzle. My fractured wrist throbs and my tired legs shake. I wish I had called my mother, although it seems pathetic, needing her rescue at my age. Maybe it's delayed shock, or relief, or just fatigue, but all of a sudden, I'm crying. How pathetic is that? All I do these days is bawl! I'm worse than baby Abby.

Shoulders hunched, I swipe at my eyes. I need to get it together. I'm not a baby. Or a hormonal teenager. I'm thirty-three and a half. An age when most people have their own families. They have real responsibilities, beyond remembering to feed their fish. A mortgage. In-laws. Immunizations. PTA meetings. And at times like this, they have people to call on—a family circle, whereas who do I have? My mom. But she's got problems of her own. And she's getting on. I shouldn't be adding to her stresses. Of course Quinn would come if I called, but I can't—not when she's barely coping with the baby. I could have called Quinn's mom, Jackie. I know she'd come in a heartbeat. She'd be furious if she knew I was out here by myself, late at night, staggering homeward. Quinn's cop husband Bruce would be equally livid.

But I'd feel embarrassed to call them, ashamed to need help. Like I was mortified to tell Colin the truth, to say: *No, I don't have a ride home. No. Nobody's here with me. Yes, I'm alone at the hospital.*

A lump balloons in my throat and fills my chest. Alone. This word hurts worse than my wrist, worse than the ache in my muscles. After tonight, all I want is to be held, to be comforted. I want someone to be relieved I'm okay, to tell me I matter. Would Josh come, if I called him?

This thought drags my feet to a stop. Would I want him here?

My tummy tilts. Warmth surges up and down my spine. Josh is like a drug—a shot of confidence and glamor. When I touch him I get high. Ordinary moments crackle with possibility. But the comedown . . .

I pull my hands up inside my sleeves and start to walk again. Those highs are followed by such lows. The second-guessing myself. The feeling not good enough, not pretty enough, not exciting enough . . . To live that way would be exhausting.

I start to walk again, my steps robotic. Josh would come if I called. I know he would. He wants me back. But I wouldn't trust his reasons for coming. He likes to win. I'm not a prize in a carnival game.

In the bottom of my purse is a wadded-up tissue. I stop and blow my nose. I'm not calling Josh. Decision made, my steps feel a bit lighter.

And Colin? My heart twists. I imagine phoning him back. I could tell him the truth. *I'm alone. I'm scared and tired. Please come get me.*

Again, my steps slow. The phone in my jeans' back pocket seems to grow heavy. My fingers find it. My whole being yearns to dial his number. But I can't. I picture his living room: the stray pink sock. He's with Miriam. Those must be her twins. An instant family. My throat constricts. Fresh tears fill my tired eyes.

There are no sounds but for the light patter of rain, my sniffling, and my soft footfalls against the asphalt. Up ahead, three streetlights in a row have gone out. It's very dark.

I hesitate, but keep walking. This is a safe neighborhood. I have nothing to fear. There's no way Lukas could know where I am. I'm just exhausted and jumpy.

In the dark, quiet street, I keep peering behind me. All lies silent: dark houses, dark bushes and trees, dark lawns, dark cars, dark sidewalks . . . My heart thumps in my chest. I long to call Colin. But I can't. He's not my boyfriend. He'll never be my boyfriend. I missed my chance. What a loser.

It's a relief to turn into my street, to see my building up ahead with its lit golden porch-light. The fake Christmas tree's multicolored lights blink on and off in the lobby. The effect is more cautionary than festive.

I look up. All the apartments lie dark. Even nosy old Mrs. Daggett must be in bed, her usual post abandoned. In my sorry state, I almost miss her.

Tonight, when I need it most, I'm completely alone. There is no one at all watching over me.

CHAPTER 31

DOWN AND OUT

I wake early, on account of the pain in my wrist, and roll carefully out of bed. My body is stiff from yesterday's exertion. I open the curtains. It's still pretty dark. Out front of my building, under a streetlight, I can see my 70-something neighbor, Mr. Garlowski, stretching in preparation for a jog. He's wearing a vintage 70s red tracksuit with an orange reflective vest over top, like Elmo doing roadwork. His bald head is circled by a fuzzy John McEnroe-type tennis headband. I bet he'd make a fortune selling his vintage duds on eBay.

I shuffle to the kitchen. A look in my fridge reveals an Arctic wasteland. The cupboards are equally barren. Various types of herbal tea, for when my mom visits. A box of prunes so old they're extra pruney. Some dusty cans of tuna. Thank god they're dolphin-friendly. A bag of quinoa, untouched since my mom gave it to me. Can I eat it for breakfast? I squint at the back. No instructions. I push the quinoa to the depths of the cupboard.

At least there's—Oh no. I tilt the tin, just in case some magically materializes. Damn. I'm out of coffee. I stare at the clock. Does Thrifty's open this early? Then I remember: my car is still at Daphne's.

I eat a sad breakfast of antique prunes washed down with Licorice Spice tea. It tastes vaguely like ouzo, but worse. And it's nonalcoholic.

It's too early to call my mom for a ride. She likes to sleep in. And Quinn? It's hit or miss. She's probably up with Abby but what if she's not? I can't risk waking her when she's already sleep-deprived. I'd feel too guilty.

Daphne's isn't *that* far. It'd take me twenty or thirty minutes to walk, tops. That might be good for my sore muscles. I'll stop for groceries on the way home, unless it's still too early.

It's not easy pulling on leggings one-handed. Brushing my teeth is hard too. I don't even try for lipstick or mascara.

I imagine my mom's dismay when she hears about last night. Since moving back to Victoria last summer, I've suffered one gunshot wound, one broken collarbone, and now a fractured wrist. So much for this place being safe and serene! My life was hectic but safe in Toronto. Here, I feel like a magnet for trouble.

I excavate my running shoes from the back of my closet. They look sad and misshapen, like relics from a lost, sportier civilization. While I shun gyms, I figured I'd start exercising outdoors, when I moved back here. So far, apart from some walks on the beach with Quinn, that plan has gone nowhere.

This could be another pre-New Year's resolution! Yesterday's frenzied run and today's walk could be the start of my new get-fit campaign! This thought lifts my spirits. I swing the shoes by their laces to shake off the dust. It's a nightmare to tie them left-handed.

Finally, I'm ready to go. When I get outside there's a little more light. Mr. Garlowski is long gone. Mrs. Van Dortmund's decrepit tortoiseshell cat is sitting on the low wall out front. When I pass, it hisses at me. I step back. I've done nothing to deserve such hostility! I swear it's got dementia. Unless it somehow knows I'm the one who keeps removing the brick from the lobby door, barring its entry and exit.

Turning to look up, I see Mrs. Daggett back in her window, glaring down at me, half hidden by her lace curtain. I wave. She pretends not to see me. I can't help smiling.

I zip up my jacket and turn right. After a few minutes, my muscles feel less sore. Despite the lack of caffeine, my brain is waking up too.

I revisit last night. Have the police arrested Lukas yet? Will I have to testify against him in court? Whose babies were those at Colin's?

With so much on my mind the walk zooms by. I'm surprised to find I'm already near Colin's street. I hesitate. Should I go another way? But my legs feel rubbery. For sure Colin—and Miri if she's there—are still sound asleep. Unless they're up with those possessed twins.

I stuff my hands deeper into my pockets and tell myself to get a grip. This is the quickest route to Daphne's. What am I planning to do? Avoid Colin's street for the rest of my life? I resist the urge to pull up my hood and turn the corner.

As I pass, I can't help but glance at his front window. It's unlit, like all the other windows in his building. I feel oddly disappointed, like part of me was hoping to catch a glimpse of him. I grit my teeth. Am I that masochistic?

I turn onto Daphne's street. Walking toward the water, the mansions and gardens get bigger. As usual, the street is deserted. That's the thing about rich neighborhoods: there's so much space and no people. Poor areas are the opposite. Everyone is in each other's faces. Sometimes I wonder what's better. Money is both a buffer and a wall, separating us from our fellow, irritating humans. The really rich end up living like they're in a six-star hotel, serene but lonely, with no one around but discreet, professionally smiley waiters.

My footsteps ring loud in the empty street. Parked out front, my little white car looks small and sad. My plan is to get it and go. But I'm surprised to see lights on in Daphne's house. She must be awake. Should I go in and say hi? While the police retrieved my purse and phone, my good wool coat remains inside. I need it for work. I may as well get it now, if Daphne's up.

I have trouble unlatching the gate with my left hand. My thighs throb as I walk down her long front path. I pray she has coffee.

As I climb the steps I feel oddly uneasy. I hesitate, then knock. The sense that something's off grows. But why? All is quiet. Ah. That's it. Where's the pig? It normally squeals like its throat is being slit. I knock again. Nothing. I turn the door handle. To my surprise, it opens.

I start to push but stop. What if Lukas is in there? But surely, this is the last place he'd hide. I hope he's been caught. Should I call Colin?

I fumble my phone out of my coat's pocket. Daphne's house lies utterly silent. Could she be out walking the pig? Are pigs walkable? I imagine Kevin in a diamanté collar.

I find Colin's number but don't press it. What if I wake him? He looked beyond wrecked last night. But better safe than sorry. I press Call. It rings and rings. Maybe he's asleep, after all. Or already at work, hopefully interrogating Lukas Dane. I send a text message: **Lukas caught yet? I'm at the Danes' place.**

I wait. There's no answering message.

I shut Daphne's door. I'll just go home. But what if something's happened to her? It's kind of weird, her front door being unlocked, especially so early in the morning.

I stuff my phone back in my pocket and open her heavy front door. "Hello?" I call. The hall lies dark and silent. I take a few steps and stop. The air smells of coffee. My mouth waters.

Another step and I see a shattered espresso cup in the middle of the front hall. Some brown stains have splashed onto the pale rug. I walk closer and crouch. Dark liquid is puddled on the hardwood.

Bending low, I sniff. It's definitely coffee. I touch it: still a bit warm. There's some pale grit in the puddle. I'm suddenly alert. Has Daphne been drugged again, in her morning espresso?

My thighs quiver as I rise and step over the mess. My heart is thumping. I call her name. Nothing. "Daphne?" I yell up the stairs. If she were on the ground floor, she'd have heard me for sure. Maybe she's in bed, drugged, like last week.

On protesting legs I climb the stairs. My ears strain for the slightest sound. The light is dim.

Walking down the hall, I look into each room I pass. Everything is neat: Lukas's teenage bedroom, the five-star guest rooms . . .

At Daphne's door, I falter. But I'd better check. I crack the door open. "Hey, Daphne, are you okay?" I call.

With trepidation, I enter.

Both the sitting room and her bedroom are orderly and empty. The bathroom is sparkling.

I retreat. Maybe she's out walking Kevin after all. The pig could use the exercise. I'm worrying for nothing.

I'm back downstairs searching for my coat when I become aware of a strange noise—a weird, background hum. White noise. It could be a fan or an engine. I tilt my head, listening. Is it coming from the basement? Does Daphne have a generator? The steps to the basement lead down from the kitchen.

Walking into the kitchen, I'm surprised to see progress on the renovations. New cupboards have been installed. The table, counters, and boxes are covered with paint-flecked tarps. Near the sink stands a stepladder. The wall by the stove bears three test swatches of paint—burnt orange, latte, and ochre. Are these Daphne's or Isobel's choices?

I listen at the basement door. The sound is louder. I open the door, cautiously. Who isn't freaked out by basements?

"Daphne?" I yell down the stairs. The hum is definitely coming from downstairs. I click on the light and creep down the steep, cement stairs. My legs are quaking.

A large, carpeted room comes into view. There's a projector and a giant screen, a huge, tawny sofa set, some leopard-print cushions. Three doors lead somewhere. The closest door is partly open. I can see a white washer and dryer. I head toward the sound, which seems to be coming from the furthest door. My heart is now threatening to pop out of my mouth. But apart from that broken cup I've seen nothing unusual. Nothing alarming.

I open the door. There's a bad, chemical smell in here. When I find the light switch, the sudden brightness makes me squint. I peer around. It's a large garage. Floor-to-ceiling shelves line the long sides of the room. There are stacks of boxes, most neatly labeled: CHRIST-MAS ORNAMENTS. FISHING TACKLE. LAWN BOWLING & TENNIS.

In the middle of the room, surrounded by empty space, stand two cars. I recognize Daphne's silver Mercedes sedan. Behind it is a classic red Mustang. Where's her Audi? Both cars look empty. The Mustang's engine is running.

I approach this red car. The smell of exhaust makes my eyes water. I raise my sleeve to my mouth. It's smoky. Who left that car on?

The Mustang has dark tinted windows. I peer into its dim interior, blinking. It's like the air is curling and twisting. Is that smoke? The car's front seats lie empty. In the back, I'm stunned to see the pig, lying on its back, short legs in the air. Daphne is sprawled under it. Her head lolls forward, tangled hair covering her face.

Sick with panic, I pound on the glass. Nothing happens. "Daphne! Wake up!" I yell. I pound harder.

Neither she nor the pig stirs. I tug at the door's handle. It's locked, as is the driver's door.

I run to the other side and claw at the handles. Neither door will open.

I look around, frantic. A metallic tube has been stuck onto the car's exhaust pipe and fed through the back window. It's held in place with duct tape. More tape covers the gap. When I tug at the tube it flies out, spewing foul smoke. I splutter and reel back. I spin around, searching.

On a shelf behind me lies a big plastic box labelled TOOLS. I wrestle it down and pry off the lid. Yes! A hammer. It feels surprisingly heavy.

I race back to the car and swing, hard. The glass breaks but doesn't shatter. I swing again. And again.

When the glass spider-webs inward I reach through the jagged hole to unlatch the front door. The fumes makes me gag. My eyes stream. Gasping from the smoke, I reach under the steering wheel to snap off the ignition.

The sudden lack of noise is startling. I hold my breath and stretch into the back seat. My fingers find the door's lock. I scrabble out and open the back passenger-side door. "Daphne!" I scream. "Get up!"

She doesn't respond when I shake her.

She's wearing peach pajamas under her quilted maroon dressing gown. I grab her under the arms and pull. The dressing gown is slippery. She's heavier than she looks. It hurts like crazy to use my right hand. I tug until she slides out from under the pig. Another heave and she's halfway out of the car. My knees wobble under her weight. Her bare feet bump onto the cement floor. I drag her in fits and starts, stopping to gasp for breath.

When her feet are level with the car's back bumper, I set her down and go back for the pig.

Kevin feels twice as heavy and five times as ungainly, like a giant sandbag. Holding the pig by its hind legs, I wrestle it out the door. It falls with a massive thump that makes me wince. I hope I didn't kill it.

I manage to tug the beast another few feet, then give up and race to the garage's front roller-door. I can't find the button or the remote to raise it. My eyes are on fire. The fumes are making me dizzy.

There's a small side door for pedestrians. I manage to unlock that and swing it wide open. For a minute, I rest, doubled-over, gulping down clean, cold morning air. Tears stream down my face. I can taste the oxygen.

Fortified, I turn back toward Daphne.

Luckily, I spy the panel that controls the garage door. In a panic, I jab various buttons. Maybe I pushed too many at once, or else the door is blocked, because it lifts a few feet and jams. The motor whines and shudders, then dies. But it's better than nothing. At least some clean air is getting in. Smoke wafts out the gap.

I race back to Daphne and start dragging her again. I pull her away from the car, closer to fresh air and the exit.

I've gone back for the pig when I realize I'm not thinking straight. I need to call for help. I sink onto my haunches and dig my phone from my coat's pocket. My fingers shake as I dial 911. I should put it on speed dial. The line stays silent. I try again. Nothing happens. Through inflamed eyes, I squint at the screen—only half a bar. There's no reception in Daphne's basement.

I'm crawling unsteadily to my feet when I hear some noise, behind me, in the basement TV room. A voice. My knees go weak. I know that voice. It comes again. "Toby? Are you here?"

Relief hits like a blast of warm air. "Colin," I rasp. "Help. I'm in here."

"Toby!" he calls again. His footsteps stride closer.

I regain my feet and start to stagger his way. Colin's here! He came! Everything will be okay!

I'm almost at the door when a scrabbling noise makes me stop.

There's a gasp and a crack, then a dull thud. I shrink back. What just happened? I hold my breath and listen.

Silence. Colin's footsteps don't start up again.

I open the door a sliver and peek through it. The room's still brightly lit. I can see the back of the sofa and the pale, thick carpeting. A heavy crystal vase lies on the floor, the decorative grasses it held now crop-circled around it. Nearby, lies an outstretched hand.

I bite down a cry. It's Colin's hand, the fingers long and strong. Hardly daring to breathe, I widen the door another inch.

He's on the floor, sprawled on his back. Through the gap, I can see his chest and his neck, the side of his face . . . His cheek is bone white.

I gently push the door a little wider. His other cheek drips scarlet.

My vision swims. He's bleeding. And unmoving. Is he dead? I want to run but am frozen.

Someone else enters my narrow field of vision—a figure in black pants and a long dark coat. He's faced away, his head hidden by a black hood. My heart accelerates. Who is it? When he turns slightly, I see a pillow clasped to his chest. It's leopard-printed.

This sinister figure walks closer to Colin and crouches. He presses the cushion to Colin's bloody face. It takes a moment to understand. He's smothering Colin!

I spin to look for the hammer. I must have left it near the Mustang. I run to find it, relieved to see it on the floor, surrounded by glistening chunks of glass. I grab it. It feels good and heavy.

I creep back to the door. My eye finds the crack. The man is still bent over Colin's inert form. I need to act quickly.

Moving quietly, I push open the door. My heart has turned into a wild horse, leaping and bucking. I tiptoe toward them and raise the hammer.

I brace, then aim for the center of his hood. Just as I swing, he turns and ducks.

My blow misses his head but strikes his shoulder.

The man staggers back and drops the pillow. With a growl, he clutches his injured shoulder. I raise the hammer. He kicks at my legs. Pain geysers up my right knee. I'm propelled backward and sideways.

I hit the ground, hard, the breath knocked out of me. I curl onto my side, gasping. I'm still clutching the hammer.

My attacker's dark hood slips down to reveal pale, watery eyes. They bulge in surprise, then narrow. His fat fingers cup his hurt shoulder. "You?" he hisses.

I blink, equally stunned. It's Daphne's son-in-law, Gerard. Glistening with sweat, his face is pale and puffy. He's like a malevolent toad, glaring down at me.

I look from him to Colin. The sight of Colin's waxy face—so still and vulnerable—sucks the air from my lungs. Is he breathing? Just the thought of him dying leaves me weak.

Pain, fear, and confusion race through my overworked brain. Did Gerard kill Stephen Buxley? Why would he want to kill Daphne? Is this all about her money?

I rise to a shaky crouch. "W—why?" I stammer.

Instead of answering, Gerard lunges.

As I jump back, I swing my hammer, desperately. While he's unarmed, I'm weak with fatigue—and using my ungainly left hand.

I miss. His fist strikes my chest. I jolt backward but stay on my feet. I reel away, gasping.

Gerard straightens. His goggle eyes blaze with fury. "You!" he says again, like he can't believe it. "Because of you, the police have been harassing my Isobel!" His voice rises in pitch. "You convinced Daphne she was there, at the *cabine*!" His flabby cheeks shake with rage. "You made the police suspect her!"

I stagger back. My chest burns. Is that why Gerard attacked Daphne? Doesn't he realize she'd do anything—including taking the rap—to protect her children?

It's hard to breathe, let alone talk. "The police know it wasn't Izzy," I rasp. Each word is a low, painful wheeze. "And so does Daphne. It was Lukas!"

Gerard snorts. "Lukas?" He sounds dismissive. "As if. He is good for nothing, that Lukas! He is too weak to kill anyone! He has no backbone."

He smiles malevolently and steps closer.

I take another step back. Pretty soon, I'll be in a corner. My panic rises.

Gerard is short and fat, but strong. He's quick too, while I'm half-drugged by the fumes and exhaustion. My chest feels locked tight. I'm shaking so hard I'm scared I'll drop the hammer. I don't dare swing again lest he grab it.

From the garage there's a noise—a strange, high-pitched wail. It takes me a second to realize: it's the pig, squealing.

Gerard turns toward the sound. His bald head turns an angry purple. "That *cochon*!" He gnashes his teeth. "I will kill it!"

That second of distraction is a godsend. With my last remaining strength, I swing my hammer. There's a sickening thud as it strikes his head.

The reverberations electrify my arm. I stagger backward.

"Umpf," says Gerard, his eyes wide with shock. He clutches at his skull and collapses.

I keep moving back, sure he'll rise and come at me.

Instead, he lies still, crumpled with one arm beneath him. A smooth magenta bump has appeared on one side of his bald head. I stop backing away.

My heart skids around my chest. There's no time to lose. On quaking legs I inch forward. I nudge Gerard's shoulder with my foot. No reaction. He's out cold.

I step over him and run to Colin. Bent close, I press my face to his. I don't feel any breath. "Colin," I cry. I find the zipper of his coat, dig a hand under his dark jacket. His chest feels warm. But is his heart beating?

Am I too late? Has Gerard killed him?

Then I feel it, a deep, solid thud against my palm. Relief pulls me forward to collapse against his chest. I bury my nose against him, inhale his fresh, minty scent. Tears fill my eyes.

But there's no time to rest. Colin and Daphne need help. Gerard could wake at any moment.

I will myself to sit up, to sway to my feet, and stagger back through the smoky garage. Daphne remains where I left her, inert in her shiny bathrobe.

I pull an old, rolled-up sleeping back down from a shelf and stick it under her head. I smooth her hair out of her face, which is the color of old parchment. "Daphne?" I say. No response. But she's still breathing.

Nearby, the pig stirs, its legs twitching, erratically, like it's dreaming. At my approach, Kevin emits a squeak. The pig is coming to.

I stumble out the side door and into the empty front yard. It looks so clear and bright. Every leaf and blade of grass sparkles in the morning sun.

I gulp down lungfuls of cold air, unable to get enough. Never again will I take this fresh air for granted—redolent of cedar and pine sap. The grass crunches with frost.

I sink onto it and pull my phone from my coat's pocket. Through inflamed eyes, I squint at the tiny screen. One bar. Two. Thank god. The grass' cold wetness seeps up through my jeans. My eyes are streaming.

With a shaking finger, I dial 911. A woman answers. My voice is croaky. She has trouble hearing me. "An ambulance!" I yell. "And the police!"

She takes down the address and instructs me to stay on the line.

I ignore her. After a moment's rest, I retrieve my hammer and head back indoors. The phone connection dies as soon as I enter the basement. I stick my phone in my pocket. The only sound is my thumping heartbeat.

After a moment's hesitation, I keep going. I must stay with Colin. And Gerard could wake at any moment.

I stumble through the garage, past the pig, which raises its head as I pass, and Daphne, still unmoving. My eyes scan various boxes: CAMPING, OFFICE CURTAINS, BABY BEDDING. Daphne had better read Marie Kondo. Although I'm lucky she didn't.

In a box marked FISHING TACKLE I find a roll of strong fishing line and a knife. This will do for restraining Gerard. It's hard to carry both weapons one-handed.

Gerard is still lying as I left him, a pale mound in dark clothes. I can't see his face. Is he dead?

Although it was self-defense, the thought brings a nauseous rush. But no, I can hear his wheezy breaths.

I stick the knife down the front of my jeans and raise the hammer, ready to use it. I inch closer.

His chest rises and falls. I'm scared to touch him, as if, even unconscious, he might harm me. Maybe he's just pretending and will sit up and grab me.

I inhale. The longer I wait, the more chance he'll wake up. I prod his back with my toe. No reaction. But even passed out, he's a malevolent presence. Again, I think of a poisonous toad. Toxic. Just touching him feels potentially lethal.

I roll him onto his stomach and pull his wrists together, behind him. His skin feels clammy. He groans a little, then lies silent. I'm relieved he's alive but more relieved he's unconscious. After securing his wrists and his ankles I push him onto his side. He grunts, loudly.

I back away, feeling sick. I rub my hands on my jeans. It's like I touched something dirty.

Colin is also as I left him, unmoving. I sink down and cradle his head. The cut up above his hairline is still bleeding.

I tug off my scarf and press it against the wound. "It's me," I croak. "The ambulance is coming. You're okay." A lie but I need to hear it. I stroke the dark, wet curls near his ear. Dried blood crusts his cheek and neck. The sight of his eyelashes, so still and dark against his white skin, makes my heart hurt.

"I'm so sorry," I whisper. "I was so lame. I should have known, sooner."

Seeing him now, it's so clear: I've loved him since we first met— the way he smiles shyly with his mouth, yet has a naughty spark in his eyes. And yet I held onto the past, obsessed with my intoxicating crush on Josh. It seems so pointless now—trading childish thrills and glamour for the real care and attention I received from Colin.

I raise the scarf, relieved to see that the bleeding has slowed.

But he's so terribly pale. His stillness pushes ice into my veins. I bend closer. "Please, get better," I whisper. There's no sign he can hear me. "Please, be happy."

I imagine him and Miriam, hand in hand, striding into their bright future. It hurts to picture them, yet I'd still be glad for Colin. They're perfect together. "I love you, Colin," I whisper. "Please recover and be happy."

I'm still talking to him when sirens close in, still cradling him when I hear running feet and urgent voices.

I turn around. "In here!" I yell. My voice is like a duck's.

Footsteps pound through the garage and stop. I know they've found Daphne.

"We need help in here too!" I cry. More footsteps pound closer.

I'm bent low over Colin when strong hands grasp my shoulders. "Are you hurt?" says a deep, calm woman's voice. I look up. It's Miriam Young.

"No." I shake my head. "But Colin is. Badly!"

A paramedic bends over Gerard. Another rushes up and deposits her bag beside Colin. "Over here," she calls to a colleague. More footsteps ring out behind me.

Miriam pulls me into an embrace. "You have to let go of him," she says gently. "They need to check him."

I allow her to lift me to my feet, to steer me away from Colin. A sob wrenches from me. I don't want to leave him.

"He'll be fine," she says. While she sounds calm, I can hear the fear in her voice. "C'mon, let's get you outside," she says.

I sway against her. The paramedics shift Colin onto a stretcher.

Walking through the garage, I lean against Miriam, all rivalry forgotten.

Daphne has been moved outside. At our approach, the pig stirs. It raises its snout, bleary but awake. "Please get the pig outside," I say to Miriam. His squeals saved my life. And—I pray—Colin's.

"We will. Don't worry," she says. "A vet's coming."

I nod. "Will you ride in the ambulance with Colin?" I ask her. I can't bear to think of him going alone. What if he wakes up and there's no familiar face, or only that of the monster who attacked him?

Miriam shakes her head. "I think that should be you."

We stumble through the door. What does that mean?

I glance at her, questioningly. While her face is serious, there's a smile in her dark eyes. Her voice is warm: "You're the face he'd want to wake up to."

For the first time, I truly look at her, or look beyond her surface beauty. I see the dark grooves beneath her kind eyes, how tired and tense she looks, like a queen whose kingdom is crumbling. She is grace under pressure personified.

She squeezes my shoulder. "Wait and see," she says. She smiles for real. For a second, her smile knocks the stress and fatigue right off her face. "I'll dance at your wedding."

CHAPTER 32:

GOOD MEDICINE

Just over two months ago Colin visited me in the hospital. Now, I'm visiting him. He got out of Intensive Care last night but wasn't allowed visitors until this morning.

I woke up early.

At 6:55 a.m. I'm headed toward the nurse's desk, armed with a bag of croissants, two takeaway cappuccinos, a terrycloth eye-mask, and a box of earplugs. I remember how hard it was to sleep in the hospital—the lights always too bright and the wards full of weird, disturbing noises.

"Bright and early," says the nurse, at my approach. She's in her fifties with short grey hair and pink cat-eye glasses. We met yesterday, when I was brought to the ER, where I was checked and released. Colin, Daphne, and Gerard were admitted. The pig is at the vet's. Everyone is expected to recover.

The nurse is dressed in powder pink scrubs. "How's your bruise?" she asks. She nods toward my chest. "You feeling better?"

"It's sore," I say. "But okay." It looks like a bottle of ink exploded against my chest. "How's Colin?" I ask her.

"Lucky," she says. A CT scan revealed he didn't need surgery, although they're keeping him under observation. Some cerebrospinal fluid was leaking. "He's awake and fairly coherent. But time will tell." She checks her watch. "He's in Room 211," she says. "Visiting hours start at seven but you may as well go in. Just remember, he'll tire easily. And his memory's pretty patchy."

"Thanks." I hesitate, suddenly nervous. Yesterday, he was unconscious the whole time. Will he be pleased to see me? Will he even know who I am? He's suffered brain trauma.

My knock elicits a muffled "come in." I push open the door. "Hey, Colin?"

Stretched out in bed, he looks very long.

His head turns. He's got two raccoon eyes. A basilar skull fracture can do that, apparently. It can also cause long-term brain damage, although the nurse said that was unlikely.

In their strange, dark sockets, Colin's eyes light up. "Toby." His voice has a slight slur. He blinks. "How are you?"

"Good." I come closer. "And you?"

"Great."

I feel an urge to laugh and cry. Great is such an overstatement. "Are you hungry?" I hold up my bags. "Or thirsty?"

It takes him a minute to answer. "Um, I'm not sure. No."

"Okay."

I deposit the coffees and my bags on his nightstand, then pull a nearby chair closer.

Colin looks so dazed and vulnerable. He shuts his eyes. From the slow way he moves, I know he's in pain. It hurts to look at him. Apart from those black bruises, he's icy pale. He looks thin, and decades older.

I take a seat and extract one of the cappuccinos from its cardboard holder. It's the perfect temperature to sip. I take a few gulps, steeling myself. "Seriously, how do you feel?" I ask, worriedly.

His eyes open, slowly. "I get dizzy," he says. "The doctor said it's . . ." He pauses, like he's searching for the right word. "Normal," he says. "I feel . . . tired."

"Your brain needs rest to heal," I say. Colin doesn't answer. "I should let you sleep." The coffee tastes unusually bitter. "I'll come back tomorrow."

His eyes open again. He reaches for me. "No. Please," he says. "Even if we don't talk, can you stay a little?"

I set down my coffee and grasp his hand. Touching him seems to unlock some tension in my neck I didn't even know was there. I bow my head and pull his hand to my forehead. "I was so scared," I whisper.

"I . . . I'm sorry," says Colin.

I sit up straighter. "No," I say. "You have no reason to be sorry. I'm sorry!"

I shake my head. There's so much I'm sorry about. But that can wait. I study Colin's hand and wrist, the IV line snaking into his blue vein. It's like blue paint on porcelain, so precious and fragile. "Waiting for the ambulance, I didn't know if you'd . . ." I gulp, unable to say it. "I was scared you were really badly hurt. That I'd never have the chance to tell you."

"Tell me what?" murmurs Colin.

"I love you," I say. I feel a strong urge to laugh. I've never said those words to any man, not since my dad left, when I was fourteen. I was scared to. Scared they'd feel like a weight hanging over me, that I'd be crushed if they drew the wrong reaction.

Yet now, I don't need him to react. I just want him to know, to feel loved. "I love you so much. I want you to be well and happy." It's a joy to say it.

Colin smiles. "I love you too, Toby Wong." He licks his chapped lips. "But you sure do cause trouble."

My heart's a soaring bird. I fight back a smile. "I don't cause it," I say. "I just find it."

He smiles and nods, then winces. "I'm too wrecked to argue. Can I have a get-well kiss?"

I rise from my chair and lean over him. "I'm scared to hurt you."

His arms close around me. He pulls me down. I'm mindful of his IV.

"Being near you makes me feel better," he says.

When our lips meet, I feel better too. It's like I was lost in the woods at night, wandering in circles, hunted . . . And now I've found the way home—seen that welcoming golden puddle of a porch light. I'll never leave home again. Never.

Our kiss goes on and on. I hope it never stops.

But then, behind me, someone clears their throat. A theatrical growl. I look around.

"Hey," says the nurse. Her voice is sharp. "Didn't I tell you not to wear him out?"

My cheeks flush. The nurse laughs. "This is a G-rated ward." She's wheeling a portable blood pressure monitor. She looks from me to Colin and pushes her pink glasses back up her long nose. "I'm kidding," she says. "Kind of. Although he does need to rest. Come back tomorrow. A daily dose of *that* will cure anything!" She laughs again. "I'm just jealous." On her feet are pink Crocs that match her funky glasses.

I smile at Colin. "See you tomorrow," I say.

He fights back a yawn. "Yes." I'm at the door when he calls out. "Toby?"

"Yeah?"

"Can I have one more kiss?"

The nurse cackles. She's got the blood-pressure belt around Colin's arm. "No way," she says. "Your blood pressure's high enough!"

She wags a finger my way. "Go home," she says. "Have a cold shower."

Again, I'm blushing. The nurse grins as she works. I wave from the doorway. "I love you," I say to Colin. Now that I've started saying it, I can't stop.

I want to sing it as I skip down the hall. I'm a romantic fool and I don't even care. I want a t-shirt: I heart Colin Destin.

I'm walking toward the exit when my phone rings. I extract it from my purse. It's my mother. "Hi, hon. How are you?" she asks.

"Hey Mom," I say. "I'm fine. I'm just leaving the Jubilee."

"Oh!" she says. "I'm here too. I'm going to visit Daphne."

Seconds later, I see her, striding toward me. She's carrying a bunch of orange chrysanthemums, wrapped in newspaper. A giant purple tote bag dangles off one skinny shoulder.

I wave and stash my phone. My mom has obviously been up most of the night. Her normally glowing complexion is dull and her eyes have a manic, overtired glitter.

"Hey Mom," I say again. She strides closer.

She's wearing a brown coat and a long, loose, navy linen dress over matching navy tights. A string of faceted black tourmaline beads circles her throat. It's the most sedate outfit I've seen her wear in years, my mom's version of formal wear. Maybe she wants the medical staff to take her seriously and not dismiss her as some aging, weirdo hippie. The look is only slightly skewed by her rubber boots, which are printed with cherries and bananas.

She studies me critically too, clearly convinced I should be hospitalized.

We meet and hug—or hug as best we can with my cast and her swathe of flowers.

"How are you feeling?" she asks again. She drove me home from the hospital yesterday morning, then spent the rest of the day fussing over me. I can still taste the vile "healing smoothie" she made me for dinner.

"I'm fine," I say, wincing when she squeezes me to her chest. "And you?"

"Me?" She leans back, surprised. "Okay, just worried about Daphne, of course." She swallows hard. "I spoke to her doctors last night. She underwent hyperbaric oxygen therapy." She says these words carefully, like she's learned them by heart. "She's doing well. The doctors are hopeful." Her optimism falters. She blinks at the shiny white floor. "But it's still too soon to say if there's lasting damage. CO_2 can cause long-term brain damage." She sighs. "No matter what, it'll be a long road to recovery."

She's got three bead bracelets on her left wrist and keeps twisting them. Smoky quartz for grounding. Citrine for optimism. Amber for healing and purifying. The last seems a good choice. I can't enter a hospital without feeling like I'm bound to catch something. All those sick people! I could never be a doctor.

My mom's shaking voice draws my attention away from thoughts of germs and crystals. "If you hadn't found Daphne when you did . . ." she says. She brushes a tear from one blinking eye.

I put my arm around her. "She'll be fine," I say, although really—

how can I know? I Googled it too. Carbon monoxide poisoning can be tricky.

My mom nods. "I know. Daphne's tough." I nod too. "Will you come with me to see her?" asks my mom.

I hesitate. She reaches for my hand. Hers is unusually cold. It feels oddly frail too. I give it a reassuring squeeze. "Of course," I tell her.

Daphne is on the fourth floor. We take the stairs. My mom dislikes elevators. I'm not sure if it's the mechanics she mistrusts, or the feng shui. We both climb slowly, without speaking. Muscles I didn't even know I had are protesting.

Daphne is in a private room. We peer around the door.

She's sound asleep. Strangely, without all that makeup, she looks younger. And she seems to have shrunk. Or maybe she's just curled up under the blankets. With her hair loose and soft, she reminds me of a sleeping child. Innocent and defenseless. I remember her passed out in that smoke-filled car.

My stomach twists. How could her son-in-law do this?

My mom inhales. She blinks back tears. I know how she feels— scared and helpless. What if Daphne is irreparably damaged?

My mom gestures back the way we came.

We both tiptoe away. "I'll come back later," she whispers.

I nod. Yes, it's better to let Daphne sleep. Like Colin, her brain needs rest to recover.

We find a nurse. My mom hands over the flowers.

We're turning to go when I notice a uniformed policeman sitting across the hall from Daphne's door. Was he there the whole time? I can't believe I didn't notice him. Is he there to protect Daphne? Or do the cops still think she's Stephen's killer? But surely, they can't think she'll escape! Can she even walk?

I turn back toward the ward's main door. It opens to emit Miriam Young, hand-in-hand with a small boy. He's got golden skin and curly brown hair. In his free hand he holds a plastic dinosaur. I recognize it: it's Buttpokersaurus.

Miriam smiles. Like yesterday, she looks dead tired. Her hair is scraped into a messy bun. She's dressed in her usual dark jeans, boots, and a black turtleneck. Today, she's got a quilted grey vest overtop. There's a blob of something white—is it bird poop?—on her shoulder.

"Toby! Ivy!" she says. "You okay? I just went to see Colin."

We nod. My mom crouches down. "And who are you?" she asks the little boy. He looks maybe two, at the most, with puffed cheeks like toasted marshmallows.

He thrusts the dinosaur at her. "Rwwwwaaaahhhh!" he roars.

My mom feigns panic. "Aaaaahhhhhh!" she mock-yells. She straightens up and brushes down her dress. "Is that a T-rex?"

"Nope." The boy scoffs, like he can't believe she'd make such a rookie mistake. "It's Albertosaurus."

"Oh," says my mom. "And who are you?"

The kid ignores her.

"Max?" says Miriam. "This is Ivy. She asked you a question."

The boy releases her hand and spins around. "Rrrwwwaaah!" he says again. His dinosaur leaps through the air. "I'm Max," he says.

I can't stop looking from the boy to Miriam Young. He looks a lot like those twins. And he looks like her. But surely, they can't *all* be hers. Can they?

"Is he . . . yours?" I ask.

Miriam smiles. "Yes."

"Oh," I say. "I didn't know you were a mom."

"I also have nine-month-old twins," she says. "Three boys."

"Oh," I say again. What I think is: *poor you!* I try to keep my voice neutral: "I think I met them at Colin's."

Miriam nods. "Colin's been a godsend."

Her right hand goes to her left, as if to touch a ring that's not there. "I transferred here a few months ago," she says. "From Salmon Arm. Messy divorce." She swallows hard. "And Max here has been having serious asthma attacks. We're at Emergency three, four times a week. Colin's been minding the twins." Her face sags, like she might cry. "I don't know how I'd have survived without him."

"My gosh," says my mom. "You're a single mom with three kids under two? I'd be happy to babysit anytime! Who knows when I'll ever get grandchildren of my own . . ." She looks at me pointedly. I roll my eyes. She digs her ancient Nokia out of her bag. "Let me give you my number," she says to Miriam.

"I can babysit too," I say. But then I remember those twins. "Although I'm not so great with babies," I add.

I can't believe I thought Colin was dating her. The poor woman barely has time to sleep or eat, let alone date! I wish he'd told me.

I need to introduce Miriam to Quinn. They can swap baby war stories. When Abby's a bit older, they can have play dates.

Miriam smiles. "You guys are so kind," she says. "But it seems Max's new asthma medicine might actually work." Her voice lifts with hope. "It's now been two days without an attack. Touch wood . . ." She looks around for something wooden to knock.

"Linen," says my mom, offering up her dress. "It's from a plant."

Miriam taps my mom's skirt. "Thanks," she says.

I want to reroll my eyes but refrain. All these superstitious people! Although sometimes, I catch myself . . .

"You know, tiger-eye can help asthma," says my mom. "Here . . ." She rummages through her massive tote and extracts a small purple velvet bag. I guess she wasn't taking any chances and brought along her set of crystal greatest-hits.

She picks out a tawny, walnut-sized rock and hands it to Miriam. "Sew that up in a sock so he can't swallow it and pop it under his pillow."

I expect a blank look from Miriam. Instead, she peers at it and looks thrilled. It's the same color as Max's hair. "Oh yeah? Wow! Thanks," she says. She zips the shiny tumbled pebble into her purse. "That's so kind," she tells my mother.

"How's Gerard?" I ask Miriam.

She frowns. "You gave him a pretty good whack," she says. "No fracture but he's got a concussion."

I shudder. The memory of hitting him—the shock waves traveling up my arm—makes me queasy.

Is Gerard here in this ward? Maybe the seated cop is here to watch him.

"Have you talked to him yet?" I ask Miriam.

We've now moved to the side of the wide hall, out of the way of passersby. Max is sitting on the floor. My mom—ridiculously flexible thanks to all that yoga—squats nearby. From the corner of my eye I see her withdraw a Matchbox car from her bag. Wow. It's like Hermione's magical beaded evening purse. What's next? The kitchen sink? Or a live pony?

"The doctors just let me question him," says Miriam. "Briefly." She looks serious. "He admitted to drugging Daphne with the Ativan," she says. "He'd been doing it for months, in increasingly dangerous doses. He wanted control of her house and cash. He claimed he didn't want to kill her, just convince her she was losing her grip. But then, when he thought Daphne was accusing Isobel of murder, he decided to get rid of her. He drugged her and the pig with sleeping meds before gassing them in the old Mustang."

I bite my lip. "Did Isobel know?" I ask. "About any of it?"

Miriam's face tightens "I don't believe so," she says. "But we're still investigating. We picked up Lukas," she adds.

I nod, relieved. For Daphne's sake, I hope Isobel had no idea what her husband was up to. Daphne will already have one kid in jail.

"How about Lukas?" I ask. "Did he confess to killing Stephen?"

Miriam looks down at her son. He's controlling the car—a red hot rod—while my mom's got the dinosaur. Their game seems to involve a lot of engine noises and roars.

Miriam sighs. "We've charged him with assault," she says. "For that attack on you. But no, he still insists he didn't kill anyone. We had to let him out on bail, like Daphne."

My throat feels suddenly thick.

Seeing my face, Miriam looks apologetic. "I'm sorry," she says. "But don't worry. We're working on it."

"Stephen and Lukas fought," I say. "I heard him admit to that."

Miriam nods. "I believe you." Her face is grim. "We just have to prove it." She takes a deep breath and draws her shoulders back. "But seriously Toby, it's all good. Thanks to you, this case is close to being wrapped up. We will get him, don't worry."

When she smiles, I know I should be reassured. So why am I not? Despite my warm coat, I shiver. I want to go home. My bruised chest feels increasingly sore.

I look at my mother. "Mom?" I say.

She looks up and rises smoothly from her squat.

She joins us again, smiling at Miriam. "Remember what I said about babysitting," she says. "Call me any time. I'd be happy to help."

Miriam blinks, like this kindness might make her cry. "Thank you," she says, softly.

My mom waves to Max. He's now clutching the dinosaur and the car.

"Bye Ivy!" he yells, like they're old friends.

As we walk down the hall I marvel at my mom's talents. She can befriend anyone, from drunken bums to billionaires, testy babies to cranky old farts, feral cats to iguanas. More amazingly still, she doesn't change depending on who she's with but is always her true, kooky self. Maybe that's her real talent.

"Want a drink?" I suggest. I already had the one coffee but could use another. Or some juice. News that Lukas is free has left me feeling shaky.

"Sure," says my mom. "I'm parched, after all that roaring."

We walk to the cafeteria. It's almost empty at this hour, one table near the back occupied by a couple of nurses. A girl in red earmuffs sits alone at a table in the middle. A tired-looking doctor talks softly on his cellphone.

My mom reaches for my hand. "Don't worry," she says. "I know Lukas seems scary. But he's not a *real* danger."

I stop, amazed.

First off, how did she even know I was thinking about him? And secondly, how could she say that, when he broke my wrist, two days ago?

"He broke my wrist," I say. "And he killed a man!"

My mom sighs. "I just . . ." She shrugs. "It's just the way I feel. I don't think you need to worry about him."

Great. I'm glad she feels reassured, but I sure as hell don't. She didn't see his face that night, or hear his embittered whining. I fight back the urge to snap at her.

My mom fingers her heavy black tourmaline necklace. She lifts it over her head. "You should wear this," she says. She looks serene. "If you're feeling edgy."

I pull away, then relent. Oh why not? It won't hurt me.

I let her slip the beads over my head. She flips my hair out from under them. My hair's now shoulder-length. I keep putting off getting a haircut.

My mom leans back to survey me. "Perfect," she says. "Black tourmaline's the best."

I nod. Yeah, yeah, yeah. I know: the stone to ward off negativity and aggression. I touch the faceted beads. Actually, this necklace is pretty.

"Hot chocolate?" offers my mom. I nod. That's exactly what I need. "You sit down," she says, pointing at the closest table. "I'll get it."

It's only when I've sunk into a chair that I realize how tired I am. It's like I've been running on fumes of fear, adrenaline, pain, and relief . . . I could sleep for days. It's tempting to set my head on the table and shut my eyes. My eyelids feel heavy.

"Here we are," says my mom. She sets down two paper cups. I wrap my hands around mine. "Thanks."

"Cheers," she says.

I smile tiredly. "Cheers."

I take a sip. It's machine hot chocolate. Below the tasty froth it's powdery, watery, and way too sweet. I drink it anyway. As the warmth and sugar spread through me, I perk up. My mom's right. It's all worked out fine. Everyone survived and is expected to recover. I'm off work today. I'll go home and sleep.

Tomorrow, I'll come back first thing in the morning to see Colin.

Colin—who loves me. How did I forget, even for an instant? He loves me! The warmth in my belly spreads to my heart.

I smile at my mother.

"You look better," she says.

I nod and try to tamp down my smile. If I keep it up, she'll get suspicious and start asking questions I lack the strength to deflect.

"Yeah. I'm relieved," I say. "I'm glad it's over."

"Me too," says my mom. She lowers her cup. She's got a hot choco-late mustache.

"Um, your face," I say. I point at my own upper lip.

She smiles. "Yeah, you've got one too."

I frown. "Well . . . what?" I wipe my lip with the back of my good hand. "Weren't you going to tell me?"

"Of course." She smirks. "But it looked cute. So not yet."

I'm freshly annoyed with my mother.

CHAPTER 33

ON A KNIFE'S EDGE

While my mom goes to the bathroom I sit and wait. A few more people have entered the cafeteria: an exasperated forty-something mother and her teenage son, in the midst of an argument about his excessive (her word) videogame playing; an elderly couple who order matching bowls of pink Jello; a guy in scrubs who looks almost as tired as me; three middle-aged ladies dressed for golf. They remind me of Isobel—skinny, blonde, and disgruntled.

I rub my eyes. The sugar surge has worn off. I slump in the hard plastic chair, feeling sore and worn out. What's keeping my mother?

Bored with watching my fellow cafeteria-mates, I skim the news on my phone. Mass shootings. Antivaxxers. More desperate refugees. The world's going to hell at high speed.

I want to go home and hide. Ideally with Colin. The thought of him perks me up again. That kiss . . . My stomach squirms happily. We could live in a bunker.

Glancing up from my phone, a flash of gold catches my eye. Is that Josh? I squint. There's no mistaking him.

He's at the far end of the room, in the line to pay. My heart gives a tiny flop, like a minnow dropped onto a dock. I can see his back and the side of his face. He turns to talk to someone.

My gaze follows his. Vonda has budged into line beside him.

I grip my near-empty paper cup. Maybe she's here visiting Daphne.

Vonda is wearing a short fur coat that's as glossy as her hair. It looks like real mink, which takes major balls on Vancouver Island. She's liable to get doused in red paint. Although it'd take a brave PETA activist to confront Vonda. Below this furry coat lie a short leather skirt, her enviable legs, and a pair of towering black high-heeled boots. Topping everything off is that raspberry beret, tilted becomingly.

Vonda deposits the bottle she's holding onto Josh's tray. She leans against him. He strokes her fluffy waist.

I grit my teeth. So they're together, after all. That didn't take long.

I wait for a flood of gloom. *Oh-woe-is-me-I've-been-replaced-by-a-gold-digging-sex-bomb . . .*

Strangely, it doesn't come. I just don't care. I pick up my cup and drain the last gluey, cold dregs. Idle curiosity inspires me to keep watching them, now at the till. They're standing so close, they look welded. Vonda pats Josh's back pocket, like she's rubbing his butt. Or is she fondling his fat wallet?

I can't help but smile. Josh is her perfect man—sure to boost her *brand image*. And him? I recall his ex-wife, who was an overblown kind of sexy. Vonda's definitely his type. They'll look awesome together on Instagram. She can pose on his yacht in extra-tight yoga gear and full makeup.

My smile widens. I truly don't care—like not one jot. Whatever a jot is. They're probably made for each other. Happiness has made me generous. I actually hope they'll be happy. May they Influence-as-one and find millions of like-happy Followers.

"Toby?" My mom is back from the washroom. She's washed her face, which is still damp, and wetted her thundercloud hair in an attempt to tame it. "Sorry I took so long," she says. "I met someone from yoga. Her husband just had knee surgery." She shakes her head. "Silly man. He just won't stop playing rugby."

I collect our empty cups and rise, then look around for a trash can.

"Hey? Isn't that Josh?" says my mom. She peers at Josh and Vonda. "Yes."

"Aren't you going to say hi?"

"Not today," I say. "I'm beat. I'm going home to sleep for the rest of the day."

Just for a second, my mom looks thoughtful. Then she nods and smiles. "Can you give me a ride?" she asks. "I walked here. And I just looked outside. It's pouring."

"Sure," I say. We walk toward the exit.

We've just gotten into my car when my mom's phone rings.

How she can find anything in that giant bag is a mystery. Yet she does. She must not recognize the number because she frowns. "Hello?" Her face lights up. "Oh, hi, Daphne! You're awake! How are you?"

I turn on the ignition and the heat but stay parked. My mom might want to hop out and visit Daphne, after all. Rain splatters against the windshield.

"Uh huh. Okay. Oh! Sure," says my mom. "No problem. Okay. Give me half an hour."

She hangs up and turns to me. "Hon, that was Daphne. She needs some supplies. A toothbrush and pajamas." She waves a hand for etcetera. "Would you mind popping by her place and dropping me back here again? I'll take everything up to her."

I want to say no. I'm dying to get into bed. But it'll take what— half an hour?

"Sure," I say. I back out of the parking spot. "Wait," I say, as we're in line to exit the parking lot. "Are you sure we can go in? Isn't it a crime scene?"

"It's fine," says my mom. "The police are done."

Rats, I think. But don't say it.

When we pull up in front of Daphne's I'm tempted to wait in the car. I'm tired and don't want to go in there. What happened yesterday is still too fresh. Too scary and raw.

I recall Gerard's pale, furious face—like a bloated, murderous Alfred Hitchcock.

My mom unclicks her seatbelt. "You coming?" she asks.

I unclick my belt too. Oh why not? I may as well. If I help find Daphne's stuff we can get out of here quicker.

We walk down the path side-by-side.

Without Kevin, it's very quiet. I wonder how it's going at the vet's. Given that the pig was stirring yesterday and Daphne wasn't, I'm guessing Kevin will soon be his greedy and mischievous self. It would take a lot to kill Kevin.

My mom extracts the spare key from beneath its flowerpot. I guess

Daphne told her where to look. When she opens the door, my ribs seem to shrink. What if Lukas is inside?

I say this to my mom. "He's not," she says, firmly. "Daphne told me. Grace drove him back to rehab. That was part of his bail agreement on the assault charge. He has to stay there."

I take a deep breath and follow my mom indoors. The hall lies dark and quiet. I shut the front door. The shattered cup has been swept up and the spilled coffee wiped away. The stained rug is gone. Perhaps the police took it.

"Hello?" I call out, just in case someone's here. My voice echoes. "What does she need?" I ask my mother.

"Toiletries. PJs. Some meds," she says. She's already heading for the stairs. "I'll get them." She shivers. "It's freezing in here. Can you check if any windows are open?"

"Um, okay," I say. My mom's right. It is cold.

I peer into the library. It's shut up tight. I pass through the double doors into the living room. Again, the windows are closed. I walk through the dim, formal dining room and into the kitchen. No open windows. The tarp over the counter has been folded back to reveal a new marble countertop. Some boxes sit on the counter. Others remain on the floor, covered by tarps. The stepladder rests where I last saw it.

Maybe it's fatigue, or hunger, or stress, but I can't stop shivering. I need some hot tea.

I peer under a tarp and find the kettle. A little more searching yields a tray of cutlery and some mugs. It feels colder in the house than it did outdoors.

Maybe the basement windows are open, to air out the exhaust fumes. They'll just have to stay that way. I don't want to return to that basement.

I bend to search various boxes. There must be tea somewhere. In the last box, there's a tin of cocoa. I hesitate. Is this the stuff that was drugged? But no, Gerard added the sleeping meds after, like the sugar.

I pry off the lid. The cocoa looks and smells fine. I spoon a generous amount into two mugs, then add some brown sugar. Carrying two mugs with one hand isn't easy. I find a tray and walk slowly, trying to keep it steady.

I'm half way up the stairs when I trip. The tray slams down and tips. Hot cocoa splashes up my front. I fall forward, onto my knees and elbows. The jolt hurts my chest and injured arm.

I straighten up. I'm not badly hurt, just startled and dismayed. Hot chocolate drips down my camel sweater and over the stairs. There are big, ugly blotches on poor Daphne's cream carpet.

I clutch my forehead, surveying the mess. "Crap," I say. If I'm not quick, it will stain. Daphne would have to recarpet the whole staircase.

With a wobble, I rise to my feet. What can I use? Baking soda? Or maybe Daphne's got some sort of cleaning spray.

I carry the half-empty mugs back down to the kitchen and set them in the sink. There might be something in the laundry.

Descending the basement stairs feels like déjà vu. My knees are rubbery. I tell myself to grow up. Gerard is in hospital, incapacitated. Lukas is in rehab.

The TV room stretches below me, quiet and empty. The vase Gerard used to bash Colin is gone, as is my hammer. The only signs of yesterday's struggle are some bits of fishing line, left where the paramedics dropped them, and a bloodstain, over where Colin lay.

I shudder. Maybe I shouldn't worry about the cocoa stains, after all. The whole house needs new carpeting. It's not like Daphne can't afford it.

But since I'm here, I may as well look. I head for the laundry room.

It's neat and bright, since there's a big (shut) window. I see a box of laundry pods and bottles of bleach and fabric softener. There must be some spray-on stain remover, somewhere.

On a low shelf sits a big plastic picnic hamper full of cleaning supplies. I pull it out. There's a spray bottle of Windex and a Toilet Duck. I rummage through various bottles and jars. Down at the bottom lies a patchwork of sponges and rags. Tipped on its side is a can. Aha—it claims to remove stains from everything.

I fish it out and grab a dark rag. The cloth's surprisingly heavy.

When I lift it out, I see it's a dark blue man's sock, folded in on itself. There's something inside it. I squish it. I can feel some hard round disks in there.

I unroll the sock and shake. Two dozen gold coins spray out. As they bounce and roll, I try to stop them. A few vanish under the washing machine. I blink, stupefied.

Daphne said Walt's coins were in the bank. So what are these? I pick a coin from the floor and examine it: On one side are the words UNITED STATES and a bird with outstretched wings. I turn it over to see a head in profile and the date 1795.

Holy cow. It must be worth something! I weigh it in my hand. It feels heavy.

I start scooping up coins. They're all different, but all old and solid gold—from the 1700s and 1800s.

On hands and knees, I peer under the washer. I can see some coins under there but can't reach them. I sit up and shake myself. It doesn't matter. I'm not thinking straight. Someone can get them out later.

I feed the remaining coins back into the sock. My mind is reeling. I get to my feet and ascend the stairs, moving slowly. The discovery of these coins changes everything.

I need to call Miriam.

The door at the top of the stairs is shut. I swear I left it open. I swallow hard, hesitating. My mom must have shut it.

I push the door open. "Mom?" I call.

My mom is standing near the sink. At the sight of me she smiles. "Oh there you are," she says. "I wondered where you'd gotten off to."

I step inside. Beside my mom stands Grace. She's washing a mug, while gazing out the window into the back yard. As usual, she's wearing an apron, this one printed with a holly pattern. As she rinses the mug, she hums cheerily. "I packed Daphne's things," my mom tells me. "Shall we get going?"

Grace turns my way. Her eyes travel from my face to the sock in my good hand. Her pink mouth opens and her eyes spark. Before I can react, she's grabbed a large knife from the cutlery tray.

"No!" I cry, but she's already seized my mother.

"Don't move," says Grace. She presses the blade against my mom's throat.

My mom jerks in surprise. Grace's grip on her tightens.

"You," she snarls. She nods her chin at me. "Put that down on the table."

I hesitate. Two dozen coins in a sock is not much of a weapon. But it's better than nothing.

Grace increases the pressure on my mom's neck. I wince. My mom is wide-eyed. I throw the sock onto the table. "That's Stephen's sock," I say. "Why were you at the cabin?"

"Poor Lukas had to eat, didn't he?" snaps Grace. "And he needed clean clothes."

I should have known. Little Lukas is way too spoiled to fend for himself in the woods. The devoted housekeeper was feeding him and doing his laundry.

"Put your hands up," says Grace. I do as I'm told. "That's right. Keep 'em where I can see 'em." She sounds straight off a bad mafia drama. I'm having trouble processing this. Grace is so helpful. So competent. So cheerful. It's like learning Mrs. Claus isn't just mythical but a real life, cold-blooded killer. I had it all wrong. Grace is dangerous.

"Now, you." She glares at me. "Walk in front. We're going upstairs." She jerks her head toward the hallway.

I hesitate. What's Grace planning? Best-case scenario, she'll tie us up and leave us in an upstairs closet. Worst-case . . . How desperate is she? Before it gets to that, we're better off trying to fight. My heart hammers. Despite her grandmotherly looks, Grace is no harmless little old lady. A lifetime of hard work has built strength beneath her matronly padding. My mom and I are lightweights. I can barely swallow. We're in trouble.

My mom blinks at me, like she's trying to send a message. What's she trying to say?

I feel desperate. If only we really were psychic.

"Hurry up!" screeches Grace.

I see a drop of blood spring from my mom's throat. I'm scared to turn my back on Grace but have no choice. Hands raised I walk slowly down the hall and up the stairs. My mom and Grace are right behind me. I pass over the spot where I spilled the cocoa.

Seeing it, Grace makes an angry hissing sound. "What a mess!" she rasps. "Who'll clean it up? Hey?"

I hear my mom gasp. Has she been cut again?

When I turn to look, Grace snaps. "Keep going! Straight ahead!" Her voice is as shrill as a drill. "Get moving! Into Daphne's bedroom."

I precede them through Daphne's sitting room and into her bedroom. We're now at the back of the house, where it's the most isolated. If we screamed, would anyone hear? The lots are big around here. It's hard to breathe. What's Grace planning?

"Over there," says Grace. "Stay away from the window."

I do as she says, then turn, slowly.

Under her pewter hair, my mom's face is dumpling-white. In contrast, beneath her dandelion-fluff hair, Grace's face is flushed with excitement.

"Up against that wall," she hisses at me. Her dark eyes glitter.

I back slowly toward it.

"So you saw everything," I say. "Stephen and Lukas scuffled, right? I'm sure Lukas didn't mean to kill him . . ."

"Shut your mouth!" shrieks Grace. "He didn't do it! That horrible man! Stephen!" She spits out his name. "It was all his fault! I had no choice—" Her mouth clamps shut and her little eyes flick sideways. On the knife's handle, her pudgy knuckles are white. "Enough chit chat," she says. "Be quiet."

My mom bites back a gasp. Grace has cut her again. More scarlet drops slide down my mom's throat and into her collar.

I reach for my own throat, feel the carved black tourmaline necklace. Protection against aggression and negativity. My stomach plummets. I took it for myself and left my mom unprotected. But now is not the time for guilt. Or superstitious drivel.

I have to distract Grace and hope she'll let down her guard. I need to keep her talking, flatter her, seem sympathetic.

"You had no choice," I say, soothingly. "You had to defend Lukas."

From the way her mouth quivers I know I'm right. I picture her wielding that iron poker. The vision makes me shiver.

"That horrible man hurt him," she whispers. "He pushed Lukas! Called him a bum! In his own home! Lukas had every right to be there, in his childhood cottage!" Grace's pink cheeks puff out. "Stephen was the interloper! The fraud!" Her white eyebrows furrow. "I only hit him once," she says, "to make him stop." She blinks. "Or maybe twice." Another blink. "To teach him a lesson."

I bet she struck him a lot more times than that. Grace licks her lips. "I won't let anyone harm Lukas," she mutters. Her eyes shine with crazed righteousness. "He's vulnerable! He needs me!"

I think of him two nights back, when he hit me. He wasn't so vulnerable then. Just another well-off white man, entitled, and angry, convinced nothing was his fault, ever. Convinced the world owed him.

"Then what?" I ask. "Did he take the coins? Or did you grab a few, hope no one would notice?"

Grace's eyes narrow with indignation. "Walt promised me those," she says. "And a whole lot more!" Again, her voice rises. "I deserve them! Thirty years I've worked here! Done all the dirty work! I raised those kids!" She jabs a finger at her aproned chest. "Walt and Daphne had no time for them. Oh no, they had more *important* things to do!" She scoffs. "More important than caring for their own children!"

I don't contradict her. It might be true. Walt and Daphne were busy people, gaining money, power, and glamor. They probably spoiled their kids with fancy stuff while neglecting them. Their housekeeper probably *did* raise the duo. It can't have been easy.

Grace yanks open one of Daphne's drawers. She pulls out a handful of pantyhose. "Get back against that wall," she snarls.

I take another step back and hit the wall. My stomach twists.

She's planning to tie us up. The thought of being defenseless around this woman turns my insides to mush.

Grace shakes out a pair of black pantyhose, ready to bind my mother.

I stare into my mom's eyes. *On the count of three*, I think. *You jab her in the gut and duck left. I'll punch right.* My cast is hard. A good whack could knock her out cold. *C'mon mom.* I think. *One. Two.*

I leap at Grace. My mom's elbow finds her tummy. My mother ducks left. I punch right. It's like a Hong Kong movie fight, perfectly choreographed. It's like we practiced.

My cast slams into Grace's head, which snaps back and hits the wall behind her.

Pain bursts through my knuckles. I see cartoon stars. My wrist feels freshly broken.

Grace turns her head, stupefied. She blinks at me. For a second she totters. The knife falls from her hand. Her legs fold under her.

My mom jumps backward.

At the start, Grace collapses in slow motion. But then everything fast-forwards. She slides down the wall and lands with a crash on the hardwood.

"Holy guacamole," says my mom. She gapes at me, then down at Grace. She reaches for the dresser to steady herself. "That was awesome!"

I step over Grace's crumpled form and go to my mom. "Are you okay?" I gasp. I pick up a pair of purple tights and scrunch it into a wad, then press it against her bleeding throat.

"Fine. Good." She nods. Her eyes are glazed with shock. "You?"

"Fine."

I look at Grace. I don't want to touch her but it'd be safer to tie her up. Even out cold, she's a sinister presence.

"I'll do it," says my mom. She bends to scoop up some more tights. I watch as she binds Grace's wrists together, behind her back.

The pain in my hand and arm is so intense I feel queasy.

My mom gives the tights a yank. "That'll do," she says. She ties a big knot, then moves down to Grace's ankles. When they're bound too, she straightens. "We'd better call the police," she says.

I reach for her arm. "Let's go downstairs."

We walk shakily, arm-in-arm, down the staircase.

I call 911 first—they must know me by now—and then Miriam. She says she's on her way.

We sit in the kitchen and wait. We're both shaking, hard. I make another batch of hot chocolate.

"Mom?" I say. I set the cocoa on the table and take a seat. Shock and relief have left me with a weird, floaty feeling.

I think back to that moment I charged Grace, how it all went exactly as I'd planned. My mom followed my instructions perfectly. Except I didn't speak those words out loud. That was all in our heads.

I rub my eyes. For the first time in my life it seems probable: my mom's psychic. And maybe I am too, or at least in her presence.

I shake my head and grasp my mug. "That was crazy," I say. "The way we subdued Grace. You . . . you read my mind."

My mom takes a sip. She cocks her head. She waves a hand, dismissive. "You think that was psychic powers?" She snorts. "Don't be silly."

Seeing my stunned expression she laughs. "I just know you," she says. She stands up and hugs me. "I'm your mother."

I hug her back. I want to laugh. And cry. The sight of that knife against her throat was so horrifying. What if . . . I pinch the skin between my eyebrows. There's no point going there. We're safe. It's over.

"We're fine," she says. "All's well that ends well." She hugs me harder.

I squeeze back. "Yes," I say. I inhale her special scent: freshly baked bread, caramel, and cinnamon.

She regains her seat but takes my hand, as if afraid to let go of me.

I grip her hand. It feels warm and soft. There's nothing like seeing what you love come under threat to make you appreciate it. I need to remember this feeling forever, and appreciate her, always.

CHAPTER 34:

HOME SAFE

After the police let us go my mom drives me back to the hospital. I need more X-rays. The technician recognizes me, as do various nurses.

My knuckles are swollen but not broken. My wrist didn't sustain any extra damage. When I'm done, everyone jokes about seeing me tomorrow.

My mom goes upstairs to deliver Daphne's PJs.

I slip over to check on Colin. Peeking around his door, I see he's awake. There's a little more color in his face than there was this morning.

"You're back!" he says, catching sight of me.

I walk closer. "I was in the neighborhood."

He must hear some wobble in my voice because he frowns, suddenly serious. "You okay? What's happened?"

"I'm fine," I say. I cross the room, then lean in for a kiss.

When I lean back he studies me. "What are you not telling me?"

I perch on the edge of his bed. Should I tell him? He's meant to be resting, not thinking about this case. But he knows something's up, anyway.

I tell him about Grace holding a knife to my mom's throat. And how she killed Stephen.

In their bruised sockets, Colin's eyes widen, then blink. "My God," he says. "Thank God you're alright." Because he's so thin, his Adam's apple seems larger now. He grips my hand. His eyes water. "You saved me yesterday." His voice is ragged. "But I wasn't there to save you, when you were in danger."

I shrug. He has no reason to feel guilty. And yet we all do, when something bad happens to those we love. Our heads cloud with should'ves, could'ves and if onlys. So many feelings overwhelm logic.

I shake my head. "But I'm okay. It's over."

He smiles wryly. "Yes," he says. "You saved yourself."

I shrug. "Let's hope there's no more saving," I say. "And from now on, we're both just safe. Period."

Colin nods, his eyes shiny and soft. His hand feels good in mine. Warm and solid. "We need a vacation," he says. "Someplace quiet and beautiful. Someplace peaceful."

I fight back a smile. People come here for that. And hasn't Colin ever watched any old episodes of *Unsolved Mysteries*? They always start the same way, with Robert Stack extolling how scenic and quiet some place is before his tone grows wary: *And then the peace was shattered* . . .

Colin is watching me. I realize he's waiting for an answer. Now's not the time for cynicism. Besides, a trip away with him sounds wonderful. "I'd love that," I say. "Just you and me. Someplace quiet."

His smile is so bright I blink. "Where should we go?" he asks.

I tilt closer to kiss him.

"Inland," I say. Definitely nowhere on a boat. We could go skiing at Whistler. Or just hole up beside a fire in a snow-covered log cabin. Nowhere to go and nothing to do except be together.

Again, our lips meet. My whole body tingles. I don't need the fire—it's already glowing, in my gut. He pulls me closer. I slide my good hand under his hospital robe, feel his shoulder blades, his smooth, hard back. Even now, when he's recovering, he feels strong and substantial.

We kiss until, behind me, someone clears their throat. It's the same nurse, the one with grey hair and pink cat-eye glasses. She's holding a little dish containing a few pills and a glass of water.

"Again?" she says, in mock exasperation. She laughs. "Didn't I tell you he needs rest?" She wags a finger.

I straighten, feeling sheepish. She laughs again and peers at Colin. "You've got more color in your face," she says. "You look much better." She tilts her head my way. "Love's the best medicine," she says. "There's nothing like it."

Faced with this woman's scrutiny, I feel shy, yet exultant. Love.

We're in love. I want to laugh out loud. Even this total stranger can see it.

The nurse hands Colin the glass of water. She presses a pill from its foil backing. Her smile widens. "Today's my twenty-fifth wedding anniversary," she says.

Colin and I murmur our congratulations.

"Twenty-five years!" She shakes her head in disbelief. "It went by like that." She snaps her fingers. "You remind me of me and Harry, back when we first met." Behind those pink frames, her eyes glow at the memory. "Ooh, you should've seen him," she tells me. "He had long, thick blond hair. Like a Viking." Another laugh. "He's bald now. And a little . . ." She holds her hands out around her belly. "Not that I care." She pats her own solid hips. "We've had our ups and downs, but when I see him, I still get that old fluttery feeling . . ." She wiggles her fingers. "It's like we're still twenty-five, on the inside."

She hands Colin the pill. He swallows it dutifully. The nurse checks something on his chart. "Good," she says, approvingly. She hands him another pill. "You'll soon be fit to go home and get on with your lives." She collects the empty glass and retreats, whistling.

I call out: "Happy anniversary!"

At the door, she pauses and turns. "Thanks. Now remember, let him rest," she warns me. Her departing shoes squeak on the linoleum.

Colin laughs. "Twenty-five years," he says, wonderingly. From the way he says it, I know he's imagining us, way down the line. Grayer, wrinklier, maybe fatter or thinner. He squeezes my hand. His eyes sparkle like peridots. "How about one more kiss?" he asks, slyly.

I tip forward. My whole body tingles. The butterflies aren't just in my stomach but swirling through every inch of me. A full monarch migration, in the springtime.

When the kiss finally ends, Colin's cheeks are tinged pink.

He exhales, happily. "Let's go somewhere remote," he says. "With no TV, phone, or internet."

I nod. That's exactly what I had in mind. Someplace to recover both in body and spirit. Although snuggled close to Colin, I know it doesn't matter where we go, so long as we're together.

"I should go," I say, reluctantly.

He brushes my cheek. "Please, not yet."

I slip off my shoes and tuck my feet up onto the bed. I lean against him. His arm tightens around me. Beneath my cheek, his warm chest rises and falls. His steady breaths tickle my ear. I shut my eyes, feel myself start to drift, pulled between tiredness and exhilaration.

I'm on the cusp of a new adventure, a journey into unknown lands. And yet I've also come home.

I fall asleep smiling.

ACKNOWLEDGMENTS

While writing is solitary, creating a book takes teamwork. Many thanks to everyone who has brought yet another dream to life: my longtime friend and mentor, Deborah Nolan; my brilliant and beautiful agent, Sharon Bowers, and her Folio Lit colleagues; my savvy editor Dan Mayer, and the rest of the Seventh Street Books team, especially Marianna Vertullo.

I'm a reader and writer thanks to my intrepid parents, Gisela and Gerry Ray, who always found money for books—even when we only had lawn chairs (and books!) to sit on. Endless thanks to my husband, Thien Nguyen, for his energy, optimism, and support. And thanks to my kids—V, S, and E, who inspired me to create Toby Wong.

ABOUT THE AUTHOR

Born in the UK and raised in Canada, Elka lives with her family in Central Vietnam. Her previous books include the first Toby Wong novel *Divorce Is Murder*; the noir thriller *Saigon Dark*; and a light romantic mystery, *Hanoi Jane*. When Elka's not reading or writing she's in the ocean.